Incanto

The Singing Gardener

ISBN- 13: 978-1484013304

ISBN-10: 1484013301

ALL RIGHTS RESERVED

The Singing Gardener Copyright 2011 Trish Doolan

Cover art by Holly Rockwell

First Electronic Book Publication, March 12th, 2013

Copyright Warning: The unauthorized reproduction or distribution of this copyrighted work is illegal. No part of this book may be scanned, uploaded or distributed via the Internet or by any other means, electronic, print or otherwise, without the copyright holder's and Publisher's permission. Criminal copyright infringement, including infringement without monetary gain, is investigated by the FBI and is punishable by up to five (5) years in federal prison and a fine of $250,000.00. (http://www.fbi.gov/ipr/). Please purchase only authorized electronic or print editions and do not participate in or encourage the electronic piracy of copyrighted material. Your support of the author's rights is appreciated.

All Rights Reserved. With the exception of brief quotes used in critical articles and reviews, this book may not be reproduced or used in whole or in part by any means existing without written permission from the copyright holder.

Applications should be addressed to the copyright holder. Unauthorized or restricted acts in relation to this publication may result in civil proceedings and/or criminal prosecution.

The author and illustrator have asserted their respective rights under the Copyright Designs and Patents Acts of 1988 (as amended) to be identified as the author of this book and illustrator of the artwork.

This book is a work of fiction and any resemblance to persons, living or dead, or places, events or locales is purely coincidental. The names, characters, places and occurrences are productions of the author's imagination, should not be confused with fact, and are used fictitiously and not construed to be real.

"Forgiveness is the fragrance the violet sheds on the heel that has crushed it."

Mark Twain

Contents

Prologue..4
1. Uno..6
2. Due..15
3. Tre...23
4. Quattro..38
5. Cinque...54
6. Sei..71
7. Sette..89
8. Otto...99
9. Nove..109
10. Dieci..116
11. Undici..125
12. Dodici..131
13. Tredici..138
14. Quattordici..147
15. Quindici..159
16. Sedici...172
17. Diciassette..188
18. Diciotto..195
19. Diciannove.......................................199

20. Venti..213
21. Ventuno...225
22. Ventidue...237
23. Ventitre...241
24. Ventiquattro...252
25. Venticinque..258
26. Ventisei..267
27. Ventisette...279
Epilogue...288
Sample From Trish Doolan's Upcoming Book........292

Trish Doolan

PROLOGUE

I had never heard him sing before the day of my mother's funeral, but they said he had a voice that made all the flowers bloom. Mourners filed down the long driveway that led to my mother's garden, their dress shoes knocking against the cobblestones. Blood red Vega roses lined the way and the wind picked up a scent of lavender and rosemary from the overgrown bushes surrounding our home. The garden shimmered, alive with creamy Casablancas, multi-colored peonies, sky blue hydrangeas and the deepest purple violets I had ever seen. Every flower looked freshly painted, but it was the willow tree, my mother's favorite, that struck me most. Draped over her casket and the ground where she was to rest, its leafy branches hung like veils, its trunk bent in what looked to be an embrace.

Signore and Signora Giuliano, dear old friends, walked beside me, heads bowed in grief. The neighbors, the LaPortas and the Finellis, offered sympathetic smiles. An older man with a thin face and pale skin, someone I did not know, stood at the edge of the crowd. He wore a short-brimmed black fedora at a jaunty angle, and was taking notes in what looked like a reporter's notebook. An obituary writer? I did not have the will to ask.

We gathered under the willow around the closed oak casket. The entire village of Castellina in Chianti seemed to press in around me. I felt a stab in my chest. What could my life be without this woman who brought me into the world? The people shifted uncomfortably, looking to the priest for direction. We weren't burying my mother in the churchyard, and few approved. But to be laid to rest here had been her most fervent wish. I'd begged the priest and made a special donation. Reluctantly, he had agreed.

Clouds dripped from the azure sky, long fingers attached to a

Incanto ~ The Singing Gardener

hand that seemed to be reaching down from heaven. The hand of God, scooping her up to take her home? It consoled me to think so.

Tall sunflowers rustled in the wind and a brilliant red cardinal fluttered past them. The priest began.

"To all who knew her, Maria Ricci was a kind-hearted soul. A role model for her only daughter, Donata. A devoted wife to her beloved late husband, Martino."

"What these fools don't know could fill their cathedrals!" This, from my mother's dear old friend, Prima. She had come to stand by my other side and pulled her black shawl around her head as if to shield herself from ignorance. The priest continued to speak, reading from a standard book of prayers.

Then, at the edge of the cobblestone driveway, I saw a man dressed in a simple black suit, a single white rose bud pinned to his lapel. He moved toward the casket.

Wavy gray curls framed his striking face. High chiseled cheekbones and a prominent Roman nose gave him an elegant appearance, and his hazel eyes glistened. He looked directly at me and smiled. I had never seen him before, yet his presence was as familiar as my own face, and an inexplicable peace embraced me.

Trish Doolan

UNO

Castellina in Chianti, 1958

Stefano Portigiani wiped the sweat from his brow and smiled down on a row of Blue Parrot Tulips not yet born. Wavy brown curls fell around his kind face, as his eyes twinkled with song. Covered in soil, he knelt and caressed the newly planted flowers.

"Welcome all my little visitors, I am here to make your stay delightful." Softly he began whispering words of encouragement, words meant only for the ears of tulips. "*Buongiorno, bel fiore.* The sun exists for your petals. You, *piccolina*, will light up the faces of all who see you." He bent kissing the Blue Parrots when a familiar voice interrupted him. "Stefano, my friendly gardener! Are you making love to the flowers again or are you taking a nap?"

Stefano looked up, startled to see the black polished shoes and faultlessly cut trousers of Martino Ricci, as he looked down on the gardener laughing. Handsome enough in his way, Ricci was a barrel-chested man with heavy eyebrows and dark, flashing eyes. He wore his thick black hair slicked back, not a hair out of place. His impeccable coiffure matched the perfectly manicured garden that Stefano tended to. Reaching in his pants, Martino pulled out a handful of *lire*.

Stefano rose quickly. "I wasn't sleeping, *Signore Ricci*. I was just making sure the tulips were securely planted."

"I know my wife loves all of these beautiful flowers, but don't ignore my olive trees and grapes. They have been in my family for generations. Flowers will come and go, but the trees, now that's where the strength is, and they last, longer than us my friend"

"I assure you *Signore Ricci* I do not ignore one living thing on your property." Stefano stood tall with his shoulders pulled back.

"That's good to hear. " Martino smiled. "At any rate, I must go to my office." He handed Stefano the money. "I think the smell of those flowers puts you to sleep. I seem to get sleepy every time I

Incanto ~ The Singing Gardener

look at them," Martino pointed to the money, "I have to work like a real man." Martino worked as a lawyer in a successful practice in Siena, about fifteen kilometers away. With a reputation for being ruthless when it came to interrogating witnesses, he was the most feared defense attorney in the region. He smacked the gardener's face playfully. "But you, my friend, you have the simple life of a gardener. You don't know how lucky you are."

Martino winked, put on his gray Fedora, and strode past Stefano to the red Zagato coupe in the driveway. Starting up the engine with a roar, he drove off at top speed. Stefano looked at Ricci's lire without interest and shoved them into his pocket.

What Ricci didn't know is that Stefano never, ever slept in his garden. No, the gardener lay in the soil only so the roots could hear him more clearly as he praised each and every flower to help them grow. Martino took for granted that he had the most stunning garden in all of Tuscany. He never questioned how, in cold and even without the luck of rain, his garden blossomed beyond measure. All the flowers were lush and fragrant, the herbs thriving, and the trees far from neglected, constantly bearing the most succulent of fruit with ease.

Once Stefano saw that Martino's automobile had gone, he made his way to the front of the house as he did every day and hid behind the willow tree, waiting. Like clockwork, Maria Ricci entered his view in one large arched window of the old stone house. Stefano watched her as she perched in her usual spot in the sitting room, overlooking the garden. Today, he noted, she wore blue. A good color for her. In her hand a tall glass of *limonata* glistened in the sunlight. Maria's dark hair spilled around her shoulders like a chocolate silk scarf. High eyebrows framed her deep-set, sea green eyes. Her nose, long and curved with a delicious little bump, rested above tiny lips that seem to curl into a point. Her skin was pale, deprived of the sun, but she preferred staying indoors and looking out.

Unaware of Stefano's admiration, on this morning as on so

many others, Maria began to cry as she stared out her window. *Perche?* Stefano wondered why such a beautiful woman should cry so much? A shiny blue Fiat sped down the cobblestone driveway and pulled up to the Ricci residence with a screech. Stefano dove to the ground and, scrambling to find his gardening tools, crawled to the boxwood hedge to make himself look busy. Mama Ricci emerged from her vehicle and marched up the front steps with a purpose. Thick arms and legs sprouted from the expensive fabric of her dress. Her gut, too, proved she had plenty of money to eat well. She carried a large wicker basket overflowing with food. Her face was round with apple red cheeks giving her an ebullient appearance. Her sizeable backside shook from side to side as she climbed the front staircase.

Stefano watched as, unable to see over her basket, Maria's mother-in-law crushed the small pot of calla lilies in front of the door. "Who put that here?" she shrugged. "Oh well," wiping her leather shoes on the welcome mat as if she could grind its fibers to dust. She grabbed the knocker, a bunch of brass grapes in the center of the door, and pounded rapidly. Maria opened promptly, but before she could even greet her mother-in-law, Mama Ricci pushed her aside. "*Ciao, ciao.*" Maria noticed the destroyed flowers on the doorstep and sighed deeply.

Spotting Stefano watching, she smiled faintly. Flustered, he pretended to be working. Without another glance his way, she walked inside the house, leaving the door ajar as if it might encourage her mother-in-law not too stay long.

"Mama Ricci, what a pleasant surprise," Maria said weakly.

"I bet you're surprised. Look at you! So frail I could pick my teeth with you," Martino's mother exclaimed. Stefano cringed at the shrill voice scolding Maria from inside the house.

Mama Ricci made herself at home. After all, it was as familiar to her as her own home. Many family gatherings were shared here. She could still smell her father-in-laws cherry pipe every time she walked in, a scent in which she found comfort. It reminded her of a

Incanto ~ The Singing Gardener

time when all of her children were running around the house, laughing, playing and full of life, but now she felt only a void and echoes of the past burrowed into the walls. The kitchen through an arched doorway had been tiled in Tuscan's finest olive green with burgundy trim. Flawless terra cotta tiles covered all the floors. Vaulted ceilings created spaciousness. Deep-set windows adorned the entire house, and heavy fabric outlined each window in royal hues. In the living room stood a shiny black piano, the one and only possession belonging to Maria. The finest Roman designer had decorated the home's interior. The tiling throughout was custom made, the woodwork handcrafted by the best in the field. The cabinets held the finest China and glassware. The drapes, linens and furniture were all the best money could buy. And although Maria was grateful for all of the beauty and luxuries, nothing in that house seemed to make Maria happy, except the piano. It was a grand jewel box missing the gem that mattered most.

The women moved into the sitting room. Not able to help himself, Stefano left the boxwood and began tending to the bougainvillea that outlined the arched window. "No wonder you can't conceive a child," Mama Ricci exclaimed, taking a seat next to Maria on the sofa. "You need some fat on your bones! Fat brings babies!" Mama Ricci pinched her daughter-in-law's stomach sharply.

Shying away, Maria cried, "Mama, please don't do that."

"What? You don't like to be touched? Ah ha! Is that the reason after three years of marriage that you don't give my son a child?"

"Mama, no…" Maria pleaded.

"Let me tell you something, my son will be upset, but I don't care." Mama began pulling food out of her basket. "When my son first brought you around nobody liked you, and I mean nobody. He is my only son as you already know." Maria stared out the window, as her finger twisted a curl in her hair. "His three sisters all went crazy. They knew he could do much better. And so did my husband, God rest his soul." She quickly blessed herself and then proceeded to make sandwiches. "Just look at you, so skinny and you come from a poor family. So why you, huh? We all wondered what he saw in you and we all fought him, but he was determined to have you. Finally I gave in, but I had my conditions."

"Oh, what were they?" Maria replied sharply.

"None of your business. That is family business. Just because you now share my family name does not mean you will ever know my family secrets, and to me you are not my family. You are Martino's family, his wife, but the only way you become my family, my blood, is to give me a baby! You owe it to me and I expect you to give it to me soon."

Mama put a sandwich in front of Maria. "*Mangia*! *Mangia*! You do realize my son could have claimed any woman in this village? Not only is he good looking and intelligent, but he has money." Maria picked up the sandwich, stared at it and then dropped it on the plate and pushed it away. "Lots of it. And this house that you live in, this was his Grandfather's house. Look around you, all these things that you have in your home are from my family's hard working hands, not yours! Now it's time for you to work a little and produce a child. This home was left to Martino so that he would raise a family here. A family! That means children! *Capisci*?"

"*Si*, I understand!" Maria moved to her usual spot at the arched window. Mama Ricci followed her with the sandwich. Stefano ducked so he would not be noticed.

"Now eat, eat. You need hips to push the baby out." Grinning, as she handed her the sandwich. I'm going to fatten you up." Mama Ricci lowered her voice and smiled as if she were Maria's friend. "And, my dear, my son must come to you every night and you must give yourself to him. Do you understand? You must do it until you throw up every morning with the sickness of pregnancy."

Pale as a lily already, Maria seemed to turn two shades lighter.

Stefano looked in the window and watched Maria chewing, tears streaking her cheeks. She spotted Stefano staring at her and

Incanto ~ The Singing Gardener

their eyes locked. She wiped her cheeks and turned away. He pretended to trim the bougainvillea.

She did not have the strength to argue with her mother-in-law. Indeed, she had married Martino at her own father's suggestion. Maria, one of the most beautiful girls in the village, found herself unmarried after her two younger sisters had wed and left Castellina. It was said that her beauty was much too threatening, that no man stood a chance with her. The truth? Few had tried. So when Martino had the courage to ask for her hand, her father urged her to say yes. Maria accepted. Her heart now weighed heavy with the knowledge that what God had sanctified, no man could tear asunder.

Finally, Mama Ricci left Maria. Grateful, Maria stood at the door and watched the car disappear down the drive. Turning to go inside, she was stunned to see the calla lilies completely restored to their perfect, bell-like grace. Delighted, she looked to Stefano as he tended the rose bushes at the top of the drive.

Her eyes held him. "I love your garden," she said softly.

Stefano's cheeks turned as red as the Vega roses. Meekly, he bowed his head. "Signora, it is *your* garden. I'm just the gardener."

Maria smiled at him and he saw the whole garden light up in her eyes.

It was three years earlier when Martino went to Maria's father, Leonardo Cavallo, in hopes of making Maria his wife. Although they lived in the poor part of town this did not discourage Martino. He had set his sights on Maria in church one summer afternoon and could think of no other. Unbeknown to her, he followed her home week after week, month after month, imagining what it would be like to talk to her, hold her hand and someday kiss her. If a woman as beautiful as Maria would have him he believed he might truly begin to value himself as a man. Being the only son was not an easy task in the Ricci home and his father constantly reminded him that he was much less of a man than he hoped for. No matter what Martino did his father was not satisfied and only told him of his disappointment. This burden weighed heavy in Martino's heart and he continued to strive for perfection in all areas. In his eyes Maria's external beauty was perfection.

Dressed in his Sunday's finest, Martino gathered up the courage to go after what he wanted, Maria Cavallo. Carrying a huge basket, he approached the humble cottage that Maria lived in with her father. The Ricci's were famous for settling all issues over good food. He fiddled with the bow on the basket and then knocked on the door. A craggily old voice shrieked on the other side of the door.

"*Avanti.*" Martino entered. Leonardo Cavallo, stick thin, gray and brittle, rolled over in his wheelchair to greet him. He could not remember the last time a visitor had stepped foot into the house. "Who are you?" A musty odor lingered in this dilapidated farmhouse, as rooster's cock-a-doodle-dooed outside.

"Ah, I am Martino Ricci, Signore." He smiled.

Looking around, Martino sensed the years of hardship this home had endured. The old wooden walls were bare and aside from a table and two chairs the only other object of interest was a black lacquered piano in the corner. Martino noticed two doorways, which probably led to bedrooms, but did not have any desire to inquire. It was neat, but dark and damp and reeked of loneliness.

"Buo*ngiorno* Signor Ricci." He extended his hand.

"Please Signor *Cavallo*, call me Martino." They shook.

"And you may call me Leo." He coughed, and coughed, and coughed.

"Ah, *bene* Leo. I brought you some lunch." Martino unloaded his basket full of gourmet cheeses, meats, big red grapes and fresh warm bread. Leonardo had not seen this much food on his table in quite some time, if ever. "And a bottle of *Brunello di Montalcino* from my family vineyard, aged over twenty years. I hope you are hungry."

Martino set the table for lunch and poured each of them some wine, Leonardo watched in amazement. Slowly sipping the wine,

Incanto ~ The Singing Gardener

Leonardo closed his eyes, and his bottom lip began to quiver. "I am very hungry. Have been for years." Martino gently patted him on the back.
"Then we shall eat and drink. Do you like the wine?"
"I used to be a winemaker. That was a long time ago, before my wife became ill." He waved his hands in the air as if to forget the past. "It aged very well. Unlike some of us." He took a large gulp and then began to cry softly. Embarrassed, he quickly wiped his eyes. "*Scusi*, it's been so long. *Grazie*, Martino." He finished his wine and held out his glass. "*Per favore.*"
"Of course." Martino obliged with a big smile.
"Why have you come my friend? I know it was not to feed me and give me wine, and although that is very kind of you indeed, I am sure there is something on your mind."
"*Si*, Signor Cavallo, I have come here today..." Martino stood up and straightened his suit and then took a sip of wine. "Forgive me." He got down on bended knee in front of Leonardo's wheelchair and humbly lowered his head. "I would like very much to have your blessing so that I may ask your daughter Maria to be my wife. I want this more than anything in the world, and if you say yes, you would make me the happiest man on earth." Leonardo stared down at Martino and could see the sincerity in his eyes.
"Get up Martino, you'll ruin your trousers." Quickly, Martino stood up. Leonardo wheeled over to the table and began to eat. Martino waited for an answer. "Sit down, let's talk a bit." Legs rocking back and forth, Martino sat next to him, poured another glass of wine, as he awaited a response.
"I promise you your daughter will want for nothing. I will cherish her, take care of her and give her anything she wishes. I assure you I will make her happy." Leonardo put down his food and stared out in front of him for a long while, too long for Martino's good.
"Will you?" He turned and looked fiercely into Martino's eyes.
"Yes, I will." Holding Leonardo's gaze, but frightened by his

intensity.

"How do you know?"

What a question, Martino thought, realizing he didn't know, but knew he had to come up with an answer. "Because I will treat her like a Queen and I have the means to provide for her."

"Does she love you?"

"I don't know yet. She doesn't know me, but she will and then she will love me. I am sure."

"Nothing in this life is for sure my friend, trust me..." He finished his second glass of wine and poured another. "I admire you, Martino, and that's why I need to warn you about my daughter, Maria."

"*E bellissima.*" His eyes lit up like a Christmas tree.

"Yes, she is beautiful, but she is complicated, very complicated!"

"Most women are." He laughed.

"Not like Maria. She is a puzzle. It would bring me great joy for her to be taken care of. As you can see, I don't have much to offer her and I assure you I have never made her happy. I'm not sure anyone can. It was hard on her after my wife died. Very hard! I just want you to be sure you know what you're getting yourself into."

"I am sure, Leo." He stared long and hard into Leonardo's eyes and neither of them looked away. They had an understanding.

"I will speak to her tonight. You have my blessing."

Martino jumped up and down and kissed Leonardo on both cheeks, as Leonardo coughed in his wheelchair.

"Thank you, thank you Leo, you are an angel. And I will take care of your daughter." He pulled out two cigars. "Would you care for one Leo?"

"The doctor said I shouldn't, but what the hell?" They both laughed and lit their cigars. "It may help me get to the grave quicker."

DUE

An auburn sun spilled out of the sky as another day came to an end in the village of Castellina in Chianti. One of the three towns that formed the triangle in the heart of Tuscany, Greve and Radda the other two, Castellina sat on a ridge of golden hills round as a woman's body.

A fortress, La Rocca, was built along with defensive walls containing well-spaced towers during the late middle ages, when Castellina was a member of the 'Chianti Alliance.' The Rocca still stands, serving now as the sleepy town hall and as a museum, as do many stretches of the walls. The original walls had two gates, one opening to the road to Siena and the other to the road to Florence. Unfortunately, both were destroyed during World War II.

One of the most fascinating archeological finds is The Etruscan tomb on Monte Calvario. Excavated in 1915, they are just outside the town on the road to Florence. The tomb holds four burial vaults designed in a cross aligned with four cardinal points. The hill claimed its name from a tiny chapel that stood at one time, on the summit, the last station of the Way of the Cross.

The Village of Castellina in Chianti held history and secrets as old as the walls that surrounded it. It survived wars and fires, which caused almost total destruction, but somehow still stands in the heart of Tuscany and demands recognition, especially when it comes to wine. The grapes that flourish in this region are incomparable to all others and can only be found in its God given soil and created vintages so delicious it made grown men weep.

As Stefano headed home, he too held a secret, which felt as ancient as the land he walked upon. Maria was still a mystery to him, yet she felt as familiar as the flowers he tended in her garden each day and she was now living inside of him. He savored her words, her smile, and the way her eyes had shone when she praised the garden. Although he had walked this way a thousand times before, this time felt like the very first. Strolling out of his employer's drive and onto the main road, he began to sing. Signore Finelli, the neighbor across the way, watched Stefano closely from his t*errazza*. The gardener had begun collecting the pine nuts that had fallen from one of the Ricci's trees.

Finelli, a jovial soul, had two patches of wiry hair on either side of his round head and a shiny space in the middle that had been stained with a raspberry birthmark. Stefano nodded to the man, shoved the nuts in his pocket and continued singing.

"I see you, gardener," Finelli shouted. Puffing on a cigar, he rubbed his belly and called out more loudly. "Hey, are you drunk?" Finelli a retired police officer found it hard to give up his spying on the village folks and believed many of them were up to no good and made it his mission to find incriminating evidence against all of them, just for sport.

Stefano stopped singing for a moment and laughed. "No, no *Signor Finelli*, just happy."

Curling his fingers into a delicate ball, Finelli shook his hand toward Stefano. "But you're always happy!"

"Not really," Stefano admitted. "I'm always *trying* to be happy. Today I'm truly happy."

"You're also truly *pazzo*."

Signora Finelli, a round little woman with a pleasant face, white hair, and warm eyes, ran out of the house with two glasses of wine. Handing one to her husband, she shouted out to Stefano. "Stefano please come by tomorrow. I have a huge dilemma."

"I promise I will stop by tomorrow after work."

"I'm counting on it. I need you. Don't forget."

Stefano vowed by putting his hand over his heart. "I could never forget you *Signora Finelli*. See you tomorrow, *Signor Finelli*." He waved goodbye to them both and continued his song.

Stefano turned back to face the imposing iron gate of the Ricci home. He began singing the last line of his song to a sky filled with clouds the shape of gnocchi. As the last bit of light cast hues over

Incanto ~ The Singing Gardener

Maria's arched window, Stefano stopped and stood for a moment in silence, the smile quickly fading from his face. He felt his happy song to be an illusion. How could he ever tell Maria the feelings he held in his heart? She was another man's wife. He turned back to Signore Finelli's house and saw the older couple, hand in hand, move to the pergola covered in grape vines and sip from their glasses as they watched the daylight slowly vanish.

"Retirement is like purgatory. As each day ends I feel closer to death." Signore Finelli complained. "I need to do something, feel useful."

"That's why I garden." Kissing her husband.

"But you're terrible at it."

"It doesn't matter. It keeps my mind busy." He began to protest, but she put her finger over his mouth. "Sshh, now keep quiet while I enjoy this moment, unless you have something nice to say."

Staring at his wife's weathered profile, he beamed with gratitude. "You are as beautiful as ever."

Without looking at him, the lines of her mouth curved into a smile. "That's better."

* * *

Arriving home, Stefano entered his humble one-room stone cottage and put a pot of water on the stove for his supper. Stefano opened a bottle of Chianti from the local vineyard, giving himself a healthy pour, and prepared his dinner. While the penne cooked, he melted some butter and cheese, reached into his left pocket and pulled out sage and rosemary trimmed from the Ricci's garden. Delicately, he broke the herbs apart and sprinkled them into the melted butter. Reaching into his right pocket, he collected the handful of *pignolis* and folded them into his poor-man sauce. He tossed the mixture over the pasta, poured it all onto a plate, and sat alone at his small wooden table.

* * *

Trish Doolan

Maria sat across from Martino at the dinner table while their young servant, Angelina, small and dark, with an ample bust and the eyes of a farm animal, served them roasted lamb over polenta on fine China.

"Angelina, *ancora!*" Angelina obeyed and refilled his glass, while Martino stared at Maria. The silence was agonizing and the boredom was palpable. "So what did you do today, wife? Wait, don't tell me. You sat watching your flowers grow and moped about the house."

"As you say," she replied.

"There's a big beautiful world out there. Why don't you ever go out? Some fresh air and sun would do you good. Maybe it would improve your mood."

"My mood is fine. Why must you always try and change me?"

"I'm sorry my darling. Please, tell me about your day." Martino undressed Angelina with his eyes. "More, Angelina. Too bad my wife can't cook like this. Maybe you should teach her. Give her something to do." Angelina served him another helping.

"Anything unusual happen today wife?" Anger fused within him.

"No." She sipped her wine, numbing herself.

"No? Are you sure?" Threat weaved into his voice.

"Oh, I just remembered. Your mother was here."

"Yes, she was." Martino narrowed his eyes at her. He and his mother were thick as thieves and Maria should have known the visit would be reported to him in detail. "Why don't you tell me what happened?"

Maria threw her fork down and let out a heavy sigh. "I don't want to talk about it. You surely already know what happened. Angelina, can you please take this away?" She pushed her plate to the edge of the table.

"You will talk about it!" Martino slammed his fist and Angelina flinched, retreating with Maria's unfinished dinner to the kitchen. He raced his fingers through his hair. "And you will talk about it now!"

Maria glared into her husband's bloodshot eyes. "Why must we go over this every single time you have too much to drink?" She rose from the table, but he grabbed her arm and jerked her back down into her chair.

"I have not had too much to drink!"

"Yes, you have. I don't recognize you when you drink. You turn into a monster!"

"A monster?" He stood up with her still in his grip.

"Why is this so important?"

Through clenched teeth, he hissed, "Because she is my mother."

"And I am your wife."

"Yes, now please tell me what happened. You know she only means well."

"She said I was too skinny and that's why I can't get pregnant. She then tried to force me to eat one of her God-awful sandwiches and told me that I owe HER a child. I feel like I am married to your mother and you're not even man enough to stand up to her. That is why she thinks she can come here, into my home and treat me like some sort of servant. I am tired of it and I am tired of you protecting her instead of protecting your own wife! You're a coward!" Maria pulled back her arm, rose from the table and quickly headed up the stairs.

"A coward!?" Martino wiped his mouth with the napkin, gulped the remainder of his wine and sprung up to chase her. "Don't you walk away from me when I'm talking to you!" Martino ran up the main staircase and after Maria.

She waited in their bedroom, already knowing what the outcome to the evening would be. Dutifully, she began to take off her clothes. When Martino arrived and saw her naked he became quiet with surprise. His knees went weak and all was forgiven.

"Let's make a baby, husband," Maria whispered without any passion. "It will make your mama happy."

Awkwardly, Martino began undressing, stumbling from the

effects of the wine. To hurry the inevitable, Maria helped him.
"Yes. It would make her so happy," he agreed, giving her a sloppy kiss. "I think it would make me happy, too." He began to kiss Maria with more fervency. "Would it make you happy, wife?"
"Please, no more talking tonight," Maria whispered. She shut the light and lowered Martino onto their bed.
"I love you."
"Sshh…" Leaving her body, as she let her husband possess it.
Once her husband was asleep not even an earthquake could wake him. Maria got out of their bed, quietly wrapping her linen nightdress around her and making her way downstairs to the sitting room. Maria sat at the piano her beloved grandmother had given her and began pressing the ivory keys tenderly and with passion, as she herself would like to be touched. She played by ear and did not know how to read music, creating songs she would reserve to memory. Closing her eyes, she pretended to be somewhere else. Her yearning notes drifted through the late night air of Castellina in Chianti.

* * *

Turning in the high narrow bed they had shared for twenty-five years, Signore and Signora Finelli smiled to themselves as Maria's music touched their ears, sending them into a deeper, more peaceful rest.
"I love when she plays," Signora murmured. "It helps me sleep better."
"He must be drunk again or she would not be at it."
"Mmm. Kiss me, *amore*." Signora Finelli curled into him, feeling lucky that God had sent her a good man for a husband.

* * *

Prima D'Amato, right next door, sat in her kitchen staring at the chair in front of her. Once occupied by her late husband Paolo, the chair had sat empty now for too many years. Tears spilled from Prima's eyes and into her glass of *Chianti* as Maria's music traveled into her window. Picking up a framed picture of her

Incanto ~ The Singing Gardener

beloved, she pulled it close to her heart and began slow dancing around her kitchen.

* * *

To the other side of the Riccis, newlyweds Carlo and Tessa LaPorta welcomed the beautiful notes weaving their way around the iron bed. The couple had money from their families and little to worry about except how to fill their time. Carlo would occupy his hours with projects. Currently, he was determined to be the greatest bread maker in all of Tuscany. Unfortunately, his bread kept turning out more like bricks, but he was not deterred. He had all the time in the world to get it right and enough money to not worry about how long it would take. Tessa on the other hand preferred shopping and good gossip. The three things they did best were fight, make-up, and make love. Now, to the tune of the piano, Carlo turned and put his hand on his new wife's angular hip. He cupped her white breast causing her to become amorous. She hummed to the tune of Maria's piano and moved closer to her husband. "I think I need to add more water. Tomorrow my bread will be perfect."

Tessa smacked him. "Please!! No talk of bread right now. I can't bear it! And it's not sexy." She shut her husband up by fiercely kissing him.

* * *

A little further up the Greve road sat the well-appointed residence of Roberto and Filomena Giuliano. They lived in a beautiful cream-colored villa with two empty wings, had never had children, and felt cursed because their land had mysteriously dried up years earlier. But they were grateful for each other. While Maria's music streamed through their upstairs window, Roberto Giuliano stroked the familiar soft lines of his wife's face while she slept. Quietly he drifted down the stairs, out his front door and found himself standing on his barren soil. He fell to his knees, blessed himself and prayed under the moonless sky.

Trish Doolan

* * *

Finally, at the end of the road, Maria's haunting tune found its way to Stefano Portigiani. Lying in his narrow bed, his eyes wide open, he listened to her music and his mouth found lyrics for her song. Unable to stop himself, he rose and followed the road back to the Ricci house. Before long, he found himself sitting in the Ricci's garden beneath Maria's arched window. There he would make his bed for the evening.

TRE

The next morning, Stefano was asleep in a bed of crisp new daffodils. Feeling the warmth of a new day on his face, he slowly opened his eyes. Maria, in bed next to her husband, opened her eyes just as slowly. Getting out of bed, dressing quietly so as not to wake Martino, she hurried downstairs to her favorite arched window.

The new beds of bright daffodils immediately caught her eye and she smiled with delight. Then Stefano sprouted up and turned to find Maria's eyes on him. His stomach filled with a field of butterflies and she gasped softly.

From behind, two hands reached around her to caress her belly. She jumped. Seeing Martino Ricci join his wife in the window, Stefano quickly crouched back into the daffodils.

"Did I scare you?" Martino asked softly.

"No, husband. But I thought you were sleeping."

"I felt you leave, my dear. I missed you," he said, whispering into her hair. "I thought we could have breakfast together before I left for work."

"Of course." She turned and headed into the kitchen to prepare the food. Martino followed, catching her by the waist as she stood by the hearth. She tried to relax under his hands as he began kissing her neck and stroking her hair.

"Last night...was amazing." Martino gazed at her as if he had never really seen her and, for an instant, she wondered if things between them might change. "Let's see if *that* doesn't produce some results." Banging the pan on the stove, Maria shook her head and laughed.

"I'm so sorry about last night. It's just that, well, I love you so much and I get a little crazy sometimes. Please forgive me."

"Don't I always?" She smiled weakly and, preparing his

pancetta and bread as quickly as possible, she prayed for him to leave. As soon as she served him, he ate his food and then lifted himself from the table and kissed her again.
"Try to have some fun today. It would do you good."
Martino walked down the front stairs and noticed Stefano clipping the boxwood topiary lining the walk.
"*Buongiorno.*" Martino smiled.
"*Buongiorno*, Signor Ricci."
"It's a beautiful day isn't it?"
"*Si, Signore.*" Stefano smiled politely.
Carlo came running up the driveway carrying loaves of bread. "*Buongiorno*, fresh bread, I just baked it. It's still hot! Feel." He pushed it in Martino's face as he tried to get in his car. "I've changed the recipe. I promise it's good this time."
"That's what you said last time. *Ciao* Carlo please give it to my wife. I have to run."
"*Ciao.*" Carlo stood dejected, and then offered Stefano a loaf, but Stefano politely shook his head.
"*No, Grazie*, I am still full from breakfast." The truth was Stefano ate nothing, but would rather starve than eat Carlo's bread. Last time it practically chipped a tooth in half.
"Very well, I will treat the lovely ladies to my new recipe." He shook a loaf at Stefano. "You don't know what you're missing out on." He marched up the stairs and grabbed the bunch of grapes in the middle of Maria's door and knocked. She opened the door with a smile.
"Signora Ricci, please, enjoy my bread this morning. I've mastered the recipe finally." The door being ajar gave Carlo enough room to peek into the kitchen and much to his disappointment he noticed several loaves of his bread in the trash.
Taking a loaf, Maria thanked him. She caught Stefano watching her and couldn't help but smile as he put his hands around his throat pretending to die from Carlo's horrible baking. As Carlo turned to walk away Stefano quickly dropped his hands from this throat and tended to the garden. Sulking, Carlo went to Prima

Incanto ~ The Singing Gardener

D'Amato's to drop off his morning offering hoping for a warmer welcome. Upon opening the door a heavenly aroma swirled through the air that made Carlo's mouth water. Prima stood with her kitchen mitts on, wearing her apron. Now she was a true baker.

"Signora D'Amato, it is good this morning, I promise. I've worked very hard." He begged her to try it as he sniffed the buttery sweet air from Prima's kitchen.

Impatiently she grabbed a loaf from him, bit into it and started to chew. Slowly her face turned sour. She spit it out into her hand. "Not hard enough. Why must you torture me this way? And the Finelli's, the Ricci's, aren't you embarrassed?

"Well, yes I am." He hung his head. "But I will get it right. I must. You'll see." She slammed the door. Carlo punched the air and threw a small tantrum before he headed back home.

* * *

Maria tried to focus on household chores. There were tiles to scrub and sheets to wash. Angelina could not be expected to do everything. Yet, Stefano's voice, as he sang in the garden enchanted Maria beyond distraction. She could not find her way to her work. His tenor sent chills down her spine. Somehow he had the ability to deliver the depth of a baritone and then sweep in with alto accentuations, which created a strong, but sensuous melody. His songs so powerful, it seemed that a quartet of musicians accompanied him, but the only thing around him were flowers. In her mind she heard the strings, horns, felt her fingers dancing on the piano. Her head became light as she surrendered to the music he produced in her garden. It was more than just the sound of his voice that captivated Maria; it was the depth from which he sang. She could feel all of his pain and longing, pouring through his lyrics. His voice touched the hearing of her heart and made her feel a connection to him. She felt as if he were singing about her, to her, as if he understood her entire life and came to her garden to sing the words she could not voice on her own. , A song that lived within and was crushing her because she did not know how to release it. Instead she buried it like the dead. The passion and pain delicately woven into Stefano's voice and his melodic ability to freely express it drew Maria to question the many other talented gifts the gardener might have. Surreptitiously, she watched from the window as he bent on the ground, the earth moving between his skillful fingers. She hummed in tune with him as she watched the sun beat down on his richly tanned flesh. His honey colored hair, thick and wavy, dipped down slightly, covering his right eye. Maria knew all the details of this man. By afternoon Stefano would take his shirt off. It would be drenched with sweat and he would hang it on a branch to dry, putting in on again before he left. Today Maria watched him without trying not to, a thrill passing through her.

He could feel her eyes on him, but he dared not look up for fear she'd see the tremor hat passed through him.

She watched his muscles quiver as he dug his hands into her garden. She could almost feel the heat of his body as the sun beat down on him. She knew this could only be a sin, to have such a desire for a man who was not her husband. But she did not turn away. The thought of being in his arms made Maria's head light. Surely it could do no harm to imagine?

Another workday came to an end and it had come time for Stefano to go home. He put on his shirt, glancing toward the arched window. But Maria was not there. He set out for home on his usual path, singing sadly.

Trimming his hedge across the road, Signore Finelli laughed. "Hey, Stefano you're not happy today?'

"Ah, Signor Finelli. I'm happy, but I'm also sad."

Signor Finelli laughed. "Ah, you're a crazy gardener. I think the flowers do things to your mind."

"They do, Signor, they do."

"Come over here please, Stefano. My wife needs your help." He set down his shears and called loudly into the house, "Elena, *vieni qui presto*. The gardener is here!"

"I can't come that quickly anymore you fool. I'm an old

woman." Mrs. Finelli emerged from their house, wiping her floury hand on her apron. She grabbed Stefano by the elbow and pulled him more than led him into their garden. "Can I trust you with something?" She looked the gardener in the eye.

"*Certo*." He assured her.

"I belong to a bridge club and every year we have a gardening contest to see who can create the most beautiful vegetable garden." Angrily she grabbed a hoe and began striking the soil. "My garden is a mess and I can't seem to make it flourish. Every year I come in second place, second, I can't take it anymore! This year I must come in first.

"*Si*, you should, you will! Who comes in first?"

"Antonietta Peragine." Digging the hoe even deeper in the ground. "I need to win, Stefano, just one time. And if you help me, I know I will win."

"What will you win?"

She stood up proudly. "I will get my picture in the newspaper, and my garden of course."

"Well then, we will make sure that happens. Immediately, he dropped to his knees to feel the soil. "Ah ha." Her tomatoes would not grow. The herbs were dry and the vegetables looked sick. The fruit on her pear and plum trees, stunted.

"*Per favore*, I'm getting desperate!" the woman pleaded.

Stefano dug deeper in the soil, moving his hands around their plants. A strange look came over his face. His eyes closed for a moment then he smiled up at the old couple.

Signor Finelli gawked at Stefano without much hope. "Is there anything you can do to help her? The Riccis have such a perfect garden. Why? Is it because you are their gardener, or because they are rich and spoiled? We are right next door and my wife's garden, well, you see for yourself, no?" He let out a belly laugh, followed by a cough. "My wife can cook, but she's hopeless in the garden. Like Carlo and his bread."

Elena Finelli elbowed him in *lo stomaco*.

Stefano smiled up at them both as gently, he began to caress the fruits, vegetables and herbs. "Your garden will be just fine, Signora Finelli. You'll have beautiful fruits and vegetables in no time. We will see your picture in the paper for sure."

"Are you sure?"

"Absolutely."

"*Basta cosí*? That's all?" Signore Finelli scoffed. "Surely you have more skill than that, my boy. A mixture of herbs in a bottle in your pocket? Something they taught you back wherever you come from...where do you come from anyway?" Smiling uncomfortably, Stefano stood up, brushing off his trousers.

"Shut up, you old fool," Signora Finelli told her husband. "Don't be so ungrateful. *Grazie*, Stefano." She kissed him on the cheek.

"*Prego*." He blushed.

"Stefano," Finelli broke in, clapping one large hand on the gardener's shoulder. "Tell me, that Martino Ricci, he's one mean bastard, no? He wins every case. I wouldn't want to be on the other end, if you know what I mean." Finelli curled up his bottom lip with disgust. "Come on, tell us. We won't say a word." He blessed himself with the sign of the cross and then kissed his fist, throwing it up to God. "Our lips are sealed, right Elena?" He turned to his wife, who nodded her head in agreement.

"I like Maria Ricci," Elena said. "She's beautiful and always pleasant, but I don't know...he...I don't like him very much. God forgive me. So superior, just like his father." She, too, made the sign of the cross and kissed her hand.

Stefano stood up and looked over at the Ricci Garden. He glimpsed Maria standing in the arched window. She stayed just long enough to take his breath away, then, noticing him watching her, quickly disappeared. Stefano turned back to the Finellis. "I guess its part of his job. Signore Ricci is all right. I can't complain."

"You're too nice! Don't you have even a little dirt on him? Tell me something *piccante*," Signore Finelli pried.

Incanto ~ The Singing Gardener

"We hear him yelling all the time," Signora Finelli added. "That poor girl. And that mother of his, *Dio Mio!*"

But Stefano could not talk about Maria, even indirectly, even to people so essentially kind. "Sometimes Signore Ricci drinks a little too much. It makes him loud."

"Ah, go on and get out of here, Stefano." Signore Finelli gave him a playful shove.

"And don't forget to check on my garden," Signora Finelli reminded.

"I promise. *Ciao.*" Stefano strolled home, resuming his song.

Early the next morning Signora Finelli woke, put on the pot of espresso, and looked out the window through the sleep in her eyes. She quickly wiped her eyelids as if to correct her vision. Who could believe it? Her garden was thriving. Tomatoes hung plump and red, heavy on the vine. An explosion of herbs tangled and intertwined on the bamboo stakes that held them. Eggplant, zucchini, broccoli, peppers and carrots sprouted from the earth. Ripe pears and plums blossomed everywhere.

Her jaw dropped. She screamed, "Tino, quick! Come this instant!"

Signore Finelli barreled in from the bedroom half-dressed. "What, who died? What are you screaming about?" He found her frozen at the window.

"What did he do to my garden?" She walked out to get a closer look. Signore Finelli followed. "It's beautiful." She repeated softly, "*Bellissima.*"

"It's about time." Signore Finelli lit a cigar. "It was probably ready to blossom anyway. He just tugged on those vines a bit. No big deal. Is my espresso ready?"

Elena Finelli walked around her garden, oblivious to her husband's demand. He threw his hands up and waved at her like she was crazy. Going inside, he poured his espresso into his favorite small cup. Carrying it delicately, he took it out onto the porch just in time to catch Stefano on his way back to work at the

Ricci's and Carlo approaching with a fresh basket of bread.

"B*uongiorno*, Signor Finelli." Carlo smiled and held out his bread. Finelli waved for him to come and join him.

"Why aren't you singing this morning, gardener?" Finelli sipped his espresso and shot Stefano a skeptical glance.

Stefano shrugged. The truth was, he hadn't found his song yet for the day, but Finelli already thought him crazy enough. "Give my best to your wife," he said and carried on.

"Eh! What did you do to her garden?" Finelli yelled after him.

"Is he gardening for you now too? How come he never helps us?" Carlo pouted, and Finelli shot him a look.

"No one can help you Carlo, now sit, we are going to talk about your putrid bread this morning."

"Nothing," Stefano replied humbly, walking on.

Finelli nodded and smiled to himself. "Nothing. You see. I knew it."

"Tell her I'll come by and check on it soon," Stefano called back. He waved to Finelli and Carlo and then turned into the Ricci's property, his heart pounding with every step along the cobblestone. As he approached Maria's garden, he could hear Finelli scolding Carlo.

"Find a new hobby please. Art, wine, anything, but baking." Finelli shouted as he broke his bread into a million pieces. "Your bread is for the birds." A bunch of birds quickly flew down to attack the bread crumbs, but even they rejected after they sampled. "You see, putrid!"

* * *

Stefano noticed Mama Ricci's automobile in the driveway next to her son's. Loud shouting came from the house. Pretending not to notice, he began working in the garden, touching the roses with his hands, brushing over the daffodils, he peered through.

Mama Ricci scolded Martino, chasing him around the sitting room. Maria sat at the window with her hands cupped over her ears. Running over to her, the older woman reached down, and pulled Maria's hands away from her ears and began yelling in one ear. Martino yelled in Maria's other ear. Stefano could not make out what anyone was saying, but clearly no one was in agreement on any count.

Clenching her fist, Maria pushed them into the table and stood up, as her pale complexion twisted bright red. Defiantly, she shouted back at Mama Ricci. The woman smacked her hard across the face and Stefano felt the blow as if on his own skin. But Maria quickly responded, matching Mama with a smack of her own. Shocked that Maria had struck his mother; Martino smacked his wife hard in the face, again and again until Maria began to cry. Stefano watched on, his fist clenched, his body trembling. Powerless to protect Maria, he finally turned away. After a little while, the front door opened and Martino stormed out.

"I won't be home for dinner tonight." He yanked the gray fedora onto his head, plunged into his coupe and sped off.

After a moment, Mama Ricci came out the door and, turning back to Maria, hissed, "See what you have done? No wonder you can't get pregnant. Your husband doesn't even want to come to you, *strega*!" Deliberately this time, she stomped on the potted plant of calla lilies, breaking the pot and smashing them to the ground. A pained look filled Maria's face.

Mama Ricci jumped in her automobile and sped off, all the while clutching the side of her face where she'd been slapped and yelling out the window, "You crazy witch! You crazy stupid witch!"

Maria stood at the front door sweating and struggling to calm her breath. Out of the corner of her eye, she caught the motion of a dark curtain in the house next door. Prima stared out the window without turning away, and Maria burned with shame. But the look on her neighbor's face was one of sympathy. Maria stood on the front step like a lost child.

"*Scusi*, Signora Ricci." Brushing his hands against his pant legs, Stefano tried to get her attention.

Instantly, she turned to him. "Please, Signor Portigiani, Maria. Call me Maria. Never Signora Ricci."

He pretended to ignore the significance of this. "Maria?" he repeated softly. "Maria." He smiled. "Then please, Maria, call me Stefano."

Maria collapsed in the doorway. Shocked, Stefano reached out to catch her. The weight of her body felt like nothing in his hands. "Signora, are you all right?" When she did not respond, he gathered her more tightly in his arms and, glancing around uncertainly, carried her into the house.

He laid her down on the upholstered day bed in the sitting room. The house, which he had never been inside of, shone immaculate. Dizzy from the immense house and all it spoke of Maria's life, Stefano took a breath and remembered why he was here. She hung limp in his arms, unmoving. Sweat dripped from his forehead. His work boots had left a trail of soil on the tile between the daybed and the door. Pulling out a handkerchief from his chest pocket, he began to wipe the droplets from Maria's brow. He noticed her delicate skin and stopped himself. His handkerchief was not clean enough to touch her!

He released her gently against the cushions and ran to the kitchen, where he spotted a white cloth. He went to the sink and quickly scrubbed his dirty hands, then wet the cloth and ran back to her side.

He knelt down beside Maria as if she were one of his flowers. Tenderly, he wiped her forehead with the cool, wet cloth and his eyes stole a glance at the length of her curving body. He took a deep breath to collect himself. Slowly, her almond-shaped eyes opened. Fixing her gaze on him, she whispered, "Stefano."

"Si, Signora." He could not bring himself to say her name again, though he longed to. "Are you all right? You fainted."

She nodded and struggled to get up.

"No, no, relax. You must rest."

"But you don't understand," she stammered.

"What do I not understand? Maria?" The name felt irresistible,

Incanto ~ The Singing Gardener

delicious on his lips. "Tell me."
Her mind raced anxiously, and her mouth felt dry. "Please, could you get me a *limonata* from the icebox?"
"Of course." Stefano got up and went to the kitchen again.
"And one for yourself," she called. "Please, have some *limonata* with me."
"Thank you," Stefano replied. Finding two glasses, he filled them with *limonata*. When he returned Maria was sitting up, a look of horror on her face.
"What is it?" he asked, handing her the drink.
"I'm doomed. What have I done? He should have just married his mother. That woman is the devil." She drank the entire glass of *limonata* as if it would be her last.
"Don't worry. She's gone now." He tried to comfort her, but he did not know where to put his hands, his eyes. He concentrated on his drink.
"She will be back, that's for sure. She always comes back and each time she does it's worse. He always takes her side and never defends me."
"Maria." Her name rolled slowly off Stefano's tongue as if it were a song.
She smiled weakly. "I like the way my name sounds when you say it. No one calls me Maria anymore." As if to challenge him, she looked into Stefano's eyes.
His stomach twisted in knots. "What do they call you?" he managed. Pools of water gathered in her eyes then were quickly replaced by fury.
"Signora Ricci, or woman. Martino calls me 'wife'."
"Wife?" He repeated.
"Yes," she admitted, ashamed. "I think it's to remind me of my place."
Not only did Stefano feel her anguish, he longed to take it away. But, sitting with her there on the edge of the daybed, he knew that he had stepped far out of his place. The maid Angelina

would arrive at any time. He became afraid. If he didn't leave in that moment, he would have to take Maria in his arms and kiss her. This would surely bring death to them both.

He drained his glass of *limonata* and set it with one trembling hand on a side table. "Signora, I'd better go now. Will you be all right?"

"I hope so, Stefano."

A soft electric current filled his veins as she touched his hand and he wondered if she felt it too. "Thank you for helping me today."

"It was a pleasure." As he turned to trace his steps back to the front door, he noticed again all the dirt from his work boots. He bent down and started to clean the tile with the cloth in his hand. "*Scusi.* I will clean this."

She rose and, bending down next to him, said, "No, allow me." She took the cloth from his hand. Her proximity made him reel. "It will remind me that something different happened to me today. You can't imagine how much I needed this."

It took everything Stefano had to pull himself off that floor and out of the Ricci home. He had never dreamed that he would actually set foot into that house, and now he felt that if he didn't leave immediately, someone would discover his secret desires and shoot him dead.

"*Ciao*, Maria."

"*Ciao*, Stefano,"

"I will see you tomorrow," he stammered. "In the garden of course. I will be here in the garden tomorrow, as usual." He stumbled out the door. Bending down to the broken pot of calla lilies, Stefano gathered up the mess.

From across the way Finelli peered through his binoculars. "Ah ha, something is going on at the Ricci's." His wife shook her head and walked away. "I don't know what yet, but I'm going to figure it out."

"You need to find a hobby, Tino." Signora Finelli yelled back. "I'll be in my garden doing something productive.

Incanto ~ The Singing Gardener

* * *

Later in the afternoon, Maria stepped outside to visit the garden. Turning on the step, she giggled like a little girl when she discovered the calla lilies restored once again to perfection.
* * *
At the end of the day, leaving Maria's garden, Stefano sang a song of hope. Before he could get far with it, though, The LaPortas were beckoning him from across the low stone wall that separated their property from the Ricci's.

"*Scusi*, gardener!" Carlo called, his wife standing at his side with a stern expression. He was as warm as she was cold, as plump as she was skinny. Stefano approached them and they prevailed on him to come through the front gate. "I saw how you helped Signora Finelli's garden," Carlo LaPorta pressed. "You see, it's our grapes. They are suffering in our hands. My father left me this place. The grapes were his jewels. I may give up baking bread and try my hand at winemaking. What do you think?"

"Making good wine is even more difficult than baking bread, but why not try? Your soil is perfect for it."

Tessa, in her cool way, tried to get Stefano to gossip about the Riccis. "I heard that terrible fight this morning," she began. "I certainly hope everyone is all right? Mothers-in-law are difficult, as everyone knows. They are like fish." Stefano looked at her with a question in his eyes. He didn't think he had ever heard her say so much. "After two days, they start to stink! And that one of Maria Ricci's?" Stefano let Tessa LaPorta talk, but only nodded, giving her none of the details she craved. Stefano examined the wilting grape leaves in the vineyard, touching them with all the love he could muster. He told the couple how better to care for their vineyard. Carlo pulled out a bottle of wine from his family's vintage. "In exchange for the wonderful advice! Please..."

"*Grazie*, but that is not necessary. It is my pleasure, truly."

Handing it to Stefano. "Take it with you to enjoy at home,"

Carlo LaPorta insisted. "After all," he said, "I am sure you have helped our vineyard."

Stefano resumed his path home and had just resumed his song when Signore Finelli stopped him.

"Gardener, come here. My wife wants you to check the tomatoes."

Crossing the road reluctantly, Stefano obliged. "You're singing a nice song today! Tell me why you're so happy. All we heard was barking like angry dogs coming from the Ricci's! Eh, is it that wine you're bringing home?"

Stefano nodded and laughed. "Carlo gave it to me. He wanted a little advice on his vineyard. He may give up baking bread and make wine."

Belly laughing, Finelli practically choked. "That will be the day. Carlo make wine? Please, he's lucky he can cook an egg, ha, make wine, what a dreamer." He led Stefano to the garden. "My wife has been waiting for you all day. Stefano was pleased to see that the garden was thriving.

"Stefano, what did you do to my garden?" she prodded, wiping her hands on her apron and coming out to greet him with a kiss on both cheeks.

"Oh, Signora, it was all you." Stefano smiled. "Don't listen to Signore Finelli. You are a wonderful gardener."

The old woman smiled back. "You're sweet and humble. I don't know what you did or how you did it, but whatever it is, I think I stand a chance to win that contest." She danced around her tomatoes like a happy child. "But enough about that. Tell us what the hell is going on over there! The whole village can hear them," Signora Finelli cried.

He hesitated only a moment, then found the words he needed. "Martino's mother is desperate for a grandchild. She's getting a little old, you know, so she's sad and wants so much for Signora Ricci to have a baby." He shrugged his shoulders nonchalantly.

"That's it? Come on!" Signore Finelli demanded.

"That can't be all," Signora Finelli complained. "I can always smell a lie. That used to be my job Stefano, sniffing out liars and thieves."

"There's nothing more. They all want the same thing, a baby. They just yell a lot because they're…passionate people." He got down on bended knee and touched the plants. "Make sure you water them, Signora. They get thirsty. And love…all living things require love to thrive, this is most important. They need love even more than water, sun or air. Don't forget this. I promise you will win the contest if you love them. Oh, and talk to them and sing to them. Like friends."

The Finellis looked at one another, bewildered. Stefano rose from the soil and kissed them both on the cheek. As he prepared to leave, they shrugged. "You have a tight lip," Signore Finelli said. Stefano smiled. It was true, he was not the kind to say too much.

"I must go. *Ciao.*" He set off down the road, glancing behind him to Maria's arched window. She was not there. He headed home singing his song, the notes deep and soaring, emerging like birds from the center of his chest, but underneath, a melody of sorrow.

Stefano would never be the same. He knew exactly how it felt now to gaze into her eyes, feel her tender skin and hold her in his arms. Everything about her consumed him. Her scent lingered in his hair and on his shirt. Her voice echoed in his head, writing lyrics on his heart.

Trish Doolan

QUATTRO

When he got far enough along the cypress-lined road, out of sight of Maria's closest neighbors, Stefano sat on a large stone and held his head in his hands. Afraid of being seen, he moved from the stone and dipped below a thick old poplar at the edge of the Giuliano residence. With so much land and so many rooms to wander, the Giulianos were seldom about. There could be little danger of being discovered here.

No longer able to contain the agony that welled inside of him, Stefano rested his head on the gnarled bark of a tree, exhaled deeply, and began to sob. All around him, he saw, truffles sprouting. And he had found a love as rare! Yes, today he had realized the depths of his feelings for Maria. But instead of bringing joy, this knowledge brought him despair. Exhausted, Stefano stumbled further into the Giuliano property and collapsed onto a barren field. Still clutching the unopened bottle the LaPortas had given him, he fell fast asleep.

Hours later, Maria's sad keys swept again through the village, waking Stefano. It was dark in the field, but his eyes caught the half lit moon and it held his stare. "Please help me forget her," he asked it. "She is not mine." These words cut his throat like razors. Stefano was in love like never before, but to fall in love with someone who is already spoken for is a sure path to misery. Was Maria happy? In Stefano's heart he knew she wasn't. So why should it be a sin to take her from the source of her misery? All these questions gnawed at him while Maria's piano called out its song of yearning.

With no one else to speak to, he spoke to the moon, "You light up the sky; that is certain. Can you shine a light on my problem? I can't breathe until she's resting next to me. Please let me have this one thing!"

Tears ran down his cheeks and dripped off his chin, falling into the soil beneath him. He grabbed the dirt and kissed it like a lover. It covered his lips. He tasted its barren years and did not cringe. Clutching more and more, he covered himself in the soil.

Spreading his love and his pain, his heart beat like a drum and he pressed himself to the ground. Crazy with wanting Maria, Stefano rose to his feet and began to dance in the desolate field, accompanied by the melody she played in the distance.

The Giuliano's field was dead. No life had touched it for decades. Even the olive trees at its edge were dry as driftwood. Stefano danced alone, but he imagined every detail of Maria in his arms. After all, he knew now what it felt like to hold her. And for a moment, even though it was just an illusion, she was there. They glided on a moonlit dance floor and he sang to her of their future together. Her green eyes sparkled with delight, mending his heart. He led and she followed, the entire field graced by the rhythm of their feet. She smiled at him. They both kicked off their shoes and let the earth absorb their bare feet.

Delirious, he fell fast asleep.

When he awoke again, morning had dawned and he lay in a field replete with Casablancas. One full acre of the trumpet-like white lilies covered the land. Stefano rubbed his eyes and then saw the hand reaching to help him up.

"Who are you and what are you doing here?" A man's deep voice poured down on him.

"*Buongiorno*, Signore. I'm Stefano, the Ricci's gardener." His eyes adjusted to the light and he made out the tall man in an elegant white suit and hat standing above him. "So sorry, I fell asleep here."

When he had raised Stefano to his feet, Signore Giuliano introduced himself. Then he looked around and caught his breath. "I don't believe my eyes. This land has been fallow for years. How can this be? Last night I said goodnight to a field of nothing and this morning I wake to a field of perfect lilies. Am I dreaming?"

"No, Signore," Stefano said, surveying the evidence of the

miracle that had passed through him. "Your soil will never be fallow again."

"I don't understand," Giuliano exclaimed.

"You don't need to. Just enjoy my simple gift to you."

"And *who* are you?"

"I told you, I'm just the gardener at the Ricci's."

"Yes, I've seen their garden. It's the most beautiful in Tuscany."

"Thank you. You are too kind."

"No, I'm just truthful and, to be honest, jealous. How did Martino Ricci get so lucky?"

"Oh, I don't know." Stefano replied. Then, changing the subject, he added. "Your soil wasn't dead, just thirsty for love. Sometimes, Signore, things appear to be dead, but in reality they are very much alive."

Signore Giuliano stood in awe, shaking his head. "These are my wife's favorite flowers."

"Why not pick a bunch and bring her some for breakfast?" Stefano offered.

"I think I will, gardener. What is your name?"

"Stefano."

"Stefano, you are an angel from up above." Giuliano bent and began picking flowers like a kid in a candy store. Stefano smiled. "How you did this I will never know, but thank you."

"It wasn't really me."

"Well, whatever or whoever did it, God bless you Stefano the Gardener. Filomena will be delighted."

As Stefano gazed across the field of lilies, he noticed Giuliano's wife standing on the front steps of their large home. She was crying, overwhelmed by the blossoming field that seemed to float in the breeze like a freshly washed sheet. The scent of the Casablancas intoxicated her. She held her heart, crying as if a long lost lover had returned to her. Signore Giuliano gathered as many Casablancas as his arms could hold and, taking leave of Stefano, brought them to his wife. Overpowered, she looked at her husband

Incanto ~ The Singing Gardener

with eyes of a virgin and took the flowers into her arms.

* * *

Stefano gathered for himself a few Casablancas and his bottle of wine. He left the field covered in dirt and smelling like a mixture of earth, sweat, and tears. The field had come to life, but his own heart remained as barren as the soil he'd slept on the night before.

Arriving at the front of his cottage, he stood in the morning sun and gave his confession to the sun, God and all the heavens. "God," he pleaded, "I wish I could lie to you. You already know because you see all that is true. I'm in love with a woman who is married, but I believe you meant her to be mine. I may be wrong. But I want her more than anything I have ever wanted. I promise to pour all my love into your soil whether or not she is with me. I know you have put me on earth to heal whatever grows. But please, God, please? Bring Maria and me together."

With this, he entered the stone cottage and shut the door.

* * *

Oblivious to all but each other, the Giulianos scarcely noticed that Stefano had left. Inspired by Casablancas, they went up to their bedroom and made love as if for the first time. Decorating the bed with fresh white petals, they delighted in the strong aroma of lilies, which became more and more potent when crushed by their bodies.

"My prayer has been answered." Giuliano looked into Filomena's eyes.

"What prayer? I thought you gave up on God?" He cried into his wife's hair. "Will you come back to church with me?"

"Yes my love, every Sunday, I promise."

* * *

The same morning, Maria sat in her arched window waiting for the gardener to come. Why was he late? Martino had never made it home the night before. Grateful for the time away from him, Maria did not care. But Stefano's absence did concern her. In all the time he had worked for the Riccis, he'd never once been late for work. Maria poured herself another glass of *limonata* and heard an automobile screech to a halt in front of the house. Martino stumbled out completely disheveled. He barged into the house, saw Maria there in the window, and stared at her in moody silence. She walked over to him and it was all she could do not to wince from the heavy odor of cheap perfume on his skin. Looking closely, she noticed pink lipstick marks on his collar.

"You should bathe," she said coldly. "Take off your clothes. I'll wash them."

They went upstairs. "I'm sorry," Martino pouted as he began to undress. "It's only that I miss you. Do you know how I feel? I get lonely for you my love." He reached for Maria, but she put her hands up to stop him. "Fine," he said sharply. "I'll get ready for work." He walked into the bathroom. She went downstairs with the stained shirt in hand. Angrily, she began to scrub it clean in the kitchen sink, all the while looking at her window wondering where Stefano could be.

Martino came down again clean and dressed for work. "What time would you like me home for dinner, wife?" He kissed her softly on the cheek.

"Angelina is coming at four and dinner will be ready by seven. But, really, come home whenever you want. If you're not here I will just put your plate aside."

"No, I'll be here. I want to be here." Martino smiled at her, and then noticed her preoccupation with the world beyond the window. Looking out, he realized Stefano was nowhere to be seen. "And where's our crazy gardener?"

"I'm not sure, maybe he had to go back home for something." She stumbled for a good answer.

"What can he possibly need? He hardly uses tools anyway. Besides, we have everything here." Martino became aggravated. "It's after nine. I'll cut his wages. I think he's out of his mind. *Pazzo*! No one knows where he comes from. Does he even have a

Incanto ~ The Singing Gardener

family? He's lucky I even gave him a job.Maria blanched. "But darling. What does it matter? We have the most incredible garden in the land."
"Of course we do. I bought the best soil money can buy."
"That's true, but the gardener is…very talented."
"Talent? Really? Martino circled her like a suspect in a courtroom. "In what way is this man so talented wife of mine?" He stopped at her side and locked on her eyes. "Do you think he's more talented than I am? Do you prefer his talent to mine? Please share with me darling. Maybe I'm missing something here." Searching Maria's eyes he realized this suspect was not budging. "If he's not here by ten I want you to tell me and I'll fire him."
Martino left the house in a huff. He walked along the garden's edge to examine Stefano's work, stopping by each of the twenty-six beds of dirt, which were planned as beds for roses. But Martino had neither the vision nor the patience to see what the dirt might yield.
Maria, having emerged from the house, watched him from the front step. He turned to her, spit on the flowerbeds and then shuffled to his coupe and sped off. Maria sighed with relief.
For hours, Maria paced back and forth from the window to the door and back again, checking the clock and then the garden. With no sign of Stefano, she came to a decision and could not stop herself. She changed her clothes and walked out the front door to the side of the house where two old bicycles rested. Hopping on one of them, she rode down the cobblestone driveway and turned onto the road towards Stefano's cottage. Passing by the Cypress tress she acknowledged their beauty with a smile. Her heart racing with excitement she sped up, as the wind blew back her hair.
She didn't know exactly where he lived, but she thought she could find it. Martino had driven her by the place once. She remembered he had pointed at the place and laughed. "That's where our crazy gardener lives."
Now she peddled faster, perspiration speckling her face.

Coming to what appeared to be Stefano's cottage, she parked the bicycle at the rustic gate and walked up to the front door. Softly, she knocked.

No answer came, but the door creaked open from the weight of her hand. She pushed it open further and ventured in. Exploring the room, she found him lying in the narrow bed in the corner, still as a stone but breathing deeply. She looked down at him in silence. Examining his face, she took in the structure of his brow, his strong nose, wavy hair, and the cleft in his chin. Last, she focused on his lips, which to Maria appeared carved by God's angels. His body beneath the sheet, she knew, stretched long and lean.

She forced herself to turn away and glance around his home. The ceilings were low and the beams dark, but it was clean and tidy. It reminded her of where she used to live before she married Martino. She recognized the aroma that belonged only to the gardener—sweet earth, the salt of his sweat, and something she could not put into words, but undeniably brought her comfort.

She found herself aroused. Pulsating hot throbs filled her groin, as her breath quickened. A mixture of fear and excitement enveloped her, while chills raced through her body. Moving in closer stirred temptations unthinkable, yet she was thinking them and could almost taste the salt of his lips on her tongue. Knowing it was much more than a kiss, which she hungered for, she turned toward the door to go, but stopped. Looking up, she made the sign of the cross and clenched her fist tight. Maria had never felt anything like this for Martino or for any other man. It terrified her. She took a deep breath, straightened her clothes and hair and then cleared her throat.

"Stefano? Stefano?" Still, he did not respond. My God, she could touch him and he might not even notice. Did she dare? When she knelt down and got closer to his face, she saw he was smiling in his sleep, dimples marking his cheeks. What was running through his dreams?

Next to his bedside, the jug of fragrant Casablancas made her laugh out loud with delight. Quickly, she covered her mouth. But

Incanto ~ The Singing Gardener

the sound had roused him, and Stefano slowly opened his eyes. Was he dreaming? How could Maria be standing in front of him? Her green eyes held his. Their smiles mirrored one another.

"Is this a dream?" he asked.

"No, you're awake and I'm here," she all but whispered.

"But this can't be real. I should wake up."

"It is real, but it's true that you need to wake up. If you don't, my husband will fire you."

Now that his eyes were open and he was talking to her, Maria felt overcome with nerves. Imagine! She, Maria Ricci standing above the bed of a man not her husband! She stammered, "*Scusi*, but that is why I came. I came to wake you up."

Stefano quickly popped up, sat at the edge of the bed, and examined the sun outside the window. "Oh my God! It must be after two. How can this be? I'm so sorry, Maria. Last night, I, I....Last night something happened." He did not know how to explain.

"Did you get drunk?" She gestured to the wine bottle on his table, not noticing that it had not been opened. "Sorry. It's not my business."

"No, Maria."

She melted at the sound of her name on his tongue.

"I did not get drunk, at least not on wine. I'm sorry. I know I do not make any sense to you, but..." He stopped for a moment, taking in her eyes, her curving mouth, and the beautiful nose he had recently noticed was just slightly, ever so delightfully crooked. This *was* a dream, a dream come true. To have her standing before him? God had answered his prayer.

"I'll wash up quickly. Thank you for waking me. I don't want to lose my job." He restrained himself from telling her he could not live without seeing her everyday. Similarly, he wanted more than anything to touch her, but commanded his hands be still.

"You mustn't lose the job. I—the garden needs you."

"There's nothing I want more than to care for it."

Each word that passed between them found them standing closer and closer. They were nearly touching and Stefano trembled, feeling naked in her presence. Nervously, she turned her wedding band with her thumb and moved away from him.

"I have to go," Maria managed. "And you, you must hurry. If Martino gets home and you aren't there it will be very bad for you."

"Thank you, Maria. I will hurry. Again, I'm so sorry."

She smiled. "I'm not sorry. I'm happy to see where you go after… after you leave me."

He blushed and turned his head, noticing the Casablancas. "Please, these are for you. I made them last night."

"You… made them?'

"*Si*. No. I mean I picked them for you. They exist for you. Please, honor me by keeping them for yourself."

She took the lilies and held them up to her nose. "Exquisite."

"Yes." He could not stop staring at her. She did not want him to stop.

Without risking more words, she rushed out of his cottage and, laying the flowers in the bicycle's basket, pedaled home.

Shaking himself, Stefano hurried to get ready for work.

Maria rode by the Finellis, smiling so widely she looked almost like a different person. Signora Finelli on her knees, sang to her vegetable garden with delight as she witnessed them blossoming with happiness each and every day. Signor Finelli, lowered his newspaper. Shocked to see Maria, he jumped out of his chair shouting from his *terrazza*. "*Buongiorno*, Signora Ricci."

"*Buongiorno*, Signor Finelli," she called back happily. "These Cypress trees are so beautiful, no?"

He frowned with curiosity. He had never seen Maria Ricci ride a bicycle down that road before. "*E' una nuova biciclietta?*"

"*Si*," she agreed. It wasn't really a lie, was it? Everything seemed new to her this morning.

"You're taking some exercise, I suppose," he yelled.

"*Si*, Signor Finelli, *si*."

Incanto ~ The Singing Gardener

Signore Finelli narrowed his eyes unsatisfied. "Elena, come quickly!"

Rushing to the terrace as fast as she could, "What is it now?"

He shook his head and puffed on his cigar. "Something is going on at the Ricci's again."

Inside the Ricci house, Maria composed herself and changed her clothes, then picked the perfect vase for the lovely Casablancas. She made herself a glass of sweet *limonata* and sat in her arched window, waiting anxiously, her heart racing.

* * *

Stefano sprung out the door and up the road, running as fast as his legs could pump. The Finelli's watched him pass. "Ah ha, see, I smell trouble."

Signora Finelli elbowed him in his big belly. "The devil is in your mind Tino because you're bored to death."

Hey, gardener, are the bees chasing you or something?"

"No Signore Finelli, just trying to get in a little extra exercise."

"You're late today! Where were you this morning?" he shouted to Stefano.

Pretending not to have the breath to answer, Stefano continued on. Signore Finelli just shook his head, and patted his enormous belly. "I'm too old to exercise."

"And too fat." Signora Finelli added.

The LaPortas stood on the their *terrazza*, Carlo waving.

"Late today?" Carlo yelled.

"Too much wine last night?" Tessa joked sharply.

"Exactly! Thanks to you two."

"Come by later. I baked some fresh bread."

"*Grazie*, I will. *Ciao*."

Carlo yelled backed. "My grapes look hopeful this morning. Thank you."

* * *

He started up the driveway to the Ricci's, relieved to be beyond the curious eyes of the neighbors when suddenly he heard a voice like an owl's calling out *"Buongiorno!"* He turned and saw Prima, drinking a pot of espresso under her pergola.

"*Buongiorno*, Signora," he responded, waiting for more. But Prima merely raised her cup to him with a nod and took a delicate sip.

* * *

Stefano filled the can from the pump at the garden's edge and began watering Maria's flowers. It was later and hotter in the day than they usually drank, but they would forgive him. Maria, seeing him, smiled with relief in the window. Stefano, waving, smiled back. He could see that she had placed the Casablancas beside her on the table. A surge ran through his body as he reached down into one of the beds of dirt Martino had spit on that morning.

Slowly, yellow roses began rising, the buds tight and brilliant. Pleased, Stefano began to sing and moved onto the next empty bed. His voice drifted to Maria's ears as red rose buds sprung up to greet their maker. Stefano nodded. "Hello, little beauties." He moved from dirt bed to dirt bed and continued his song. Like a giddy girl, Maria watched through the window as one variety of rose after the next began to emerge.

Before long, Angelina came walking up the cobble stone path. She stopped and, thinking no one was watching, admired the gardener as much as his garden. Such a strong man. Though no one knew where he came from or from what kind of family, how could a simple girl go wrong with a man so nice to look at? Politely, he smiled back at her and the maid, giggling, sauntered into the house.

From her window, Maria watched. She never minded when Angelina caught her husband's eye, but fire ran through her veins at the thought of Stefano and Angelina together. Could he prefer the younger girl to her? Guilt stabbed her heart. If he wanted another, did he not have every right?

By the time the sun was beginning to sink, twenty-six beds of roses in various colors had emerged from the dirt beds.

Stefano had finished his song and was washing his hands at the

Incanto ~ The Singing Gardener

water pump when a familiar hand grabbed his shoulder. Startled, he turned to find Signore Giuliano standing before him, dressed in yet another immaculate white suit.

"Stefano the Gardener. How lovely to see you again."

"And you, Signore."

"I'm going to make some money thanks to you."

"*Bene, bene.*" Stefano waited curiously.

"Yes, I've made deals with several markets. They want to buy my lilies and it's all because of you."

"It's your land, Signor Giuliano."

"But it was you that healed it. I owe you something."

"No, no," Stefano answered, raising his hand in protest.

"Yes, my friend, I will reward you. I must. We will think of how. In the meantime, please take this as a small token of appreciation." Signor Giuliano handed him some money. From across the way, Finelli spied through his binoculars as he puffed on his cigar.

Stefano felt embarrassed, but Signor Giuliano insisted. "I will be insulted if you do not take this. Please don't make me upset."

With a nod, Stefano folded the money into his pocket.

"Excuse me now." Giuliano smiled as if he knew a secret. "I have some business to conduct here."

Stefano nodded as the older gentleman walked to the house. Angelina admitted him, casting a twinkling eye at the gardener and shutting the front door behind the visitor.

Inside, Maria greeted Signor Giuliano with surprise. So seldom did anyone but Mama Ricci come to the house. She asked after his wife and he smiled broadly. "She is magnificent." Maria nodded at the curious expression and they shared *limonata* while chatting about the Ricci's beautiful garden.

Suddenly, she heard Martino's coupe in the driveway. The car door slammed and the front door opened. After handing his coat to Angelina, Martino stalked into the sitting room, pulling at his tie, a scowl embedded on his face. Seeing Giuliano, he brushed at his

suit and composed a cold smile.
"Oh, I did not know we had guest."
Signore Giuliano rose from the chair to greet the man of the house, extending his hand warmly. Reluctantly, Martino shook it. His eyes followed Angelina's body as she hung his coat in the front closet.
"*Ciao*, Signor Ricci," the older gentleman began. "I'm your neighbor, Roberto Giuliano."
"Yes, I know who you are." Abruptly, and to Maria's embarrassment, Martino left the room. He went to the kitchen sink and washed his hands. Coming back, he stared out the arched window. "I see our crazy gardener showed up today after all."
"Yes, right after you left." Maria could not help but gush a little. "Did you see all the roses?"
"I saw them." Martino's voice had a hard edge. "That doesn't excuse the fact that he was late. If I were late for a trial I would be fired. No wonder he's just a gardener. Only a real man understands responsibilities. Do you agree Signor Giuliano?"
"Perhaps," Giuliano acceded. "But I do think gardening is an extremely important skill, an art in fact."
"Ha," Martino mocked. "An art! Plant the seed, water it, and watch it grow. This is art? You're as crazy as my gardener…and my wife. Do you know he actually sings to the soil? I even catch him sleeping in it. Does that sound like art to you?"
Maria lowered her eyes.
"Most great artist are strange, that's what makes them artists."
"Please stop calling it art! We are talking about flowers for God sakes!" Martino demanded a glass of wine from Angelina without offering any to his guest. "What can I do for you, Giuliano?" he asked.
"Actually, Signor Ricci, I came over here to ask if you'd be willing to part with that gardener of yours. He's not an artist, after all." Giuliano smiled. "And I can find you another gardener."
This request shocked Martino, but not as much as it did Maria. At the thought of losing Stefano, her stomach turned upside down.

Incanto ~ The Singing Gardener

As Angelina handed Martino his glass of *Chianti*, Maria grabbed the maid's arm.

"Please, Angelina, bring me some, too!" Then, remembering her manners, she asked if Signore Giuliano would like wine as well. Politely, he declined. When Angelina brought her full glass, Maria drank a little too quickly.

"Are you crazy, Giuliano?" Martino sputtered, taking no notice of his wife's strange behavior. "You want my gardener?"

"Yes."

"But your land is dead. It has no chance of producing for you."

"It was dead, but now that has changed. It is very much alive and thriving. I'll need someone with skill to keep it up."

Martino looked out the window. Stefano stood singing, holding tulips in his hands. Martino couldn't help but laugh.

"Look at him. Who would want such a fool?"

Everything inside of Maria wanted to scream out, "I!" She tasted her wine and tried to still her fluttering mind.

"I want him," Giuliano said simply.

"And what do I get?" Martino signaled to Angelina for more wine.

"Martino we can't…" Maria interjected, desperate to stop the transaction.

"Quiet, wife! I will make the decisions in my house. Is that understood?"

Maria sipped her wine quietly. Signore Giuliano cringed. No man should ever speak to a woman that way. "Well," Giuliano answered, keeping his tone civil. "We can discuss that once you decide, but I will find you another gardener and pay his wages for the first six months."

Martino smiled and Maria could see that nothing she could say would stand in the way of his greed. "Your land is the joke of the town."

"*Was* the joke Signor Ricci. I assure you things have changed. Please come and see for yourself. Come now if you like."

51

Trish Doolan

"I will think about it, Signor Giuliano. I will let you know." Martino walked over to the table and picked up the vase of Casablancas. "Where did these come from?" he demanded.

Maria's stomach tied itself into a knot. They did not have Casablancas in their garden and because he was a lawyer, Martino had a keen eye when it came to discovering evidence. Desperately, she found herself looking out the window toward Stefano, as if he might rescue her from a lie.

Signor Giuliano sensed her fear though he did not know its origin. "My wife had me bring them to your wife," he offered. "From our new and fruitful garden." Giuliano smiled.

Maria could not meet her neighbor's eyes, but her voice held all her gratitude. "Wasn't that a lovely gesture, husband?"

"You expect me to believe, Signore Giuliano," Martino scoffed, "that these flowers came from your decrepit land, which everyone knows has been dead for years?"

"Yes, I expect you to believe that and I beg you to come and see for yourself."

"Then let us go right now. My eyes can't wait to behold the source of such perfection." Martino began laughing hysterically. "You must come, too, wife, since you love flowers so very much."

* * *

Thus they found themselves on Giuliano's land, amidst an acre of lilies pure as fresh snow. Each flower waved in the breeze and Martino could not help but feel they were mocking him. Signore Giuliano and his wife stood alongside the Riccis. Martino's mouth hung like a spatula. Maria, overcome, felt as if she were dancing on a cloud.

"Now do you believe me, Signor Ricci?" Giuliano pressed.

Martino could barely speak. "This makes no sense." The lawyer had no proof or evidence to build a case that could deny miracle.

Signora Giuliano grabbed Maria's hand. "Please take as many as you like for your home."

Maria responded. "Thank you, but the ones you sent earlier

Incanto ~ The Singing Gardener

were more than enough."

Signore Giuliano winked at his wife and she said no more. He turned to Martino, "Please think about my offer."

"I will give it great consideration."

"Please do. I want only the best gardener for my land and you, my friend, have him. I believe he is an artist and you do not appreciate him, so why not replace him and make a profit?"

Martino was still having trouble absorbing the field of white blossoms. "Beautiful," he murmured. He took a deep breath and a smile filled his face. "They even smell real."

"That's because they are real," Signor Giuliano replied with a delicate grin.

"If I didn't see this with my own eyes I would not have believed it." Martino reached for Maria's hand. "Giuliano, may I take some home with me?"

"*Si*, take as many as you like," the older man replied.

Martino began picking lilies, stiffly at first, but then gathering them like an eager child. Maria scarcely recognized him.

That night Martino placed Casablancas all around the bedroom, laughing.

"What are you doing?" Maria asked, puzzled.

"I'm going to see how long these things live. There's got to be a trick. They're probably all defective." Stepping back, he stared at the bloom-filled bedroom. "But I must admit, they do look pretty." He laughed and, regarding Maria with sudden desire.

He pulled one of the flowers from the side of the bed and gently rubbed it along her chest. The fragrance opened Maria's senses. Her husband laid her down on the bed. "Say my name," Martino urged. But the only name that came into her mind was *Stefano*.

Trish Doolan

CINQUE

Martino walked into the sitting room the next morning carrying the Casablancas that had decorated the bedroom the night before. They remained as fresh as when he'd picked them. Maria was sitting staring at the garden. He bent down and kissed her cheek.

"Maria, last night was...fantastic. You were so different. I don't know what it was." The sound of her name on her husband's lips made her cringe. With a sinking realization, she understood why.

"Yes, I was different." She could never be the same.

"Maybe it's because you conceived last night," Martino said, coming to stand between her and the window, bending to caress her cheek.

Maria's body went weak at the mere possibility. "Yes, husband, maybe."

"Mama would be relieved, no? And so would I." Suddenly, Martino appeared a small boy again in Maria's eyes, trembling at the thought of his mother's rage. He went on. "She would leave you alone. And we could be a family, happy together. That's all I have ever wanted my dear wife. I do cherish you." He kissed her over and over and then nuzzled on her neck until she began to laugh. "Ah ha, I knew I could get you to smile. You fight me, I know, but I do make you happy my dear, do I not?"

"Yes, you do." She removed herself from his grip and walked to the stove.

His heart ached as she slipped away. "Do I? I can never tell. You wouldn't lie to me, would you my darling?" Desperately wanting to change the subject, Maria turned on the burner, but then realized she had nothing to cook, or boil or any reason to even be by the stove.

"No, I would not." Frustrated, she turned back to her husband and focused on the Casablancas in his hand. "And why are you

Incanto ~ The Singing Gardener

holding all those flowers?" she asked him.

"I'll bring some to Mama. That will make her happy. Who would have thought that crazy gardener could create such beauty?" Maria's eyes fell down to the floor. Martino waited for her to respond. "Can you believe how pretty these flowers are?"

"Yes, of course," she blurted, without thinking.

"Oh really, why is that?" Here was the hard tone she was trying to avoid.

"He's very... passionate about his work." Her skin began to burn at the mention of Stefano. But she went on. "He seems to be such a hard worker. Hard work always pays off. That is what I'm trying to say," she fumbled.

"I work hard." He moved in to kiss her mouth, but she pretended not to notice and turned away. Bristling with rejection, knowing how much the garden meant to her, he said, "Maybe I will let Giuliano have the gardener. My garden grows by itself. I can get anyone to water it. Why should I pay for a gardener to sing to the flowers? He's crazy anyway." He raised his arm and made a twisting gesture by his head. " And Giuliano? He's even crazier. Imagine how stupid he is to pay for our new gardener for six months? I would've given him away for free. Get someone more reliable. Yes, I might just do it," he exclaimed.

Maria jumped in her chair. "But why?"

"I just told you. What do you care who we have for a gardener?"

"You know I love that garden!"

"Yes, I do, but no one is taking your garden away. I'm talking about replacing the gardener."

"But..."

"But nothing." He laughed. "Why? Do you have a special interest in our gardener?"

Maria fell quiet, staring at her wedding band.

"I leave for Rome tomorrow," Martino said. "I'll decide while I'm away and give Giuliano my answer when I return." As Martino

55

left her, Maria's stomach churned. She buried her face in her hands.

Martino was getting into his car just as Stefano came walking up the drive for work. "*Ciao*, gardener." Ricci chuckled strangely. "Nice lilies."

"*Buongiorno*, Signor Ricci. *Grazie*." Stefano smiled politely.

Martino turned and noticed his wife staring at the gardener through her favorite arched window. He sank into his car and drove off. Stefano watched his employer pull out and waited until he had driven out of sight. Then he turned toward Maria, a smile of anticipated pleasure on his face. But when he saw her, her figure heavy with sadness, he knew that something was wrong.

Stefano walked up the front steps and gently knocked on the door. After a long pause, Maria opened it, the old wood creaking.

When she saw Stefano on the threshold, sun shimmering on his face, Maria thought she would break down. The hues of gold made him look like an angel in a painting.

"*Buongiorno*, Maria." His words poured out like a melody.

She melted before him. "*Buongiorno*, Stefano." Then, turning away as if the sight of him were too much to bear, she asked. "Shall I get you some *limonata*? It's hot already."

"No, Maria. I'm not thirsty for *limonata* right now." He stood firmly. She faced him again and their eyes held each other's gaze until Maria broke it. She could not chance the feelings coming over her.

"Well, I will have some," she said. "Excuse me. I'm rather hot this morning." She went to the kitchen and opened the icebox, leaving Stefano in the doorway. Instinctively, he moved to follow her, but quickly remembered his place and position. Glancing down at his dirty boots, he saw they were dirtying the beautiful terra cotta tiles that protected the floor. What had he been thinking?

"I suppose I should begin my work for the day," he said when she came back. He noticed that she had no *limonata* in her hand. She struggled to keep her eyes from catching his. "Maria, is there

something wrong?"
Looking into his eyes, she could not lie. "Yes, Stefano."
"What is it? Tell me," he pleaded.
She began to speak. "You…Martino…" He deserved a warning that he might lose his job, but she could not get the words out. Noticing that the door hung wide open, she ushered him in and slammed it shut. Stefano looked at her with surprise.
"I'm sorry if I upset you somehow. I will go now, Maria."
Tenderly, she covered his mouth with her finger. "No, sshh, no Stefano I do not want you to go!"
"Maria, I should not be here."
"But you are and so am I. Do you want to go, Stefano?"
He moaned. "Never, Maria. I never want to leave you." He began caressing her face delicately. Her breath grew deeper. Her whole body began to shake with desire.
"Oh my God, we can't!" she cried, but she was already touching his face with her fingertips, following each curve as if tracing a map that would lead her home.
They smiled and then, as if a wind were pushing them from behind, they embraced. Their hungry lips found each other.
"Oh, how can this be?" She managed to catch her breath.
"How long I have waited, Maria," Stefano gasped with relief.
"I, too, have waited."
Knowing it could not last, Stefano savored her taste--lemons and sugar and something fresh and clean. He felt lost, wondering how he would ever recover. Would he ever want to?
"I am yours," Stefano whispered softly into Maria's ear.
The smell of spring rain permeated her hair. She folded into his arms and realized that she, too, belonged to him, but should not say so. Still, the truth burned to be shared. Maria succumbed to the wave of her desire. "And… I am yours," she confessed.
He pulled her away and, gripping her arms, looked into her green eyes. "But, Maria, you aren't mine and you can never be."
She wished he had not said it, but it was true. Confusion and

guilt stirred inside of her. She looked into Stefano's open face. "You are right," she said, her voice hollow. She stepped away from him and he felt as if he'd been ripped apart.

"But we can find a way," he broke in. "Surely, God would not present such a love to us only to take it away."

"Perhaps," she worried. "But perhaps this temptation does not come from God."

With that, he could not bear to look at her any longer. He could not find words to sway her. "If that's how you feel, I suppose I'd better go back to the garden."

"I--yes." She watched him walk out the door and when it closed behind him, felt that someone in her own family had died.

Signore Finelli passed the binoculars to his wife. Looking through, she witnessed a dejected Stefano trudging back to the garden. Lowering the binoculars she shook her head and handed them back to her husband. "No, I cannot believe it. He's too good. It's not what you think. I'm sure he's just being helpful to Signora Ricci."

"Helpful? Eh, whatever you say." Finelli puffed on his cigar with satisfaction.

* * *

Maria clutched her stomach. A dull ache pierced her guts. How could she have let him go? How could she let him stay? No answers came to her. She savored his taste in her mouth. She longed for him to kiss her lips again. Standing frozen, confusion swirled through her mind. All at once, she knew she must take herself to church. There she might be consoled, might find answers to her questions. Running upstairs, she washed her face and changed her clothes. She could not go to the house of God with Stefano's scent lingering on her.

Making her way through the village as if in a dream, she passed the ancient walls of the castle and ran her hand along the stones for balance. The ground below her seemed to move further and further away, and her head spun. Perspiration misted her brow and the

Incanto ~ The Singing Gardener

palms of her hands. Her hair hung hot against her neck. With each step, she felt she marched to her own crucifixion. But this was the only way she knew to cleanse her soul, to come back to herself again.

As she walked past shops and cafes, Maria imagined the eyes of the people of Castellina scorching holes in her. She might as well have been wearing a sign. Stones might fly at any moment! Finally, she made it to the church only to notice Mama Ricci exiting. The portly woman bustled down the front steps with an air of satisfaction, as if she had just given the priest or God a piece of her mind. Heart racing, Maria quickly turned away and hid around the side of the building until Mama had moved out of sight. Catching her breath, she headed up the front steps and pushed open the wooden doors.

As she entered the church, the thick scent of frankincense and myrrh pricked Maria's nostrils. She glanced around. Three older women dressed in black sat in a pew muttering their prayers. As she passed, they gaped at her as if they knew her to be a sinner. Why else would she be coming to confess, after all? Maria could almost smell the years of mourning on their musty dresses. Genuflecting, she took a seat in the pew near the confessionals and focused on the tile floor. Each tile had been imprinted with a royal blue cross in the middle of a yellow and orange spiral. The pattern made her dizzy and her stomach clenched in a knot.

    No one waited before or behind her, but Maria noticed the red light on above the booth, signaling that someone else was confessing. Suddenly, a thin, nervous man with strange blue eyes pushed away the heavy curtain and, adjusting his short-brimmed black fedora at an angle, stalked by Maria, sulking. Oh no, Maria thought, Father DeSanto must be in a bad mood! But her turn had come and she rose.

    Entering the booth, she let the darkness behind the heavy curtain engulf her, and knelt on the red velvet cushion on the floor. The moldy air reminded her of past confessions, but none had come close to what she was about to reveal. Alone in the wooden box, her heart pounded through her dress and pulsed through her hands, cupped in prayer. The sliding window opened abruptly, its criss-crossed grate appearing before her like a picture frame. A strange light passed through the opening that separated her and the priest and Maria felt more exposed than ever. But what else could she do? Blessing herself and taking in a sharp breath, she began.

"Bless me, father, for I have sinned. It has been one week since my last confession." Her mouth dry, she could feel the sweat in the creases behind her bent knees.

"Yes, my child. I'm listening." To her surprise, the unfamiliar voice did not belong to Father DeSanto. No, this was a kind, soft voice. She exhaled with relief. Father DeSanto must be away. It would be easier to reveal herself to a stranger.

"Father, I have done a terrible thing. I have kissed a man who is not my husband. And... I want to do more." As her words tumbled from her mouth, his silhouette leaned in closer to the window that separated them. "I'm a married woman," she went on, "but I must confess I do not love my husband, not the way I believe God intended love to be." Just saying these words aloud, Maria felt a weight begin to lift from her chest. At the same time, she was terrified. Nervously, she continued. "Until now, I did not know I would ever meet the right man, the man that I believe God intended for me to be with. But I've met him now and it's too late. I'm already spoken for." Tears streamed down her cheeks and agony twisted her voice. "Father, I can't stop thinking about this man. He's in my heart, my soul, my skin. When I look at him, I see myself. I see everything I ever wanted. I know it's a sin to feel this way. I know I need to forget I ever met this man and try harder to love my husband, even though..."

"Even though what?" The voice coming through the grate resonated in Maria's chest.

"Even though I cannot bear him," she answered. "My husband is a good man father, he is kind to me most of the time, and I know he loves me. Forgive me, Father, but sometimes I cannot bear to make love to him. When he drinks too much he is mean to me, even violent. I know he's unfaithful and I don't blame him. I don't even care. I only care about…this other man. I beg for your forgiveness." Maria let out a heavy sigh. She waited for the priest to pronounce her penance and admonishment.

"My child, you must know that God wants you to be happy," he said gently. "He can only rejoice if you are living a truthful life. He did not create you to suffer, but to follow your heart. Now go and examine your consciousness and your motives and act accordingly to God's will."

With that, the silhouette made the sign of the cross and blessed her through the tiny window. "God be with you."

Maria felt awash with peace and light. Could this be real? She felt like laughing aloud and wanted to reach through the confessional window and kiss this priest. But the grate slid closed. She stayed kneeling in prayer for a moment, looked up and, trembling, whispered, "Thank you." She took a deep breath and pushed aside the heavy red curtain. There were still no others waiting behind her in line. The three widows had gone. The red light on the confessional booth had gone out and a young priest hung a sign on the doorknob that read 'closed.' *How strange*, Maria thought. She never saw this priest before. He must be new.

As her eyes adjusted from the dark to the light, she noticed the imposing figure of Father De Santo standing in the front of the church. He was talking to a small group of parishioners in his usual severe manner. Feeling lucky that God wanted her confession to be heard, but not by Father DeSanto, Maria looked up and gave thanks. The young priest nodded his head and smiled at Maria, as he walked up to join Father DeSanto. She nodded back, and managed to walk down the aisle and out the front doors. Drifting through the piazza and all the way home, the swallows twittered about her and she felt accompanied by angels.

* * *

Martino sat with his dear friend and head of the most reputable bank in Sienna, Enzo Antinori. They sat in Enzo's private chambers. Comfortable leather chairs sat on either side of Enzo's Mahogany desk. Enzo, had tiny brown slits for eyes and wore his black hair slicked back. He had a terrible habit of smiling all the time, even if a situation called for tears. Enzo smoked cigarettes as if they were pure oxygen and constantly shook his head. Sorrow filled Martino's eyes as he sat in front of his friend. "I feel that I am losing her, Enzo."

Enzo smiled. "No Martino, that's not possible. Your wife loves you. I know she does." He inhaled his hand rolled cigarette deeply while he rolled another. "Bring her some nice flowers. That always works with women."

The color drained from Martino's face at the mention of flowers. "Flowers will not work, Enzo." Close to tears, Martino held his head in his hands and tried hard not to embarrass himself. "I have a plan, but I need your help."

"Si, si, my friend, whatever you want." Enzo laughed. "Please don't worry. Everything will be okay. Women can be difficult to understand sometimes, but she will come around."

* * *

That afternoon, a knock came on the Ricci's door. Maria pulled herself from the corner where she had exiled herself and opened it.

Prima D'Amato, the neighbor she knew least of all, stood on the threshold of her home. Dressed as always in her widow's black, she held a beautiful pear *torta*. It smelled fresh from the oven, and Maria looked at Signora D'Amato with surprise. Up close, she appeared more striking than Maria had imagined. She had a wide, open brow and eyes like moons. She carried herself like a queen, and Maria could see that as a young woman, she must have been stunning.

"B*uongiorno*, Signora Ricci. I hope I'm not interrupting you." Prima smiled.

"No, no, *Buongiorno* Signora D'Amato. What a nice surprise." Maria smiled tightly.

Incanto ~ The Singing Gardener

"I brought you something." She pushed right by Maria and started towards the kitchen.

"You are too kind," Maria managed.

"No, I'm not kind," she assured her. "I just do what I want to do."

"Thank you, Signora D'Amato."

"Please, please, call me Prima!" the older woman nearly scolded her. "My husband has been dead for years and no one says my Christian name anymore." She paused, searching Maria's face for understanding. "Besides I hate the formalities, don't you? May I call you Maria?"

Amused, Maria responded, "Yes, of course. That is my name after all."

"*Si*, Maria! It has been years that we lived next door to each other. A shame we have never truly spoken."

"*Si*, Signora D'Amato, I'm sorry, I should be more social."

"Prima, please, Prima!"

"*Si, si, scusi*. Prima." Maria smiled and invited her guest in to the kitchen.

Prima placed the *torta* on the marble table and, without asking, dove into a drawer to find a knife. Maria's attention was drawn out the window to her garden where Stefano sang to a row of tuberose. Could it really be all right with God to follow love, no matter where it led? She smiled sadly, realizing that Martino might decide her fate for her. He might soon take away the one sweetness that tempered the bitterness of her life.

Knife in hand, Prima watched her hostess "Shall we have a little something to sweeten the day?"

Charming as this neighbor was, Maria suddenly found herself wishing Prima would disappear. She wanted to rest her eyes on him while she could. It was all she could do to remember her manners. "Of course, Signora..." Then, heading off the inevitable protest, "I mean, Prima."

The woman nodded, pleased. "Something sweet always makes

you feel better, don't you find? Sugar is good for melancholy."

"*Si, si,*" Maria answered blankly. Following her hostess's gaze, Prima looked out the window and saw Stefano bent to the new roses.

"Your garden is lovely," Prima said.

"Yes, the garden is lovely." A heavy sigh escaped from Maria's chest.

Prima cut a small wedge from the *torta* "A rare find, your gardener." Maria listened as if in a trance. Prima put a piece in front of her. "I made it this morning."

Maria slowly lifted her fork and took a small morsel into her mouth. Prima watched closely as the young woman's expression took on life and pleasure.

"Mmm, Prima. So delicious! You must give me the recipe."

"Ah, no, Maria. Then you'd make it yourself and you would not need me. Friends keep their recipes a secret. This keeps the friendship strong. We need our friends for the things we don't know how to do for ourselves, *si?*"

Maria smiled uncertainly. "Thank you, Prima."

"You're welcome. Now that you have a taste for my *torta*, I have an excuse to see you more." She put her hand, freckled with age, over Maria's smooth white one. The two women moved to the sitting room, where they chatted comfortably until Prima took her leave.

* * *

All day, Stefano labored. He felt Maria's eyes on him and ached to taste her lips, but could not bear to return her gaze. Tears streamed from his eyes and fell onto the petunias, which immediately grew to full blossom. So many questions raced through his mind. The power of love vibrated through his veins. But today he felt lost in this garden, which had always been so familiar. He could not remember which path led to the tulip beds and which to the grape arbor.

And Maria? She looked out on the same garden from her

Incanto ~ The Singing Gardener

familiar window, but everything seemed different. Each plant, each flower, stood more sharply defined against the blue sky. Her hand glided to her lips where Stefano had kissed her. Biting her finger, she knew one kiss would not be nearly enough to fill her insatiable need. She reached for more of Prima's pear *torta* and bit a forkful of sweetness. Her body hummed with electricity as she swallowed the fruit, Stefano working only yards away. The only thing that separated them was a beautiful garden.

* * *

Martino took the still thriving Casablancas not to his mother but to one of the women of the night he liked to visit in the city. Welcoming him into her room, she took the flowers and drank in their perfume. "*Grazie, bello!*" she gushed, and moved to kiss him on the mouth. But Martino turned away. He never let these women kiss him or look into his eyes. He needed them only to satisfy the urges that he could not ever fully satisfy with Maria. In his heart, he knew that his beautiful wife had never loved him. He could not make her love him and the bitterness of this knowledge was steeping Martino's heart in poison.

* * *

Early evening brought another visit from Mama Ricci. "Would you like to join me for mass? You could use some help from God."

"No, thank you Mama. I already went today."

"So did I, but you cannot visit God too much."

She smiled proudly. "Look, Mama," Maria assured her, showing the woman Prima's nearly empty baking tin, "I ate almost an entire *torta* today! Soon I will be fat. Just the way you like. Did you like the Casablancas Martino brought you?" she went on.

Mama looked at her as if she were mad. "Martino, bring me flowers? I hate flowers. They make me sneeze."

"*Scusi*, I must have misunderstood."

"Yes, that is part of your problem. You should pay more attention to your husband," With that, Maria's mother-in-law gathered herself to go to evening mass and left.

* * *

Martino returned home late that evening drunker than ever. He slammed the door of his coupe, and for an instant, froze at the sound of the beautiful music pouring from Maria's piano. Walking through the garden, he noticed the new petunias, their rich colors so striking he stopped in his tracks. Staring into the folds of tiny petals, he felt tears begin to gather in his eyes. But he shook his head, wiped his eyes and forced out a boisterous laugh. "Silly gardener. I don't need him. Water is all I need. Money and water," he mumbled under his breath. Stumbling into the front door, he hollered, "What's for dinner?"

Maria heard her husband's voice, sighed heavily, and went on striking the black and white keys in front of her. Martino stumbled across the room and over to the piano. "Where's Angelina?" he slurred.

"She left hours ago. It's very late." Maria remained calm, continuing to play as she spoke to him.

"Then why are you playing that stupid piano if it's very late?" he shouted.

"Because it makes me happy." She played on.

"You pay more attention to this damn wooden box than you do me." He slammed the piano lid down hard, grazing her fingertips, as she removed them from the keys with a start.

* * *

Next door, the abrupt end to the music and the loud bang on the piano alarmed Prima D'Amato. To the other side of the Ricci's, the LaPortas broke off an argument over what a mess Carlo left in the kitchen every time he baked bread. What was that horrible racket coming from the Ricci's? Even the Finellis across the way became concerned at the terrible noise.

* * *

"Why did you do that?" Maria cried, standing up in protest.

Incanto ~ The Singing Gardener

"You know my grandmother gave me this piano."

"Because I don't want you to play!" Martino shot back. "I want you to talk to me while I eat my supper."

"If you were home when you were supposed to be, I would. Instead you went off with God knows who and now you want me to keep you company?" Shaking with rage, Maria drew in a breath and managed to walk away from him.

Martino followed, grabbing her arm. "That's right! You're my wife and that's what a wife is supposed to do. You do what I say, when I say it! Do you understand?" He squeezed her arm hard and he shouted into her face.

Staring at him with hatred, she spat back, "Yes, I understand. You hate everything that I love and want to destroy anything that brings me happiness."

He smashed his plate full of food to the ground. "Like your garden?"

"Yes, like my garden."

"Like your music?" He threw the vase full of Casablanca's on the floor. Glass shattering everywhere.

"Yes, my music."

In a cold frenzy, Martino picked up a heavy paperweight from the desk in the corner and lifted the lid that covered the piano keys. Maria screamed, but he could not see straight. Like a madman, he began smashing the keys with the heavy glass ball. Maria pulled at his arm and tried to stop him, but he would not be stopped.

The cacophony had the entire village of Castellina up and at their windows listening. Maria broke down, sobbing and pleading, but Martino seemed spurred on by her pleas. The piano destroyed, Martino marched out the front door, grabbed a shovel from the side of the garden wall, and stormed into the flowerbeds. He made his first stop the petunias that had nearly caused him to cry. Lifting the shovel high, he pounded its metal edge down onto their stems. He ran through the garden destroying as much beauty as he could— roses, bougainvillea, even the grape arbor—while Maria watched on helplessly. He even approached her willow tree as if he could fell it, but seemed to know he was no match for its strength. Breathless, stumbling, he threw the shovel down and wiped his hands with satisfaction. All of the neighbors were up and peering out their windows at the show Martino was putting on.

"Let's see your wonderful gardener fix all of this now, eh!" he shouted at the top of his lungs. Then he charged back to the house screaming obscenities. Paralyzed at his rage, Maria remained silent, standing stock still in the doorway. He twisted her arm hard, bending it behind her back. Then, from a cabinet in the front hallway, he pulled out a pistol she had not known was there.

"I want you to see this. Do you see?" He waved the gun in front of her face until she trembled in fear. "I could kill anyone I want anytime. Anyone! Even you, wife, and get away with it because I know the law. Do you understand me?"

Maria felt a profound stillness come over her. If she died now, she would not see Stefano again. She knew it would only be hours before Martino left for Rome. If she could just get through this moment, this night, she prayed, if she could just have one more day to see the man who made her feel alive again, she would endure anything.

"Yes," she said calmly, "I understand."

"Upstairs now!" Martino sputtered, shoving the gun back into its place. "I need a son and you better give me one or else…!"

* * *

Across the way Prima listened from her window to the ominous silence. Such quiet after so much noise could bode only ill.

* * *

In his cottage down the road, Stefano felt a chill come over him. He had heard the noise of her piano being broken and the terrible yelling. "Maria," he whispered to himself, frantic. Sweat poured from his brow. He jumped out of the bed and went to the basin, splashing water on his face. He looked at his reflection in the mirror, and the fury in his body pumped fire through his blood.

Incanto ~ The Singing Gardener

Gripping the basin, his knuckles bulged and the veins in his hands protruded through his skin. Images of Martino hurting her raced through his mind.

* * *

When Martino and Maria reached the bedroom, he began ripping her dress off and angrily kissing her while pinning her down to the bed. "You are MINE, yes MINE!" Repulsed, Maria numbed herself and tried to drift away. She tried to find Stefano in her mind while Martino took over her body. Martino could barely undress himself through his drunken stupor, but he forced himself into her. She lay like a corpse, praying for it to all end quickly. He controlled her body in that moment, but never could he possess any part of her heart or soul. As he thrust himself into her for the last time, he grunted and immediately passed out on top of her. She rolled him off quickly and locked herself in the bathroom, sobbing.

* * *

Stefano ran down the dirt road toward the Ricci house praying that Maria was safe. Only the heavy sound of his breathing filled the road.

In her bathroom Maria looked in the mirror and cried at the woman she saw before her. A limp vessel. No better than the prostitutes she suspected he used. Worse! She ran the bath water and grabbed a bar of soap. She scrubbed her skin hard, as if she could rip it from the bone. She tried to wash every trace of Martino off of her. Climbing into the tub, she washed between her legs. Then she lowered her entire body and, lifting a heavy stone that acted as a doorstop, she submerged her head under water. She held her breath, weighted down. Perhaps it would be better never to return from this calm abyss. There were many reasons to remain under the water and she entertained each one of them. She stayed this way for a very long time until one thought, one voice found its way into her tortured mind.

Below her window, Stefano stood singing. His voice echoed

through the water and lifted all the darkness that rushed inside of her. His smile, his touch, his voice and the way it sounded when he said her name. Here was a reason to stay on earth. Maria raised the heavy stone from her chest, popped up from underneath the bath water and gasped for air. Catching her breath, she coughed water from her lungs. *I will live for him*, she thought, *only for him.*

Incanto ~ The Singing Gardener

SEI

The roosters began crowing at five. Maria woke and looked over at Martino, still sleeping. The smell of alcohol on his breath made her wince with disgust. It would be so easy to just take a knife from the kitchen and stab him in the heart. Or that pistol of his. She would never have to worry about him touching her again. But Maria could not commit murder. Hastily, she packed his leather suitcase wishing he were already in Rome. She headed downstairs to prepare breakfast. Stopping at the bottom of the stairs, she observed in the daylight the damage Martino had inflicted on her piano. The black and white keys were cracked in half, pieces littering the floor. The wooden box that once produced music was scarred with holes.

* * *

Martino and Maria sat in silence while he ate his breakfast. She barely touched hers. He looked at his watch and quickly gathered his belongings. "Well, wife, I'm off," he stated plainly. No apology. No mention of the piano or the garden. "Oh, one thing before I go." Reaching into his pocket he pulled out a check. "I need you to go see Enzo at the bank and deposit this check for me. I didn't have time to get there yesterday." He placed the check on the table. "My mother can take you if you want. It would be nice for the two of you to spend some time together while I'm away."

"Have a good trip." She gave him an obligatory kiss and he grabbed his suitcase and left, gunning his engine as he sped off.

Maria stood in the front doorway and when Martino drove out of view, she let out a sigh of relief. From the other side of the stone wall to her left, a woman's voice called out, *"Buongiorno,* Maria."

Prima sat under her pergola sipping her morning espresso.

"Buongiorno, Prima," Maria answered, a little stiffly. "And

how are you today?"

"Very well, thank you." The older woman had set down her cup and walked to the wall that separated their properties. "And you, Maria? How are you?" Her wide, weathered face brimmed with concern.

Maria bent her head as if to discover her answer. To her surprise, she realized that she felt light, even happy. Martino had gone. He would not be home for five days and four nights. "I'm very well, Prima. Thank you. Very well."

"I can see that. It suits you." Prima laughed.

"What does?"

"That smile that you're wearing this morning."

Maria caught herself. "Oh yes, well, I'm happy this morning."

"I would be, too, if I were you."

They both stared at the garden in silence. The devastation Martino had left behind would seem to warrant little joy. Most of the flowers had been squelched before reaching full bloom. The beds looked as if they'd suffered a malevolent storm.

From across the way, Carlo shouted out.

"Signora Ricci, would you like some fresh hot bread. I just took it out of the oven, still have the burns to prove it." Laughing, he held up his hands, revealing blistered fingertips. Tessa stood behind him.

"*No Grazie*, I've already eaten!" Maria shouted back politely with a smile.

Tessa stood behind Carlo forcing a smile as she waved and spoke through her phony smile.

"She's lying. She never eats. Just look at her." Squeezing her husband' pudgy cheeks. "Next time you need to be more charming."

Prima rolled her eyes at the newlyweds. "Or bake better bread."

"Good morning, Signora D'Amato." Carlo and Tessa waved.

Prima half-heartedly waved back and then whispered to Maria. "Have you ever tried his bread? I'd rather lick turpentine. Look how thin his wife is. He can't even get her to eat it." They both

Incanto ~ The Singing Gardener

howled with laughter.

"Would you like to come over to help me finish the rest of your *torta*?" Maria asked, wondering why she felt no shame with this woman. Prima had surely heard every part of the fight the night before, yet she seemed to take no relish in scandal.

"I thought you'd never ask." Prima walked to the small gate and followed Maria into her house.

The two women sat, the morning sun beaming through the arched window. "It's not too early for *torta*?" Maria smiled.

"Of course not. I hope it helped you yesterday?"

"Helped me? I suppose it did." Maria looked at her curiously. "Prima, why haven't you come by sooner?"

"Ah, a good question."

"Yes, we've lived alongside each other for years and I didn't even know your first name."

"Well," the older woman began, "I had to wait until you were ready." Prima turned and Maria saw that the older woman's round dark eyes were speckled with golden flecks.

"Ready?" Maria pressed. "Ready for what?"

Prima smiled widely, revealing gums along with strong, white teeth. "Ready to change."

Maria shifted uncomfortably in her chair. No one had ever spoken to her so intimately. "Don't worry, Maria. I'm here to help you, not harm you," Prima assured her.

Without thinking, Maria responded, "How can I be sure?" What if Prima was some sort of witch? She wore the black kerchief and dress of an ordinary widow, but there was something far from ordinary about her.

"Trust your intuition," Prima said simply.

Maria's intuition told her to pour out her heart and confess all of her innermost secrets. But she felt afraid for her life. Then she considered the previous night's brush with death and knew she had nothing to lose. How liberating it would be to tell one person out loud the secret she kept in her heart. If she told another soul it would mean the seed was real. Telling might make it grow.

Prima watched Maria's struggle. It showed itself on her brow and in her clear green eyes. "Be sure of this, Maria!" She looked directly into those eyes. "That gardener truly loves you. No distance or absence will ever diminish the passion he holds in his heart for you."

"Prima?" Maria gasped.

"Don't worry, dear. I won't tell a soul. I'm happy when I see true love. It is so rare." Prima grinned, and began recalling to Maria her own true love.

As a girl from a good family, Prima had what others said was the ill fate of falling for Paolo Sangiacuomo, a mere shoemaker. Prima would watch Paolo working in his father's shop from her upstairs window every day. She saw that a smile always lit the young man's face and that he worked hard to satisfy each customer. Prima knew, with a burst of clairvoyance the first of many she would experience in her life, that despite his low station, this man was meant to be her husband.

Being a shoemaker's wife did not offer a very promising future for a girl of her class. But, as fate would have it, it was true love. And true love, Prima knew, always wins in the end. In the years after the war, shoes were becoming more important than ever, especially to the wealthy. Paolo's father had always told him, "A good pair of shoes is more important than the comfort of a woman, for tomorrow the woman might be gone, but still we must walk through our lives." This served as inspiration for him to learn the trade well, but it did not stop Paolo from searching for the perfect woman. When Prima came into the shop one day with a request for her father, he fell deeply in love. And when she agreed against her family's wishes to be his, Paolo's father declared, "A good woman is very much like a pair of good shoes, hard to find, but easy to wear!"

With Prima at his side, Paolo became the greatest shoemaker in all of Italy. The wealthiest men would travel all the way to Castellina in Chianti to meet Paolo and for him to make them shoes that would carry them through until the end of their life. Paolo's shoes lasted through all weather, travel and the most difficult of times. "But winter comes to every life," Prima told Maria. "That's why we must enjoy the spring."

"What happened?" Maria probed, caught in the throes of Prima's life.

"Oh no, not now, Maria. There will be plenty of time for that. Now we must talk about you and the gardener. There isn't much time."

"No, there isn't." Maria's heart sank.

"But you must make use of the time you have. What will you do?" Prima asked.

"I don't know, Prima." Maria blushed, scarcely believing she was having such a scandalous conversation. "I suppose I must tell Angelina not to come this week."

"Yes, you don't need her around," Prima agreed.

"What will I say?"

"Tell her you don't feel well and Martino's gone so you won't be needing her."

"Yes, but then she'll tell Martino when he returns." Maria felt nervous about lying.

"Then tell him you got sick and didn't want him to waste extra money on her cooking for you. Are you kidding? He'll be relieved." Prima took Maria's hand. "Now, back to the gardener."

"Yes, Stefano. Maybe he will not make a move and I...I...cannot!"

"My dear, you don't have to do anything except surrender," Prima assured her.

"Surrender?" Maria asked.

"Yes, surrender to the truth that stirs your heart. Let yourself go to the place your heart longs to be." Prima spoke in a gentle tone, her husky voice that of a prophetess.

"And where is that, Prima?" Maria was still struggling.

"Into the arms of your true love! The one who has been waiting for you. The one who has traveled and searched to find you. He is the one, Maria. He is your home."

Tears streaked Maria's cheeks. "You're right, of course. But how can this be? How will I ever get through this?"

"Maria, you can't think about how right now. You must trust. All of this is happening exactly the way it supposed to," Prima said calmly.

"Four nights! Four nights are all I have, all we have!"

"Four nights that will change your life," Prima said simply.

A chill ran up Maria's spine.

The last of the *torta* sat between them. Maria looked into Prima's smiling face.

"More sweetness?" Prima gave a lighthearted laugh.

Maria smiled, grabbed her fork and jabbed it playfully into the crust. Prima grabbed her fork and matched Maria's enthusiasm. "To the sweetest time of your life," Prima toasted, raising her full fork.

"Oh, Prima." Maria stopped.

"Yes Maria."

"Do you believe it's possible?"

"Maria, stop asking questions now and eat."

They each took a bite, Maria savoring the taste as if it were Stefano's kiss. She smiled with delight. Prima laughed.

"Now, you're going to need my help," she said. "So let's plan."

"Prima," Maria answered with anguish. "I can't be with Stefano in my house."

"No, you can't," her new friend agreed.

"Than where can we go? I can't risk going to his cottage. The neighbors might see me on the road and then Martino will surely find out."

Prima smiled, turned and looked out the arched window and into the garden.

"Oh! The garden?" Maria exclaimed. "Yes, the garden. Perfect."

"Surrender to all of it, whatever may come." Prima waved her

Incanto ~ The Singing Gardener

hand in the space in front of her. "Maria, not everyone gets a chance like this in life." The older woman hesitated and a shadow seemed to darken her clear brow.

"What is it Prima? Please tell me."

Prima stopped and took a deep breath. She closed her eyes and sat in silence for a moment, Maria watching and waiting. After what seemed an eternity, Prima opened her moon-like eyes. They glowed with intensity as if a force greater than herself were speaking through her.

"If you do not take this chance with him, you…you will not have another."

* * *

Later that morning, Stefano arrived singing. As he neared the entrance to the Ricci's, Signor Finelli waved to him.

"*Buongiorno*, Signor Finelli," Stefano called out.

"*Buongiorno*, Stefano!" Finelli bellowed.

"How's your wife's garden coming along?" Stefano inquired.

A woman's hearty voice yelled from garden. "*Bellisimo*, Stefano, you are an angel."

"You made the wife very happy. When she's happy, I'm happy!" Finelli added. "It is a beautiful day, no?"

"You were right. They love when I sing to them and praise them. I am going to win."

Stefano laughed. "*Si*, I am sure of it. *Ciao*"

"*Ciao*," the Finelli's waved.

* * *

From the other side of the Ricci residence, Carlo LaPorta yelled out, "*Buongiorno*, Stefano."

"*Buongiorno*, Carlo. How's your wife?"

"We both had too much of my wine last night!"

Stefano laughed. "And the vineyard?"

"*Molto bene. Grazie.*"

Stefano waved goodbye to Carlo and walked up the driveway

of the Ricci residence. When he saw in the daylight the damage Martino had left for him, he did not feel surprised. He knelt as if in church and began tending to the beds and flowers, the sun beating down on him. Stefano blessed all the plants whose lives had been cut short by Martino's anger. Why would such a strong man harm a little flower? He sang to the dead flowers and delicately stroked their petals.

In her bedroom Maria darted about looking for the right thing to wear. She pulled out dress after dress from her closet, and a pile grew alongside her bed. Filled with excitement, she smiled in the mirror and liked what she saw. Pushing through her closet, she tried on nearly her entire wardrobe. Making her way to the very back of the closet, Maria felt the paper covered wedding dress and nearly lost her breath. Her hands slowed. Delicately, she lifted the dress out of the wrapper and off the hanger where it had rested for many years. She stroked the pretty white linen, her long fingers trembling, as she pressed her face into the soft cloth. Her tears flowed but then a laugh escaped from her mouth.

Standing before the mirror with the dress pressed up against her, she admired its beauty and remembered the first time she ever saw it. Her grandmother had sewn it by hand with the intention that Maria be married in it.

Nonna had designed the dress to bring Maria luck, blessing each and every strand of the hand-woven fabric, decorating the neckline with jewels believed to bring protection. But her grandmother had died a month before the wedding. Nonna had disagreed with her only son, Maria's father, about encouraging the girl to marry Martino. "He is not right for our Maria," the old woman scolded him, but Maria's father would not listen. Then, as Nonna lay dying, she called for Maria. "Yours is the last face I wish to see," she whispered. It was then that she presented Maria with the dress and told her she must wear it. "It possesses a power," Nonna told her. Maria believed what her grandmother said, that this dress would ward off any evil or harm that tried to touch her. She believed that it would help her through all obstacles.

"Wear it for me, *piccolina*. It is the last thing my two hands created on this earth."

Maria promised Nonna that she would wear the beautiful gown, but when Martino's mother saw the dress she threw a fit. Mama Ricci screamed at the top of her lungs in horror. "No bride of Martino Ricci will be married in a peasant's wedding dress! No son of mine will marry a girl who considers wearing such a thing!" Martino's reputation at stake, although he was afraid of Maria's reaction, he threatened to call the wedding off if she wore the dress in question. Shattered, still reeling from grief at her nonna's death, Maria went along with the Riccis to satisfy her father.

As she held up the wonderful dress to her figure now, she realized that it was never meant to be worn for Martino. No, she was never truly meant to be his bride. All the wishes and prayers her nonna's hands had sewn into the dress were meant instead for Maria's true love.

Delicately she placed the dress on the bed, as if it were her lover. Touching it the way she wanted to be touched, her nerves dancing with anticipation. Approaching the window, she looked down to find him. Not seeing her, Stefano sang as he dug his hands into the soil. Quietly, she began singing the same song as he. Just when it seemed he had heard her, she sprung away from the window and went to the bathroom to wash her body. There, she experimented with different scents and perfumes that lined the cabinets. She opened each bottle and sniffed. If the scent delighted her, she splashed a little behind her ears, on her neck, in between her breasts and on her wrists. She danced naked around the room, feeling a freedom that she had never known.

In this moment, she was not Martino's wife. She was not his mother's daughter-in-law or even her father's child. She was just a woman, a free woman. She looked at her wedding band and removed it, and stuck it in a drawer. As she slammed the drawer shut, a wedding photo of her and Martino crashed to the floor. She grabbed it, looked at it for a moment and clearly saw for the first time how sad she appeared. In a cold silk gown and gloves ordered from Florence, she looked almost like a corpse. Martino grinned uncomfortably by her side. Shaking her head, Maria stashed the picture into a drawer next to her wedding ring.

She hung up all the dresses except for Nonna's. Finally, she imagined, this dress would touch her flesh, bringing all her grandmother's hopes for her to fruition.

She slipped the dress over her head and as it slid down her body she could almost see Nonna smiling and clapping from heaven. She looked at her own image in the mirror. Happy tears filled her eyes. Finally, she knew the feeling that comes over a bride-to-be on the day of her wedding. Taking a deep breath, Maria fixed her hair. Giggling, she ran downstairs for her morning *limonata*.

* * *

At home, Prima brewed a fresh pot of espresso. As she waited, she watched Stefano working and singing in the Ricci garden. When the coffee had brewed, she poured herself a cup and drank it almost to the bottom, leaving enough so that she could read the grinds. She turned the espresso cup over and let the grinds fall into place. As she looked at the pattern they had made, a smile rippled across her face.

"A week to remember." Then, searching the black specks more deeply, she cringed. "Oh, but how they will suffer, equally in pain as they do in bliss."

Stefano looked up and caught Maria gazing at him from the arched window of her sitting room. This time she did not try to hide her smile. Something had changed in her. He began to walk toward the house.

She poured another glass of *limonata* and walked to the door. He knocked and, almost instantly, she opened the door.

The white dress draped her body like water, showing off her delicate figure and the curves he longed to caress.

"*Buongiorno*, Maria," he managed, almost stuttering.

"*Buongiorno*, Stefano." She smiled. "Would you like a

limonata?"

He nodded and she handed him the glass. He drank it in one gulp, his thirst unquenchable.

"Is your husband gone?" He inquired anxiously, knowing the answer.

"Yes, he is."

"Oh, well, that is good." He was blushing now, unsure of himself. "Is it good?"

"Yes, Stefano. It is good." She pulled him inside and closed the door. The world shut out, her decision made, she began kissing him. Startled, he let his *limonata* glass fall onto the tile floor, where it smashed into tiny pieces.

"Oh my God, I'm so sorry…Let me…" he stammered.

She put her finger over his lips. "Sshh, forget the glass." Unable to resist, she gave him yet another kiss, this one deeper and more passionate than the first.

Entangled in each other's arms, they kissed as if sampling the finest delicacies of life. Never before had either tasted anything sweeter. Never again would either long for any other's mouth. Stefano lifted Maria easily, placing one hand on the small of her back and the other on the nape of her neck. She threw her head back in surrender.

"Maria, this dress is perfection. You've never looked more beautiful. " He stroked the fabric of her gown and continued to kiss her outstretched neck.

"I have never felt so beautiful, Stefano." She lifted her head and brought her face into his. "Whatever you want, whatever you want from me, I am yours."

Looking into her infinite eyes, a chill passed through his body. Could this be real? It seemed his whole life had led him to this moment. Yet at any moment he might wake up from this delicious dream.

"Maria, Maria…"

"Yes, Stefano."

"Are you sure?"

"Yes, I'm sure."

He reached under her wedding dress and his hands glided along her silky skin, rousing a commotion in his heart. The heat stirred inside of them both. She loved his strong hands on her skin. They seemed to feel the rhythm of her body and move accordingly. Consumed by her grace, he could barely breathe.

"Oh, Maria." Ever so slightly, he bit her lip and then found her tongue with his. Their tongues danced into and around each other, perfect partners. He could taste the bitterness of her childhood, her coming of age and longing for love, the sharp fear that marked her marriage to Martino and the delight she found herself enjoying now, with him.

Neither of them wanted this kiss to end. But Maria pulled away. "We cannot be in this house."

"I know," Stefano said, taking her hand.

"You know?" Maria looked at him curiously.

"Yes, Maria. It is not right for us to be here."

"Where do you think we should go?"

"Into the garden, Maria," he responded without hesitation.

"Yes."

"I've been preparing for this for years."

"You have?" She looked deeply into eyes.

"Yes, Maria. You must know that you are the only reason I'm here." His eyes held the truth.

"Thank you."

"It has been my pleasure, Maria." He took her hand in his. "Now, may I show you?"

Maria melted as Stefano whispered softly in her ear. "Show me!"

He began to lead her to the door. Looking around the room where she spent so much of her days, Maria sensed that she was about to leave behind her old life. She thought of the pistol in the cabinet, of her mother-in-law's fury. But the change churning inside of her frightened her most. "Stefano," she confessed. "I'm scared."

"Don't be. I won't let any harm come to you." He took her hands and looked into her green eyes. "I'll go out first. Meet me under the sunflowers in five minutes?" She nodded and he ran his fingers through her hair and then pressed his face into it. "Maria, your hair smells like lavender."

She laughed.

* * *

Stefano lay under the seven-foot tall sunflowers and stared into the sky. A wind blew and the black and yellow beauties swayed above him. When Maria appeared five minutes later, he sat up like a happy puppy

"You came."

"Of course I came. Did you think I wouldn't?" She smiled and pressed her lips into his. Her hair draped around his face. He took a strand, brushed it under his nose and inhaled.

"Ahh Maria, I am intoxicated by your scent."

She pinned him into the earth. With their black faces and yellow petals turning toward the sun, the *girasole* protected them from the world's view. She also knew that Nonna's dress would let no harm come to her.

"And I love the scent of you, Stefano."

"What would that be? Sweat, dirt, earth?" He laughed.

"Yes, all of it!" she protested. "Because it's all you. And I love all that is you."

"Maria, oh my sweet Maria, I love you. I always have."

"You do?" She asked, suddenly unsure of herself.

"Can there even be a doubt in your mind? I love you with all that I am. With you I can't tell a lie."

"Nor can I." She kissed him, but this time a kiss was not enough. "Can anyone see us?" She asked him.

"No, Maria." He continued to kiss her.

"How can you be sure?"

"I'm sure."

Trish Doolan

* * *

Signor Finelli was snoring on his terrace, as Signora Finelli danced and sang for her luscious and colorful vegetable garden. The LaPorta's were busy in the kitchen arguing over Carlo's bread recipe. Tessa insisted he give up this hobby, but he was sure he finally created the recipe that would redeem him.

* * *

Slowly, Maria began to unbutton Stefano's shirt. His body trembled with anticipation, as she touched his muscular chest with its silky hair. She stroked him with her fingertips as the sun blazed through the yellow and orange flowers above them. Maria and Stefano knelt before each other ignited with the sun's fire. She removed his shirt and slowly, slowly, he lifted her wedding dress over her head, placing it down carefully beside them as if he sensed its sacred origins.

The vision of Maria's naked figure before him, time stood still for Stefano. Pain dissolved and no one else existed. He bit his lip as if afraid to spoil her, then began caressing her breast. His hands glided around her nipples, so excited to receive his attention, but he would make them wait and ache for him. Kissing the fleshy pathway that led him down to the center of her chest, he stopped at her heart. Lingering there, he seemed to have a private conversation. He slowly lowered her body to the soft earth, all the while whispering promises into her heart, promises not even Maria would ever know.

Stefano found his way back to her breasts and began to adore them, giving them unimaginable pleasure with his tongue. For the first time Maria understood what it felt like to be with a man who had the power to move her.

"I could live right here forever," he whispered from between her breasts. Lifting his face up into hers, he kissed her mouth passionately.

"I want to feel you," she whispered, "inside." Burning with a deep ache, she sunk her body deeper into the soil.

Incanto ~ The Singing Gardener

"You, Maria, are the most beautiful flower in all of this garden."

"And you, the only one who can make me bloom."

She helped him remove his trousers. He folded his naked body over hers and found they were a perfect fit. Pressing his body gently into hers, he discovered home. She spiraled from dark to light, skin tingling with ecstasy, a burst of heat causing pleasure and sweet pain.

"I know, Maria. I know what you need," he whispered.

Maria discovered that love, a mysterious animal, had carved a pathway into her lonely heart. Savagely, it would rip her apart in exchange for rapture. Euphoria gripped her and nothing existed except Stefano and the garden.

Gently, he pulled away from her and the two of them caught their breath. It was in this separation that she began to feel her fears rising up again like crows.

"I need to tell you something," she said, looking up at the sky through the flowers.

"Yes, Maria, I'm listening."

"I--I'm damaged," she confessed.

He looked at her, a smile of disbelief on his lips. "In what way are you damaged, Maria?"

"I feel like I am cursed and cannot have children," she said softly, with shame.

"No, Maria, no," Stefano answered her. "You are perfectly healthy. Of this I am certain."

"But I haven't been able to get pregnant for years," she explained. "My husband blames me. His mother blames me. And the doctors say that he is fine. So it must be because of me."

"It is not because of you, *amore mio*." Stefano smiled knowingly.

"Then why?"

"You are not in love with your husband and you should never bring a child into this world when it is not born into love. Have

you honestly wanted to get pregnant?"
"Not with my husband," she admitted.
"That is why, Maria." He caressed her cheek. "Nature thrives on love."
"So you don't believe that I'm damaged?"
Stefano delicately kissed her lips and then moved to her right cheek, then her left. He kissed her chin, and forehead, neck and down to her breast, where he suckled her nipple. Burning with unbearable desire, she released a moan of hunger. She longed for him again, but he was singing softly now, directly into her belly.

As he finished the last line of his song he entered her and penetrated deeply, all the love he felt streaming inside of her. Guardian sunflowers bowed their heads as the diminishing rays of light sprinkled from the Castellina sky.

* * *

Throughout the village, sparks of love ignited all who resided there.

* * *

Prima, in her wine cellar, touched each wine bottle with tenderness. Some bottles she clutched to her chest with deep yearning. She began dancing through the oak racks of wine, tears of joy streaming from her eyes.

For no apparent reason, Signor Finelli woke up and went into the garden where his wife stood proudly admiring her work. He came up from behind and embraced her, dipping her in a kiss as if he were a film star. "I want you now, Signora Finelli."

"Why, Signor Finelli, are you drunk?" She laughed, taken aback.

"No, my darling. I'm not drunk, just alive." He danced around her, his two left feet momentarily graceful. "And you, you are more beautiful than the night we married." She smiled, swooning.

* * *

The LaPortas, in the middle of their quarrel, suddenly went

silent and stared at each other in the kitchen. Ravenous, the newlyweds knocked all the baking items to the floor as they cleared the large butcher-block table. The flour, butter, salt and mixing bowls splattered all over the tiled floor, but neither seemed to care. They moved into each other's arms with sudden passion, all was forgiven. Carlo easily lifted Tessa onto his bread making station and climbed on top of her. Finally, a recipe was put on the table that she could enjoy.

* * *

Down the road, Roberto Giuliano ran from his prospering fields into the large house he shared with his wife. Filomena moved about lighting candles in the front room. When she saw him, she set down her long match and curled like a cat on the sofa, all but purring. He went for her like a lion.

* * *

Yes, the entire village of Castellina in Chianit had come alive. No one knew why, but there was no denying the passion that filled the air. As evening fell upon the curving hills, the people did not stop to question their good fortune.

Maria and Stefano made passionate love underneath the sunflowers all through the night, exploring every detail of each other's bodies. They hadn't had anything to eat or drink, but it hardly seemed necessary. Stefano nestled his head into Maria's chest.

"Rest, my love," she cooed. In one moment, all else but peace washed from his mind and she felt the years of worry go as his head became heavy on her breast. He drifted into sleep as her fingers found their way through the curls of his hair. Maria gazed into the forgiving sky. Stefano's body melted into hers and they were one body, one soul, one moment in time that would eclipse all others.

Maria kissed his head and glanced over at the wedding dress. At last she had carried out the promise to her grandmother. She drifted with Stefano into deep slumber, the sunflower bed their wedding bed.

SETTE

Dawn shimmered over the horizon and the sunflowers began to lift their heads. Maria, too, stirred to wake, careful not disturb Stefano. It did not matter that her arm had fallen asleep or that she could no longer feel her legs. It did not matter that she had not moved a muscle in hours. He was still sleeping comfortably in her embrace. She never wanted this moment to end.

How had she survived this long without love? How could anyone live without it? She began to ask herself how she could ever go back to being Martino's wife when she knew for sure that her husband was right here with her now. Everything else was a lie. Slowly she felt herself coming to life, yet she also thought that if she were to die in this moment her life would be complete. She wished everyone on earth could feel the same lust for life that inhabited her this very morning.

As her mind raced with possibilities, a circle of bright cardinals flew overhead, alighting on the sunflowers. Looking down on Maria and Stefano, the birds began talking to each other in their own loud language. Maria pursed her lips together and shushed them, but they would not be silenced. Stefano's strong and lean body stirred on top of her, as he came to life. He opened his eyes to the chirping cardinals. A smile filled his sleepy face as he gathered Maria, too, into his sight. There she lay, the woman of his dreams, naked and real as the day she was born, smiling back at him.

At first, they did not speak but their eyes carried on a beautiful conversation. Gently he rubbed his nose to hers and, bit by bit, kissed her face, each tiny kiss whispering 'good morning.' "You are the most beautiful morning of my life," he said. Smiling, his mouth melted again into hers.

She whispered back, continuing the kiss. "And you are mine. I'm sorry that the birds woke you."

Stefano laughed. "I'm not, Maria. They come to me every morning like an alarm clock. Besides, I'm grateful. Being awake with you is much better than being with you in my dreams."

"What shall we do today, Stefano?" Maria asked, languid in his arms. If they did nothing but this, she would be quite happy.

"First let's get dressed and then I have a surprise for you," he answered.

Maria looked at him, curious. How could he have a surprise already when he had just woken up? But like a child on Christmas morning, she quickly put on her dress. Stefano laughed and drew his clothes on, too. While dressing, they held each other's eyes. Then Stefano took Maria's hand and led her through the seven-foot sunflowers. The cardinals protested the disruption, and then flew off in a burst of red.

Stefano whispered, "Maria, cover your eyes." She filled with excitement. "Keep walking, a little more." Then he stopped her and put both of his hands over her eyes. It occurred to her that she had never been given a surprise before. She'd not had a surprise party or even a party for that matter. Yes, her Nonna had given her the piano and other gifts before, and the wedding dress *was* a surprise of sorts, but never had she been asked to cover her eyes in this delicious way. She kept her eyes shut tightly underneath Stefano's hands, loving the smell that lived in his skin and the scent of their lovemaking lingering on his fingers. Feeling safe, she waited patiently, a wide smile filling her face. Finally, Stefano removed his hands from her eyes, leaned into her and whispered, "All right, Maria, you can open your eyes now."

But Maria kept her eyes shut for a moment longer. She did not want this feeling to end. She took a deep breath and prepared herself, delighting in the rich fragrances exploding in the air. Then she opened her eyes.

At first she could not take in what she was seeing. Perhaps she was still asleep under the seven-foot tall sunflowers and this was a dream. Or maybe she suffered from a hallucination. Before her, her name, *Maria*, had been written across the garden in flowers.

Incanto ~ The Singing Gardener

Different arrangements formed each large letter. 'M' rolled white as snow, scripted with glorious Casablancas. The deep red 'A' formed itself from the tallest Vega roses that any garden had ever produced, their buds like sculpted hands holding a heart. Maria began to cry and laugh all at once. The next letter of her name, 'R', had been designed by peonies in pink, orange and yellow. Stefano had created the 'I' with sapphire blue hydrangeas puffy as clouds. And the final 'A' was laced in purple violets deeper than amethyst. Each color shone more brilliant than the next, her name alive with the colors of the rainbow. Maria was speechless as she circled and touched his gift to her.

Stefano watched on as she took pleasure in what he'd created for her the evening before as she slept. Each flower seemed to hold a secret for Maria to unravel. She looked at him playfully. "Can I run through them?'

Stefano laughed. "Maria, do anything you wish. It's all for you. You can jump, run, dance, whatever pleases you."

"You please me, Stefano," she said with a certainty that touched him. "Very much." She giggled and then ran into the scripted flowers. She began to dance around each letter as if she were a captive just given her freedom. Losing herself in the design, she rediscovered the meaning of her name.

It had taken Stefano only five minutes to prepare the gift. One minute for each letter of her name. He had gone over his design a million times in his head before, but never had the opportunity to realize it without the threat of Martino Ricci catching him. He hoped Maria would cherish this moment. Sadly, he knew he would have to make it all disappear soon enough. He could not risk anyone seeing.

But for now he delighted in each giggle that tumbled out of her. He memorized her dress and how perfectly it fit her figure. Her hair danced wildly as she wove in and out of the many flowers. Stefano never imagined that watching another person could bring him such pleasure. Unable to contain his feelings, he began to cry,

She looked over and saw him and rushed over. "Stefano, you are crying. *Perche?*" She gently kissed the angles of his cheeks.

He kissed her mouth, tasting the salt of his tears and smiled. "Because I'm happy." He began to laugh. Her lips traveled over his wet face. She grabbed his thick curls in her palms. The sun hit his hazel eyes, and they glistened and changed color. "I'm in love with you, Maria."

She smiled. "And I am in love with you, Stefano." She kissed him deeply and he pulled her back into the hydrangeas.

Fiercely, as if it were a matter of life and death, he told her, "I've never felt anything like this in my life, Maria. I'm overwhelmed with what's stirring inside of me. I feel like I want to fly and to die all at once."

Maria listened to the words that described exactly what she, too, was feeling.

Unsure if he should say anymore, but unable to help himself, he went on, "Maria." He took a sharp breath. "Maria, my love, my love, I'm so afraid to tell you what I feel in my heart, for you may not feel the same." He turned away.

Gently, she turned his face back to hers. "Please, Stefano, tell me. You're safe here with me."

Looking into her sweet face, Stefano decided to say the words he had kept locked away for so long. "I will tell you, then. I—like to think I'm a man of honor and would never covet another man's wife."

She cringed at the mention, however oblique, of Martino.

He went on. "I don't know myself right now and yet… I finally feel I am myself. I feel…that you are my wife, that the heavens acknowledge our love. You should be by my side! I—I do not even feel guilty. I know you are not in love with Martino. How can I feel guilt when I know what we're doing is so right? I don't want you to ever leave me. You're the reason for all I do, all I am."

Tears streamed down her face, too, as her heart drank in his words.

"I fear that when your husband returns all of this must go away,

Incanto ~ The Singing Gardener

and yet I know nothing can ever erase what we have shared together. I'm confused. What will come of our union? Forgive me, Maria, this isn't coming out right."
Maria stopped him. "Stefano, I'm following every word."
To bring himself comfort, he touched one blue hydrangea, caressing its stem without picking it.
"I believe we were meant for each other, Maria. I never want to touch another woman, breathe in another, or kiss any other lips but yours. Finally, I have found my home in you. I don't know what I'll do if this ends."
"My love," she answered him, "this can never die. What we share between us can never end." She kissed him, trying to wash away his fears. But Stefano could not let them go.
"I want you to go away with me," he said.
"Where shall we go?" She laughed.
"Anywhere you say. I can garden anywhere. We can go to France or Spain maybe even America."
She laughed again. "America! You *are* a big dreamer, Stefano."
He tried not to notice that she had not agreed to go with him. Instead, he laughed, too. "Yes, I am. I have a dream that you and I will walk hand in hand through our very own garden, watching our children grow before our eyes." The words bloomed in her chest. "I dream that your face will be the last gift I see before I leave this world and I dream of giving you all that you deserve, but have missed until now. Now that I have found you I can't imagine being without you ever again."
"You'll never have to be without me. I belong to you," she whispered. "Now please stop talking of doom. This is the happiest day of my life and I won't have you spoiling it with your silly fears." She knew full well his fears were not silly and they were burrowed deep inside of her as well, but she could not admit this to Stefano or to herself.
"You're right, Maria! I'm sorry. *Basta!*" So that she would be happy, he shifted his mood.

"So, what shall we do today?" She looked at him with excitement.

"Well, I think we should eat an enormous breakfast!"

"Yes!" she squealed. "Eggs and pancetta with tomatoes and onions, fresh bread, apricot preserves. Mmm, finally, I feel hungry."

"But where can we find a breakfast like that?"

She grabbed him. "Come with me. I'm taking you to Prima's. She'll be happy to have company." She knew they'd be safe at the house of her new friend.

Stefano put his hand on her arm. "Go ahead. I'll meet you there." Gesturing toward her blossoming name, he said softly, "I must erase this so no one else will see."

Maria's smile disappeared. His words echoed in her head and she buried the feelings of shame that they sparked. Must this love really be kept a secret? For how long?

All the flowers must die. The memory of them would last forever, but the fragrance would only be in her mind. She stood before her name and breathed in the heavenly scent. "Wait, Stefano," she begged him. Pulling one flower from each of the letters of her name, she created a radiant bouquet. "You showed me what my name truly means."

"You are beauty itself, Maria," he said.

Sauntering away from him and through the garden, Maria carried her bouquet to Prima's.

When she had gone, Stefano knelt before his creation. Lifting his arms, he offered his hands to heaven and asked God to bless them with the strength to erase her name.

* * *

Signore Finelli looked out his window. He leaned out and put one plump hand on the shutter. It appeared to him that the name *Maria* had been written there in flowers, and that the crazy gardener was circling her name like a panther. How could that possibly be?

Incanto ~ The Singing Gardener

* * *

Walking around her name slowly, gliding his palms over each letter, Stefano sang a melancholy tune. Waving his hands as if conducting an orchestra, he finished the song and in one gesture the flowers vanished. A stabbing sensation gripped Stefano's heart. Falling to the ground, he held his chest and fought back tears.

* * *

Finelli quickly downed a cup of coffee, rubbed his eyes and ran to find his glasses. After putting them on, he looked again. Now he could see clearly. Stefano down on his knees in the garden as usual. Not a trace of *Maria* written in flowers. Finelli shook his head and laughed. His old eyes had been playing tricks. He poured himself some coffee, grabbed a cigar and let out a sigh of relief that he wasn't missing a Friday after all.

* * *

Stefano gathered his strength, willing himself to rise from the empty earth. He looked at the space, which now cried for something new to fill in the void. Staring at the blank soil, he could not see what wanted to live there. No, it was too much to consider at this very moment. Maria awaited him for breakfast and he did not want to lose another moment with her.

At Prima's house, he found a scrumptious feast spread across the kitchen table. It had been quite a while since someone had prepared a meal for him. He felt like a king.

"Please," she said, imploring him to sit. "Enjoy." Everyday that she admired him in her garden, Maria had been dreaming of feeding his long, lean body. Stefano did not eat very much nor did he usually hunger for food. But happiness brings an appetite with it and he was ravenous now.

He nodded to the lady of the house and Prima smiled as Stefano took a chair at the head of the old oak table. The older woman had made apricot preserves and baked fresh semolina. Maria, covered in a red apron, fried ham in a skillet.

Stefano watched as, in another pan, she sautéed fresh roma tomatoes, basil, parsley and eggplant from the garden. Smiling over her shoulder at him, she grabbed a whisk and began scrambling eggs in a bowl. Love raced through her entire body and vibrated off of her fingers, each bit of food she touched infused with passion.

She poured the eggs over the vegetables and herbs, and the frying pan sizzled. Prima sliced the bread and put a spoonful of apricot preserves atop it for Stefano. He thanked her and watched Maria coming alive in the brick-lined kitchen. As she poured him coffee and cooked for Stefano, Maria wished she could do so every day.

In one long draw, Stefano inhaled and held his breath. He never wanted the smell of this moment to escape his lungs. Prima's simple kitchen made Stefano feel very much at home. The flowers that Maria had saved from his morning surprise were arranged in a blue clay vase in the middle of the table. And the breakfast smelled so good he could hardly wait to savor it.

Maria shaved some fresh fontina over the eggs and served Stefano a generous portion. He took the first bite, pleasure passing his lips and tickling his tongue. He swallowed a mouthful of her love and it spread out to every part of his body. Prima switched on her old radio and '*Funiculi, Funicula*,' by Enrico Caruso filled the air. Stefano reached over and held Maria's hand. Finishing her own food, Prima excused herself.

She smiled. "I will be gone for hours. Please make yourselves at home." Prima wrapped a kerchief around her grey hair, grabbed her bag and made her way to the front door.

"Thank you," Maria called out.

Stefano chimed in. "Yes, Prima. Thank you so much."

Prima chuckled devilishly. "My pleasure. Really, you have no idea." With that, she darted out the door.

Stefano's hunger was no longer that of food, but the tastes of Maria. Taking hold of his hand, she left the dishes on the table and sat on his lap.

Incanto ~ The Singing Gardener

They kissed and, biting his bottom lip, she giggled. "I have a surprise for you."

"You do?" He continued to kiss her while she led him upstairs.

"Now it's your turn to cover your eyes," she said as they reached the top landing. She covered his eyes with her hands and led him to Prima's bathroom. Heavy curtains covered the windows, creating the illusion of nighttime. Dozens of candles lined a pathway to the old tub. When they arrived at the edge she whispered into his ear. "Are you ready?'

"I think so." He suddenly sounded as shy as a boy.

She removed her hands from his eyes, revealing a tub full of multi-colored rose petals.

Mesmerized by the floating garden she had created, he said, "It's perfect, Maria. Just perfect."

She began to undress him. "I want to wash every part of your body."

After he was completely undressed, he slipped off Maria's dress with ease. The two of them stood before each other completely naked again. Flames from the candles jumped up and down, causing shadows to dance on the walls. Maria caught their reflection inside a long oval mirror in the corner. Their separate bodies leaned into each other.

"I love the way we look together, Stefano," Maria whispered, blushing.

He turned to the image. He recognized her, but had never seen himself this way. He saw a man and a woman united as one. Slowly, he began to stroke Maria's skin, outlining every curve and defining each feature with the elegance of his fingertips. Watching his hands dance on her flesh excited both of them. Stefano knew just how to touch her. He pulled her to the rug on the floor and they began making love yet again.

Mesmerized, Maria watched their reflection undulate in the mirror. Their bodies melted into one another, flesh on flesh, light on light, and a love so powerful that the whole room seemed to vibrate with it. Maria took her finger and ran it along Stefano's reflection.

They rose from the floor and stepped into the still-warm water of the tub. Sitting first, he rested his back against the cool porcelain and then guided Maria down to rest between his long legs. Leaning into him, she rested her back on his chest. Arms wrapped around her, he sunk more deeply into the warm water. The rose petals swam around them, sticking to their skin.

They washed each other. The candles flickered across their bodies.

Stefano cupped his hands, gathering multi-colored rose petals, then let them trickle again onto Maria's body.

"Who knew that life could bring such joy?" she sighed, sinking more deeply into his body. The bathwater rustled.

OTTO

Hours passed and Prima did not return. Maria and Stefano felt eternal in each other's arms, he tracing the slight bump on her nose, she rubbing her hand over his chin and laughing when it tickled her skin.

"May I shave this beautiful face?"

He blushed then smiled. "Yes, that would be nice." No woman had ever shaved him before and he hoped he could keep still. Sitting him in a chair in the corner of the bathroom, Maria lathered his face with cream. She found a blade in a drawer—Prima kept everything of Paolo's as shiny and new as if he were still alive and needing his things. Expertly, she navigated the blade around each and every curve on Stefano's chiseled face.

"I love this face." Rinsing the blade in the basin, she returned it to his cheek.

She continued with precision. When she had finished, she took a warm wet cloth and wiped him off, rubbing her lips against his freshly shaved cheeks. She giggled. Handing him a silver mirror, she urged, "Look at yourself!"

He barely recognized the face that stared back at him from the glass. Not because it had been freshly shaved, but because all the love he had received in these days was transforming him. The lines had disappeared from between his brows. He looked sturdier, more substantial. The change was apparent in his eyes, his face and in his glowing reflection.

"What shall we do tonight, Maria?" he asked her.

"What would you like to do?"

"I have an idea, but I don't want to presume," he admitted.

"Tell me!" "Well, if Prima would lend us her car, I have a place I would like to take you."

"And where is this place?" Maria had never heard him speak of

anyplace beyond Castellina.
"The Mancinelli Villa is in the mountains, overlooking the ocean. It's where I worked before I came here. The air smells like jasmine every night, and honeysuckle in the morning. The people who own it are the kindest I've known. When I left they told me to always consider their home my own." His body filled with excitement as he recalled this place that he loved so very much. "The birds come each morning and sing. Fruits and vegetables grow in the garden and each night you could pick all that was ripe along with herbs for dinner, everything so fresh it makes your mouth water. Lush vineyards stretch around the property and the cellars are always full of the best vintages. Oh, and the ocean air Maria, it is so crisp and clean there," he said. "And best of all we could stay without fear of being seen. It's three hours north, near the place where I was raised, but we could leave tonight and come back whenever you wish."

At first, Maria was filled with excitement, then with fear and skepticism. How could she leave her home and not get found out? What if the neighbors came by? What if Mama Ricci arrived unannounced as usual? Or if the Finellis or the LaPortas saw her go?

"Stefano," she began. "What is this place? And who are these people?" More fears gripped her. She remembered Martino yelling about how no one knew where Stefano was from or who his family was. "I—I know so little about you."

"Oh! Is that what worries you, my love?" He searched her face. "Then let me tell you the short story of my life!" She sat in the chair across from him and he took her by both wrists so she was facing him. "I began working for the Mancinellis as soon as I was old enough to work. They took me in and let me apprentice with their own gardener, a master from *Firenze*."

"And they…took you in from where?"

"I was raised in the orphanage of the church of San Salvatore."

Maria knew this place. It was famous for its fresco of the enthroned Madonna, her golden crown held aloft by small angels, her baby perched on her lap. Maria imagined Stefano as a small boy without any mother but this Madonna and she almost cried.

"Don't look so sad for me, Maria," Stefano laughed but underneath, she sensed, lay sorrow. "In those days, so many parents could not care for their children. No doubt I was one of many babies needing more food than they had to give. And there was enough to eat at San Salvatore. The gardens there were always full. Two nuns took very good care of me and helped me to understand my gifts in the garden."

"What were their names?" Maria asked. "What were they like?"

"There was sweet Sister Camilla and stern Mother Giloria." He laughed. "They were the women who raised me along with many other boys. Sister Camilla gardened. She was my first teacher. Most of all she taught me that all life comes from God, that all that lives is precious in His eyes."

"When I turned seventeen and it was time for me to leave the orphanage I was given the last name of the mother Superior. Mother Giloria had come from the Portigiani family."

Maria imagined meeting the nuns who had been so kind to him. She would like to see this villa he spoke of but she wished even more that she could see the humble orphanage where Stefano had spent the early years of his life and became a *Mage*.

"Those women gave me everything," he mused. "Sister Camilla? She told me that I must not be afraid of my God given gift in the garden and I must not waste it. 'It makes God angry when you do not use the talents he blesses you with,' she said. I learned to use the pain and love in my heart and channel it for good instead of letting it destroy my soul. And Signore Mancinelli waited so patiently until I was old enough to come and work for him. He had wanted me since I was eight. He and his wife treated me like I was their son. But the nuns told him that all great things take time. They did not want me out on my own until they felt I was ready."

"Why did you leave the Mancinelli's Villa? It sounds like heaven."

He smiled, a distant look in his hazel eyes. "I could not explain it then, but I felt a pull to find...another place." He did not say that he felt he had been pulled by her.

"I would love to go, Stefano..." Maria's voice trailed off weakly. "I would."

"But?" Stefano saw from her face that this trip away might be too much to ask. "I'm sorry, Maria. It's not fair of me to ask such a thing."

"No, no, Stefano. It's a lovely thing to ask. It would be a lovely thing to do. I'm just afraid, that's all. I'm afraid."

"Of course, I understand." Stefano tried not to show his disappointment. Of course it could be nothing but a far-fetched dream. Why had he thought he could ever take Maria away?

"Stefano?' she pressed.

"Yes?"

"This place you speak of sounds magical, wonderful."

"It is."

"I don't understand. If you love it so much why do you live here? You can garden anywhere. Anyone—these Mancinellis, too—would be lucky to have you."

His face grew somber. Did she not understand his heart? "I'm here, in this village, in your garden, for one reason only. I'm here because of you."

A wave of pleasure filled her, then guilt. To think that he had sacrificed an easier, more beautiful existence for her sake caused her pain. She pictured him living in his tiny cottage. She remembered the place that she grew up in. Shivers crawled up her spine just thinking about her father's shack and struggling again. Yet, he put up with all this to see her face everyday?

"It was a foolish idea," he told her lightly, unable to bear the torture he saw played out on her face. "We're fine right here."

"For now," she said.

"Yes, for now." His heart sank.

Incanto ~ The Singing Gardener

They had thousands of hopes and one million days planned for their future together. But fear kept washing away their sandcastle.

"It's not foolish Stefano, it's just that...well...we cannot be seen together." Her words pierced his heart like daggers, as his eyes revealed the wound. "*Capisce, vero?*"

"Yes, Maria, I understand." He turned away from her, but then could no longer handle the pain in his throat caused by words unspoken. "No Maria! NO! I do not understand. The only thing I understand is the way I feel when I'm with you. And that is the only thing that matters, what can be more important? If you feel the same then there should be no doubt in your mind where you belong."

These new feelings Stefano churned up had made her question everything in her life, and the very meaning of life itself. She had never really been taught to fulfill her desires or reach for the things that she dreamed of. She had not even been encouraged to dream. Her dissatisfaction in life was strong but also familiar. She felt powerless. Flashing Stefano a small tight smile, she tried to pretend that everything was fine.

Stefano knew that Maria had hidden her feelings her whole life, even from herself. He didn't want her to fake anything with him and he imagined he could face anything that happened as long as she told him the truth.

"Where are you right now, really?" he whispered gently.

"I'm here with you of course, in Prima's bathroom." She batted his arm playfully.

"No! You're far, far away where I can't reach you. Where do you go when you get so afraid?"

She felt him reading her like a book, but didn't not know how to explain herself. "I get so lost, Stefano. I feel I don't know anything. I've been asleep for so long that I can't tell what's real and what's a dream." She began to cry and he reached out to comfort her. "You've brought me to life and opened my eyes. It will be impossible to go back to sleep, but it... it's difficult to be awake."

"Why, Maria? Why is it so difficult?" He searched her face.

"Because I have to make choices and they terrify me. I don't want to lose you and I don't want to be without your love," she blurted, weeping now.

"Then what is so difficult?" he coaxed.

"What will people say about me? I'll bring shame to my family, my father! You know our church and country don't allow divorce. No matter how much love we have for each other, I took a vow before God. I--I'm married to Martino." She covered her face with her hands as sobs racked her body. "I know he loves me and I feel guilty because I can never love him the same way. Yet, I feel responsible for his happiness."

He pulled her into a troubled embrace, holding her tightly as if she were a small child.

Downstairs, Prima bolted through the door with bags and bags of groceries. "I'm back, I'm back!" she shouted in warning. She didn't want to interrupt anything. Prima turned on the radio and began humming to the upbeat music, dancing and unpacking bags of groceries.

Hearing the radio, Stefano and Maria felt relieved. They went down to join Prima. Entering the kitchen, they began helping Prima unpack the array of food she'd brought home.

"I have just the thing for this occasion," Prima said, pulling a bottle from a hidden shelf. She popped open the champagne and, as it spilled over her hands, laughed a throaty laugh. Maria and Stefano joined her. Maria quickly grabbed three flutes from the cabinet. The bubbles leapt over the tops of the glasses as Prima poured. Still dancing, she held up her glass.

"To true love!" she said. "To living life and choosing what brings us happiness." Stefano and Maria lifted their glasses, smiling at each other. The three touched their glasses together, punctuating the music from the radio with a *ting*. Each one of them tasted and swallowed the champagne as if it could grant their deepest desires. Prima's cellar held magic, and anything seemed possible.

Prima wished for these two young lovers to follow their hearts the way she once had. Seeing Stefano and Maria together had awakened long forgotten feelings, feelings that had given meaning to her life. She wished she could be with her husband again, despite the veil between the worlds that separated them.

Maria wished for the courage to leave her life of bitterness for a life that promised her sweetness.

Stefano wished for her to realize the destiny of their souls and have the courage to choose a life with him. He prayed that their love would conquer her fears, and that they would be together until the end of their days watching their hair hue grey with age.

He observed her as she finished her champagne too quickly and realized how desperately she needed to escape her reality. He sipped slowly to keep his wits about him. When she turned and kissed him full on the mouth, her lips were pungent with champagne. His heart ached as he kissed her back.

A long silence lingered as the three of them drank in the moment. Prima broke it. "To capture time in a glass! But good as it is, even this champagne doesn't have such powers. Why don't we dance?"

As evening began to fall, music from the radio lightened their hearts as the drink lightened their heads. Before long, Prima set a leg of lamb on the table and the three of them gave thanks. Roasted carrots and potatoes complemented the meat and a fine *Brunello di Montalcino*. Bounded by the Orcia and Ombrone rivers, the Montalcino hills rose above the plains of Tuscany like a golden ocean. The soil there grew grapes that made some of the most delicious wine in the world. "This *vino* was Paolo's favorite," Prima said.

Stefano carved the tender meat, gliding the knife through it with ease. The pink roast yielded juice that made their mouths water with anticipation. True, Maria and Stefano might have done without food in favor of each other, but they knew that Prima needed this evening. And as they all ate and drank together as a family, they felt nourished beyond the physical world. Here was a family that did not judge, a family that did not expect or demand, a family that wished only the best for their loved ones. Stefano wiped his mouth with the pretty yellow cloth napkin and sipped his entire glass of wine. When everyone had finished, he pushed back his chair.

"Ladies, I must go. The garden waits." He bowed his head with respect.

"What do you mean you must go?" Maria protested. "We haven't even had dessert."

"Maria," Prima interjected, in her throaty voice. "The sweetness he longs for no chocolate can conquer. Let him go. It won't be forever."

Stefano blushed, and set out for the door. "But I don't want you to work," Maria pleaded.

"I'm not working, I promise you. I'm doing something which brings me great joy." His eyes sparkled.

Maria gave in, understanding then that he must be preparing the garden for another evening of love.

"Before you go, my dear," Prima stopped him. "Please taste something very special." She went to the cellar and chose a bottle. Wiping off the dust, she kissed it and looked up. "It is time my love," she whispered into the air. She came back with an ear-to-ear smile, holding a bottle. She told Maria and Stefano that she had been saving it for her twenty-fifth wedding anniversary, but that Paolo had died a year too early. "I promised myself never to open it. But this...this is such a special night."

"Prima, *sei sicura*?" cried Maria.

"Never more sure! Hand me the corkscrew." She shook the dust from the wine cellar out of her hair and sat at the table as if she had just returned from a very long journey. After a deep breath, she revealed the label. Maria gasped when she saw that this bottle had been saved since 1902. "A Consorzio!" she exclaimed. The Consorzio winery had been passed down from generation to

Incanto ~ The Singing Gardener

generation for hundreds of years.

"Yes. This bottle was produced during the Consorzios' luckiest year and should only be enjoyed when it reached its full maturity," Prima told them. "It is said that all who drink this particular wine will find their full potential."

The lovers paused, absorbing her words. "Maria, please go to the China cabinet. I have some glasses in there that have never been used."

"Are you sure?" Maria asked.

"Yes! I've been waiting. Huh, could you believe it? I've been waiting for...I don't know what the hell I've been waiting for, but I'm tired of waiting! This is the night that my wedding crystal will finally be put to use. Paolo and I never got around to using it. We were saving it for something special. Well? Is this night not special? Let's celebrate!" She laughed, then gripped the corkscrew and pierced the top of the cork. Winding the screw in, she pictured all the years that led to this point and all the celebrations that had never taken place because she didn't allow her desire to overcome her grief. "Why is it when you're young you think that you have to wait for some perfect moment to do the things that are dearest to you. Trust me, if I could do it all again I wouldn't wait for anything or anyone. I would just grab life by the nose hairs and pull as hard as I could." Prima popped the cork and poured the rich red liquid into the three wide goblets.

As the wine met the crystal, it created a song that true wine lovers appreciate. Sweet in melody, robust in harmony, rich in its strings and deep in its chords, The scent of blackcurrant and liquorice escaped from his glass as Stefano brought it to his nose.

"Stefano, please make a toast," Prima urged.

He nodded. "To the two most beautiful women I know," he said simply, regarding them both with an expression of joy. They drank. Maria let out a satisfying moan. Maybe this excellent wine really could give her the courage she needed to choose Stefano?

"Prima, I can see why you have saved this bottle," Stefano said.

"It's superb." Noticing the dying light in the window, he told them he had to go.

Prima smiled and refilled his glass. "Take this to the garden."

Stepping out, Stefano inhaled the scents of the soon-to-be evening air. Almond trees and the distant smoke of a hearth. Moisture cooling and the smell of red earth. Crossing the wall and finding the deepest part of the Ricci garden, he chose the spot where he and Maria would share the night. He laid his hands upon the soil then knelt down to kiss it. He spoke into the earth, asking it to bless him and Maria with a bed of tulips. Months earlier, he had buried the bulbs there and now love streamed through his fingertips and he watched as the stems seeped up through the soil, weaving into a Queen Bed just on the edge of blossoming. Flame Parrots popped up their heads to create the first layer. Then came the White Fire Parrots. Stefano dug more deeply into the soil and called up Emperor Fosterianas in white, yellow and red, then Swan Wings with their fringed edges to outline the bed. Blue Herons and Burgundy Lace grew up in the spot where Maria would rest her head. Ice Sticks and Sweethearts sprang where her feet would lie.

When he had finished and the flowers shimmered in the fading light, he realized they did not provide adequate privacy. Something tall. He needed something tall to hide them.

Stefano shut his eyes and when he opened them, he was standing inside a circle of shuddering corn plants as high as his head, the tulip bed alive at its center. He fell to his knees and bowed his head. Never before had he felt so much power running through him. He knew Maria to be its inspiration, and God its source.

NOVE

Prima swirled the wine around in her glass and examined her goblet as the wine became still. "You can always judge a wine by its legs."

"Its legs? Maria laughed.

"Yes, look at them." Prima held her wine goblet up to show Maria the streaks the fine wine formed along the glass.

"Oh my, it does have legs. I never knew."

"Paolo taught me that." She smiled sadly. "When it is good," Prima looked directly into Maria's eyes, "It gets better with time!"

"Are we still talking about wine, Prima?"

"*Amore e vino*, it's the same Maria. Both take years to cultivate, need careful attention and all the elements must line up perfectly to create a magical combination that is unforgettable. Once you've tasted a truly fine wine there is no way to go back to drinking crap, like Carlo LaPorta's across the way, *Dio Mio*, it's terrible It's almost as bad as his bread." Maria burst into laughter, as Prima savored another sip of love from her glass. "Believe me, Maria, you never forget a perfect wine, it lingers on your tongue, fills up your senses and burns stars into your memory."

"You are the older sister I never had." Maria hugged Prima. "You give me so much."

"Thank you *bella*, but I'm old enough to be your mother."

"Another thing I never had, well, for a short time, but it almost feels as if I never knew her. I can't remember anything about her. Isn't that crazy?"

"How old were you?"

"Seven. The only thing I remember is her funeral and then I feel like I fell asleep for years. As a matter of fact, Prima, I feel like I've been asleep up until now, right now in this very moment. I finally feel awake, alive, and I think I'm happy."

"Well, that's for sure! You're glowing like a street lamp."

"Am I?" She became as giddy as a seven year old.

A gentle knock came at the door. Maria jumped, nearly spilling her wine. What if it were a neighbor? How could she explain her presence? Unworried, Prima motioned for Maria to answer. On the other side, to her relief, Stefano was standing with a big smile on his face and an assortment of beautiful tulips in his arms. He also held Prima's empty wine glass. "Maria, would you join me for the sunset?"

Maria jumped up. "I would love to." She looked at the flowers and smiled. "Oh! I love tulips."

"Well, these are for Prima." Stefano grinned and playfully held the bouquet out of Maria's reach.

"Should I be jealous?" she joked.

Stefano smiled and stepped further into the room. Kissing Prima on both cheeks, he presented his offering. Their hostess took the beautiful flowers and his empty glass. "Stefano, you shouldn't have! But thank you." She stuck her nose to the tulips and breathed.

"Thank you, Prima, for your kindness."

She began filling his empty glass. "Please, Stefano, have some more," she insisted.

"I won't argue. It is delicious!" He took his full glass from her. "But I have to get back. Maria? Will you come?" Prima filled Maria's glass, too.

"Remember? It's supposed help you reach your fullest potential. Your...deepest expression!"

Maria blushed, thinking of the evening to come. Nervously, she turned to Prima's tulips. "I've never seen so many different colors before."

"Yes, they're lovely. I'll put them in water now and admire them all night." Standing to do so, she said over her shoulder. "Now you two leave me. You have each other to admire!"

Maria liked to think herself very familiar with every detail of her garden. After all, she spent every morning looking at it, and

Incanto ~ The Singing Gardener

most of her afternoons walking through it. But as she followed Stefano to the spot he had chosen, chills made the faint hairs on her arms stand on end. A cornfield! How strange. Why had he turned her beautiful garden into a cornfield? The tall green stalks rustled as if inviting her to find out. He parted them and drew her after him, deeper into the center of the maze.

At first, she closed her eyes and let the corn stalks tickle her arms. And then she gasped as her eyes took hold of the multi-colored tulip bed at the maze's center. All of her senses were jolted, as she placed one hand over her heart. She should not have been surprised given all the wonders she'd seen him perform. Given his gift to Prima, she had expected to see tulips. But so many, in so many colors?

"How is this possible?" She could barely speak.

"Maria, all things are possible," Stefano said, putting one warm hand on the small of her back. "We only need to believe they are so." He invited her to dip into the layers of tulips. They sank together, the cool petals brushing their skin. Maria felt as if she were lying in clouds of silk.

The daylight had begun melting toward the horizon. He took her hand in his and reverently they stared at the canvas of the sky. The sun dipped slowly into clouds, casting out bolts of glowing colors. Deep blue held the orb and a burgundy waterfall spouted from its side. Rose outlined each ray of light. As it sunk more deeply, the orange ball bled into red, spraying out buckets of gold. The hills drank in the color, and the sky kissed the earth one more time.

From her kitchen window, Prima watched the day disappear, and then clutched her heart. She whispered, "Drink it now."

Stefano lifted the glass of wine to his lips and waited for Maria to do the same. Together they sipped the elixir chosen by Prima's crafty hands. As the wine swam inside of them the entire world went away. All that remained were Maria and Stefano and the tulips. Their vision became sharper and brighter, every smell more potent, and every touch more sensual. Every thought was more profound. Prima's choice elixir was one of pure ecstasy. Stefano held a sip of wine in his mouth. Crawling across the springy flowers, he arrived at Maria's face. Placing his mouth over hers, he slowly opened his lips. Maria parted hers, as well, and *vino* trickled from his mouth into hers. Their tongues swirled into each other and they broke apart, the kiss almost too delicious to bear. He took her wine glass and placed it in the mouth of a Swan Wing. He sat his glass beside hers near the mouth of a Blue Heron.

Maria sat up in the tulip bed. Stefano collected the hair that fell around her face and swept it back to feast on her green gaze. Their eyes remained fixed on each other. She began to touch his face, the kindest face she had ever had the pleasure of knowing. It seemed that hours had passed, and they had not moved. They scarcely had to touch each other in order to make love. But still, but still.

Slowly, Maria began to remove her clothing. She watched Stefano's eyes change as her naked body was revealed. She wanted him to breathe in every inch of her body, to do whatever he pleased with her. Mesmerized, Stefano did not help her undress. His flesh tingled with each inch of flesh Maria revealed. When she knelt completely naked on the tulip bed, he went to her, feeling the heat releasing from his skin as he got closer. He slid his hands just above the surface of her body, not touching her yet. The energy that pulsed from his hands had Maria aching. He held his palms an inch from her breast and the sensation made her nipples harden with expectation. He put his mouth close to hers, but did not allow their lips to touch. Each could feel the gentleness of each other's breath. Careening his hands around her body without touching it, he created a force field around her. She basked, enraptured, awaiting his next move.

He removed his clothing bit by bit while Maria remained still. Not a single thought entered her mind except Stefano. He finished undressing and Maria sprung forward to touch him, finding his mouth in her kiss. Dusk fell as Stefano entered Maria.

That night, Stefano taught Maria that making love was not just an act between two bodies. Not the mere satisfaction of indulgence. No. Making love was an art that could only be mastered by the most passionate souls, an exchange so powerful that it transported them beyond their earthly bodies.

They made love the whole night through, no longer two bodies or two souls, but one. Together, they glided swiftly through space and time, intertwined.

The sun began to breathe light into the Castellina sky. Maria took in the magnificence of the tulips. Her hands lingered in particular on the Ice Sticks, their teal buds blushing to pink, their white petals dipped in pink and royal blue. Stefano plucked one colorful stem and ran it over Maria's lips.

"*Buongiorno*, my tulip."

Maria giggled. "*Buongiorno*, my beautiful gardener." She pulled him down into her again and the tulips swallowed them.

* * *

It was Stefano who forced himself to remember the demands of the morning. Soon the neighbors would be waking up. They would expect ordinary life to go on in the ordinary way. He knew he must protect Maria. It would be difficult to make their incredible tulip bed disappear and it would break both of their hearts, but he had no choice. Maria gathered her clothes and kissed Stefano with a flower-stained mouth.

"Meet me at Prima's for breakfast." She grabbed the wine glasses that she promised to return and slipped away. Stefano watched her go and then dropped to his knees and hung his head. He felt happy and sad, grateful and terrified. So in love he felt he could fly above the tulips, above the garden and above the whole of Italy. He could barely contain the love passing like a wild river through his veins.

"Thank you, God for blessing me with this gift. I do not take it lightly and know that it's rare. Forgive me now." It had come time once again to make the beauty Maria inspired disappear into the earth, to return the garden to its normal state. He began to sing, digging his hands deeply into the tulip bed, as he finished his song the flowers vanished into the earth, followed by the tall corn plants.

From across the way Signor Finelli peeked out his open kitchen window. In the Ricci's garden, a tall plant he could have sworn that was corn vanishing before his eyes. The coffee cup fell from his trembling hand and smashed to the ground. Burned, he screamed and began to wipe himself off. He quickly grabbed his binoculars from the kitchen table and ran back to the window and looked out again. Stefano was on bended knee tending to a bed of dirt. Finelli shook his head and sat down for a moment. What if, in his old age, he was going crazy? It had happened to an old aunt of his. It might run in his family. "*Porcamiseria!*" he exclaimed.

Signora Finelli ran into the kitchen to see if her husband was all right and found him sitting quietly staring into space. She went to him and sat down, too. He smiled softly at her, and then gently placed his hand on hers. "Did you burn yourself, you silly man?" she scolded. She got up to get him a cool cloth and, at the window, glimpsed Stefano. "He's in the garden so early this morning," she commented, and forgetting the rag, went out to the *terrazza*. "I didn't see him leave yesterday."

Signor Finelli came and stood by his wife as they gazed at the Ricci garden. "Yes, I thought the same thing," he said. "Yesterday he was here at the same time," he added.

"He works so hard," she said in disbelief. "That's why his garden is the prettiest. And now so is mine. Two more weeks. I can't wait until Antonietta sees my garden. I can finally shut her up."

Realizing he had an audience, Stefano looked over and waved. "*Buongiorno*, Signore and Signora Finelli," he shouted.

They both waved back in unison. "*Buongiorno*, Stefano."

"Aren't we lucky to have such a beautiful day?" He smiled at them and waved, turning slightly to find the watering can by the shed.

"Yes, we are," Signora Finelli shouted back.

Incanto ~ The Singing Gardener

Signor Finelli shook his head. "I thought you were planting...corn this morning."

"Corn?" Stefano laughed. And then he waved as if dismissing a joke and went back to work.

When he had walked out of sight, Signor Finelli laughed uncomfortably. Signora Finelli elbowed her husband. "Corn? How ridiculous. In the middle of a beautiful garden?"

Signor Finelli scratched his head. "Something's not right over there."

Signora Finelli smacked him. "Forget it please."

"I don't know yet, but I feel it," he said, a worried look troubling his pudgy face.

"Shut up and have some coffee. That's what's wrong. You need more coffee." Not paying him any mind, his wife walked back in the house.

DIECI

Bustling about Prima's warm kitchen, Maria gathered all she needed to make another breakfast. She slid pastry into the large brick oven. Taking eggs from the icebox, she cracked them into a bowl, chopped vegetables and meat, and poured the frittata in a pan.

"You're very animated this morning," Prima teased. Maria blushed. Prima was accustomed to seeing Maria trudge around in a lifeless shell she called a body. Now her smile glowed from within. "And you look about ten years younger." Maria shot her hostess a questioning look. "Not that you looked old before!"

"Ah, but I *was* old before," Maria answered. How much effort it had taken to live in a state of constant fabrication, to pretend to be fine when she had been anything but. "Since…since Martino left, I'm not tired even though I've hardly slept. My mind is racing with…"

"With endless possibilities?" Prima finished.

"Exactly! I feel like a child again. Oh, and what a playground he has made me! The roses. The tulips…"

Prima smiled. Some things could not, it seemed, be expressed in words.

When the frittata was done, Maria dished it out among the three place settings. She lowered the skillet on the stove and began suddenly to cry. "Prima, the truth is I'm terrified!"

Prima hugged her. "I know, *dolcezza*, I know."

"Is this really happening to me, to us? I do thank God, Prima….but I also question Him." Maria sat down and sobbed into her hands. "I love Stefano so much it hurts."

"Yes, you are definitely in love. It's certain."

"Why does it hurt so much, Prima?"

"Because it's real Maria, it's so real that it has awoken the

Incanto ~ The Singing Gardener

sleeping dragon inside of you. When the dragon awakens it breathes fire into the battle we will have to fight in order to hold onto love. Once you find real love, my dear, you find adversity. The world, for the most part, will be jealous of such a love. But once awaken the dragon can never be put to sleep again. Only death itself can make the dragon fall back into a state of endless sleep."

Maria felt that her sleeping dragon had awakened and would fight to the death to hold onto this love that she shared with Stefano. "Do you think Stefano's dragon is awake?" Maria asked.

Prima smiled. "Maria, Stefano's dragon has been awake since his birth. It has been battling its way to you ever since. There is nothing that can put his dragon to sleep. You are the love of his life, and the only woman who his heart beats for."

Thrilled to hear what she already knew, she wiped away her tears and wondered what her gardener was up to out there among the flowers. Surely nothing could surpass the surprise he gave to her the morning after they first made love. How magnificent her name had looked in flowers! Then the tulip bed hidden in a magical field of corn. Now on the third day of their time together, she couldn't help but wonder what he was preparing.

Stefano arrived at Prima's with an appetite like he had never known. Maria sat him down in front of his plate and Prima poured an espresso. Both women fussed over him and he accepted it all gladly. "Mmm, these eggs taste like they were prepared by angels!" Stefano moaned with pleasure as he ate Maria's food.

"I'm glad you like it." Maria kissed his cheek. Prima nodded approvingly.

After breakfast, Prima again announced that she would be heading into town for a few hours, that he wanted them to feel free to stay in her home and enjoy their time together.

"Thank you, Prima," Maria said, touched by her friend's generosity.

"Yes, thank you," Stefano echoed. But then a look of worry

passed over his face. "But I must go home for a little bit."
Maria objected. "*Perche?*"
"Why? I have been wearing the same clothes for three days!" Maria and Prima laughed.
"Really, I'd like to put on a fresh shirt and some clean pants." At this, Maria began sniffing his shirt. She even dug her nose deep into his armpits.
"You don't need a fresh shirt," she exclaimed. "I love the way you smell, like tulips. Please don't change." She put her lips close to his and gently whispered. "I love the smell of you."
Prima remembered Paolo's wardrobe, kept in tact at one side of her closet. She had never been able to throw away his clothing or the scent that they held.
"Stefano," she said. "I would like to offer you the clothing of my late husband. You and he were about the same size. If you feel comfortable wearing them, I will let you choose from his wardrobe."
Taken aback by Prima's kind offer, Stefano murmured, "I don't know what to say."
"Say thank you and let's go dress you so that you don't have to leave!" Maria broke in, delighted.
Prima showed them Paolo's clothes. As Stefano touched one of Paolo's crisp shirts, a chill passed through him, and the hairs stood up on his arm. Running his hands over the carefully preserved wardrobe, Stefano smiled. He could feel the love that Prima and her husband shared through the shirts that once hugged her husband's flesh.
He turned to Prima and held her kind, wide eyes. He didn't need to speak for she knew every thought that passed through his head. Stefano grabbed Prima like a sister, kissed her on the top of her gray, wiry head.
"Thank you, Prima. It will be an honor."
She smiled, tears springing to the corners of her eyes. "I'm happy. It will be nice to see his clothes moving on you. It will make me feel like he is with us."

Incanto ~ The Singing Gardener

"He is with us, Prima," Stefano assured her.

"I know, Stefano, I know," she agreed. "Still, it's not the same." Maria and Stefano gave her looks filled with sympathy. "I'll go now and leave you to select whatever pleases you. I only ask that you do not touch the navy suit. He wore that on our wedding day."

"I understand, Prima," Stefano assured her.

She kissed Maria and Stefano goodbye on both cheeks. "Enjoy, my darlings and please use the place as if it were your own." She left the room. While Stefano stood before Paolo's wardrobe, choosing, Maria ran after Prima and caught her before she left the house.

"Prima, Prima…" Prima stopped and turned to face Maria. "I don't know what I would have done without you. I don't know how I ever made it through a day before I met you. You mean the world to me."

"I know, Maria, I know. I want you to enjoy your time with Stefano. It will go too quickly."

The way she said this made Maria's heart sink. "For now Prima, but we'll have so much more time. It's only beginning."

"I'll return with a dinner that will make all of our tongues dance with joy." Prima left and shut the door.

Maria found Stefano dressed in some of Paolo's nicest clothing. In timeless black tailored slacks with a seam down the center and a royal blue buttoned down shirt that complimented his muscular chest and arms, he looked dashing. A black leather belt fastened the ensemble together and, adorning his feet were a fine pair of black leather shoes, created by Paolo himself. Stefano loved the way it felt to be in Paolo's shoes. He somehow liked this man he'd never met. He could feel Paolo's kindness through the fabric of his clothes. Stefano turned to Maria and spread his arms.

"So what do you think?"

"I think you look spectacular. I should go home and put on a special dress to match your elegance." She got excited at the

notion.
"Then you should. Let's get dressed up and celebrate. What is today?"
"Thursday," she blurted.
"Then we must celebrate because it is Thursday. This will be a Thursday unlike any other, a Thursday we'll never forget." He didn't realize that he had never spoken truer words. "Happy Thursday, Maria." He smiled at her.
"Happy Thursday, Stefano." She bit her lip and wondered how many people in the world would think of such a thing. He made every day so special. Maria jumped up. "Don't move! I will return immediately. I only live next door."
"I know Maria I'm your gardener, remember?"
She smacked him playfully and ran out. "I'll be right back."
"I'll be right here waiting for you."
Maria ran home and opened the front door. Stepping onto the terra cotta tiles, she felt sick to her stomach. Fighting nausea, she made her way upstairs.
The house was haunted with reminders of her life with Martino. His irritating cologne lingered in the air. She could hear his roar bellowing through the house and remembered his hands trying to hold her down while he controlled her body and the gun, yes the gun. Flashes of the weapon that could take her life and Stefano's at any moment, kept haunting her. She tried to shake these images and stick to her mission, but her head began to swim. She told herself to shut it all out and to forget about Martino for now. He did not exist and she must hurry and get back to Stefano.
She rushed to the bathroom to splash cold water on her face. Looking in the mirror, she found her eyes. "Come on, Maria, you can do this," she said to her reflection. She turned back and saw the tub, where only a few nights ago she had almost taken her own life. How could things have changed so fast? She opened her closet and did not even recognize her own clothing. How many dresses had she bought because Martino wanted her to? Or her mother-in-law wanted her to? How many had she chosen because she

Incanto ~ The Singing Gardener

genuinely loved them? She knew the answer. Shuffling through the closet, her heart raced with panic. If she could only choose a dress, she could get out of the house and everything would be all right.

But disapproving voices in her head threatened to trap her. The voices were loud and convincing, yet they were not hers. They were her father's, Martino's and Mama Ricci's. She could hear the neighbors, the parish priest and the churchgoers. "Sinner!" "*Putana!*"

"Pick a dress, Maria," she urged herself. Sweat rose in every pore. Running to the sink, she looked at her reflection once again. The color in her face had drained, leaving her pallid. Struggling, she tried to regain her composure. "What's happening to me?" The room began to spin, and a narrow tunnel formed in her eye line.

Next door, Stefano worried. What was taking her so long? He ran down the stairs and checked for any nosy neighbors, than ran out of Prima's door. He leaped the stone wall and ran into the Ricci residence. Inside, the air was thick with sorrow.

"Maria, Maria where are you?" he called out. No response. Stefano checked each room for her. Entering the living room, he noticed Maria's piano, smashed and lifeless, and anger seized him. He ran up the stairs and into the bedroom where she had collapsed on the floor. He picked her up just as he had on the very first day that she fainted before him. Carrying her to the bed, he laid her down and ran to the bathroom for a cold rag, which he placed on her forehead.

"Stefano, you came for me." She smiled into his worried eyes.

"Of course, Maria, I will always come for you." He was racked with concern, but he managed to put a tease into his voice. "I know what the problem is, my love. You have been missing your *limonata* and your body is experiencing a terrible withdrawal. How many days has it been since you've had the one thing that sustains you?"

"Three days without a drop of *limonata*." She managed to laugh.

"Ah ha, this is unacceptable. I'll make a batch right now and it will restore you." He got up to leave.

"No, Stefano. Not here. You must make it at Prima's. Pick out a dress for me and take me out of here, please I beg of you." Tears streamed down her face.

"*Si*, Maria." He quietly approached the closet and examined her dresses. One in particular caught his attention, a teal cotton, a beautiful color for her eyes. Its flared skirt and thin waist would compliment her figure. When he held it up for her approval, she murmured in delight. The dress was one of her favorites. She remembered the day she'd bought it. Martino had disapproved of her choice, but she insisted and he reluctantly gave in.

And now Stefano had chosen the very dress that she chose for herself. He lifted her up in his arms, the dress dangling from one hand. "I've got you, Maria," he whispered in her ear.

This one small sentence meant the world to her. Never before had she felt so completely understood and cared for as she did in the arms of Stefano. When they got to the front door, Maria stopped him.

"I can walk now, Stefano," she convinced him. "I love being carried but I think it is best if I walk on my own."

Stefano agreed. Besides, what would the neighbors think if they saw him holding her in his arms as if they had just returned from their wedding? It was not far from the truth, but not everyone can be trusted with the truth.

* * *

When they got to Prima's house, Stefano went immediately to the lemon tree in front of the house. Arms full of the pungent yellow fruit, he came into the kitchen and went to the icebox.

"I'll make your *limonata* while you change into your dress," he told her.

She kissed him on the mouth. "No," she said, "Wait."

Needing to find home again, she dropped her dress and went to him. He released the handle to the icebox. They enveloped each other.

"I want to bathe with you again," Maria whispered fiercely.

"Shall I make you your *limonata* first?" He knew that she needed the drink as the flowers need the sun.

"Yes, please. I like it sweet. I'll run the bath." She laughed into his mouth.

"Sweet, I know. I've tasted your *limonata*." He watched her pick up the teal blue dress and head upstairs.

Stefano made a huge batch from the fresh lemons, adding plenty of sugar. He poured two glasses and turned on Prima's radio. Happy music filled the house. Prima's house made him feel welcomed. He noticed all the pictures of her and Paolo that decorated the mantle above the fireplace. The two had never had children. But Stefano could see how happy the two of them were in each and every picture. Each still photograph captured a moment in time, never to be replaced. He held up their wedding photo and studied it, brushing the edge of the frame with his finger. He placed the photo back on the mantle, grabbed the two glasses of *limonata* and ran up to Maria.

Stefano could smell a fragrance all the way up the stairs that calmed him. Entering the bathroom, he saw Maria before him, completely naked and waiting for him to join her in the tub she had sprinkled with dried lavender. He handed her an ice-cold glass of *limonata*, which she took gratefully. She sipped it and released her tension into the steamy water.

"Ah, Stefano, you made it perfect, just how I like it. *Grazie.*"

"*Prego.*"

Maria took another sip and found her way to the bottom her glass. Stefano smiled and took the empty glass from her. Placing his own glass close to the tub, he removed his borrowed clothes and hung them up so that they wouldn't wrinkle. He slipped into the tub and then swooped behind Maria so that she might rest her head upon his chest. As the water soaked away her tension, she remembered that she was not in Martino's house right now, but resting in the home of her lover's arms. With that thought, she drifted off into a deep sleep.

Stefano, too, dozed as Maria saturated into his skin, the lavender restoring their bodies while they slept.

UNDICI

Thursdays were Signora Finelli's bridge club day. They alternated homes to accommodate the five women members. Whoever happened to be the hostess each week, would show off their winning recipes, or extravagant wine, or in Antonietta Peragine's case, clothes and money. Even though they were only playing cards she dressed as if she were hosting a ball. Hair and accessories included. She always had to prove she was better and wealthier than the rest. Signora Finelli gaped at Antonietta, her nemesis, as she dealt the cards.

"The contest is in two weeks. Are all you chickens ready?" Antonietta giggled annoyingly. "I can't wait to have my picture in the paper again. I already have my outfit picked out. And I'm having my hair done by Francesco." She stopped and looked directly at Signora Finelli.

"What are you looking at? Am I that beautiful? You can never seem to take your eyes off of me." Signora Finelli pointed out. "I know you're jealous, it's okay. I don't care who does your hair or picks out your clothes, this year belongs to me."

The other three bridge members, Gemma, Jacopa and Lena felt the usual fight coming on and were actually anticipating the thrill it brought. They lived for their bridge club. It was the most excitement they could find all week. Each woman more bored than the next looked forward to this weekly gossip and drama that was almost always guaranteed.

"Your garden doesn't stand a chance. I've got the most expensive seeds and the best soil."

"Ha, you think that's all you need? You don't know the first thing about gardening."

"Really? Is that why I win every year?" She threw down some cards. Jacopa followed with a card, and then Lena picked up, but their eyes were transfixed on the real game at hand.

"You won every year. And I let you. This year I'm taking the title. And my picture will be in the paper."

"We'll see!" Furiously picking up cards. "No one can garden like me."

Signora Finelli laughed. "I bet you pay a gardener to come in and help you." Antonietta's mouth opened in horror and all the ladies went quiet for a moment. She looked around as they all examined her. She felt caught. "I do not. I have the greenest thumb in Tuscany. And I buy the best seeds money can buy."

"One thing you can't buy is love, you ignorant woman." She threw down her cards. "Bridge!" All of the other woman hemmed and hawed as Elena collected the pool of money in the middle of the table. "You don't know how to love anything, but yourself." Scorned, Antonietta put her hand over her heart. Gemma tried to break the moment, as she grabbed the basket of sweets.

"Biscotti anyone?" Jacopa and Lena burst into laughter.

* * *

Later that afternoon, back from the market, Prima put together a cheeseboard of selections from her favorite stands. "The stinkier the cheese, the better the taste," Prima reminded herself. There was an aged gorgonzola, bigio and a sharp provolone. She sliced up red pears and green apples from her trees and draped burgundy grapes around the cheese board. Cracking open a local Chianti, she poured a glass of the intense ruby red with its scent of violet, sipped, and enjoyed the warmth flowing through her blood. Then she put out a mixture of green olives with pimientos and yet another stuffed with garlic. Last, she sliced fresh bread and placed it in a basket. "A perfect snack for lovers!" she exclaimed, pleased with herself.

Looking at the food reminded her of the feelings love brings. A ravenous hunger for your lover's body. Thirst unquenchable but by a long, deep kiss.

* * *

Stefano and Maria entered the kitchen glowing. Maria's teal

dress fit her like a second skin but it was the sight of Stefano in Paolo's clothing that made Prima's breath rise.

"You look so beautiful, Maria! And Stefano, so handsome." Tears streaked her cheeks. "It's nice to see you in Paolo's clothes. They suit you." She went to Stefano and turned him around for a full view. "*Bellissimo!*"

"*Grazie*, Prima." Stefano smiled and gently kissed her on her cheek, tasting the tears that salted her skin.

"I have the perfect wine for you two tonight. You must finish the bottle, for the deepest gifts are in the very last drops." Prima held up the jug of Chianti.

"Then we'll drink it all," Maria assured her.

"But not before tasting some of this delicious food!" Stefano cried out. "Are you as hungry as I am, Maria?" When she nodded, he took a section of pear and dipped it into the Gorgonzola and slid it into her mouth. She smiled and rolled the flavors around her tongue, but all she could taste was Stefano.

Ravenous, he sampled each cheese and gathered a few hunks of bread. Looking out the window, he saw that, sure enough, the sun had begun to sink.

"I think I should pretend to go home tonight. Signore Finelli should see me leave as usual. If he doesn't he might get suspicious and run his mouth. Even though he is retired he still has to patrol the village."

"Those neighbors!" Prima exclaimed. "*Impiccioni!* So nosy!"

He worried about protecting Maria. "I need to change back into my own clothes or Signore Finelli will notice. He notices everything. And if not him, the LaPortas."

"You're going to travel all the way home just to turn around and come back again so that old Signore Finelli doesn't suspect anything?" Maria protested. "I think it's ridiculous.

I get tired just thinking about it." She pouted.

Stefano did not have the heart to scold her, to tell her that all of this was for her own protection. Kind as the Finellis were, he knew they could never resist spreading good gossip. Nor could Carlo and Tessa LaPorta. "It's a good thing Prima fed me with all this cheese. Now I'll have enough energy for the whole night." He ran upstairs and quickly changed, grabbed some more bread and cheese and, kissing Maria, headed out the door.

"He's crazy," Maria blurted. "I hate being away from him even for a second." She looked at Prima. "I know this isn't good. He's more necessary to me than the air, the water, anything. God, it's all mixed up inside of me. Do you know this feeling Prima?"

"Yes, Maria, I know it very well." She grabbed her young friend's hand. "What you have to do is breathe or you'll float away like a balloon."

Stefano walked home on his usual path in his usual way. But today he sang a particularly happy song, and an extra bounce punctuated his stride.

"Ah, there you are. We haven't seen you lately." Tessa yelled out.

"How was work today, Stefano?" Carlo LaPorta yelled out, fishing.

"*Molto bene, Grazie.*"

"He seems very happy today, doesn't he, Carlo?" Tessa LaPorta asked, loudly enough for Stefano to hear. "Maybe a little too happy."

"I'm happy, Signora, thank you. *Ciao.*" Stefano waved and continued on.

The LaPortas looked at each other. Tessa raised a thin eyebrow.

* * *

Stefano passed Signor Finelli sitting on his porch, puffing a big cigar and sipping a glass of Chianti.

"Ah, Stefano, another day's work done." He puffed on his cigar and rubbed his large belly.

"Yes, Signor Finelli. And the sunset is beautiful no?" The sky glowed, awash in rose, violet, and lime.

"Forget the sunsets. Where have you been the last two nights? I

Incanto ~ The Singing Gardener

didn't see you go home.." Finelli did begin to laugh. Quickly it turned into a cough. At that moment, Signora Finelli ran out with a sack full of food, saving Stefano.

"Stefano, here, for you! Take it, it's from my garden." Stefano took the heavy flour sack and looked inside. Tomatoes, eggplant, basil, oregano, parsley all overflowed in rich colors that pleased the gardener.

"Thank you, Signora. You are too kind."

"And you are a brilliant magician."

"And you are a joy to see everyday!" He placed his hand on his heart and nodded his head with respect. "You have done everything I told you and that is why your garden must win for sure."

"How can you be sure?"

He reached in the sack and took out a tomato and bit into it. "Ah, the heavens live in this tomato, *Dio Mio*, you gave it so much love."

"I did!! But how can you tell?"

"I can taste it. I assure you, everyone will vote for you. You've earned it. You should be very proud. Shouldn't she Signor Finelli?" Stefano shouted to Signore Finelli, but he waved him off.

"You didn't answer the question gardener."

"I am proud!" She kissed Stefano on both cheeks. "Thank you Stefano."

Signore Finelli gulped some more wine. "Elena, what time is supper?"

"Don't act like you're starving to death. Just look at that belly." She winked at Stefano.

He winked back. "*Buonosera*, Signora. Signore." Stefano quickened his pace and continued on his path.

"Good night to you, gardener," the Finellis called.

As Stefano trotted off, her husband gave her a knowing look. "He's up to something."

"He does seem different, more happy, if that's possible. It is

129

none of our business why he is so happy. I'm just glad someone around here is." She walked inside.

 Singor Finelli eyed Stefano carefully as he traveled home on the dirt road.

Incanto ~ The Singing Gardener

DODICI

When it was dark Stefano headed back towards Prima's. He made sure Signor Finelli was not on his *terrazza*. Looking into their window as he passed, he saw the Finellis sitting across from one another in the dining room, sharing supper.

A little further ahead he saw the LaPortas through their front window, and caught the muffled sounds of their screaming match.

When he got to Prima's, their hostess had already gone to bed and Maria sat waiting with the jug of wine at the kitchen table. He offered her his arm. "Are you ready?"

"Yes. I'm not sure where we're going, but I'm ready."

"Good." He led her out the door, over the wall, and through her garden. "Tonight I'm going to take you on a tour through my favorite garden and tell you the meaning behind each and every wonder planted in your soil."

"My *professore!*" She laughed.

A warm breeze swept over them, and flowers waved in the wind. "But first you have to remove your shoes," he instructed. They both kicked off their shoes. Though Maria had walked through her garden many times before, she had never done it with Stefano. Nor did she know the intention behind every plant that lived in her garden. She only knew that without the garden her life would be monotony, black and white shades devoid of color and possibility the flowers offered. Now, she walked arm and arm with the gardener who brought her world to life. As they strolled barefoot through the soil, Maria could feel the cool texture on her feet. The earth lived, pumping life through her heels just the way it pumped life into the seeds Stefano planted. No wonder they grew so beautifully. She'd never realized the earth's force could be so powerful.

"The garden comes alive at night," Stefano said. "Trust me. It does things you can't imagine." He held her hands and gazed into her eyes sincerely, his words calming her.

"I trust you." She squeezed his strong hands.

"Then let's explore."

They journeyed in more deeply. Roses of every color sprouted through the ground as they walked, creating a silken floor of petals for their every step. Maria was speechless, but she followed Stefano wherever he led. With every step, heavenly scents consumed her. Never before had she experienced such aromas.

"As we come upon each new group of flowers notice how the air around you changes and shifts your mood." He whispered in her ear. "If you close your eyes you can tell when we are upon a new flower just by the scent. Each fragrance will make you feel a different emotion if you let it. Go on try it! Close your eyes and walk. Stop when you sense the shift in the air."

Maria shut her eyes and slowly moved forward. When she reached the Petunias she stopped abruptly. "Ah, I feel it."

"Keep your eyes closed. What do you feel?"

She inhaled the fragrant air. "I feel young, innocent." She giggled like a child, and then dug her feet into the earth. "And the soil feels different in this spot. It's warmer."

"Very good. Keep walking."

She moved toward the blue lacecap hydrangeas and sweet hyacinths, honeysuckle and jasmine. "Oh my, it changed again. She breathed in the aroma. "This makes me feel...sexy!"

"Yes, open your eyes." In front of her were orange and yellow marigolds. Yellow flag irises. And a host of blossoms she could not name. Her senses danced with delight.

"I never knew flowers could be so much fun."

"Fun yes, but they are very complex creatures. Each flower has certain needs. A conscientious gardener must listen carefully to his charges and provide them with the right ingredients to flourish." Maria realized she had taken the intricacies of the garden for granted. All she'd been seeing was the beautiful end result, with no idea how difficult the task had been to bring the landscape to perfection. Never again would she look at a flower the same way. What a world Stefano inhabited!

He led her through a pond and over a bridge made of Passionflower, rambling roses and wisteria. They walked across the bridge to a pergola clad in Clematis. He led her to the part of the garden in which, were he to admit it, he took the most pride in.

The orchids made up a garden within the garden. Their rich smell permeated the air and the diversity of their shapes and colors astonished her. Why had she never taken in their full beauty before this evening? Perhaps it was because she had never taken in her own beauty fully either.

"This is my favorite flower of all."

"Really?" Maria was curious. "Why? I want to know all of your favorite things."

"Well, to me, it is the most sensual to look at, but the history fascinates me. Orchids existed as many as five centuries before the birth of Jesus Christ." He delicately pulled one from its stem and held it up to Maria. "They have long been associated with human sex organs. Because of their shape, they had been attributed with the powers of aphrodisiac. The Medieval Europeans used to dry them out and mix them in potions to encourage conception of children," he told her. She giggled, bending to study them closer.

"Some looked like women, others like men. Still others like mythical beasts." Stefano pointed out the different parts of the orchid, three sepals and three petals and, most fascinating, the lip that protected the flower's reproductive parts. Maria tried to listen to these facts as Stefano's knowing fingers touched the orchid in question, but she couldn't really concentrate. The thought of him touching her in the same way made her light headed.

Walking through the garden with Stefano was like floating on a cloud in heaven. He had stories about the lilies, the peonies, roses and daffodils. He had songs about the iris, the sunflower, and the bird of paradise. The flowers had faces, and Maria could swear that each and every one of them flashed smiles as they passed. The garden seemed endless, the moonlight inextinguishable.

Saving the best for last, Stefano led her to her favorite willow tree. Its coats of rough bark told a story of two hundred years of strength. The tree had weathered every storm and still stood proud. Its feathery hair brushed across their faces and Stefano grabbed Maria's hand, gathering her under the tree's protection.

"The willow has the power to take pain and send it into the earth, rejuvenating us with the courage to go on." Stefano hugged the tree and kissed its bark. As he embraced the ancient tree, she could sense its healing power. "The power these old trees have is something we take for granted. It's a shame. They are the most reliable creatures alive."

He took Maria's hand and placed it on the base of the willow. She felt a current pulsate through her palm and up into her arm. She, too, embraced and kissed the tree. She spread her arms wide, hugging as much of the weeping willow as her arms could hold. Stefano spread his arms, too, and wrapped them around from the other side. Their fingertips almost touched.

Maria silently confessed her fears and dreams into the rough bark. Then she moved away from the trunk and into his arms. "You are my willow, Stefano." She kissed him deeply.

"I want to shelter you from all storms." She wrapped herself in the willow leaves and he ran his fingers through her hair. In an instant, ropes of pink and purple Bougainvillea fell from the willow, forming a kind of ladder.

"How on earth?" Maria exclaimed. But the answer came to her. They stood on an earth she was only beginning to know. Stefano stepped onto the Bougainvillea to make sure it held sturdy. He held the wine Prima had given them in his hand and climbed into the tree. Reaching a point where he could rest on a flat surface, he stretched his hand down to Maria.

"Come. I will guide you."

Without stopping to question, Maria began climbing the flowery ladder. When she reached Stefano, she was shocked to find a room, a kind of child's clubhouse, in the middle of the willow tree. The shimmering moonlight illuminated the spot. Maria didn't want to question how any of this was possible. Stefano held up the bottle of wine. "Here's to a night we'll never forget." He handed the bottle to Maria. Her eyes fixed on his, she swallowed her sip of wine knowing full well that this was a moment in her life to which no other would come close.

Tonight, in this moment, Maria had come awake and alive. She smiled into Stefano's eyes and took in every detail of his face. He was burned into her heart. As they finished every last drop of Prima's wine, intoxication set in, but not because they were drunk. No, they saw the world as it was, as it was meant to be seen, vibrating within, around, above and below them.

Maria let her head fall back in Stefano's lap. "Did you know, Maria, that the willow is the tree of the moon, of water, and the goddess? It's considered a tree of deep emotions, intuition and dreaming." Maria understood why she had always been drawn to the willow. "The ancients believed the willow held a healing spirit and enchantment for all those who chose to draw from its source. And when one of its branches is severed, it can grow into a whole new tree if it only finds some water and soil."

"If only," Maria repeated, and Stefano paused. Searching her face, he seemed to come to a decision. In one swift movement, Stefano reached down into the hollow part of the tree and pulled out a ring. He held it up to the moonlight, and Maria could see that it was gold, the craftsmanship exquisite. He looked into her eyes with the question and, overcome, she nodded. Before slipping it on her wedding ring finger, he showed her the inscription engraved in curling script on the inside. She read it aloud, "*From this day on we are forever.*" She ran her finger over his words, her tears falling freely.

"Thank you, my love. I don't know what to say."

"Say yes." He kissed her softly. "Now you are weeping, just like the willow." She let out a gentle laugh. "Will you wear it?" His voice trembled.

When she nodded through her tears, he slipped the ring onto her finger, a perfect fit. Electricity shot through their bodies.

She moaned, "I need you."

With pleasure, he took care of her need.

* * *

The morning birds sang to the dawn and the lovers climbed out of the tree and began to walk towards Prima's. Maria turned back to look at her weeping willow once more and let out a gasp. The Bougainvillea ladder had vanished. Then she turned with a shrug and tiptoed after Stefano. Every day more miracles.

Neither of them wanted the neighbors' attention, so they did not talk. They slipped into Prima's for their ritual breakfast. Prima poured her famous espresso so strong it could make a dead man dance. Maria prepared some brioche with fresh butter and jam. Stefano set the table with a fresh arrangement of orchids.

Maria and Stefano ate their breakfast like they were teenagers again.

Prima sat and took each of their hands in hers. "I need to tell you two something."

"What is it, Prima?" Maria shuddered, afraid of bad news.

"Nothing bad! Last night Paolo came to me. At first I thought it was just a dream because each night before I go to bed I ask him to visit me in my dreams, but last night…" She turned to Stefano and smiled. "He was right before me. I actually touched him and he touched me."

"Well, what happened?" Maria asked.

"There are some things too sacred to share," Prima replied, and the lovers shot each other a glance. "One thing I will tell you is that Paolo told me he likes you wearing his clothes, Stefano. It makes him feel alive." Tears spilled from her eyes. "God, it was good to see him." She lifted her hand to her heart and then gulped her cup of espresso.

"Tell Paolo thank you from me. I feel him with me, too."

"Tell him yourself. He said he's around all the time and that he would show me signs. I don't know what they are, but he said I would recognize them."

Stefano smiled and looked up to the sky. "Okay then." He shouted up. "Thank you for lending me your clothes, Paolo." He laughed and then out of nowhere Prima's radio turned on by itself and a song began to play, "*Parla mi d'amore, Maria,*" by Gino Federici. Prima's eyes widened as if she had just seen a ghost.

"This was our wedding song!"

Maria and Stefano looked at each other, shocked. Prima began to cry, a wide smile on her face. Slowly she began dancing in the middle of the kitchen. She felt Paolo and wrapped her arms around his image. From Stefano and Maria's point of view she appeared to be dancing with her partner.

Stefano extended his hand to Maria. "May I have this dance?" She jumped up into his arms and they danced alongside Prima and her invisible, ever-present love.

"By the way, I noticed Finelli spying with his binoculars. I don't trust him, or anyone for that matter." Prima continued to dance.

"What shall we do Prima?" Maria panicked.

"Don't worry! I have a plan." She spun around the room confidently as she delighted in her secret scheme.

Trish Doolan

TREDICI

Prima headed out the door with a two *tortas* that she had baked especially for the neighbors. The Finellis would get the pear, the newlyweds the apple.

Smelling the butter in the crust, Signor Finelli greeted her with a smile. He could not resist food and he certainly had no willpower when it came to sweets. Signora Finelli, too, ran to the door.

"*Buongiorno*, Prima," she said, an edge of suspicion in her voice. "It's been too long!"

"*Buongiorno*. I brought you two something I hope you like." Prima smiled.

"Thank you. It looks absolutely sinful!" Signore Finelli narrowed her eyes. True, Prima liked to bake, and everyone knew she was a master. But why was she here?

Signore Finelli took no notice of his wife's suspicion. He patted his belly in anticipation of the treat. "Eh! I did not see Stefano in the garden this morning. Is he over there?"

"*Si, si*, you know him," Prima answered in a low tone. "He's probably lying in the dirt singing to the flowers."

They both laughed, relieving Prima of any further explanations.

"Thank you so much, dear neighbor. You're too kind," Signora Finelli added. Was Prima after her husband? That woman had been alone so long, and the way to a man's heart, especially her man's heart, was through his stomach.

"What are neighbors for if not to add a little sweetness to your life?" Prima held up the other *torta* and Signora Finelli noticed it for the first time. "I don't want the LaPortas to feel left out. I better get over there." She prepared to leave and Signora Finelli realized, ashamed of herself, that maybe *she* had been jealous for nothing.

Signor Finelli asked, "And what kind are the LaPortas getting?"

Prima answered, "Apple."

Incanto ~ The Singing Gardener

"I love apple, too, Prima." He laughed and his wife shot him a sharp glance.

"I'll keep that in mind for next time! Divertiti!" Prima walked away.

Signora Finelli smacked her husband for being such a pig. It was he, not Prima, she had to worry about!

* * *

Prima strolled over to the LaPortas and received a welcome as warm as the *torta*. As Tessa LaPorta opened the door, a thin smile animated her pale lips.

"How kind of you!" She took the pie and called to her husband. "Carlo!"

Before he could come to the door, Tessa turned to Prima and whispered. "Did I see the Ricci's gardener go into your house this morning?"

"Oh, *si*, *si*, I always ask him to come and give me tips on my garden. I give him a cup of espresso in exchange."

"I see. Well he does a very good job with the Ricci garden, why not ask for help with yours? He's helped us, too. And how is Signora. Ricci? You two have become quite friendly, no?"

"She's well," Prima said simply.

"I haven't heard her play the piano in a while."

Carlo came to the door, greeting Prima with a smile and saving her from Tessa's interrogation.

"Thank you so much!" he exclaimed. "This wife of mine never makes sweets. It will go with my coffee."

Tessa shot him a cold look, but Prima broke in. "Any time you want a baking lesson, Tessa my dear, you are very welcome. And you too Carlo. I bake bread you know."

Carlo kissed her. "I would be so grateful. I know my bread is ghastly, isn't it Prima?"

"Eh, you need a little help, that's all." She patted his cheek like a baby.

"A little!" Tessa rolled her eyes. "This looks devilish Prima.

Grazie."
"*Grazie* Prima."
"*Prego.*"
Prima smiled and headed back home empty handed. The gifts she had just delivered would satisfy many appetites.

* * *

The Finellis dug into the pear *torta* and groaned with satisfaction. They had never tasted anything more delicious. Insatiable, they began shoveling piece after piece into each other's mouths. They laughed at themselves. When they had finished, they hungered as much for each other. Signora Finelli ran to the bedroom, squealing, and Signor Finelli ran after her.

* * *

The LaPortas could not understand how a simple *torta* could taste so magnificent and how they could have finished it all in one sitting. Then the desire for each other ignited, they began making love on the kitchen floor.

* * *

In the broad daylight, Maria and Stefano walked hand-in-hand through the garden without fear of being seen. Thanks to Prima, they were to experience one day of freedom, a small taste of what it would be like if they could be together as they wished.

In the garden Maria and Stefano sat under the willow tree. The silence drifted between them and they reflected on their time together. Maria worried whether to tell him that Martino had plans to get rid of him. But she did not want to speak her husband's name. She did not want to think about the fact that Martino would be home tomorrow and how everything would change.

Maria knew she had to find a way to leave Martino. But if she and Stefano simply disappeared, Martino would use all of his power and connections to track them down and destroy them. She could not put Stefano, in particular, in jeopardy. Should any harm come to him, it would be worse than her own death. Without

thinking too much, Maria told herself that everything would be fine, that she and Stefano would be together soon. Somehow. Stefano saw Maria's body fill with tension.
"Don't worry, my love. I'm here." He squeezed her hand. She tried to ignore the nagging voice that filled her head.
"I know, Stefano, you have always been. I just wish I'd found you sooner," she admitted.
"We have to trust, Maria. We did find each other and that's the most important thing, isn't it?"
"Yes, you're right," she answered sadly.
"Why are you so sad?" He touched her face. "Tell me what haunts you?"
"I've never felt like this about anyone. I'm meant for you. I did not live before you walked into my garden and now that we're about to return to a world of unknowns I'm so afraid. What do we do?" she pleaded.
"I don't know, Maria, but we'll figure it out. We have to be together whatever it takes."
But Stefano's heart, too, filled with fear. He didn't have the money to take care of Maria in the way she was accustomed to, nor to take her far away to America. He'd spent everything he had saved on her ring. He wanted to give her everything, yet he knew he had nothing to offer right now except his love. His little cottage was barely big enough for him. How could he ever bring the wife of Martino Ricci there?
Stefano's heart sank. Now that he had finally found his true love, was it possible he could lose her? No! He must find a way to earn enough money to change his position in life. He thought of how many more gardens he could tend to. He would work night and day for her. No matter what he had to do he could not lose Maria.
Now, it was Maria who felt Stefano's fears. She began kissing his neck tenderly. Her fingers danced across his chest and then her lips found their way up to his ear. She bit his ear lobe gently and

then whispered into his ear.

"I, Maria, am in love with you, Stefano."

Tears ran down his cheeks and every fear melted instantly. He turned to her. She kissed his lips.

"And I, Stefano, am in love with you, Maria. Un amore profundo." He put her ringed hand over his heart. She felt it pounding. "Can you feel, Maria?" The entire world went still in that moment. The power of her words, her scent, her eyes and her love jolted Stefano so that he began to weep. She cradled his head on her chest and wove her fingers into his curly mane.

She could hardly believe that tomorrow Martino would return and expect to find his wife, Maria, at home and tending to his every need and demand.

Stefano raised his head from her breast. They smiled at each other and tried to convince themselves that everything would be all right, but a hollow ache of sadness washed over them.

"Maria, I've told you where I was raised. But I haven't told you this. There was something Sister Camilla told me that's always stuck in my head. It is this saying that applies to us." Stefano had her complete attention. *"Non si puó promettere domani."*

She repeated his words, "Tomorrow is promised to no one." So true. Neither of them knew what tomorrow would bring, nor could they stop the clocks that moved their destiny forward.

* * *

Prima walked up the cobble stone driveway to the Ricci property. Spotting them, she observed their body language. To her it looked like a crushing goodbye scene. Their pain was palpable and permeated through the garden. She headed over to the willow tree.

"It is a good day." Prima smiled at them. "Sometimes we miss the gift of the present because we are so worried about the future."

"Speaking of gifts, how did the neighbors like the *torta's*?" Stefano asked.

"When they wake up, all they will remember is that they made wonderful love. All the rest will be a blur." She cackled. Stefano and Maria smiled, grateful for the distraction.

"When will they wake up?" Maria asked.

"Tomorrow morning just before noon. And then all will return to normal." Prima's words also applied to Maria and Stefano. "So you two have one more night to be free from interfering eyes. I know you won't waste it." With that, she walked away.

* * *

It began to rain, a soft caress at first, then a more insistent shower that even the willow could not shield.

"Can I sleep with you tonight?" Maria asked him. "I want to be in your home, in your bed."

"Are you sure? You've seen where I live. It's not much."

She was very sure.

"*Si*, Maria, I would love nothing more than to have you beside me in my bed tonight." He kissed her.

Maria knew she would have to leave before the sunrise, but she had no fear. The neighbors were taken care of and Martino would not arrive before noon. Besides, this would be her last night with him before God knew how long.

Lightning sliced the Castellina sky as they made their way to Stefano's cottage.

The storm clapped against the loose tiles on the roof, creating a symphony. Glowing candles lit the rooms. Stefano held Maria in his arms and they danced in time to the rain. A bolt flashed outside the window.

"It's beautiful," she murmured.

"Yes. Too bad the Finellis and the LaPortas are sleeping right through it!" Stefano laughed.

Maria buried her head into Stefano's chest and he held her head upon his heart as they floated around the room. She ignited fire in his belly. He did not have to simply accept what was given him any longer. With this power he knew he could win her love and keep it.

He stopped dancing and she stood still before him. Gracefully, gratefully, he removed her clothing piece by piece. The lightning cracked, ripping white light through the room, engulfing Maria's sculpted figure. Stefano knelt before her, worshiping her body. He knew just how to kiss her and how to touch her. Each time they made love it got better and better, behind his every move a purpose.

Rising from his knees, he lifted her into his arms and carried her to his bed. He snapped the top sheet off, revealing the petals of a thousand roses, and then lowered her onto them. Her skin responded with goose bumps. He undressed; she waited with her eyes fixed on him. The lightning cracked again, flashing through the room. Soon after, thunder rumbled through the sky.

"The storm is close," Stefano whispered.

"It is here." She touched her belly, then his. Stefano and Maria moved and glided as if they could read each other's thoughts and desires. On this night they would not speak any more at all. They would taste each other and hoard the food they would need to help them survive in leaner times. Maria wanted Stefano to devour her; she could not give him enough. She wanted him to crawl inside her skin and live there so the two of them would never be separated.

Was it really possible to love like this? This question ran through Maria's mind and was followed by yet another, more profound question. *Is it possible to love like this and let it go?*

Stefano penetrated Maria deeply as she moaned with pleasure. He was her very core, her truth. Martino's face flashed before her eyes and she realized he would be back sooner than she could bear. He would demand things of her and expect her to make him happy, but the thing she dreaded most of all was the thought of him on top of her. She belonged to Stefano. How could she ever let Martino touch her again or be inside of her? She cried as Stefano held her. He did not ask why she was crying. He already knew.

The storm was passing. Though neither of them knew, this would be the last rainfall for quite sometime. He laid her back as the candles lit up her beautiful face. Scooping up as many rose

Incanto ~ The Singing Gardener

petals his hands could hold, he held them above her, releasing them like the raindrops that pitter-pattered on the roof. He took a rose petal and wiped away her tears and then he opened his mouth and placed the salty petal on his tongue. He chewed and swallowed it.

She watched him in awe. Never did she imagine she could be loved so completely. But Stefano loved her without hesitation or judgments. A love so sure had no limitations.

It rained softly through the night and they continued to indulge in every minute of lovemaking they could steal.

Maria's hair caressed the white linen case that covered the pillow. Stefano dipped his nose into her and let her scent permeate his senses. They stared into each other's eyes and cried, then laughed, then cried again. The rain lifted and they fell into silence. The early morning birds began their song and roosters greeted the new day.

Maria dressed. Stefano watched her, his heart breaking. The woman he loved more than anything in the world was walking out of his door and possibly out of his life yet his hands were tied. He wanted to scream, "Please, Maria, don't leave me, not now!" But he couldn't speak. Thorns from bitter roses pierced his tongue. He couldn't breathe. He lay paralyzed on the narrow bed. Finally, he managed to place his hand on the sheet where he could still feel the warmth of her body. But even that warmth would soon be gone.

In a fever, he jumped up.

"Maria?" She turned and looked at him so simply, so purely, that tears gathered in his eyes.

"Yes, Stefano?" She smiled sadly.

"I don't want you to leave." He collapsed into her arms.

"I don't want to leave, either. But it's just for now my love, just for now," she told him. Anything else would be too much for either of them. She had to find a way to go home to her husband and pretend. She kissed Stefano and he responded almost listlessly.

"I will see you later," she whispered into the saddest eyes she had ever seen.

"Yes, Maria, I'll be in the garden this morning." She opened the door and stepped out into the dawn. As soon as she closed the door behind her, Stefano crawled to his bed, curled up in the rose petals and cried. But nothing could absorb his anguish.

Incanto ~ The Singing Gardener

QUATTORDICI

    Roosters screamed to the morning sky as Maria traveled the path Stefano had marked so many times before. She consoled herself by imagining him singing as he walked to her garden, perhaps touching the low stone walls by the road, maybe even stopping to smell the wild irises that grew knee high. Swallows chirped, answering the roosters, and she let the birds' song carry her as she knew it carried him every morning. Last night's rain had made everything look luscious, and the smell of damp earth filled her nose.
    The beauty of the morning did not erase Maria's grief, but she couldn't deny that life had a way of moving on, no matter what. Nothing could stop the day from coming, the night from falling, or the day from coming again. Maria felt Stefano everywhere she looked. At a gnarled fig tree, she stopped and ripped a tiny fruit from its vine. Biting in, all she could taste was him.
    The pain ripped her heart in half, as she felt their separation begin its evil course. Up the cobblestone drive to the heavy front door she trudged. Entering her own home, she felt like a stranger in a foreign country. Looking around, she realized that nothing in this house was important to her. Nothing meant a thing if she couldn't be with Stefano. Her clothes, at least, still smelled of him. And she still wore the ring he had given her. Oh God, the ring! What would Martino say if he saw it?
    She rushed out of the house in agony and ran to the willow tree. Hugging its trunk again for strength, she removed the golden token and tucked it into the hollow Stefano had drawn it from. "I'll be back for you soon," she said aloud.
    Then she ran back into the house and spotted the check Martino left for her to deposit. Her heart raced. "*Dio Mio.*" She picked up the check and ran to Prima's. Barging in as if someone had just

died. "Prima, please you must help me! I must get to the bank in Sienna immediately. I forgot to deposit this check and Martino will be very suspicious." Prima grabbed her scarf, wrapped it around her head and lead Maria out the door.

"You must calm down Maria. You look like you just killed someone." Maria cried even harder realizing that she may have.

Cigarette smoke filled Enzo's private chambers as he sat across from Maria. Smiling uncomfortably, Maria handed Enzo the check. He noticed circles of sweat pouring from her armpits and through the fabric of her dress. "Is it too hot in here for you Maria?" He smiled and shook his head as he inhaled deeply on his cigarette.

"*Si, si fa troppo caldo.*" She wiped beads of sweat from her forehead as the color drained from her face. Finding it hard to meet Enzo's eyes. "Martino asked me to give that to you. Is there anything else before I go?" Getting up to leave.

"Yes, there is. Please sit Maria. Are you in a rush to get somewhere?" He laughed.

"Well, my husband will be home soon and I wanted to make a special lunch for him."

"How sweet. What a good wife. My wife is a great cook." Enzo examined the check. "Didn't Martino leave days ago?"

"*Si.*"

"I was expecting you days ago. Why didn't you bring me the check sooner?"

"Oh I was busy, very busy." Maria looked down and focused on the floor as her legs trembled underneath her dress. Her heart beating like a drum. Enzo sensed that she was not herself and maybe Martino was right. He smiled, shook his head and then pulled out Martino's banking information. He slid some papers across for Maria to see.

"Martino wanted you to sign these documents." He laughed for no reason at all, lit up another cigarette and then handed her a pen.

With a trembling hand she reached for the pen. "I don't understand. What is this?"

"Ah, this is your husband's account and by you signing it makes it a joint account. Half is yours and half is his." He came around the desk and stood behind Maria. Looking over her shoulder he pointed to where she should sign and then pointed to the amount that was in the account. "Ten Millioni is a lot of money. Your husband is a very wealthy man, and you are a wealthy woman because of him."

"Ten Millioni," Maria screamed out in shock. "I had no idea. That is a lot of money. I'm confused Enzo, why does he want me to sign this?"

"My darling Maria, he is making sure that if anything happens to him, God Forbid, that you are protected and comfortable for the rest of your life. No one else can come between you once you sign." Enzo laughed loud. "Not even his mother. He told me she is jealous of you and wanted you to know you really are his priority." Collapsing in her chair, Maria's body dropped to the floor. Enzo went to her, grabbed a glass of water from his desk and began fanning her with the papers. "Maria, drink, drink! Are you okay?" Slowly she opened her eyes and saw Enzo looking down at her, his cigarette dangling from his mouth.

"It's too much." She managed.

His inappropriate habit kicked in once again, as he laughed out loud and shook his head. "What is? The money? The heat? Come now, let's get these papers signed so that you can go home and make your husband lunch. He deserves it after all, eh?" Laughing again. "It must be nice to be so loved." He picked her up off the floor, put her in the chair, handed her the papers and the pen and waited for her to sign. Maria knew that this was more than just a signature. She was making a deal with the devil and it would seal her fate. Sweat poured from the palms of her hands causing the pen to slide out. She wiped her hands on her dress and stared at Enzo. Sensing her trepidation, he went in for the kill. "So Maria, what did you do with your free time while your husband was away?" Smiling into her eyes, as he puffed on his cigarette.

Looking down at the papers before her, she felt trapped. "Not much, chores, not much."

"How is your garden? My wife and I pass by all the time just to admire it. Martino tells me it's your favorite thing in the whole world." An eternal smile plastered on his face.

"It's fine. Yes. It's just fine." Maria thought perhaps she had been spied on and was now about to vomit. Feeling as though she had no other choice, she quickly signed the papers, but scarcely recognized her own name on the paper beneath her. She got up abruptly. "Thank you Enzo. Now I must go." Maria rushed out of the bank. As she turned the corner she leaned on the building for support and threw up. Prima rushed to her and helped her to the car.

* * *

Arriving back home, Maria ran upstairs to bathe, crying at the thought of washing Stefano's scent off of her body. Time was running out. Martino would be here soon. She scrubbed herself, but all she could think about was Stefano. She went to the drawer and put her old wedding band back on. She pulled out the sad picture of her wedding day feeling sick inside.

* * *

Stefano walked his usual path to work. He looked down and noticed the footprints Maria had left just a few hours earlier. Stepping inside each one of them, he tried to imagine how she had been feeling as she walked to her house this morning. Passing by the Finellis--they were still sleeping under Prima's spell--he began to sing a sad song. When he arrived at the Ricci garden he realized it would need some adjustments. The topiary had grown a little ragged, and the places where he and Maria had been together were bare now. Stefano went to all the spots where he and Maria had made love and dug his fists in the soil. When he pulled out his hands, blooms sprung up in somber purples and blues. His tears watered the soil.

* * *

Incanto ~ The Singing Gardener

Maria watched Stefano working from her arched window as she sipped Prima's strong espresso. She touched the glass of the window, her heart bleeding.

"Oh my God, Prima. I am doomed. I cannot hurt Martino. He is good to me. He does not deserve my betrayal." Then she turned to Stefano working in the garden. "But, oh I love him so much it hurts," she cried.

"Yes," the older woman said. "Love hurts like hell, doesn't it? He's suffering just as much as you." Prima held her hand.

"How can you be sure?"

Prima pointed out all the dark blossoms sprouting up throughout the garden.

"Look at all that! Do you think that he could possibly do that without feeling inconceivable love? And just look. They are all the flowers of melancholy."

"What have we done?" She could barely get the words out, as she clutched her heart. "I cannot believe how much my heart aches. Why Prima? Why does it physically hurt my heart so much? I cannot breathe."

"It's giving you a warning that it is unnatural for you to be separated from your true love. The pain is a signal telling you that it is broken, split into two parts when it should be joined as one. That's why the pain is so deep Maria. You heart is crying with bitterness."

Stefano looked into Maria's arched window and caught her looking out at him. He smiled and shrugged as if to say *I'm sorry, this is all I can do*. In his imagination, he kissed her through the glass that separated them and she kissed him back.

Martino's Zagato roared into the driveway. Stefano stopped his work and stood to watch this man returning home, this man who would soon have his hands on Maria. The thought of it turned Stefano's stomach.

Martino got out and stared at the garden, truly taken aback by its beauty. "Sometimes you don't appreciate things until you are away from them." He said out loud and then noticed Stefano. "*Ciao*, gardener," he yelled out, walking over to greet Stefano. He put out his hand. This confused Stefano. In all the years he had worked for Martino Ricci, never had the man extended his hand in this kind of friendly gesture. Stefano wished he hadn't. But, shaking Martino's hand, he could not help but feel the other man's vulnerability, despite all his bluster.

"*Buongiorno*, Signor Ricci, welcome home."

"Thank you. It's good to be back. The garden looks good!" He smiled. "Is my wife inside?" Martino asked. *Mia moglie.* How Stefano hated those words. How could any other claim Maria as his wife when she belonged with him? He pretended not to hear Martino and reached into the soil. "Did you hear me, gardener?" Martino repeated more loudly.

"*Scusi*, Signor Ricci, did you say something?"

Martino laughed and shook his hands at Stefano. "Ah, you have not changed, never mind. I'll go and see for myself, where else would she be?" Martino retrieved his valise from the car, walked up the front steps and, easily as he pleased, entered the house.

Stefano sank into the earth, stabbing a trowel into the edge of the lawn to sharpen its line. He watched Maria open the door. She forced a big smile for Martino and then kissed him. Martino had been missing her. He grabbed her waist and made the kiss a long one. Stefano felt as if the trowel had been thrust into his heart.

When Martino finally pulled away, Maria noticed Stefano's eyes on her. The last thing in the world she wanted to do was to bring her lover pain, but there could be no way around it. Her green gaze captured the sorrow in Stefano's eyes as he stood lifeless.

As Martino entered the house, he put his suitcase down. Maria slowly closed the door. Gripping her breast with pain, Maria shut the door prepared to hide in a world of lies.

Stefano lost his breath and felt trapped in a nightmare. How could it all be washed away with the slam of a door? He told himself that Maria had to act this way or Martino would suspect something. The next time they were alone, Maria would assure him. She would explain that this was all an act with Martino, that she was working out a plan so they could be together.

An overwhelming fear shot through his body, as he realized that he did not know the next time he and Maria would be together. They had made no plan. He stumbled further from the house. The garden began to spin and sweat dripped from every pore in his body. He could not feel his legs beneath him. He dropped to his knees and hid beneath the sunflowers, digging his hands deep in the earth and praying to God to have mercy on his soul, to lift the pain piercing his heart. Stefano had never felt the intensity of grief, and it was swallowing him up like quicksand. "Please don't take Maria away from me. I can't be without her," he prayed. "Please help me, dear God and I will never ask another blessing from you."

* * *

Prima could feel Stefano suffering in the garden and she, too, began to cry. But what could she do? She tried to catch glimpses of him out her window, but he was nowhere in sight.

* * *

Inside the Ricci house, Maria presented Martino with a plate of food. "I thought you might be hungry."

He kissed her on the cheek. "I'm not. Giuliano will be here in a couple of hours."

Maria started. "Giuliano? So…so soon?"

"If he wants that gardener, let him take him. Martino said cheerfully, walking up the stairs. "I'm going to lie down. I had a very tiring trip." From upstairs he yelled. "Did you get to the bank?"

"*Sì*. Thank you Martino." She bit her lip and began to weep and then collapsed in the chair by her arched window. She covered her mouth so that Martino would not be able to hear her sobs. There was nowhere to run. She didn't know how to be in the house with Martino, yet how could she step outside with Stefano? Her life had become a riddle.

Tortured, she turned to the window and looked out to the garden only to find Stefano standing before her. He stood closer to her arched window than he had ever before, not caring who saw him. Her heart leapt into her throat and anxiety flooded her limbs. He stood staring boldly as if trying to pull her back through the glass to him.

She stared back, placing her hand on the window. He reached his hand up to mirror hers. With tears in her eyes, Maria turned away. Feeling like a corpse, she began to go about her chores, sorting Martino's dirty laundry from his suitcase, relieved to have a task. As she examined Martino's clothing she couldn't help but smell the fragrance of a woman's perfume. She also found lipstick on several of his collared shirts. So he had betrayed her as well, and not for the first time.

A knock came on the front door and, drying her hands on her skirt, Maria went to open it.

Signore Giuliano stood smiling on the other side. "Signora Ricci, so nice to see you."

"And you, Signore. Please come in. I will call Martino."

She felt sick knowing why he was here. In moments her Stefano would be ripped out of her garden, their garden, and her life would never be the same. She walked to the staircase as if traveling in slow motion. A weakness came over her and she could not even call up to Martino. The breath left her body. Signore Giuliano noticed Maria stumble. "Are you all right, Signora?" He went to her.

"Yes, thank you." She placed her hand on the banister for support. "Maybe I should just go up and get him." She could not find her voice. All the color drained from her face and she slowly lowered herself to sit on the stairs.

Very concerned, Signore Giuliano repeated, "Are you sure you're all right? Can I get you something?"

Maria remembered the time she'd fainted and Stefano took her inside, the moment that had started everything. She wanted to go back to that day, to stop time. Impossible! She looked up to Signore Giuliano.

"Please, could you get me a glass of *limonata*?" He immediately ran to the kitchen and poured a glass, then rushed it to her.

"Thank you," she said, taking it. "I'm sorry I haven't been feeling well."

"Please, don't apologize. But forgive me. Maybe you should see a doctor?" Signore Giuliano asked.

Just at that moment Martino appeared at the top of the staircase. "See a doctor for what? What's wrong with you?" he asked harshly.

Quickly, Maria rose to her feet.

"Nothing, nothing, I'm just a little light headed is all."

Signore Giuliano was shocked at how quickly she changed in her husband's presence. The three of them came down the stairs, and it was Giuliano who watched to make sure Maria didn't fall.

"Ah, she's always got something wrong with her!" Martino teased. "Inventing illness, if you ask me, for lack of anything useful to do." Maria winced, and so did their neighbor. "So, Giuliano, are you here to take my gardener?" He laughed.

"Yes, if you are willing to part with him." Signor Giuliano looked to Maria, who turned her eyes away. The conversation was all too much for her to digest. She walked to the kitchen to pour herself more *limonata*.

"Have you found me a gardener to replace him?"

"Yes, I have. I think you will be very happy."

"And you will be paying him for the first six months, right?"

"Right." Giuliano put out his hand and Martino shook it. "Then we have a deal?"

"Yes, we have a deal." Martino turned to find Maria's eyes welling with tears. "Well then, let's go see the gardener, shall we?"

He led Giuliano to the front door, and the two of them walked outside. Maria stood in the doorway and watched from a distance as they approached Stefano. He had moved and was kneeling down above a section of the garden he had designed in the shape of a heart. The heart had been created from ten different varieties of African violets in shades of night and half night. He knew that Maria would find the heart that he was leaving for her, but that Martino would likely never recognize the symbol.

Signor Giuliano, though, spotted the romantic shape right away. He was wise enough to admire it silently. The violets were exquisite, and inexplicably he felt an ache in his heart as he beheld them. Stefano rose up to his feet.

"Signor Giuliano, it's so nice to see you."

"And you, Stefano." Giuliano smiled warmly.

Martino looked at Stefano and an uncomfortable laugh escaped his mouth.

"Well, gardener, this is your lucky day, or should I say my lucky day? Giuliano would like to have you as his gardener and I've made a deal with him."

Martino continued to speak, but Stefano could not hear him. He turned to Maria, who stood in the doorway like a statue. She wasn't even meeting his eyes. His hands swung down to his sides in surrender. Stefano could not help but feel shocked that Ricci, so strangely friendly earlier, would give him away like a pair of old shoes. In fact, Stefano felt as if he'd just been punched in the stomach. Had she known?

"*Scusi* Signor Ricci, did I not care for your garden properly? Did I do something wrong? I tried to make you happy and make sure the garden pleased you. Did I not do my job?"

"Oh you did your job, but anyone can do your job. I know you made my wife happy while you were here, but she too agrees that anyone can water the grounds and watch the flowers grow. She might miss your singing." He began to laugh. "But I need a gardener, not a crooner."

Ever the gentleman, Signore Giuliano added, "Stefano I hope you will be happy with me. I think we'll work very well together." He put his arm around the gardener, who stood transfixed on Mrs.

Ricci in the doorway. Giuliano worried that Martino would see what he was seeing. Finally, Maria turned, walked into the house, and shut the door.

With her back up against the door she looked up to God. "Why did you bless me and then curse me all at once?" she whispered.

Outside, Stefano turned to Signore Giuliano and Martino, trying to hide his anguish. "Well, I guess it's all settled then. When do I come with you?" Stefano did his best to speak calmly, but his voice cracked.

Signore Giuliano smiled with a heart-welcoming smile. "Now, Stefano. I'm here to take you back with me today."

Stefano wiped his hands with resignation and looked around the garden one last time. His eyes landed on Maria, who had been unable to resist moving to her arched window to watch him. There she stood, more beautiful to him than in the days before they had shared love, and more tragic. He locked this picture in his memory for eternity. Nodding his head to her ever so gently, he placed his hand over his heart. When he turned back to Martino and Giuliano, he pretended to be wiping his dirty hands on his chest.

"I'm ready."

"Now someone else can pay you to sleep and sing your silly songs on their property." Martino laughed and patted Stefano on the back.

Stefano did not smile or laugh or pretend to suffer Martino's rudeness. He wanted to spit on this man. "Goodbye, Signor Ricci. Thank you for allowing me to tend to your garden all these years. It will remain forever in my heart." He stared at Martino for a moment and then turned away.

Giuliano led Stefano to his automobile. He opened the door for Stefano and the gardener reached down and grabbed a handful of dirt from the Ricci garden and shoved it into his pocket. He turned and looked for Maria one last time, hoping perhaps she moved to her favorite arched window but it was empty. He got in the car and sat staring straight ahead, as they pulled away from Maria's

Trish Doolan

garden.

QUINDICI

The Giulianos, sat Stefano down in their airy kitchen and Signora Giuliano herself served a delicious meal of truffle risotto she had been preparing since early that morning, complimented by a delicate Chianti her husband had taken from his cellar. Stefano was moved. It was unusual for a gardener to be treated with such hospitality.

"My wife, she's a wonderful cook. No, Stefano?" Giuliano smiled.

"Leave him be," Signora Giuliano scolded mildly, embarrassed. "Eat, Stefano. There's plenty more."

"*Grazie*, Signora. This is very kind of you, and it is delicious." But Stefano ate and drank slowly, unable to think of having more, unable to think about anything but Maria. "Signore Giuliano," he managed politely, "you are a lucky man."

"Please, Stefano, we are friends here. Call me Giuliano."

His wife broke in. "And I'm Filomena."

Giuliano went on, "We consider it our good fortune to have you here as our gardener. If you do well for me, you will do well for yourself. I'm a fair man, Stefano. I know a good thing when I see it." Signore Giuliano poured him some more wine.

"I'll do my best to please you." Stefano sipped his wine and began to feel a little better. The only reason he remained on the Ricci property for so long had been to be near Maria, but now he knew he must find a way for them to really be together.

Signore Giuliano looked at his wife and gave her a look and a nod. She smiled and excused herself. After she had gone, Signore Giuliano placed his hand on Stefano's shoulder.

"You know that we have plenty of room here. You're welcome to stay here with us."

"No, no I couldn't do that. I have my own home and am

comfortable. Thank you, thank you very much, but no." He finished his wine. Signore Giuliano poured him some more.

"I don't mean to insult you." He tried another approach. "You might be able to...to save more. You wouldn't have to pay us anything to stay." He got up and began to pace. "Stefano, I know that I would not have anything growing in my garden if not for you. With fertile soil we can grow not only olives and grapes for wine, but fruits and vegetables as well as beautiful flowers. I've already spoken to the vendors that I worked with in the past and they're just waiting for my land to produce."

Giuliano, usually so smooth, seemed nervous as he paced the kitchen.

"Signore Giuliano," Stefano said, "I'm your gardener now and can make all these things grow. You don't have to worry."

"Stefano, I'm not worried at all about your abilities, but I need this garden to produce for me. More than you know."

"I'll do everything in my power to make that happen."

"But now you'll see my selfish motive. I must be sure. That's why I'd like you to stay here. I want more than just a pretty garden like the Ricci's, Stefano. What I want is a second chance. I want to revive my family's good name and make money, lots of it. I want to give Filomena everything she deserves and more. And if I do make money, I promise to take care of you, too." Giuliano paused for effect. "But you're going to have to work very hard, harder than you have before!"

Giuliano's fervor did not bother him. "So you want me right her under your nose!" Stefano laughed.

"*Preciso!*"

Stefano thought that it might be the best thing for him to work and work and do nothing more. Besides, what could his small cottage hold for him but painful memories?

"I know we can do this. Together we can."

Giuliano paced even more quickly around the kitchen as if he were racing against time itself. The Giuliano property had a long history of success and before its demise, had been known to all of

Incanto ~ The Singing Gardener

Castellina in Chianti, and all of Tuscany for its fresh produce and healthy florals. As a younger man taking over the property, Giuliano had not understood all that was required to keep the land happy. In the past his father and his father before him had much help. They had kept five gardeners on the property. Giuliano tried very hard to keep the land fertile, but soon grew overwhelmed with the responsibility and lack of knowledge. He took the land for granted and had treated his workers casually, poorly. He had been paying for his mistakes ever since and knew that the land had been cursed because of his neglect. Now that the curse had been lifted, he could not chance making the same mistake.

"You can save plenty of money and make plenty of money. And then? Stefano you can get on your feet and let them take you wherever you need to go next."

With Giuliano's offer so sincere, Stefano did not question his intentions. Still, he didn't answer right away. Having been ripped from Maria, his nerves were raw. It would be too much to jump into a new life now.

"May I take some time to think about it?"

"Of course, Stefano, please take all the time you need." Giuliano stopped pacing and took hold of himself. "There will be no work today, but I would like to walk the grounds with you."

Stefano smiled. "I would like that very much."

"This land has belonged to my family for many generations and we have always taken pride in its history." He led Stefano along the outskirts of the farm. "The Giuliano family had supplied fruits, vegetables and flowers to many villages for hundreds of years. We were known for being one of the most reliable farms in Tuscany." He stopped and gazed out over his property. "When it all dried up and could not produce I felt I was letting my family name fall into the mud."

"It was not your fault. Bad luck." Stefano tried to comfort him.

"No, I was a very spoiled young man. I killed the land with neglect. A man can have money in the bank and food on the table,"

Giuliano added, "but if he has no strong purpose in the world, his manhood withers and dies."

As they walked across rolling fields, still covered in Casablancas, Stefano felt the history buried beneath the ancient soil. Giuliano had so many fields, along with groves of failing olive and almond trees, and vineyard land perfectly positioned to drink in the sun. Stefano was grateful that he had a huge task to undertake. A distraction he truly needed. He vowed to throw himself into this project, day and night, and to make Giuliano's land yield beyond anything that the family could imagine. Yes. His work on Giuliano's land would be a roadmap that would lead Maria back to him.

Stefano examined the land carefully to determine how to separate it into sections that could supply all the demands that he and Giuliano would be making of it. Closing his eyes, he envisioned the incredible garden he would create, the fields that would burst with food. Now was no time to be humble, or to hide his gifts, as he had had to do at the Ricci's. Optimism filled him. His black mood began to lift and he reached out to clap Giuliano on the shoulder.

"We shall begin in the morning," he said. "Do you have someone who will buy the Casablancas?"

"I have a few places that might be interested."

"Good. We'll need the field for other things. In one week you won't recognize this land."

It was unlike Stefano to boast. Giuliano beamed. "Thank you, Stefano. Now go home and think about my offer. The guest house is beautiful and…very private." He kissed Stefano on each cheek and left him.

* * *

Stefano went home that night and found Prima sitting at his dining table with an open bottle of wine and two glasses.

"I hope you don't mind me breaking in!" she said, "But I needed some company." He rushed to fold her in a warm embrace.

Incanto ~ The Singing Gardener

Next to Maria, she was the person he most wanted to see in the world. He kissed her on both cheeks. "I didn't get a chance to say goodbye to you. I'm sorry."

"Stefano," she said. "It's I who am sorry, sorry for you."

They sat together at the table. Prima poured the wine and then took his hands in hers. She looked into his sad eyes and he let her look. Though she already knew what she would find there, she began to read his heart. Tears trickled down his face, but he did not look away. Prima could feel all of his sorrow spinning inside of him.

"Drink some wine, Stefano."

"Prima, I have to be at work very early tomorrow. I have a lot to do."

"Yes, I know. Giuliano wants you restore the family fortune. He's smart, and a life of mistakes has taught him well. At least you'll finally be appreciated. You deserve money, lots of it! See to it that he gives it to you."

Stefano shrugged.

Prima scolded lightly. "You must promise me that you will accept every nickel that man offers you. Promise me you will never refuse his money." She knew that he would need all the support he could find in the months and maybe even years to come. These days, money could hold a person up above water.

"I promise, Prima." Stefano sighed.

"Now drink up," she insisted.

"Knowing your cellar, you've probably chosen just what I need. But please. I don't need to sleep too much. Tomorrow's my first day of work. I can't be late."

"Stefano, don't you trust me? I promise you'll be at work even earlier than usual and the vintage won't interfere with your powers in the garden in the least"

"Then what will it do for me, Prima?" He refused to drink it until she answered.

"This wine will do nothing more than take away all the pain in your heart for a while. I can feel what you're feeling there, Stefano, and it pains me."

"Well," he said ruefully. "While I don't want you to be hurting…"

"Yes, for me, please," she interrupted, pushing the glass towards him. "We'll drink it together."

He pushed the glass back to her and corked the bottle.

"Prima, it's more than thoughtful of you to try to soothe this grief in my heart, but I don't want it to go away. I want to feel all the pain to the very depths of my soul. It reminds me that what happened with her was real! Don't you see? If I feel my broken heart than I can feel Maria?"

"You two are surely made for each other." She sighed.

"Oh Prima, do you really believe that?" He searched her eyes.

"Absolutely." She grabbed the wine. "Well, I'm going home. Maybe I'll just drink this whole bottle myself. Unlike you and Maria, I don't like pain." She began to walk out of Stefano's cottage.

"Thank you, Prima. And Prima?" The older woman turned to face him. "Please tell Maria I love her."

Prima turned back and smiled widely.

"As if that is really necessary! But I will." She looked around the dark cottage. "And Stefano? It's a good time to move. Too many memories are here, no? You need to be around people, good people. The Giulianos are good people."

With that she closed the door.

He went to his bed and curled up in the spot where Maria slept just the night before. He rested his head upon the pillow she'd slept on, and the scent of her hair made his body go weak. Inhaling her pillow, he fantasized about making love to her. How could everything change so quickly? He wanted to run to her and tell Martino and tell Signore Finelli, all of Castellina, and the entire world that he was in love. It wasn't fair to have to hide it away in secret.

Perhaps Prima had a point. Everything seemed to be changing

in Stefano's life, why not where he lived? He was a grown man and didn't have any roots or a home worth keeping. There was nothing of value or anything worth selling. He allowed himself to picture what the future held if he could really make enough money to buy a home to be proud of. A place where he and Maria could live together! He could buy her a grand piano. Their children--yes their children--would have a place to grow and play.

He sat up in the bed and opened all the windows, the fresh evening air invigorating his mind. Tomorrow held the chance for a new life. Maria needed him to be strong and prove that he could take care of her, didn't she? He couldn't collapse now. This new work at the Giuliano's would be a gift to them, but also a gift of freedom for himself and, he prayed, for Maria, too.

His heart raced and his head pounded. At two o'clock in the morning, unable to sleep, he decided to get dressed and head to the Giuliano property.

As he passed the cypress tree where he had first laid his head the night he made the land fertile with his tears, he thought it strange that he would find himself here once again, on the very soil that had absorbed his longing for Maria. He remembered that night and the promise he'd made to God. How he would use his gift no matter what. But he hoped God would see fit to lead Maria to him. Once again he fell to his knees on Giuliano's land and made a new pact. He began picking all of the Casablancas except for a small patch. He piled them high in stacks to the side of the garden. He then blessed the earth with all the love he felt in his heart for Maria. He committed to nurturing its soil, as carefully as a lover. He reached down and began to create a vegetable garden. Slowly lowering his hands over the land, he named a spot for each vegetable. He began to sing the song that played in Prima's kitchen the morning they all danced together, *Parlami D'Amore Mariu'*. Tears poured from his eyes as he imagined Maria in his arms. In between his lyrics he orchestrated the new garden.

"Tomatoes." Slowly, a row of vines blossomed with the

brightest red tomatoes in Italy. "Zucchini, spinach, green beans, lettuce, eggplant, peppers, broccoli..." He walked back and forth while vegetables sprouted up beneath his hands. His eyes remained closed, as he relived his time with Maria in the Ricci garden. He could taste her, smell her, feel her. He let himself be inside of her. Feeling his love, the land responded like Eden.

When he opened his eyes he smiled at the creation their love had sown. He then went to the edges of the land and asked, too, that the Giuliano's trees should bare fruit. For this, he had to dig deep into the earth, and let his entire energy spill into the soil. He started with a lemon tree, than an orange, a grapefruit, a fig, an apple, a pear and, last, a cherry. Truly exhausted, Stefano was also obsessed.

He pulled a bunch of cherries and started to eat them. Sweetness spread through his mouth. He picked an apple, a pear, an orange, a grapefruit, a fig and a lemon. He tasted them all to make sure they were as good as he hoped them to be. Indeed, everything tasted divine.

As the sun rose over the dry hills of Castellina, Stefano felt a sense of great relief and a quiet sort of renewal. This was a new beginning. Anyone who tasted these fruits and vegetables would taste all the love that had created them. Everyone would want produce from the Giuliano gardens. Stefano knew he still had work to do. He had to design the area where all the newborn flowers would live, but for now his body felt depleted. He sprawled out under an orange tree and let himself sink into the earth. Taking advantage of exhaustion, he shut his eyes and slept.

Signor Giuliano woke up early. He, too, was excited to greet the new day and begin on the project of a lifetime. When he walked out into and saw all the work that Stefano had already done, he froze. Speechless for a long moment, he finally blurted out to his wife.

"Filomena, come quick!" She came down from their bedroom still in her silk robe and stepped out onto the terrazza. Looking out, she began to weep.

"Oh my God, he is a magician!"

"Please, darling," Giuliano implored her, "go make Stefano a big breakfast, one fit for a king." He looked up to the heavens. Some might fear Stefano's power as dark, but Giuliano knew that such a gift could only come from God, and he felt God smiling on him, too.

He walked the grounds, dizzy-with-delight, stunned by all the new life Stefano had infused into the soil just over night. If the man could do all this in a night, what more could be done here over time?

He stopped at each new plant, delighting in the bounty that had exploded all around him. Life vibrated beneath his feet. The soil felt awake and eager to please. Hard to believe, Giuliano thought, that just a short time ago he had walked on the same land and felt his own death approaching. The soil had held all his life's deprivation, but now all of that had changed. A rush of adrenalin filled his body and he searched to find Stefano. The gardener must be close by.

"Stefano!" Giuliano called, but no answer came. Then the fruit trees on the edge of the property caught his eye. Fruit trees where hours before there had been nothing? Not only that, they were heavy with the rich colors of plum, pink apples, bright lemon yellow and orange and red pear that shone through the green leafy branches. Giuliano felt he was in a dream. The trees looked like oils on a canvas, painted by a great master. He reached up, picked an apple and bit into it. The crunch loud, the juice sprayed in all directions. Giuliano laughed, ecstatic, as the taste filled up his mouth. Then he picked a fig and savored it on his tongue. Like a fool, he began to dance.

As he swirled under the tree he noticed Stefano sleeping nearby. At first he was startled. Had the poor man collapsed from all of his hard labor? Giuliano rushed to him, but found his breath even, his face peaceful.

Aware of another presence, Stefano woke up to find Giuliano

standing above him.

"*Buongiorno*," Stefano said with a smile, the sun gleaming in his hazel eyes. Slowly he began to lift himself up.

"No, no, Stefano! Rest, please," Giuliano protested. "Filomena's making breakfast for you. I'll bring it out." It seemed the gardener felt at home under the trees. "Unless you would be more comfortable inside?"

Relieved that Giuliano understood the way he worked and did not accuse him of being drunk or sleeping in the garden, Stefano said he would join the Giulianos inside.

" I—I hope you don't mind." Stefano smiled. "I had a hard time sleeping last night and thought I might as well begin." Stefano rose to his feet.

"I'm mesmerized by all that you have done." Giuliano gave an almost imperceptible bow. "I can't begin to tell you how happy I'm that you are here. Have you thought about my offer?"

"Yes," Stefano answered. "I think I would like very much to live here and help as much as I can with the land."

Giuliano clapped his hands in joy and embraced Stefano warmly. He grabbed Stefano's hand and ran to the house. They arrived at the front door and Giuliano began to shout.

"Filomena, Filomena! He said yes!" He pulled Stefano into the house. Filomena beamed and clapped her hands.

"*Bravo!*" she exclaimed. "Oh, we're so happy, Stefano." She kissed him on both cheeks and sat him down in the chair, putting a huge plate of food in front of him. Stefano looked up at her.

"Thank you. You are too kind."

"Don't be silly. It is nothing." She put a plate down for Giuliano and then one for herself and they all dug into their first breakfast together.

Afterwards they took him to the guesthouse and showed him where he would be living. Modest but sound, freshly painted in Tuscan yellow and olive greens, it struck Stefano as charming. The clean kitchen had a stove and an icebox and large terra cotta tiles on the floor, its counter tiled in midnight blue with champagne flowers in the center. Each glazed flower was accented with orange trim and the room opened into a comfortable dining area. A large bed covered in fresh white linens and big fluffy pillows sat in another room, and had a private bathroom. The guesthouse was three times the size of Stefano's cottage and windows adorned each wall. The natural sunlight gave it a cheerful feel. "Perfetto," he whispered. The Giulianos looked at each other, relieved.

"E molto privato," Giuliano said. "We won't ever disturb you here."

Filomena had just cleaned the guesthouse and prepared it. A large vase overflowed with beautiful Casablancas from the garden. Filomena opened the icebox and showed him that it had been stocked with fresh cheeses, milk, butter, eggs, juice and fresh preserves. Stefano was speechless.

"I...I don't know what to say. It is all so beautiful."

"Stefano, we want you to feel at home. We understand how hard you work. We would like to add a little joy to your life is all." Giuliano grabbed his shoulder and smiled into his eyes. "Now, we'll leave you to get settled."

"Thank you." He smiled and watched them leave then walked around his new home feeling hopeful. But he did not want to linger there. He wanted more than ever to create the most abundant garden in all of Tuscany. There was much to do. The more quickly he succeeded, the more quickly he and Maria could be reunited.

* * *

Stefano collected all of his belongings into two boxes and brought them to his new home. He pulled out the pillowcase that Maria slept on and placed it over his new pillow. He held it to his face and inhaled her for a short time, but then quickly put it down. Her scent made him weak with the memories of her flesh touching his. He could not think about her right now. At least not in that way. He could only think of the goal he must reach.

* * *

The Giulianos invited Stefano to share dinner with them. Afterwards, Stefano explained to Giuliano the particular ways he wanted to design the layout of the garden and why he felt it would be advantageous.

"Please, my friend, you just take charge. I have complete faith in you."

"All right!" Stefano smiled. "Just tell me what you can sell and we will have it in the garden."

"Filomena, he is a man of the soil. Magica! He can grow anything! Vero Stefano?"

"Yes, I suppose that is true." Stefano had never spoken so proudly, and he felt compelled to add, "But it isn't really me."

"*Certo*," Filomena joined in, "All gifts come from God."

"But you know how to use your gifts," Giuliano protested.

"God talks and you listen, no?" Stefano bowed his head.

"Stefano," Giuliano pressed. "When can you have the garden ready?"

Stefano replied quickly. "When can you have the buyers ready?"

Giuliano hoped he wasn't pushing too hard, but he knew that once the word got out that he had gone back into business there would be a great demand. The Giuliano name still held some sway. "Can you be ready in a few months?"

Stefano took a deep breath. "Yes, I will have it ready. Make a list of all the biggest demands and you will have plenty of all of it."

"This calls for a celebration," Giuliano exclaimed. He ran down to his wine cellar and pulled out the finest bottle of champagne he could find. Upstairs again, he popped it open. Filomena moved to take down three flutes, but Giuliano began drinking straight from the bottle. "Ah, who needs glasses?" He passed the bottle to Stefano who took a celebratory sip then passed it to Filomena and she did the same. They danced around the kitchen and passed around the champagne until they had emptied the bottle.

"Life is good!" Giuliano shouted.

Incanto ~ The Singing Gardener

Life *was* good, but for Stefano, not yet complete.

Trish Doolan

SEDICI

    The judges, three men and three women, for the bridge club's vegetable garden contest surveyed each woman's garden with expert examination. The way the contest worked was that all five women would go from home to home, with the judges, and after the last garden was inspected they would talk amongst themselves and return with their verdict. The newspaper reporter followed them with a photographer documenting each garden in case it was crowned the winner, but only the winner would get their picture in the paper with a personal story about the victor.
    Antonietta's garden was magnificent. Each vegetable stood proudly and demanded to be noticed. The colors all strategically placed to look like an Italian flag. She thought that would surely win the heart of the judges. The other women thought it was a cheap shot and quite tasteless, but in the end it didn't matter what they thought. It was out of their hands. Signora Finelli was sweating bullets as they made the rounds. Her garden was to be judged last being that it was the furthest down the road. The anticipation was nerve wracking and kept her pacing back and forth at each garden. When the judges eyed her nervous behavior, she would stop and smile politely, hoping she wouldn't lose respect for being a bundle of nerves. Her only competition was Antonietta. However, Gemma did have gorgeous squash, which impressed the judges, but not much else of anything noteworthy.
    Finally arriving at Signora Finelli's garden, the crowd gathered around. Tessa and Carlo came by to support their neighbor. Antonietta's jaw dropped when she saw Elena's garden. The vegetables all looked fake, too good to be true. The tomatoes so red and deep you could taste them through the air. The judge's mouths were watering just looking at them. They began writing in their pads with excitement. The broccoli sprouted up like huge

Incanto ~ The Singing Gardener

trees that one might climb and the eggplant looked like giant chocolate raindrops, slick and supple. Her basil blew in the wind like green veils and the rosemary and parsley brought solace to everyone as they inhaled the rich air. "Impossibile!" Antonietta exclaimed. All six judges shot her a nasty look. Quickly she covered her mouth. "*Scusi*, it's just, never mind." She didn't understand how Elena's garden could have transformed so drastically from last year. Everywhere the judges turned there was another wonderful creation to scrutinize. Bright orange carrots strategically placed along happy yellow squash seemed to look like a sunset in the middle of the earth. Cucumbers, artichokes, spinach, kale and yellow, red and orange peppers created a bouquet of splendor. The Finelli's beamed with pride as their neighbors smiled. Capturing every angle, the photographer flashed wildly careful not to miss one inch of this extravagant garden.

As the judges huddled by the six-foot high tomato vines, the women waited for their decision. Gloom grew like weeds over Antonietta's face. The judges returned with a unanimous vote. "The winner of the 1958 Bridge Club's vegetable garden award goes to Elena Finelli. Everyone applauded except for Antonietta Peragine, who stomped away in her high heel shoes. The photographer snapped pictures of Elena as she lifted both hands to the sky, the champion. A smile so wide he had to back up to capture it in the photo. The Finelli's hugged and Tessa and Carlo congratulated them and then asked if they could have some vegetables to take home. Gemma, Jacopa and Lena lifted Elena up and carried her around the garden.

"Finally, someone shut her up." Jacopa screamed with joy.

The next day Signora Finelli's face and garden adorned the *La repubblica* newspaper. Her wish was granted, thanks to Stefano. She made her way to Guilanno's to show him.

"Oh Signora Finelli, nothing could make me happier. You see, I told you you would win."

Leaning in, she whispered "I would have never won if not for you." He shrugged. "And I know you came by last night because my garden did not look that magnificent when I went to bed."

"Ah, I thought you could use a little extra love." She held up the paper to show him the quote below her picture. It read, 'Elena Finelli says her garden is a winner because she learned how to love it and love helps all things grow more powerfully.' "*Bene, bene,* this is good. I am proud of you." He kissed her on both cheeks. "May I keep this newspaper?"

"Of course. I brought it for you. I have twenty more at home." They laughed.

* * *

Stefano spent every day and night in the garden.

Filomena brought his meals out to him and he only went inside to the guesthouse, his new home, to bathe. Driven by pure love, he felt no need to sleep. Giuliano, too, spent day and night making arrangements with his buyers. He went to over twenty markets, studied their produce and researched prices. Leaving no stone unturned, he asked each store and each market to get their trucks to his garden. He would give them a discount for picking up the food themselves.

The months flew by, everything going as planned. Giuliano came home one Thursday afternoon with a photographer and a reporter from the newspaper in Siena. They took pictures of the garden and of Stefano. Giuliano explained how they met and how he believed that Stefano had certain powers. He told the reporter about how Stefano sang to the flowers, the trees, and all of the plants. The man was skeptical, but could not deny the bounty of the garden, nor the sweetness of its fruits and vegetables. And whether true or not that the gardener possessed some kind of power, it did make for a good story. Giuliano promised future customers that they would find the finest produce and flowers in his garden or be given their money back. "It's human nature to challenge guarantees," he explained to Stefano, "and there's nothing better than controversy to keep business booming."

Incanto ~ The Singing Gardener

* * *

That evening Stefano walked up the road passed Signore and Signora Finellis, the same road he had taken every day when he worked the Ricci garden. He was carrying a large basket of fruit from Giuliano's land. Signore Finelli called out to him and waved him over, but Stefano could not bear to stop and talk. He could not bear to be so close to Maria's driveway. Could he trust his legs not to walk to her door? His hands not to gather her into his arms? He gave Finelli a brief wave and a nod and walked on to Prima's.

His friend answered the door as if she'd been waiting for him "Stefano!" she exclaimed, "Come in!"

"I'm sorry, Prima, I can't stay," he told her. "I only came to ask a favor."

"A favor? You know I'd do anything for you, my dear." She regarded his basket of plums, pears, apples and lemons. "Those are beautiful!"

"Please, Prima," he began, staring at his feet. "Will you give this basket to Maria?"

"Of course, of course," she assured him.

"And please take some for yourself."

With that, he told her of the progress he'd been making at Giuliano's. "I can't stay," he added. "Tomorrow's a big day."

"*Certo.* I understand. *Ciao* Stefano." She watched him walk away, his shoulders hunched, his gait weary. "I trust tomorrow will bring you hope," she called to him.

* * *

Friday morning's paper ran the story on Giuliano and the infertile garden that had been brought back to life by the "magical powers of one Singing Gardener, Stefano Portigiani." A photograph of Stefano working the garden, squinting into the sun, ran next to a picture of Giuliano and his wife in front of their home.

Prima ran over to Maria's with a pot of her jolting *espresso*,

Stefano's basket of fruit and a copy of the newspaper in her arms. Maria was delighted to see her neighbor's face. Grabbing two cups, she ushered her to the sofa, where they sat down together. Prima pulled out the paper. "Did you see this?" She opened to the page and when Maria saw Stefano's picture, her heart stopped.

Maria began reading the story and didn't know whether to laugh or cry.

"I'm so happy that he's doing well," she said faintly.

Prima pushed the basket of fruit toward her. "He sent this for you. All made with his very own hands, for you." Prima popped a luscious plump red strawberry in her mouth. It exploded with sweetness on her tongue. "Delicious!" she exclaimed.

"Of course it is. It came from Stefano what do you expect?" Maria's voice was sharp. But she popped a strawberry into her mouth and felt overcome with sweetness.

"It's all for you, you know." Prima wanted the foolish young woman to realize.

"What is?" Maria asked, confused.

"Giuliano's garden. He's doing it all for you." Prima poured the espresso. Maybe it would knock some sense into Maria, who seemed to be asleep on her feet.

Maria delicately caressed the fruit, fantasizing about Stefano's long, lean body moving next to hers. She looked out her arched window almost expecting to see him smiling back at her, but all she saw was the balding old man Martino had hired to water, and destroy, it seemed, all her precious flowers. Prima, too, scowled at the sight of him.

"How's the new gardener working out?"

"He's awful," Maria cried. "Nothing looks as pretty as it did when Stefano was here."

"No one cares the way he did," Prima assured her.

"Did?" Maria asked peevishly.

"Does, does!" Prima sipped her espresso and shot Maria an evaluating look. "He's going to make a lot of money soon, you know."

Incanto ~ The Singing Gardener

"That is wonderful news, Prima." Maria said listlessly. And then, a flash of desire animated her face. "Prima, please will you go to him and tell him that I think about him all the time and that I miss him?" she cried. "No, maybe I should not tell him anything. He must know how I feel. I don't want to make things worse."

Prima put her freckled hand over her friend's smooth one. "Maria, what can be worse than the two of you being apart?"

"Nothing!" Maria answered quickly, looking down at his picture. She began to cry.

* * *

That night, Martino pulled into the driveway as usual. He stepped out of his automobile with a newspaper in hand and stopped to examine the garden, clearly a mess. He felt a strange sensation in his feet and looked down to see his shoes being swallowed in the over-watered soil. Annoyed, he wiped his muddy shoes on the step before entering the house.

Angelina, at least, continued to do a good job. The house sparkled and dinner sat ready on the table. She had said nothing to him of her absence, as Maria had asked her not to trouble him with silly details. A course of pasta followed by veal cutlets was set before him. Maria tried to be pleasant as they sat down for dinner. Her heart was not here with Martino, but she must carry on as if it were.

"How was your day?" she asked him

He threw the paper down on the table, the page opened to Stefano's and Giuliano's pictures. "Ah, look at that crazy gardener in the news today. Could you believe it? Maybe I should go get him back. Our garden is going to hell. You must tell that stupid man not to water it so much. He's killing it."

Maria tried not to say too much. But she couldn't stop herself from telling him, "I suppose gardening is much harder than you thought."

Martino shot her an angry look.

"What are you trying to say? Are you saying I made a

mistake?" he yelled.

The maid was removing plates from the table quickly.

"Angelina," Maria kept herself as cold as ice, "that's enough for tonight. I can clean up. Go home."

Angelina quickly grabbed her belongings and backed out the door. Martino glared at her and then turned to Maria.

"Don't look at me like that," he said. "I know what you're thinking."

"I'm not thinking anything, husband. Nothing at all." In fact, she felt nothing but boredom.

"You think if I had kept him we could be in the paper."

"I don't care about being in the paper."

"What do you care about my beautiful wife? Do you care about me? Or is it just your stupid flowers that brought you happiness." He got up and began to circle around her as she gazed out the window. "Was it the garden that brought you joy, or was it the gardener?"

"I'm going to bed. I don't feel well." She rose from the table.

"You never feel well." He stood in front of her, but she wouldn't look into his eyes.

"So it's my fault that you are not happy? Look at me when I'm speaking to you." He commanded. "Because I gave your gardener away? You miss him, don't you?"

Maria could not look at him for too long. "You were never nice to Stefano. You hardly paid him and your never showed him any appreciation and now that he's gone my garden is a mess and yes I am depressed about that." Maria was now screaming.

"Since when do you call that peasant gardener Stefano?"

"It's his name. What do you want me to call him?"

Martino rose and, turning beet red, put his hands around her throat. "I don't want you to call him anything. I don't care about him, but I can see you do. You wish he was here, don't you?"

Maria did wish for that, but she wasn't about to say so. Martino could choke the life out of her, and she would surrender. When she didn't fight his grip, he released it.

Incanto ~ The Singing Gardener

"I'll find another gardener," Martino muttered.

"It will never be the same," Maria said softly, and turned to walk away, leaving the dishes on the table.

"What, do you think 'The Singing Gardener' has magical powers too?" he mumbled under his breath and picked up the newspaper with Stefano's face on it. He slammed the paper down. "Well, you and everyone else have gone crazy." He angrily poured another glass of wine, drank it down and then smashed the glass over the newspaper. Glass splintered into a thousand pieces over the picture of Stefano and his new garden.

* * *

The Giulianos had invited Prima for dinner and insisted that Stefano come and eat with them. He felt happy to see her again and, after the meal, he took her to the guesthouse and showed her his new home.

"It's so nice for you," she said. "I'm glad. And you looked so handsome in the newspaper."

"Prima, I am making very good money now and I am saving so that I will be able to take care of her" He showed her a box full of money. "Then she'll feel comfortable leaving Martino," he finished, a quiver in his voice.

Prima gave him a hug. "I am so proud of you."

"Prima, tell me how she is."

Prima smiled at him. "She's struggling Stefano. She wanted you to know she thinks of you always, and misses everything about you."

Stefano's heart filled. "She said that Prima?"

"Oh yes, and she said your strawberries were the best she had ever tasted."

" Prima, everything will change after we open Monday morning. Once everyone tastes our produce we will be selling to all of Tuscany. Do you think we'll do well?"

"I know you will Stefano."

"Thank you. Now I know I can't fail."

Trish Doolan

***

That weekend Giuliano brought in workers to help pack the boxes. He wanted to make sure that he didn't run out of anything. Giuliano had promised twenty markets one box of each fruit and each vegetable. Just to be safe, the workers packed hundreds of boxes. He promised the men that if everything went well, he would hire them for good.

Sunday night had arrived and they were ready. The boxes stood packed and lined before the stone wall that bordered Giuliano's land, poised to be loaded on to trucks that would take them away. Giuliano, Stefano, and Filomena filled with excitement and anxiety. What if no one showed up? The Giulianos worried. Stefano assured them that people would come because Prima told him so. "And she's never wrong," he added. "She can see into the future."

That night, Stefano slept in the garden under a bright blanket of stars. He made wishes on every star he could see. He saw Maria's face in every constellation. He sent her all his love and hoped she felt it. He asked God to let this land bring happiness to all who ate from its garden. He blessed every fruit, vegetable and flower in the garden that night. He asked for the happy customers to receive magical blessings, good fortune, and most of all love.

***

It didn't feel like he had been sleeping too long before he heard trucks pulling up one by one to Giuliano's land. He thought that maybe he was dreaming because the sun had not yet come up. Popping up from under the cherry tree, he found at least a dozen produce trucks lined up one by one. He ran to the main house to get Giuliano and Filomena, but when he got there they had already heard the trucks and had come out to greet them.

Giuliano smiled and hugged Stefano. "Prima was right, Stefano! They have come." The two men went out to talk to the drivers and help them load their trucks. It was only four o'clock in the morning, and Giuliano could not believe the line of trucks.

Incanto ~ The Singing Gardener

They had arrived before the roosters' calls.
An automobile whizzed up to the front of the line and the reporter and photographer who had done the story announced that they were here to do a follow up. "You are very welcome, gentlemen," Giuliano beamed.
He noticed more trucks pulling up with their headlights on. Stefano tried to count, but the line went too far back. The photographer began taking pictures. One by one, the two men loaded the trucks and collected the money. The sun came up and they were not nearly done, but they were full of energy, as they packed up each truck, smiled and waved goodbye to the customers.
"We'll see you very soon! *Ciao*," Stefano shouted.
Hours passed, but the trucks did not stop coming. Giuliano was expecting ten at the most, but he hadn't really been counting on all of them showing up. This went beyond his expectation. The newspaper must have attracted all the others.
Over twenty trucks showed up and Giuliano didn't have enough boxes packed to serve them. But Stefano assured him that they could supply the produce needed. The reporter documented every detail of the day and the photographer continued to snap pictures. Between furiously packing new boxes, Stefano made sure that the reporter got to taste all the luscious fruits and fresh vegetables, explaining that their produce was different.
"How is it different?" the reporter asked him.
"Can't you taste the love in every bite?" Stefano grinned.
Giuliano and Filomena ran through the house and brought out every last empty box and bag they could find. They moved with the speed of a much younger couple, and never did they exchange a sharp word.
"It's like a big party!" Filomena managed, catching her breath.
"One with many more guests than you planned for," the reporter said.
"Yes," Giuliano admitted, "but we want to make sure every guest feels like they *were* invited, and let them know that next time

they would surely be on our list!"

The long day came to its end and Stefano and the Giulianos stumbled into the kitchen, exhausted. Filomena prepared a light dinner and opened up a fine bottle of Barolo. They barely had the strength to eat, but knew it was absolutely necessary. Stefano sipped his wine and ate Filomena's delicious primavera.

"Filomena, your cooking is stupendous," he said.

"My cooking. Your peas, zucchini, carrots and tomatoes..." she answered.

"Hey! Maybe we should start a restaurant, too" Giuliano joked. The other two looked at him as if he were crazy.

"This man wants to make more work!" Filomena said. "Do you see what I have to put up with, Stefano?"

"Say what you like, but I think all of Tuscany was here today," Giuliano boasted.

"True," Filomena mused. "I saw people I haven't seen in years and other faces I've never seen before."

"Was it nice for you, Stefano, to see all the people coming to share a piece of your garden?" Giuliano asked him.

"Not everyone from Castellina came." He put his fork down, brooding a bit.

"Stefano?" Giuliano had never seen the gardener so gloomy. "You need to rest. You look very tired and I don't want you to get sick. Take the day off tomorrow. You earned it."

Stefano knew he could not afford to have idle time on his hands. He did not want to give his heart time to feel any pain.

"No. I'd rather not if you don't mind. I need to work. Besides, we have to get ready for the rush of buyers that will surely be back." Stefano got up from the table. "*Scusi*, I will rest now." He left his food and wine unfinished on the table and headed for the door.

Filomena shot her husband a troubled look. He shrugged.

"Stefano," he called out, rising to his feet and walking over to his friend. "You have saved me." He hugged him like a son.

"And you have saved me. Now buona notte." Stefano left the

Incanto ~ The Singing Gardener

main house and retired to the guesthouse.
* * *

When he had gone, Giuliano went to Filomena and hugged her tightly. "*Ti amo.*"

She looked at him sweetly. "Oh, my darling, I love you, too. And I'm so very proud of you." They kissed. But she broke away. "Stefano has a heavy heart," she worried.

"Yes, he doesn't talk about it and I don't want to push him, but I know he suffers from love."

"Get him to talk to you, Roberto. I know you can help him. You're so good with him," Filomena encouraged.

"In time, my dear. I want to give him time to come around to me."
* * *

The next morning brought a procession of automobiles and trucks beyond imagination. *La repubblica* had put the story of Giuliano's success on the front page. The headlines read, "One Taste of The Singing Gardener's Produce and You, Too, Will Be Singing." A picture of Giuliano and Stefano loading the trucks with big smiles accompanied the story, which went on to talk about the wonders of their produce, the reporter admitting that he had never tasted fruit with so much flavor. "And the produce is a magical drug that erases everything bad from your life, leaving only the happiness that your mouth is experiencing in that moment." The story mentioned, too, the camaraderie between the Giulianos and their gardener. The last line read, "Isn't it comforting to know that everything is grown with such love and care?"

Giuliano stepped outside and, seeing the trucks, froze with shock. Filomena came out after him and could not believe her eyes. She looked around, but did not spot Stefano. Giuliano looked at her in panic. "Please! Go find him."

Filomena ran to the guesthouse and found Stefano sleeping in his bed. Finally, he had surrendered. She knew he needed to rest, but there were so many people waiting to buy from the garden. Gently, she shook his shoulder.

"Stefano, wake up!" Slowly, he opened his eyes to find Filomena above him.

"*Buongiorno*," she said. "How do you feel?"

"Fantastic," he answered, with a curious look on his face. "I had a funny dream. Everyone showed up in the garden for fruit, but there was none left because I fell asleep." He let out a sleepy laugh.

"I'm not so sure it was a dream," she exclaimed. "Come and look." She pulled him to the window and he looked out, rubbing sleep from his eyes to make sure he wasn't seeing things. He looked at Filomena and didn't know whether to jump for joy or crumble from nerves. How would they satisfy all of these people? Stefano began to dress. "Tell your husband I'll be right out."

Filomena ran to Giuliano. Stefano quickly washed up and took a deep breath.

* * *

In the garden, Giuliano and Stefano stood together surveying what remained. They certainly had enough to supply a small portion, perhaps a quarter of the people that were waiting. But all of these trucks and cars? *Porcamiseria*!

"Stefano, what should we do? We just don't have enough."

Stefano looked at the long line of automobiles and trucks. People waved the newspaper out of their windows, and some had even begun to call out questions about when they would open.

"Hey, Singing Gardener, I'm here to taste your magic!" One woman shouted, and Stefano blushed. He looked at Giuliano, a little nervous.

"*Andiamo*," he said.

"Stefano, look at all these people! It is pointless. We're not prepared. Not even you can pull this off. I must send them away."

"Trust me, we can do this." Stefano turned away from Giuliano and dropped to his knees in the garden. He spread his arms out to the heavens and then dug his hands deeply into the soil. He pictured Maria's face and let the tears that were never far from the surface, fall. He then placed his hand over his heart and stood up, singing. Walking down each row of vegetables, he extended his hands over them. Immediately, the plants flourished before his eyes. Tomatoes ripened on their vines. Eggplants glowed deep purple in the sun. And snap peas seemed to *ping* with new life. The vegetables grew so fast that they fell onto the soil ready to pack.

Giuliano stood in amazement, tears spilling from his eyes. Stefano kept his eyes closed and walked through the entire garden. He carried Maria in his heart every step of the way. He hugged the beautiful trunk of each tree and kissed the bark with all the love he held inside. Plum. Apple. Orange. Peach. Lemon. The trees began dropping fruit from their branches like rain. There were puddles of fruit under every tree and plenty to supply the long line of automobiles.

Giuliano's felt chills from head to toe and he could barely speak or move. Stefano knew he had to snap him out of it so they could service all of the people. He shook him. "Giuliano, I told you to trust me. Now let's give these people what they came for."

Unaware of the miracle that had just occurred, every customer wanted to talk about the newspaper and get Stefano's autograph. But he humbly refused.

Stefano was busy helping an older woman with a bag of lemons and oranges when he looked up for a moment to find Maria and Martino standing before him. Suddenly, he could scarcely breathe. Martino held the newspaper up with the front page exposed. He began laughing. "Look at you, gardener. You're quite the sideshow now, aren't you? Maybe I'll take you back and give you a raise."

Martino continued to talk, but Stefano could not hear a word the man said. The whole world went away for a moment, leaving only Maria in his view. She was wearing the teal dress that set off her green eyes. She smiled at him and lowered her head.

Approaching the Riccis, Giuliano noticed what he suspected all along to be true. He jumped in to save his friend from embarrassment. "Hello, Signora Ricci. Martino, so nice to see you."

Martino held the paper up. "You must be doing well, Giuliano."

"We're just getting started, but it looks very promising."

"I guess I misjudged my gardener."

"Si, but he's my gardener now." Giuliano said jovially.

"Well this changes everything," Martino shot back. "You didn't tell me all that you intended to do with my gardener. If I had known, I would not have let you have him. My garden is in need of his services and I want to be compensated."

"You must be joking?" I paid your new gardener for six months up front."

"Yes, you paid him to ruin my garden and you have made my wife miserable."

Stefano said nothing. He just stood and stared at Maria.

When she looked up her heart raced wildly. She was afraid she would rush into his arms. She wanted to kiss his warm, soft lips, to feel his body close to hers.

He felt all of her desires and longed for her the same way. Standing amidst a crowd of customers, Stefano didn't care who could see his love for Maria. It had been months and he didn't know when he would see her again and he wanted to capture every moment her face remained before him. He would need to store up these moments for later, when he found himself alone again.

In the face of Martino's coarseness, even Giuliano grew impatient. He pulled out some cash and shoved it in the man's thick hand to appease him. "Here's another two months. And that's it. You didn't appreciate him. Now be a man about it." Martino smiled and slid the money in his pocket.

Stefano cupped his hands and dug them into a basket full of red and purple berries. When he pulled his hands out, they overflowed with color. He blew on them and handed them to Maria. "For you, Signora Ricci," he said.

Incanto ~ The Singing Gardener

Terrified, Maria looked to Martino. Martino grabbed Maria's hand. "Come on we don't need these berries."
Maria pulled her hand away with a start. "But I do. I'm so hungry." She looked at Stefano with haunted eyes.
Martino could not think a thought that would steal his manhood from him so completely. He dug his heels in the ground and, spinning, headed for his automobile. "Hurry up, woman."
Giuliano averted his gaze and pretended not to notice how tortured they both were.
Maria cupped her hands in front of Stefano. He placed his hands above hers and slowly let the berries fall delicately in her hands. The mere touch of his hands aroused her. Martino had walked far enough away so that he could not possibly hear them and Giuliano, too, had left them. Maria held Stefano's fingers.
"I miss you, my love. I don't know what to do," she whispered. "What should I do, Stefano?"
"You must come to me with a free spirit and of your own free will. It's not my decision to make. I'll be right here waiting for you."
"I'm kissing you right now." He felt the intensity in her eyes.
"Lean in so I can smell your hair. I want to run my hands up and down your body, and never let you go." Maria leaned her head into him so that her hair rested just beneath his nose. Breathing in the silky ropes brought him some tranquility and he whispered the words she had heard before, "Ah, Maria, I could live in your hair."
"I have to go for now." She gently moved away.
"Please don't leave me waiting too long, Maria," he said, but she was already walking away. She held the berries as if they were treasure, and she was bringing a piece of him home with her.

DICIASETTE

Martino sped around the winding roads of Castellina, as Maria held on for dear life. "Please slow down Martino. You're scaring me." He accelerated even more.
"I am not an idiot." He burned holes through her with his eyes, neglecting the road in front of him.
Maria screamed, as they headed toward an oncoming car. Martino swerved, barely missing it. Laughing maniacally. "Maybe I will just kill us both? Then I won't have to look at your miserable face anymore." Tears came streaming out, but he wiped them quickly. "Why don't you love me? I have given you everything."
Maria feared for her life and tried to calm him down. "I do love you Martino. Please, let's go home." She lovingly put her hand on his arm.
"No, not yet! We are going to visit your father."
"Why? I don't want to."
"You never want to. He is your father and he misses you." He began to slow down.
"I don't like coming back here and you know it!" She was filled with anxiety.
He pulled up in front of the dilapidated farmhouse. "Let's go! Maybe you need reminding of where you came from." He took Maria out of the car and led her into the house.
Leo was pleased to see them, but could see how uncomfortable Maria was. "Hello Papa." She kissed him on both cheeks.
"My Maria, *come' stai*?" Tears filled his eyes.
Her body shuddered with memories, as she held herself tightly and unconsciously rocked like a little girl. "Fine, just fine. We cannot stay Papa. I just wanted to say hello."
Martino eyed her. "Why don't you show me the room you use to sleep in?"

Incanto ~ The Singing Gardener

Horror flooded her entire being. "No!"

"Why not?" He insisted, as he walked toward the two closed doors. Leo watched realizing there was more going on then just a friendly visit. He rolled his wheelchair in front of Martino.

"Martino, this is my house. It may not be much, but it's mine. My daughter is obviously troubled right now and I suggest you respect her wishes and leave before I get up out of this chair and remove you myself."

"I'm sorry Leo. We will go. It's just that your daughter is very ungrateful and I don't know how to make her happy."

"Well here's a bit of advice. Never push somebody's past in their face to force them to behave like your puppet. They will only resent you." Joy filled Maria's heart, as she watched her father defend her for the first time ever. Rushing to his wheelchair, she kissed him sweetly.

"I love you Papa, thank you."

"I love you to my sweet angel, more than you'll ever know." He glared at Martino and then shook his fist. "If you hurt her I'll kill you."

Frightened by his intensity Martino nodded with respect. "I will never hurt her Leo. I love her. It is she who hurts me, every day." With that he left and slammed the door.

☆ ☆ ☆

Stefano poured everything he had into the work, and Giuliano's garden thrived, bringing a stream of business. Giuliano hired the crew of workers to do most of the hard labor, picking and boxing. In this way, Stefano could tend only the land. One day, about a month after opening, Giuliano brought Stefano to the bank. "You must set aside money for your own needs," Giuliano urged. Thinking of Maria, Stefano opened his first account. It was a time of firsts, and Giuliano also took him shopping in Siena for new clothes.

"You never give me a day off!" Stefano joked. "When will I have time to wear these things?" But he had to admit that he liked the figure he cut in the tailored shirt, pants, and jacket Giuliano suggested for him. *I will be a man worthy of her love*, Stefano thought. *I will give her the things she deserves.*

It had been months since Maria and Stefano had been together and, when he could admit it to himself, Stefano knew he was beginning to feel hopeless. His pain was growing even more acute than it had been on the day Martino returned home from his trip to Rome.

On one of their trips to outlying villages, Giuliano took Stefano into a small church built of ivory colored stone. "I haven't talked to *Il Signore* for a long time," he explained. Giuliano put money in the box for each of them to light a candle. Kneeling in the presence of God, Stefano felt exposed, his heart broken wide open.

Giuliano looked over at his friend. He saw tears welling in Stefano's eyes. He wrapped an arm around his shoulder.

"My friend," Giuliano spoke in a low tone. "I'm here to listen to anything you might have to say. You must know in my eyes you can do no wrong. I know your heart."

Stefano looked up to God, Mary's son cast in bronze and dying on the cross for their sins. Then he looked to his friend. How he longed to unburden himself.

"I'm in love, but can't be with the one I love." Stefano took a breath. "No one must know or I could cause her pain."

"You have my word, Stefano," Giuliano assured him.

"It is Maria that I love, Maria Ricci." He buried his face in his hands.

"I know, Stefano," Giuliano said, smiling wistfully.

"You know? How do you know I love Maria?" Stefano's voice rose in surprise.

"Anyone with a little bit of sense can see what's between you. It's clear she loves you, too."

Stefano lowered his head and took a deep breath. He felt naked, but also relieved. "You can see that she loves me?"

"Stefano, she loves you. I can tell you one thing for sure, she does not love Martino. How could anyone love him?" He blessed himself quickly. "Forgive me, God."

"But I don't know what to do, Giuliano." Stefano rubbed his hand over his eyes and shook his head.

"Do nothing, Stefano," Giuliano said weakly. "God will show you the way."

The two men finished praying. They blessed themselves and kissed their clenched hands, then stepped out of the church onto the bright piazza.

When they returned home that evening, Maria was sitting in the kitchen with Prima and Filomena. Dressed in blue, a strand of chestnut hair from her chignon escaping across her face, she looked like a saint to Stefano. He caught his breath. Could it be that his prayer had been answered so quickly?

Warm greetings were exchanged between all but Stefano and Maria, who stared at each other as if there were no one else in the room. A bright moon rose in the sky and the Giulianos invited Prima outside with them on the pretext of touring the fruit orchard. "I know you'll find some delicious pears and apples for your famous *tortas*," Filomena told her.

When their friends had left the kitchen, Maria sat quietly, afraid to look at him. Stefano pulled a chair alongside of hers. Her skin glowed in the lamplight. She turned to him and suddenly they were embracing, sharing a passionate, long-awaited kiss.

"Maria," Stefano whispered, "I can't believe you're here, but you are and that's all that matters." He kissed her long and deeply and, trembling, she did not fight him. When the kiss ended, Maria pulled away, remembering her purpose.

"Stefano, we have to speak." He could not tell if she was troubled or full of joy.

"Speak, Maria, I'm listening." He held her face in his hands.

She took her time and just when he thought he would burst, she began to cry softly. Then she smiled like a little girl and said, "Stefano, my love, my life, I'm...I'm pregnant."

Stefano's heart soared. He gathered her into his arms and open her twice around the room. "How many months?"

"Three." She laughed, but sadness stained the laughter.

"Maria, what's wrong?" He hadn't for a minute thought the baby might not be his, that it might be Martino's. But now a shadow crossed his face. That, certainly, would be reason for grief. Stefano knelt before her. He lifted her face to his. "Why are you sad? Is this baby...our baby?"

"Oh, yes, my love. I'm sure that it's your baby. In fact I knew the moment I conceived. So for that I'm very happy, but..."

"But what?"

"Now I have to think about my child--our child's wellbeing. I'll have to rely on Martino even more." She looked away from him, biting her lip.

Stefano hung his head and felt ashamed. She was right. How could he possibly move her into the guesthouse, especially now? It would cause a great scandal. He was not yet in a position to take her away from here and the repercussions of Maria leaving Martino while she was pregnant would ruin her reputation for the rest of her life. It would be a terrible beginning for them, a terrible beginning for a new life. But there had to be a way! Stefano could not bear the thought of her living in Martino's house with his child inside of her.

"Maria, I'll be making a good amount of money soon, very soon. Giuliano may even make me a partner. Then maybe...?"

Maria put her hand over his mouth.

"Please, Stefano, don't." It was more than just the money. Maria struggled with all the voices in her head. She questioned everything, including whether she had ever really been given free reign to follow her heart in the confessional. More than likely, she had imagined it, found a way to do what she wanted to do. What kind of God lets us do whatever we want to do? Wasn't life about sacrifice? Especially when you have a child? She longed for Stefano, but being with him had come to seem more and more impossible with every passing day.

She had decided. She would have to make the best of this

situation and stay with Martino, the man to whom she'd yoked her fate. She would be a mother now. A child should not have to battle the judgment of the world because of a mother's mistake.

Resolution came over her face like a shroud, and Stefano felt sick. Clearly Maria had made her choice. He had no say in the matter.

"Does Martino know you're expecting?" he asked gently.

"No, not yet. I wanted to tell you first." She began to cry.

"You're the baby's father and you always will be." Stefano gathered her up in his arms and held her, trying to sense the child inside of her.

"Maria, this is not right. We're meant to be together. You know it. I know it. And God knows it." He rocked her and whispered in her ear.

Maria cried even harder. "But I'm married Stefano, a man that I damn every night. Still, he's my husband and my hands are tied. I must go. I must go now." She kissed him long and deeply. Both of them wept, their lips tasting of tears. These might be the very last kisses they would ever exchange. Maria pulled away, but Stefano kissed her again. She released a moan, her body weak with desire.

"Please, Maria, come back to me, please."

Maria could not bear the pain in his eyes. If she did not leave immediately she felt she would die. She rose and began to walk out the door.

"Prima?" Maria called out at the threshold.

Prima came from the orchard to meet Maria in the doorway. She set down her basket of fruit and took Maria's shoulders in both hands, searching her face. Then, without a word, she released the young woman and went into the kitchen to Stefano. He looked shattered.

"My poor Stefano!" she could not help but exclaim. She went to him and kissed him on either cheek. "I'll be back to check on you soon." She smiled sadly, but he did not respond. He looked at her blankly, evidently in shock.

Maria had already started to walk away. Prima followed. The sound of their footsteps on the gravel echoed in Stefano's ears. The doors of Prima's car slammed and the engine started up. There was nothing he could do. No way to stop Maria or convince her that their love would overcome all of this. There was nothing left for him, no reason to carry on. If he could not be with her and their child, if there was no chance of a future together, why work? Why live?

When Giuliano and Filomena came into the kitchen, Stefano's eyes were vacant. He refused Filomena's offers of food and rejected Giuliano's companionship. Running out of the house and into the garden, Stefano fell to his knees in a patch of sunflowers. He looked up at the full moon hanging low in the sky. Its glow lit the garden, painting a silver sheen on all the trees, plants, and flowers he had worked so hard to cultivate.

Suddenly, a rush of anger came over Stefano. "Why God? Why create such beauty, such fertility, and withhold from me the one thing that could nourish me? Why would you play such a trick on me? Why did you allow me to find her, but only lend her to me for a short time, to learn what she feels like, tastes like, smells like, only to rip her away from me? I do not understand." He cried out to the empty sky. "Why do you make it impossible for us to be together?" Stefano cried. Please God take me please, I cannot bear this pain or this life without her. Please take me."

DICIOTTO

Weeks had passed and Stefano could not eat or work. He stayed in the guesthouse, ignoring the invitations of the Giulianos, gentle at first then more insistent, to join them. He shut out all human noises. If he had been asked to say his own name during this time, he would not have been able to. Darkness had entered his heart and no boundary existed between him and hell.

But one morning, this fever seemed to break. A strange idea had come to him and he stumbled to his feet. His eyes wild as a mystic's, he went into the garden and began packing a basket full of fruits and vegetables.

He would bring it to the Finellis. He needed to see the things that he used to see on the way to Maria's garden each day, to follow those same stone walls, to hear the birds sing above his head as they led him to her. He needed to find familiar things that could remind him of who he was. To see Signore Finelli's fat belly and round Signora Finelli standing by him, scolding. To hear the LaPortas arguing over nothing, oblivious to their luck in being together.

By the time Stefano arrived at the Finellis, the walk had restored him a bit. He was greeted warmly. The couple, grateful for his presence, expressed how much they missed him singing up and down the road every morning and evening.

"You were the beam of bright sun in our day," Signora Finelli told him.

"That bastard Ricci did not deserve you," Signor Finelli said. "But it's our loss, too."

"He doesn't deserve Maria either," his wife added. The mention of her name stabbed Stefano's heart. "Poor thing hasn't played the piano for quite some time."

"I heard that pig broke it. We used to love to hear her play."

Signore Finelli puffed on his cigar.

"The whole village loved it. It helped me sleep better." Signora Finelli shook her head mournfully. "And Stefano," she added, "You would not believe the state of the Ricci garden." She served him a cup of espresso.

Stefano did not press her for details. He could only imagine how the devastation in his heart would be reflected in Maria's garden.

The Finellis had saved both newspapers with Stefano's pictures and had them framed above their fireplace alongside Elena's big gardening competition photo.

"My wife, she loves to save everything." Signore Finelli laughed.

"Everything important." Signora Finelli shot back. "But you were the one who cut these out!"

"The point is," Signor Finelli said, turning to Stefano with a rare, serious look on his plump face, "You have a gift. And we are honored to know such a man."

Stefano lowered his head and took a deep breath. He, too, felt honored to be in the presence of these humble people. In that moment, he understood why he had to go on. To deny a gift that brought so many hope, health, and nourishment would be equal to suicide.

He left the Finellis tired but full of gratitude. Stepping outside and looking over to the Ricci residence, he could see the garden and Maria's arched window. It was empty.

* * *

The next morning Maria sat at the kitchen table waiting for Martino to come downstairs. She had prepared a special breakfast of mille fogiole pastry cradling dollops of chocolate and cream. Martino walked into the kitchen in his usual rush, pulling at his tie. She smiled at him.

"I made you breakfast. Won't you sit for minute?" Pulling on his jacket, Martino looked at her and at the pastries on the table.

"Thank you, but I don't have time to sit. I'll take one with me." She went to him and put her hand on his arm to stop him. "Please, Martino, I must talk with you."

"Not now. I have to go." He pushed her away.

"But I—I'm pregnant," she blurted out miserably.

Martino stopped and searched her face as if she were lying. "You? Pregnant!" He sat at the table and stared at the pile of pastries. "Ha! I knew there was nothing wrong with me." He grabbed a pastry and put into his mouth, chewing with sudden gusto. "It's about time. Mama will be so happy. Do you think it's a son?" Jumping up from the table, he exclaimed, "Very good! I'll tell Mama and everyone else." Looking at his watch, he added, "But now I really must go." He paused, looking at her with a clinical eye. "Make sure you eat. I want a healthy baby boy."

When the front door slammed behind him, Maria let out a heavy sigh and waited until his car disappeared. She all but ran to Prima's house.

When Maria rushed in, Prima had the espresso brewing on the stove and a raspberry *torta* fresh out of the oven. Maria refused the coffee—she could not hold it down these days—but not the *torta*.

"That smells heavenly Prima."

"I used Stefano's raspberries."

Maria took up her fork and dug it into the crust as if to devour a piece of forbidden love.

"*Madona mia*, the berries! I can taste him." She finished her piece quickly and began to cut another, tears pouring onto her plate. Prima looked at her and smiled. "Don't look at me that way Prima. I'm eating for two now."

"I know, my dear. It's wonderful." Prima clasped her hands together. "Oh, Maria, you're going to be a fantastic mother."

Maria laughed through her tears. "I hope I'll get so fat that Martino never wants to touch me again." She stuffed *torta* into her mouth like a child.

"At least you have a sense of humor." Prima chuckled, but then her face took on a serious cast. "Tell me, Maria, how did Martino take the news?"

"He wants a boy. His big fat mother will be so happy and he's so proud of himself. Of course, I could have nothing to do with it." She laughed, and the venom in her voice surprised Prima. "Little does he know that *he* had nothing to do with it!"

Catching herself, Maria could not believe the words that had flown from her mouth. Her eyes widened with shock and Prima spit out her *torta* to avoid choking from laughter. It was better to laugh than cry.

Martino went to his mother's house and hugged and kissed her the way he should have hugged Maria. Mama squeezed him back, excited.

"I knew it wasn't you, my son. We must tell everyone. When is she expecting?" Martino looked at her blankly and realized that he didn't know. He shrugged, embarrassed.

"Well, you need to find out! We're going to have to prepare for the baby and I want to have everything ready in time."

"I will find out, Mama. I will find out everything." Martino kissed her again and rushed out of the large house. He got into his coupe and felt strangely ill at ease as he drove along the winding roads. Pulling up to a small house with crackling red plaster, he parked in a back alley, came up to the front door and knocked three times quickly. A woman opened the door wearing a silk bathrobe. She opened it to reveal nakedness underneath. Martino pushed in the door and began to grope her breast. "I'm going to be a father," he said. She shut the door behind him with a hoarse, sharp laugh.

DICIANNOVE

As Maria's belly grew with new life, her garden continued to die. She stared out her arched window every day while gardener after gardener tried to restore the former beauty of the grounds. But they created nothing but a world of wilting, pallid flowers. Even her weeping willow seemed to blow aimlessly, devoid of any human touch. She could not even think of the ring hidden in its trunk, much less go out to try it on.

Mama Ricci came by with her usual basket of food and presents all wrapped in blue, as she barreled through the front door. "I'm here." She shouted into the house. Making herself at home, she placed the presents down and began to pull food from the basket. "Where are you?" Maria came walking in slowly.

"Hello Mama." They kissed politely. Mama had become more bearable now that Maria was pregnant, but it was only for the baby's sake. She knew once the baby came her mother-in-law would become a witch again. "So Maria, you are now five months along, *si*?"

"*Si*, Mama."

"Why didn't you tell us sooner?"

"I wanted to get through my first trimester, to be sure I was strong enough to carry it."

"Hhmm, so that means you got pregnant right before my sons trip to Rome?" Her tone became accusatory.

Shocked, Maria tried to remain calm. "*Si, si* the night before actually. Why?"

"I was just trying to figure it all out in my head, that's all." She smiled wickedly. "I like to know all the details. I'm a mother." She prepared lunch and served Maria, but wouldn't let up. "I cannot wait to see what this baby looks like." Mama added, as dread spread through Maria's skin. "You know, I came by the house a few times to see if you wanted to come to church with me while Martino was in Rome, but funny thing is you were never here, even funnier is you're always here. You never go out. So how come all of a sudden you weren't home, eh?"

"Oh Mama, I was at Prima's right next door. We have become very friendly. You should've came for me there." Laughing uncomfortably.

"Ha, why would I ever knock on some strangers door looking for you? You think I'm a mind reader or something?" Narrowing her brow, she examined Maria's every move. "And since when did you become so friendly with neighbors?"

'Since Martino left for Rome," she smiled. "It's nice."

"Hhmm," her face twisted. "I don't like it, not one bit. That's all I have to say right now."

* * *

Finally Mama Ricci left. Maria waited until she could no longer see her car and then ran to Prima's for solace. "Prima, may I play your piano?" She had been the one to bring over a tray of pastries this time.

"I was wondering how long it would take you to ask." Prima smiled.

Maria sat at the piano in the parlor. "I still can't believe he destroyed my grandmother's piano." She stared at the keys. "Of course I believe it. He's destroyed everything precious to me."

"Well, you can play this one anytime you want. I can't play a lick. It was Paolo's. It would do me good to hear music from it again."

"I've had a song in my head for weeks now. The baby has been filling my heart with music."

Maria closed her eyes, and her fingers glided along the keys with a confident elegance. An enchanting melody filled Prima's home; a tune of gentle pleading that had Prima melting into the couch. Maria's body moved with the music and her long fingers

Incanto ~ The Singing Gardener

stroked the keys with precision. What a shame Maria had been deprived of her piano, Prima thought. Maria smiled and realized how much she loved the black and white keys, the floor petals and the full sound the wonderful instrument created. She let herself be transported to Stefano and felt the two of them together again. When she finished she opened her eyes and brought herself back to Prima's living room. Prima wiped the tears from her eyes and clapped her hands.

"That was beautiful, Maria. You are to the piano what Stefano is to the garden."

"Thank you, but I could never be like Stefano. Oh how I wish I could. Maybe then we would be together." It was too much for her to think about. "I have missed my piano." She looked at the keys longingly. It was Stefano she missed most of all.

* * *

All the neighbors were out on their terrazza's listening with ear-to-ear smiles.

* * *

Stefano kept his distance despite his desire. He didn't want to cause her any more confusion or pain. He had renewed his efforts in the garden and he and Giuliano had established a consistent, lucrative venture together. Giuliano made him a partner as promised. "Why shouldn't I?" he said, "How could any of this even exist without you?" In addition to becoming famous for the taste of their olives and grapes, they were the top produce garden in Chianti. Stefano was making more money than he ever had and his bank account began to grow. He enjoyed the demand for his services and it kept him mercifully busy.

One day, Stefano and Giuliano went into Sienna to pick up some special items for the garden. Walking down the main street, Stefano spotted a grand piano in a storefront window. He stopped, his eyes feasting on the instrument. Giuliano took him inside and they talked to the shopkeeper. Stefano asked if he could make a deposit to hold the piano and the shopkeeper looked at him skeptically. But when Giuliano said, "Do you not know the Singing Gardener when he's standing right in front of you?" the man stammered apologetically and stumbled over himself to assure Stefano that, yes, they could work out a schedule of payments. Thrilled, Stefano agreed and Giuliano assured him he would be able to pay it off in a couple of years.

* * *

 Pleased with the success of his garden, Giuliano invited Stefano and Filomena to a special restaurant in Florence to celebrate. Stefano dressed himself carefully in his new clothes and they drove the few hours to the city. Navigating a maze of busy streets, Giuliano parked near the Ponte Vecchio. The three strolled over the arched bridge, so lovely that even the Germans had not been able to destroy it during the war. "It's good to know that some beautiful things do survive, eh?" Giuliano asked him. Stefano nodded. Stopping midway across, he gazed out over the Arno, which was placid in the twilight, dotted with a few small boats. The sky shone a rich violet. He could see all of Florence—*Il Duomo*, the red tiled roofs of the buildings and the mountains beyond. Church bells rang out and for the first time since he and Maria had parted, he felt the preciousness of his own life.

 "There's our place!" Giuliano pointed out a modest restaurant sheltered underneath the stone bridge. They made their way across to the street and found the front steps that led down to the dining room.

 Giuliano took Filomena's arm and Stefano followed. The smell of sautéed garlic filled the air.

 Inside, champagne colored walls glowed in candlelight and happy-looking diners gathered at large tables sharing food and conversation. Stefano and the Giulianos were greeted as people of great importance. The maitre'd led them to a special table in the corner and bowed as they seated themselves. Giuliano told Stefano that the restaurant now used only the vegetables grown on his land.

Incanto ~ The Singing Gardener

"That's why they know us here."

The owner, a small man with an eager face, soon came over to their table and kissed Giuliano and his wife. Stefano, he hugged like a son.

"Bellisimo, I can't believe you're here." Stefano stood up to greet him. "You're amazing! Do you know that my business had doubled since I've been using your produce? My customers say there's something special in the food. They keep coming and bringing more and more people. I don't know how to thank you." He kissed Stefano again on both cheeks.

Stefano laughed. "Thank you It's my pleasure to help you."

"Now if only you can make it rain for us! *Dio Mio*, it's been months."

"*Si*, I wish I could. It's very bad. But only God can help us with that."

"Let's pray he does." The owner shouted to the waiter, "Bring them a bottle of our finest champagne. Anything you want tonight, it's on the house." The man shook Giuliano's hand and kissed Filomena again. "Let me know if you need anything at all." He walked away, but midway across the room, spun on his heels and came back to the table. Overcome, he kissed and hugged Stefano once more, thanking him profusely.

The waitstaff laid course after course before them. First came eggplant rollatini, zucchini flower with marscapone cheese, and fresh water mozzarella over succulent tomatoes with leaves of basilico. After the first course, they finished the champagne and began on a bottle of Brunello diMontalcino. The second course consisted of a penne sautéed with olive oil, fresh garlic, tomato, rappini, sausage and peccorino cheese. With this came a platter of grilled peppers, onions, radicchio, asparagus, broccoli, sweet potato, turnip and spinach all marinated in port, mustard, garlic and sundried tomato. As they ate the extravagant meal, Stefano marveled the array of tastes. He understood why customers kept returning to this restaurant. Giuliano lifted his glass for a toast,

"To Stefano, the Singing Gardener. Your gift brings so many people joy. Salute." The three touched their glasses together with a clink.

"Thank you, Giuliano," Stefano answered, "But it's really our chef who should be saluted. He makes me look good." Stefano sipped his wine.

"In life we all need people to help us along and let us shine." Giuliano paused, looking to Filomena, who nodded quietly. "Stefano, there's a special reason we brought you here tonight. We have a present for you. A little reward for all of your hard work."

Stefano shifted nervously in his chair. "You've already done so much for me," he managed. "I couldn't take anything else from you."

"Just consider this a gift from friends. You never told me when your birthday was. When is it?" Giuliano was curious.

"It's August…August seventeenth," Stefano answered hesitantly.

"So consider this an early birthday present," Giuliano joked. Then he pulled a key from his pocket and put it into Stefano's hand. "This, my friend, is a key to freedom, a key for you to explore things you've never seen before, to go places you only dreamed of." As Giuliano spoke, Maria's face flashed in Stefano's mind. She was his dream, his freedom. Giuliano went on, "This key is yours and it fits into your new car."

Stefano lost his breath and began to shake. He looked into the eyes of Giuliano and Filomena, two angels that God, whom he had questioned and damned only a short time ago, must have sent to protect him. Stefano reached over and hugged Giuliano with all his might, his chest heaving with emotion. Filomena, he kissed.

"I have no words," he said. "I don't know how to accept this gift or to ever repay you for all you've given me."

"It's nothing very fancy," Giuliano cautioned. "But it will get you from place to place. We'll go pick it up tomorrow."

In this moment, the waiter brought out the next course, rabbit alla campagnola garnished with parsnips, carrots and beets accompanied by a side of whipped mashed rosemary garlic potatoes.

"*Perfetto!*" Stefano declared. They finished the meal with Zabaglione poured over fresh mixed berries, baked apple tart and a tiramisu accented with a glass of anisette. The only thing missing was Maria. For now, though, Stefano tried to appreciate all he had.

* * *

The next morning Stefano and Giuliano went to pick up Stefano's new car in Siena. The small Fiat 600 suited him perfectly. He got in on the driver's side and Giuliano got in on the passenger side. Stefano grabbed the wheel, looked over and smiled.

"Is she really mine?"

"She's really yours." Giuliano laughed. "Start her up."

Stefano inserted the key into the ignition and turned it. The engine roared and he jumped back like a child.

"Powerful!"

He delicately shifted the gear and stepped on the gas pedal. The vehicle began to roll gracefully forward.

"Stefano, let's drive by Maria's and show her," Giuliano suggested.

"Oh," Stefano's face fell. "I don't know if that's a good idea."

"I think it is. You haven't seen her in months. If Martino is there, I can say we came to bring him some fresh vegetables." He held up a sack of produce and smiled. "If he's not, at least you can see her."

Stefano drove in silence, taking the curves in the road to Castellina as if he'd been navigating them all his life. Maria was all he could think about. He'd wanted to rush to her and show her the gift to make it real. Without her, what did it matter? Maybe now she would realize he could take care of her, take her away. He looked over to Giuliano.

"All right, let's go." Stefano tried not to think about the consequences. Instead, he told himself that, if nothing else, it would also be nice to see Prima and take her for a spin in his new toy.

"*Bravo!*" Giuliano smiled, clapping his friend on the shoulder. They headed to Ricci's.

* * *

From her arched window, Maria saw the unfamiliar car pulling up the driveway. She was not expecting anyone and Mama Ricci had just left. At seven months pregnant, it was a chore for Maria to lift herself from the chair. But she managed to go to the door to see who was coming. As the vehicle got closer she thought her eyes must have been deceiving her. Stefano? Behind the wheel of a brand new Fiat?

From across the way, Finelli peered through his binoculars. "*Andiamo* Elena." Signora Finelli ran out. "It's the gardener, driving a new car. I told you something is going on over there." She grabbed the binoculars and looked for herself.

Tessa and Carlo came out and stood on their porch. "Looks like the gardener is back for a visit." Tessa smiled like a imp.

Stefano parked and he and Giuliano popped out. Maria covered her mouth and began to cry when she saw Stefano's gorgeous face smiling at her. Without care or a thought of Giuliano or anyone else, she rushed as fast as she could manage to his arms. He held her tightly.

It seemed that not even a moment had passed since they had been together in the garden, yet at the same time it felt like a lifetime. Gently, he held her away from him and rested his eyes on her face.

"Let me look at you." His eyes took in her round belly and softened features. Her skin glowed. "My God, you look even more beautiful pregnant, if that's possible."

Maria felt she would melt with pleasure.

"May I touch?" He held his hand over her belly.

She smiled. "Of course, Stefano! It's your child." He placed his hand on her belly. When a strong pulse moved under his palm, he

jumped back and laughed.
"It kicked! *E un miracolo!*" He kissed her belly and whispered private messages to his child. Maria couldn't help but remember the first night they'd made love under the sunflowers, how he sang to her belly then. She understood now that he had been sowing the ground for her to conceive.
At this moment, Prima came walking over with a peach *torta*. "What's the matter, old friend, have you forgotten me so soon?" she called, her throaty laughter ringing out. Stefano hugged her warmly and she greeted Giuliano as well. He and Prima did not mean to intrude on the lovers' time together, but all of them knew that the neighbors would be watching. Best to shield Stefano and Maria from prying eyes.
"Do you like Stefano's new car?" Giuliano asked the women.
"This is yours?" Maria managed.
"Yes, Maria," he said. "I can go wherever I want, whenever I want."
"It's beautiful, Stefano," Prima told him. "But don't forget to keep your two feet on the ground."
"I've seen your picture in the newspapers," Maria went on. "I knew you were doing well, but I didn't know you were rich already," she teased.
Giuliano jumped in. "Oh, but he is. We're going to be getting another property so that we can keep up with the high demand for Stefano's creations."
Stefano looked over the garden, heartbroken at what had become of it. He shook his head, knowing how much Maria needed to be kissed by the beauty of the garden each morning as she gazed at her arched window.
She looked at him with despair. "Everything is a mess since you left. Everything."
Conscious of the neighbors' eyes, Prima invited, "Let's go in and have something sweet, shall we?" They all went into Prima's home.

* * *

Lowering the binoculars, Signora Finelli turned to her husband. "If I didn't know better I would say they are in love." Spying from across the way.

"Ah ha, you see! I'm not crazy after all." He let out a victorious laugh and lit up a cigar.

* * *

Carlo and Tessa were out peering into the garden as well. "How come we never get invited over for her espresso?" Carlo pouted. Tessa handed him a dishtowel.

"Silly man. Finish up the dishes, it's your turn today." She sauntered back into the house imagining what was going on with Stefano and Maria.

Prima served everyone her peach *torta* in her kitchen. Stefano held Maria's hand while they ate.

"How are you feeling?" Stefano asked with genuine concern.

"I'm fine, Stefano, just fine, I guess." She tried to sound convincing.

"Can I do anything to make you feel better?"

Stefano's words warmed Maria's heart. She knew he meant what he said. She also knew he was still a pillar of strength, and that she could lean on him if she chose.

Maria's mind raced with all the things she wanted for Stefano to do and be for her, but she stopped herself. It was futile to think about. She tried to keep things light hearted. "Yes, Stefano! Fix my garden so that I can be happy each morning when I look out my window." She touched her belly. "I want her to experience the joy of your flowers, just the way I always did." She pulled his hand to her belly. "I think it would make her happy," she said, putting her hand over his.

Prima laughed. "You said 'her'. So you know it's a girl, do you?"

Maria covered her mouth. It had just slipped out.

"Prima, you are terrible! But yes, I feel it is a girl."

Incanto ~ The Singing Gardener

Stefano and Giuliano looked to Prima for validation and Prima nodded her head, yes. Stefano jumped up from the table, grinning. "*Bella donna*, I hope she looks just like you!" Stefano grabbed her and swung her around the kitchen with happiness. "We're having a girl, a little baby girl!" They laughed and kissed and then, realizing they would not be together much longer, stopped.

Stefano sat down and put his head in his hands. Maria rested her hand lightly on his mane of thick hair. He began to sink into despair. His child would be born and he might never have the opportunity to play with her or teach her things that a father teaches a daughter. She might never even know that he was her father!

He raised his head and forced a smile. If Maria felt sad the baby would feel it, too, and, as much as it seemed impossible to prevent, he did not want his little girl being born into the world with a heart full of grief.

Giuliano sensed Stefano's pain and thought it would be best to protect him. "We have so much to do back at our garden, Signora Ricci, Prima," he said. "I hope you'll forgive us for leaving so soon." They all walked out to Stefano's new automobile.

"Prima," he said, "I'd love to take you for a ride soon." Maria wondered if he would go to the coast, to the Mancinelli's villa, the one he had spoken of to her all those many months ago.

"I'm counting on it." Prima hugged Stefano and kissed Giuliano goodbye. She nodded to Maria and walked back to her house. Giuliano got into the passenger side while Stefano stood with Maria by the other side of the car.

"Maria," he said, "I'm with you every day."

"And I with you, Stefano."

"I don't know how to go on each day without you so I tell myself that we'll be together again soon." What had he to lose by being honest? He had never been able to be otherwise with her. "Will we, Maria? Will we be together again soon?"

"I don't know, Stefano. I honestly don't know." Maria felt as though she would crumble. Her answer left him bewildered.

"I love you, Maria. More than life itself. You are my life."

"I love you, too. You must know that there's nothing that you're feeling that I'm not feeling also. Whenever you question my love for you, know that I feel exactly as you do. Now go. Before I break into a million pieces."

She began to cry as she hugged him goodbye. He inhaled the scent of her hair, to bring it home with him. She broke away and walked quickly into the house while Stefano started up his car and headed back to his life without her.

* * *

As night fell over Castellina in Chianti, Stefano walked the familiar pathway to the Ricci residence. He snuck by the Finellis and peered through their lit window. They were enjoying their evening meal together, waving their hands in animated conversation. At the LaPortas', he did not hear any fighting and he smiled and carried on his way. When he got to the Ricci's cobblestone driveway, he slowly crawled along the ground so that he would not be seen. He looked in the arched window and saw Martino eating dinner as Maria sat silently staring at her plate.

All of the sudden, she seemed to sense his presence and turned her head toward the window, but Stefano ducked down deeper into the dried bougainvillea. He rested his body in the soil and looked around at the neglected garden. He thought of his little girl to be and wondered what she would look like. Would she have Maria's green eyes?

Stefano waited until Martino and Maria had finished dinner and gone upstairs. Under brilliant stars, with no other light than theirs and the light that burned in his heart and hands, he began.

Maria woke up the next morning and trudged over to her arched window. When she looked out her heart soared. Stefano had turned the entire garden into a sea of yellow wallflowers, accentuating their brilliance with bright red tulips. The baby began kicking vigorously and Maria laughed out loud. Martino, walking down the

stairs at that moment, asked her sharply, "What's so funny?"
"The baby just kicked," she told him. "Do you want to feel?"
"*Si*." Gently placing his hand on her belly for a moment. "My God, that's amazing. He is so strong. It must be a son with a kick like that." Martino kissed her on the cheek. "I'll be late tonight." He walked out the front door to his car, then stopped in his tracks to regard the gorgeous wallflowers. "Ah, see we don't need that stupid singing gardener after all!" he muttered.

* * *

Not even the beauty of the flowers he'd given her could bring Maria to leave Martino for Stefano. She expressed her gratitude, asking Prima to relay her message, but she also told Prima that she could not see Stefano again. The joy of seeing him had been beyond measure, but the time it took Maria to calm down, she felt, could not be healthy for the baby. Seeing him in the flesh and then watching him go yet again had felt like death. She had put him and the love they shared in a box on a back shelf in her heart. Seeing him had opened up that box and caused all the contents of her life to spill.

"Prima, I never want my daughter to struggle like I did. Seeing the house again terrified me of living like that again."

"But you wouldn't Maria. Stefano is doing well now."

"For how long? My father was a man of the soil too, but then they no longer needed him. There were days he barely had enough to feed us. I had to share a tiny bed with my two sisters. I never had new clothes and I had to take care of my father because he became so sick, heart sick really and I just can't have that happen to my child. It's not fair to bring her into a world of struggle. I would rather allow her to have everything and I unhappy for her sake. She will want for nothing and I will go without. I know what's best for her."

"Maria..." Prima wanted to reason with her, but Maria was firm.

"Please, tell him not to come again," Maria asked her friend, and the older woman hung her head in sadness, nodding. *No good will come of love rejected*, Prima thought.

VENTI

As drought parched Stefano's heart, the land, too suffered. The strong Tuscan sun refused to give way to rain. A terrible heat had struck the region. Tuscany's gardens were dying. Daily masses in every church in every village were packed with people praying for moisture. The farms, orchards, and vineyards withered. Surrounding lakes, ponds and tributaries had evaporated and all the crops were suffering. The biggest terror of all? That the wine vineyards and olive groves might fail. The vineyards were drying up, the olive trees on the verge of decimation. The government stood on the alert, rationing water and cautioning farmers not to panic. But what powers does a government have compared to Mother Nature?

Giuliano's land was not immune. Every plant on the property had started to wither. Stefano walked the property listlessly, more concerned about Maria and the baby than his work. She was expecting soon and he wanted to make sure she was all right. He drove to Prima's with gallons of water taken from Giuliano's trickle of a spring and asked Prima to please give them to Maria. "I will replenish Maria's garden every so often," he told her. "I want her and the baby to…to be happy when they look out the window."

It broke Prima's heart to see him in so much pain. Heavy and lethargic in her final weeks of pregnancy, Maria took the water without question. Stefano kept coming in the evenings after everyone was asleep, receiving nothing in return. How empty he must feel inside, Prima thought.

Each time Stefano came, he left her and the baby a colorful surprise. Close to them both, separated only by the stone walls of the house and by Maria's choice not to be with him, he drew easily on his gift. He had only to think of his daughter and the love he felt for her and her mother for the power to surge in his hands. His tears of love were the only watering the soil needed.

Away from Maria's garden, he found it more difficult to hold onto this love. Every other flower, tree or vine hung limp and lifeless in his hands.

Worried, Giuliano confronted Stefano one day beneath the browning grape vines of the pergola.

"I know there is a drought, my friend, and some things even you can't change. But surely you can do something! Everything is dying again!" he cried. "If this keeps up, I'll have to sell this place."

"Be patient. The drought will pass soon." Stefano assured him. "But the hell I feel inside of my soul might never pass." He grabbed a handful of grapes and crushed them as the juice stained his hand. Opening his clenched fist, he licked the liquid in his palm. "See, the vines are still alive."

"And so are you." Giuliano reminded him.

* * *

Hot and uncomfortable, Maria was ready for the baby to show herself. She could think of nothing but how she wanted to hold her baby in her arms.

It was the middle of August and still they had not had any rain. The crisis reached its peak. The regions had called for a meeting of all the farmers, crop growers, wine makers and gardeners. They wanted to see how they might remedy the situation. Everyone had been losing money and much more would be lost if all the crops failed. The people would be deprived of the necessities for living.

Giuliano and Stefano arrived at the piazza and entered *il commune*, the public building where the meeting was to be held. The date was August seventeenth, Stefano's birthday and the room was packed with worried souls. The mayor and all the important politicians sat on a raised dais at the front of the room. The newspapers, too, had sent reporters and photographers. Even Martino Ricci was there. Tragedy can be good for business, after all. Men who had never spoken in public, old farmers and winemakers and olive growers, got up to the podium, took off their caps, cleared their throats, and spoke with passion. "The land is our life," one old man shouted from the back of the room. "Without it, we cannot go on." Stefano turned to find the old man protesting from his wheelchair. Stefano felt an immediate connection to this man. Many cried with despair, afraid to lose everything they had worked so hard for, fearing they would not be able to support their families.

A priest from Greve stood up. "Please everyone, I urge you to pray each day for rain. If you do, if we all do it faithfully, God will surely hear all of your prayers and bless us with rain," he said. But his words were met with stony silence. Had they not been wearing the knees of their trousers thin with praying for months on end with no result?

"God has forsaken us!" one voice cried out. And when the priest tried to find the blasphemer, no one would point him out.

Stefano and Giuliano walked to the back of the room. Stefano sensing the waves of despair that were threatening to drown the people of Chianti. He extended his hand to the man in the wheelchair. "I am Stefano Portigiani." Leo grabbed Stefano's hand with a desperation that gripped his broken heart. Stefano knelt down to him.

"I am Leo Cavallo. We need your help. My daughter's baby can't be born into a drought. I cannot have one more curse plague my family."

Looking into this man's desperate eyes he recognized the eyes of his true love. "You are Maria's father?" Stefano's eyes filled with tears.

"Yes, how did you know?" Leo was taken aback.

"She has your eyes." He kissed Leo on both cheeks. "Do not despair my friend. Your grandchild will not be cursed, I promise."

"I believe you." Leo whispered into Stefano's ear.

Full of purpose Stefano walked up to the podium to speak. A hush came across the hall.

"My name is Stefano Portigiani and I may have a possible solution. In fact, I assure you I do."

The room stirred with chatter. Some voices sounded hopeful, while others hissed in suspicion. "I cannot promise you water, but I will come to each one of your fields and orchards to rejuvenate them. From there, it is true, we can only pray for rain."

"How are you going to do it?" One of the winemakers shouted. "Are you Jesus? We need a real solution and you're talking about a miracle. It's not possible." The crowd grew angry and began throwing things at Stefano and making threats. Giuliano ran up to the podium to protect Stefano.

"Please let him finish you fools. Have you any better solutions?"

"I've seen the state of your crops, Giuliano!" another man added. "If he hasn't done anything for you, why should he for us?"

Giuliano held his temper. "Some of you do not understand why I say this, and the truth is that I don't understand his gift either. But I have witnessed it with my very own eyes and I know it's possible. What have we got to lose?"

The room became silent and camera bulbs began to flash. Stefano whispered something into Giuliano's ear. "There is one condition," Giuliano said. "Stefano must be free to do this in whatever way he wishes. And for those who don't believe what they cannot see? I want pictures taken of all the damaged crops and gardens before he works on them and then after. Everything will be documented." Reporters wrote furiously in their notebooks, and the room buzzed with comments. Giuliano went on. "Take care of him generously if you are satisfied with the outcome, won't you brothers? And have faith."

When Giuliano stepped down from the podium everyone, even the most skeptical, rushed to make arrangements for Stefano to visit their land.

Martino Ricci looked at the gardener, who was quickly being

engulfed by the crowd, and began to laugh with scorn. To the man standing next to him, he muttered, "Has everyone gone mad? That peasant sings to flowers and does nothing but sleep in the garden."

The man looked at Martino with disdain. "I don't care if he pisses over all of my land! If he can make my olives grow then I'm behind him."

Another man chimed in. "What else are we going to do? Are you going to save our crops?" he challenged Martino.

"My garden is fine." Martino fell into brooding silence. He watched everyone huddle around Stefano, treating him like a hero. "Bah! I don't know what all this fuss is about. He's a gardener and nothing more! Anyone can water flowers! All we need is water!" He shouted out trying to get anyone's attention, but no one paid him any mind. Martino slipped out the back door and found himself heading to a certain woman in a certain red house. She had a harsh laugh, but always kept good whiskey by her bed and didn't expect too much from him, least of all love.

After many hours talking with farmers from far and wide, Stefano and Giuliano drove home in Stefano's car discussing how much time Stefano would need to replenish each property. They had almost reached home when Giuliano looked at a newspaper on the front seat and noticed the date. "Stefano, today is your birthday!" he exclaimed.

"Yes. Just another day." The gardener's voice was listless.

"Just another day? Nonsense. It's a day of celebration. Happy birthday, my friend."

"Thank you, Giuliano."

"Is there anything special you want to do before we go home?"

Stefano was about to sigh and shake his head when another impulse gripped him. "Yes," he said, "I want to see Maria. I need to see her before I begin all of this work. It will help me to do what needs doing."

Giuliano shook his head in agreement.

"I know she doesn't want to see me, and maybe it's selfish, but

I can't do a thing if I don't see her face."

"Of course, Stefano, we'll go right now." Giuliano had seen Martino at the meeting and guessed he was not the type to go home early.

When they pulled into the Ricci driveway, Giuliano could not help but notice the beautiful garden, now blanketed in pink and red peonies in full bloom and billowing like succulent clouds. "Funny, Maria's garden does not seem to be feeling the drought." Giuliano suspected where Stefano's efforts had been going and felt a pang of envy. But the romantic in him could not fault his friend.

"You can do this for her, but you haven't been able to grow a cactus for us?" Giuliano laughed and punched him in the arm.

"Because of my daughter I can do this," Stefano replied, serious. "I don't know how to explain it to you. I just have to feel it."

"Well you better go feel something soon because all of Tuscany is depending on you to save their land."

The men got out of the car and across the low stone wall, Prima opened her door to greet them, bustling through the gate to embrace Stefano.

"I was just about to go to your house and bring you a cake!" She carried a large chocolate cake with "Stefano" written across the top in white. Stefano hugged and kissed her.

"Thank you, Prima, for remembering my birthday. I feel like a lucky little boy again." The sun had begun to set, the heat lifting just a bit.

"Shall we go inside and eat some?" Prima suggested. As if reading his mind, she added, "I'll just fetch Maria."

When Stefano stood speechless, Giuliano broke in. "Good idea. We'll wait for you," he replied, marching Stefano toward Prima's house.

Maria had heard the car but had not moved from the sofa. When Prima came to fetch her to share the cake, she hesitated, but something in her friend's eyes drew her up and out of the house.

Inside Prima's kitchen, upon seeing Stefano, Maria fell quiet.

She spoke to Stefano with her eyes.

Prima opened a bottle of wine. "Paolo asked me to open this one for Stefano's birthday." She poured the Barbaresco as Maria took the cake into the other room and decorated it with long thin candles. She lit the candles and came back in the room singing *Buon compleanno*. Everyone joined in and she placed the cake in front of Stefano. When they were finished, he closed his eyes and made a wish. Looking up into Maria's green gaze, he held it for a moment.

"I met your father today. You have his eyes." He then blew out the candles. Giuliano and Prima clapped.

"You did?" How is he?" Maria cut the cake and served each of them a piece.

"He is worried about you and the baby, but I assured him you would both be fine." Stefano smiled into Maria's face and could not have been happier to spend this birthday moment with three of his favorite people. Giuliano told Maria and Prima about the meeting and what Stefano was about to do for the countryside. Prima nodded her head as if she knew. "The gifts God has given us we must not waste."

At that moment a look of terror came over Maria's face and she cried out, "*Dio Mio! Madonna!* Oh God!"

Liquid seeped from between her legs, darkening her dress.

"Her water has broken," Prima said, her wide face calm. "It's time."

The men jumped up and began running around the table in circles, not knowing what to do with themselves. Feeling Maria's forehead as she laid her on a daybed, Prima spoke sharply.

"It's time to have your baby."

"Here?" Maria cried. "Now?" Racked with a contraction, she moaned.

"Yes, my dear," Prima told her. To Stefano, she said. "Go put on a big pot of water on the stove." He obeyed.

"Should we get the midwife?" Maria looked at Prima.

"If you want," Prima said, "But this wouldn't be the first baby I delivered."

"Prima," Stefano said, "You never stop surprising us."

She smiled, showing her bright teeth and her gums. And then the directions began in earnest. "Giuliano, go get me a stack of towels and some sheets." Giuliano ran upstairs, sweating. "Stefano, go to the garden and get me lavender, and bring in some of Maria's favorite flowers. Roses, for sure, we will make rosewater to calm her nerves." Stefano nodded. This he could do.

Prima held Maria's hand and walked with her around the room, helping soothe her through each contraction. Maria began to moan, a deep animal sound that surprised and even embarrassed her a little. But Prima told her this sound would help her push deep from within.

Stefano came back with an armful of flowers and herbs. At first she wanted to smell only the calming scent of lavender, but soon that became too strong and she demanded rosewater. Stefano soaked a rag in the magical water and delicately dabbed her entire body with the fragrant cloth. Surrendering to his touch, she lied down. Stefano placed his hand over her belly and kept it there. He kept talking to the baby, through Maria's taut skin, giving words of encouragement for the passage she was about to make. He assured her it would be safe to come into the world, that he and Maria would be waiting to greet her.

Prima laid a sheet across Maria's legs and monitored the baby's progress. "This will be quick," she exclaimed. "Now push!"

Maria undertook the work of her lifetime. Pushing and groaning, she felt there was no way to stop the wave moving through her. All she could do was hope the pain would end soon and produce a healthy child. With Stefano at her side, rubbing her head and massaging her stomach, Giuliano standing ready with supplies, and Prima watching the baby crown, Maria gave her final push. Prima caught the new life in her freckled hands.

"A beautiful girl!" she exclaimed, and Maria reached for her right away. They were a family welcoming another generation. It didn't matter about the drought. It didn't matter that Stefano and Maria were not together. It only mattered that this baby girl had arrived, healthy, happy, and with her whole life in front of her.

The baby began to wail, a pure strong sound that made Stefano's heart sing. Prima cleaned her up and placed her on Maria's chest with the umbilical chord still attached.

Maria cooed, lips pressed against the baby's soft head, and held her tightly to her breast. Right away, she began to nurse as if she'd been doing it forever. When the baby finished, Prima held up a big knife she had sterilized in the flames of the stove.

"All right, Papa, time to cut the chord."

"Oh no, Prima. I leave that to you!" Stefano looked pale. Maria laughed and when Prima was done, she held the baby out to Stefano.

Gently, he gathered her in his arms. He looked down at this gift from God and began to weep. He saw Maria's face in this little newborn. "She looks just like her mama," he breathed.

He held the infant close to his heart. Giuliano and Prima watched on, overjoyed that Stefano could be with Maria for the birth of their child. When he invited them closer to look, they admired her tiny round face and perfect nose. Her eyes were closed still, but they had Maria's almond shape. Chestnut hair covered her head. Her tiny lips were perfectly curved and pink.

Prima touched the baby's face with her pinky finger. "She's a gift from God." Prima smiled.

"That's what we'll name her, Donata, our gift from God," Stefano declared, looking to Maria with a question on his face.

"*Bella*. Donata it is," she said.

"Hello, Donata!" Giuliano gave her a delicate kiss on the cheek.

Stefano looked down at the baby in his arms. "Hello, Donata welcome to the world, my little angel." He could not take his eyes off of her.

Maria, having passed the afterbirth and recovering from her

labor with Prima's attention, adored the way Stefano looked holding their daughter. Clearly, he had fallen in love with his child and never wanted to let her go. Maria smiled at him and pulled him down so that she could whisper in his ear.

"Happy birthday, Papa Stefano." She gave him a delicate kiss on his ear that nearly made his knees buckle. But he had to be careful. He was holding a treasure.

Stefano looked down at Maria, the mother of his child, and knew that he would love her forever. He smiled and kissed Donata.

"Happy birthday to you and happy birthday to me. We are born on the same day, Donata! What do you think about that?" He spoke to his little girl with such tenderness.

Maria was exhausted, and Stefano placed Donata to sleep on her chest. He burned this vision of the two of them into his mind, storing it so that he might call on it again when the sun rose and he was not with them. Never before had he felt such love. Different than the love he felt for Maria alone, it required nothing but his breath to access. He kissed mother and child, who both stirred gently without waking. With profuse thanks, he and Giuliano left Prima and headed home.

Maria woke once in the warm night. Prima led her and the baby back to her own house and bed. Prima sat in the chair beside her, dozing, and when Maria woke again, led her downstairs to make her breakfast. Stepping gingerly, Maria took Donata to her arched window. The entire garden was resplendent in bright Pink Sweet Peas, their ruffled petals as delicate as the baby's features.

* * *

Martino barged in at nine o'clock in the morning, hung-over and miserable. But when he saw Maria in the window, holding little Donata, he brightened.

"You....last night? Here?"

She nodded, trying hard to contain the bliss she was feeling. She did not want it trampled.

"Buon giorno, Martino. We have a baby girl, Donata." She

ushered him to look at the little being swaddled in a soft white blanket.

"A daughter?" Martino tried to cover his disappointment.

Taking a deep breath and saying a silent prayer to the Madonna, Maria handed over her daughter to the man she would know as her father. He held her awkwardly.

"She's beautiful," he admitted. It was undeniable. Surprised by the feelings that stirred inside of him, he sat down so he didn't fall.

"She looks like you."

"Yes, she does." Maria smiled. "Prima thought so too." Prima was in the kitchen, cleaning up the last of the breakfast. Martino nodded to her.

"I wanted a son. Mama wanted a son. But we have a daughter," he stammered. "All right, I don't know what I'm supposed to do with a daughter, but I guess we will figure it out. Right?" He looked to Maria.

"Yes, husband, we will figure it out."

"I have to wash up for work."

He handed the baby back to her, took a deep breath and went upstairs.

Maria turned back to the garden. Little could penetrate the bubble of happiness surrounding her and Donata. Enchanted by the Pink Sweet Peas in the garden, she began humming a tune to the baby. Prima came in with a pot of espresso, and pulled out two cups. "Are you ready for coffee again?"

Maria nodded. Suddenly, she had a taste for it again. Amazing how much could change in a day.

"That garden looks like God sprinkled on earth the very meaning of a baby girl," Prima whispered.

"I know. Isn't wonderful?" Maria beamed.

* * *

When Martino left for work, he noticed that the garden had changed once again. "What the hell is going on? Pink, pink everywhere. I hate pink!" He ran back into the house.

"Oh, husband," Maria started. "Shall I call Mama or would you like to?"

"Tell me how our garden is thriving when Tuscany is in a drought?" Pounding his fist on the kitchen table. Maria looked at him blankly. "Ah, you don't have an answer, do you? Don't worry, I will find out." With that he left.

Prima and Maria looked at each other and laughed. Maria refused to let Martino's indifference spoil her joy. "Prima, I want to play the piano today," she gushed. "This is Donata's first day on earth and I want her to know I'm happy." Prima was delighted by her strength. "But first I want to introduce her to the garden. She should see all the beauty her proud papa left for her." With Prima's help, she rose and dressed in a light shift. Outside, she began walking Donata through the garden, showing her the pretty flowers. She picked a sweet pea and tickled the baby's cheek with it. Maria could feel Stefano with every step she took.

She walked to the spot where Donata had been conceived, recalling the night that she and Stefano slept beneath the *girasole*. She remembered the tulip bed and the willow tree. With Donata asleep on her chest, she relived every moment of their days together in her mind. She knew that the baby could feel everything she felt, and this made her happy.

The walk in the garden renewed Maria. She took Donata to Prima's and was delighted to see that her dear friend had set up a bed for the baby girl next to the piano. Maria placed the infant down and began to play a simple lullaby. The music brought serenity to Donata, Prima and the neighbors in Castellina once again. And there could be no fear of Martino coming over to Prima's and breaking the piano. She could play whenever she desired.

* * *

Down the road, resting in his bed in the Giuliano guesthouse, Stefano heard Maria's music and could not for the life of him stop smiling.

VENTUNO

"Well, my friend, are you ready to go to work?"
Giuliano and Stefano sat sharing a breakfast with Filomena, one prepared in celebration of Donata's birth. The woman cared not at all that Stefano and Maria weren't married. When love bloomed, she felt, it was only right to appreciate its beauty. For his part, Stefano was so filled with love over the birth of Donata that he felt he could heal all of the land in one night.

Giuliano laughed, believing that Stefano's adrenalin was tricking him. "Step by step, papa!" he cautioned. Giuliano wanted Stefano to go from property to property as planned.

In the days that followed, he drove Stefano to all the farms in need so that he could get an idea of how long it might take to restore them. Passing through the thirsty countryside, Stefano was saddened by the damage the drought had wrought. It was much more serious than he realized. Hundreds of properties suffered. Owners were doing everything in their power to be first on the list for Stefano's help. They offered extra money, even portions of land, but Giuliano wanted to be fair. Photographers from the local newspapers accompanied them to each property and took pictures of the withered crops and vineyards. Giuliano and Stefano examined all the properties and chose the most critical to attend to first. Stefano would work his way through all the others.

Back at Giuliano's, reporters began to interview him. One man, who wore a short-brimmed black fedora and identified himself as Dante Deloria from *La repubblica*, asked, "Eh, Singing Gardener what makes you believe you can manage such an enormous job? Do you really think it's possible to bring the land back to life?" Doubt twisted the reporter's thin face.

Stefano considered his answer, then replied, "I know it is possible. Love can heal all things. Combine love with intention and... what you want to happen? It will happen." Pencils scribbled furiously against pads.

Deloria shouted out, "Is it really true that you sing to the soil?" Everyone stopped to listen. The man awaited his answer.

Stefano smiled. "Why, yes, I do."

Dante shouted back, scorn in his voice. "Why would you do such a thing?" Stefano looked at all of the reporters and photographers and did not know how to explain his gift. He turned to the man who had asked the question. "Signore Deloria, is it?" He nodded. "Have you ever had anyone sing to you?"

Dante laughed. "No." The other reporters laughed with him.

"Of course you haven't. If you had you would never have asked such a question!" Stefano went on. "When someone sings to you, just for you, it makes your heart come alive and for that moment, you feel the meaning of your life through song. Song brings hope and inspiration to every living thing. Flowers, plants, trees--all are living, no? I sing to them and they express their thanks by blossoming."

Silence greeted him. They had stopped even writing in their pads. Even Dante Deloria became silent for the moment. Dante was known as ruthless, both in his work and in his life. There wasn't a woman he'd been with whom he hadn't hurt. And when he wasn't working or chasing women, he was drinking. No one who knew him could believe that this loud-mouthed reporter had nothing to say.

After assessing the land, Stefano told the press, he felt that it would take at least a month to accomplish the task. He began that evening.

The reporters and photographers waited outside the first property. Giuliano reminded them not to disturb Stefano or they would be sent away. Stefano began with the largest vineyard in the land. Before the drought, Gianarro Vineyards had produced the very same wonderful wine Stefano had sipped in Florence on the night Giuliano surprised him with the Fiat. He recalled its rich, delicious flavor and the happiness that evening had brought him.

Incanto ~ The Singing Gardener

Walking through rows of dry vines, he blessed the land so that it would bring many more happy moments to others. Stefano pictured the future and then pulled into the very moment through the power of his mind and body and ignited his vision into the soil. He saw all of the people in the region smiling and toasting with the wine that this vineyard would produce after it was healed. He thought of Donata, and how he and Maria might drink a toast to her birth.

Slowly the grapes transformed themselves from shriveled, dried up lumps to luscious ripe globes that would be ready to pick in the morning. The soil bubbled as it became moist again. Dead brown twigs changed into green vines that twisted and turned before his eyes. Stefano walked out of the garden smiling. Rushing in after him, the reporters and photographers were paralyzed by what they saw. Dante Deloria, too, took in the rebirth. Without lingering, or stopping to consider that he was disregarding Stefano and Giuliano's request that Stefano be left alone, he ran to catch up with the gardener. After all, there was a story to be seized.

At the Gianarro vineyard, the other reporters rang the front bell of the owner. Signore Gianarro had not yet gone to bed and now he turned on all of the lights and came outside. Seeing his land, he dropped to his knees and kissed the ground crying with gratitude.

"*E un miracolo!*" The photographers snapped pictures, and the reporters jotted down every detail they could. Signore Gianarro prepared to alert his workers that the grapes would be ready to harvest in the morning.

Stefano had arrived onto the next property, also a vineyard. The family here had suffered greatly and they, too, were in dire need of help. Stefano walked among the rows of grapes, happy as he remembered holding Donata in his hands. The vision of Maria still pregnant as he held his hand on her belly the night before Donata's birth filled his mind. Digging his hands into the earth, Stefano infused it with all of the love he felt for his daughter and began to sing. Dante, who had followed him unnoticed, waited outside the property. He had come for a scoop and nothing more, but Stefano's melodious voice streaming through the evening air melted his icy heart. Looking up to the violet sky, listening to the gardener's song, Dante thought maybe Stefano really was blessed with a rare gift. Surely, the man had a stronger purpose on earth than anyone else he had ever encountered. The song, a haunting aria, brought tears to Dante's eyes. It was the kind of song that made him want to be in love and made him question why he never has been.

Dante was so inspired he pulled out his pad and wrote with an ardent fervor. The other reporters and photographers came running up the road, but Stefano was already done, and he walked out of the vineyard. They ran in to see what Stefano had done. Dante went, too. Once again, the vines had come alive in Stefano's hands, the grapes hanging like jewels, the soil rich and dark.

Stefano visited over twenty vineyards along the road that night and into the morning. He did not tire, for he carried with him thoughts and images of his baby girl every step of the way. Though she might never know the truth about who he was, he wanted to make her proud. Yes, he felt happy to bring life to the decimated vineyards, but nothing had given him more happiness than bringing life to Maria's womb.

Never again would Stefano be the same. He didn't know how he would be able to carry on with the lie without it destroying his soul. The idea of Martino Ricci holding his little Donata, and believing she was his, tore at Stefano's heart. But he stopped himself thinking about it. He knew that he must only think of love now, as anything else would interfere with the work he had to do.

Intrigued by the gardener, Dante no longer cared just about the story he was writing. He suddenly wanted to learn from Stefano. But learn what, exactly? Dante's head spun and he felt almost drunk. But the intoxication was with the possibility of changing his life.

As Stefano arrived at the next vineyard, he realized that someone was following him. He turned to Dante, who stood with his hands at his sides. The man had no notepad, no pencil dancing with excitement across the page. He did not snap pictures. He did not say a word. Stefano stared at him, noting the man's strange blue eyes, and Dante began to cry.

To his dismay, Dante could feel all of Stefano's pain. "Come with me," Stefano called. Together, they went into the vineyard. Dante could not speak, as he glided with Stefano through the rows and rows of staked grapevines, surveying the damage.

At the end of one row, Stefano took his right hand and, asking permission with his eyes, placed it over Dante's heart. Every pain that the reporter had ever suppressed in his life seemed to rise to the surface. Dante fell to his knees and wept like a child. Then Stefano took his right hand and dug it into the soil. He sang a song for Dante's lost years. The reporter watched from his knees as the vineyard restored like a grand illusion. The soil, which had been dry and flaky, now seeped through his pant legs. The vines thrived with healthy grapes and the whole vineyard seemed to be glowing. But it was no illusion. Dante realized that maybe his whole life up to this point had been the illusion.

"How do you feel?" Stefano asked him.

"I—I feel I must change my life." Stefano looked at Dante and sensed a soul longing for its purpose. Stefano put his arm around the man.

"You look familiar," he said. "What's your name?"

"Dante Deloria." He could barely speak.

"Ah, the ruthless reporter."

"Si, *scusi*. I can leave if you wish."

"No. Come with me, Dante. I can see you understand now what I do."

* * *

The reporters all attempted to tell their own version of the miracle they had witnessed. If they hadn't seen it with their own eyes, they would have never believed it.

Each morning, the papers followed the events taking place in Chianti. Quickly becoming a household name, Stefano Portigiani had gained notoriety beyond celebrity. The newspapers sold out every day and the publishers had to double the number of copies printed. Each morning Prima, the Finelli's and the LaPorta's would fight at the local newsstand over who should get more copies, as they bragged about Stefano.

"He's my closet friend." Prima boasted.

"He likes us the most. I know this for sure. Right Tino?" Signora Finelli topping her while her husband nodded in agreement.

"He helped us with our vineyard. You should all buy my wine now. The Singing Gardener touched my grapes." Carlo and Tessa shouted to everyone.

More and more people had become fascinated by the Singing Gardener, enchanted with fabulous tales they yearned to believe.

And Dante Deloria? He had not handed in one story since meeting the gardener. It had been two weeks and his editor was furious. The only reporter in the entire bunch that had written nothing, Dante had jeopardized his job. The editor threatened to fire him if he did not produce a story soon. "What's wrong with you, Dante?" the man shouted at him. Dante shrugged. He couldn't explain what was happening to him. "You pick a hell of a time to take a vacation!"

Giuliano, too, appeared in the papers everyday. As the hero who found Stefano, he had been paid handsome sums for the restoration of the properties. Giuliano continued to build Stefano's bank account to assure him security and stability for the future.

One day, Stefano took Dante into a field that produced olives for the finest cold pressed virgin oil in Tuscany. The drought had caused such a thirst that the prettiest olive branches were now decrepit and starved. The olive branch, symbol of peace and forgiveness, could hardly stand for much at all in such a state. Nor could it produce the delicious, rich olive oil that made this land famous. Stefano lifted a branch and, brittle, it easily cracked in two. Dante watched him and waited.

"Stefano," he said. "I'm so sorry I doubted you and mocked

you." Stefano just smiled at him. "I'm lost." He looked to Stefano for help.

"No, my friend, you are finally found! It's just that you're unaccustomed to the new feelings that stir inside of you."

"They want me to hand in a story on you, or I'll be fired."

"So do it." Stefano did not understand the man's dilemma. "Isn't that why you've been following me all this time?"

"No." Dante tried to explain. "Well, at first yes, but then when I heard you sing I no longer wanted to write about you. I wanted to... *be* you." They both laughed. "Well," Dante went on, "At least to feel what you feel, and know what you know. I want to change the world like you do. Can you help me find a purpose?"

"Let's see what we can do." Stefano made everything sound simple.

"It's not that easy, Stefano. My whole life has been a waste and now I've met you and I can't go back."

Singing, Stefano took his hands and extended them over the olive branches. They began to sway in the wind. Dante watched the olive fields explode with life before his eyes. Stefano broke off one of the restored olive branches, its silvery leaves shimmering in the light, and offered it to Dante.

"Forgive your past. From now on, be true to yourself."

Dante took the branch hoping it would guide him to an answer.

"Write your story," Stefano went on, "but not to win or be the best. Write it because you can't keep it inside of you, and you need to express the truth. Write from your broken heart and expose the vulnerability that a man experiences, but denies because he is afraid of being judged. Make the world believe in song again, and how it can heal even that which is most damaged. Use your gift to change the world, Dante. Don't rob us of your eloquence."

Dante went back to his hotel room that evening and found himself writing like never before. In the past he had manipulated his stories to serve himself, to create gossip and appeal to the devilish nature in all his readers. On this night his hands shook as he typed. The truth of his experience with Stefano bled onto the page. He wrote of the songs that had begun to change his life and heal the soil of Italy. "The drought in Chianti has saved my wretched soul. If not for this misfortune I may have never been blessed with the bounty that the Singing Gardener has taught me to claim. It cannot be bought or sold or won, no, this wealth comes from so deep inside one's soul that it is God in the truest sense. As I witnessed this simple and beautiful man love the land, it turned from black and white to color, from despair to hope and from dead back to life. The grapes, olives, flowers and soil respond to his touch, his love, the way a crying baby would when given it's mother's breast. My life has meant nothing until now. I can see so clearly when I stand beside this mage who vows to heal the land with no expectation of receiving any reward except to make all living creatures thrive. He claims no credit for his deeds, but turns to God and is humbled to be a channel for his gift. In his presence I realized my life has been a sham and I strive to be half the man Stefano Portigiani is." That was only the beginning. There was so much more to write and yet he realized no words could ever describe the experience he was witness to. Writing relentlessly, his hands did not belong to him. Finally, finishing his last sentence as the sun came up, he smiled.

Reading over what he'd written, though, Dante felt a pang of fear. This was not a typical news story. He had not followed prescribed structure, had, in fact, broken every rule. The story had none of the biting edge he'd become known for. But Dante decided that he would hand the story in and risk being fired. He went down to the head office at the *La Repubblica* and, with shaking hands, gave the pages to his editor. He remained unshaven and had not slept in days, but his eyes were gleaming. The editor looked at him and began to read the front page to himself. "I pray that we can all find a little piece of the Singing Gardener inside of ourselves," he read.

Before finishing, to Dante's great worry, the man excused himself. The truth was he locked himself in the bathroom so he could finish without crying in front of another man. It was the most beautiful thing the editor had ever read. Not only did he want to run the story, he wanted more.

The next day, *La Reppublica* published Dante's story with a picture of Stefano on the front page. The paper sold more copies in any day in its history. Prima bought fifteen, Giuliano twenty, and the Finellis bought out one entire newsstand as they fought with the LaPorta's, finally they decided to split them equally. All of Italy was buying copies up, even saving them in plastic because, no doubt, they would be worth money someday. Dante had once again become the envy of every reporter, but this time it was different. His colleagues admired not his ruthlessness, but his bravery.

When the editor called him in for a promotion, Dante thanked the man and regretted to say he had to quit. "But I don't understand!" the man protested. "You can't go now."

Dante felt tired of fighting for stories, fighting for angles. He wanted to find something to be passionate about. All of his senses had been rejuvenated and he wouldn't go back. He could smell the gardens, hear the birds sing, and see all the beauty around him. But most of all he could feel his heart, which had been closed for so long, beginning to open.

His editor urged him to reconsider and pointed out the record-breaking sales, but Dante was not moved as he might have been in the past. He did not even get excited when his story won the award for best story of the year. None of it mattered to him anymore. He promised himself that the only writing he would do from this point on would be for passion and never for money or fame.

* * *

After Martino left for work, Prima brought a stack of papers to Maria. She would not dare come when Martino was home. After all, he was furious about all the attention being paid to his former gardener. He felt that Giuliano had robbed him, and became bitter whenever someone mentioned Stefano's name. Martino suffered from Maria's rejection and even though he was married to her, he felt she didn't belong to him. To avoid any further damage to his heart he turned cold and distant to both Maria and Donata. He stayed out late every night and did not even try to touch his wife anymore. He slept in a guest bed and left the bedroom to Maria and the baby. He could not get past the gut wrenching feeling that this child might not be his.

* * *

Maria read the newspaper as she nursed Donata. Despite herself, she began to cry.

Prima scolded her gently. "That's bad for the baby, *Bella*. Smile instead! Doesn't he look handsome?" Prima held another paper up, showing off Stefano's picture. Maria touched his face.

"Yes, very handsome, as always." Donata's little hand reached out for the paper, too. Maria smiled. "Papa, that's papa." She took the baby from her breast and, handing her to Prima, began to weep uncontrollably.

* * *

Little by little all the vineyards, crops, and farms in the land were restored. When only one property remained, Stefano invited all the reporters to come and watch. This was a plain brown truffle field studded with poplars, worth its weight in gold when fertile. The owner could hardly contain his excitement that the land might be healed just in time for truffle season, and that all would be able to enjoy the delicious enhancements that truffles provided even the simplest dish.

Giuliano and Dante stood on either side of Stefano as he committed himself to this last bit of soil. He realized it had been a month since he held Donata in his arms, a month since he'd gazed into the endless green of Maria's eyes. He did not know what he would do when this work ended. It had kept his mind off of his hopeless situation.

Just as he was about to begin, and wondering where he might draw the power to heal the truffle field, a familiar figure made her way to the front of the crowd. Wrapped in her widow's black as usual, Prima had come to watch Stefano's last 'performance'. His heart beat with joy at the sight of her dear face and she came to him and kissed him on both cheeks.

He whispered in her ear, "How is she, Prima?"

Prima pulled him in and whispered back, "Donata saw her father in the newspaper this morning."

Stefano felt happy and sad all at once. He looked down to the needy soil and grabbed Prima's hands, knowing that they had just been touching Maria and Donata. She did not protest. He felt the spirits of the two he loved most in the world pulsate through Prima and he began to sing a sad, sweet melody. The reporters watched as Stefano plunged his arms deep into the earth, reaching to the truffles planted deeply in the soil. He begged the earth to rejuvenate. He lifted his arms and spread them high up into the sky, tears streaming down his face.

The truffles began to grow, little balls of precious flesh bursting to the earth's surface.

But for Stefano, another ending had come. What would he do now? Stefano could not bear all these endings. He thought of the day she had left his cottage. He was doomed, it seemed, to long for the one thing he could not have. No longer able to take the pain, he cried to the heavens and begged to be set free.

All of the reporters watched him moan like a wounded lamb. His pain was contagious. After all, the entire village had grown to love Stefano as he selflessly healed their land and they could not bear to see him in so much agony. His grief became their grief. All of the people in Chianti began to weep with him and in that moment, the sky cracked open. An electric bolt and drums of clapping thunder exploded in the atmosphere. The clouds released the first rainfall in months, drenching Castellina and surrounding villages.

"*Pioggia*! *Pioggia*!" the people called out, laughing now and crying at the same time. Everyone danced in the truffle field and complete strangers hugged and kissed each other like old friends. The cameras flashed and pens flew across the page, but no photograph or news story could ever capture such a moment. The only ones who would ever know exactly what happened that day were the ones standing right there in the mud.

VENTIDUE

The drought in Tuscany had changed the course of every life it touched. Out of desperation, the people had put their faith in a man, in a dream. In return they had witnessed a miracle. And the man himself? He, too, had changed.

Stefano continued to work with Giuliano and their business grew more successful than ever. After all that Stefano had done, produce he touched came into in greater demand. His legend grew. He was becoming wealthier, business better and better. Still, he felt completely empty inside. Or should it be said that he felt too much? Indeed, he walked through his days full of love, but with nowhere to place it. Stefano was torn. He did not want to cause Maria or Donata strife, but he could not understand how Maria stayed in Martino's house with their child. How, day after day, did she manage to pretend that everything was fine? Divorce was unheard of, especially in Italy and God forbid if you were Catholic. Yes, were she to go with him, she would suffer gossip and scorn, but such trifles they could overcome. At least he believed they could. What Maria believed, he could no longer say.

Stefano's heart was not turning away from Maria, but for the first time he began to think of himself. He needed to be held, to be touched and cherished the way that he cherished her. With each and every day his patience grew thinner. Donata's birth and the drought had taught him that he could not live any longer with such thirst. If Maria was unwilling to quench it, he must find another way to drink. Or die.

Although he did not say a word of his pain to anyone, Stefano had become thinner and weaker. All day long he would sleep in the garden under the fig tree, curled up like a baby in his mother's womb. Soon, he grew unable to work and could not seem to make anything blossom.

Giuliano watched his friend wither with each passing day. Stefano would drive to the Ricci residence during the day, sit outside the garden and observe gardener after gardener try to tend to Maria's sanctuary. But the ground, which seemed to sense lack of true love, suffered terribly. Stefano hesitated to put anymore of his affection into Maria's garden, and he had stopped coming at night.

Prima, seeing Stefano from her window, knew that his wound cut deeper and deeper. But she could not intervene. She met with Giuliano and Filomena. They all prayed for a miracle to come and mend Stefano's heart. Filomena had made dinner and Giuliano went next door to invite Stefano. He knocked on the door of the guesthouse but no answer came.

"Stefano, please!" Giuliano began to fear the worst. "Prima's here to see you!"

After a pause, the door opened and Stefano looked at him and nodded wearily. He followed Giuliano to the kitchen and kissed Prima listlessly on both cheeks. She had brought a special bottle of wine, which her host uncorked and poured for all of them. Stefano drank it freely and hoped that she had chosen well. Now he wanted to be relieved of the grief that swallowed his heart even if it meant forgetting Maria. Actually, he was praying it would erase her from his memory all-together.

Prima didn't tell him that she had chosen this vintage from the deepest reaches of her cellar, one of the oldest bottles she had. It was meant to protect a broken heart from further damage. The love in which Stefano had invested so much of his soul was but a moment in time that would never be again. But he would always have the memory. Prima hoped this wine would help him to accept the reality of his situation and find the will to carry on even through deep disappointment. Giuliano and Prima waited until the wine had sunk into Stefano's body. Prima grabbed his hand firmly. He knew she was about to give him news that he dreaded.

"Stefano, you must move on from Maria," she said.

Stefano shook his head and set down his glass. Giuliano

Incanto ~ The Singing Gardener

grabbed his other hand. "Stefano, we're worried about you. Maria has Martino and Donata now. She's settled in her life. She has no intention of changing it no matter how much she loves you." Giuliano found it difficult to express the truth, but he wanted to be a good friend. Pretending could do Stefano no good.

Stefano pulled away. He knew that his friends were right. But only he could decide if he should move on. Maria and Donata owned his soul. They were the reason he was born into this excruciating world of turmoil. He could not yet accept that he would never be able to freely love either of them the way his heart desired. No, he would not accept it. Giuliano and Prima watched Stefano struggling. As Filomena's food grew cold before them, Stefano wept. "But I know she loves me."

"Yes," Prima answered. "But in this world love is not the only thing that brings two people together. And it is certainly not what keeps them together."

Stefano shook his head again. "How can there be anything else?"

No one knew what to tell him. Stefano drew his own conclusions in the silence. Maria offered him nothing but pain and sadness. She offered no hope of a future for them and their daughter. She spoke only of all the reasons they could not be together. He wondered what had happened to the woman he'd made love to over and over in the tulip bed, under the sunflowers, and in the willow tree. Where had that woman gone? Had she not been with him sharing in a love like no other? Yes, he knew, she remained with him in her heart. But she wouldn't fight for their love now the way he had hoped, the way he himself was willing to do. He dropped to his knees.

"Why, why, why? Why did God flavor me with her taste and then turn my tongue to bitterness? Why did he let me sink into her green eyes and then drown me with sorrow?"

Giuliano and Prima lifted him up, and Filomena fussed over him with a glass of water, but Stefano could not be consoled.

Giuliano tried to stop him from leaving, but Prima held Giuliano back. "It will be settled in the eyes of God," she whispered. Stefano ran out of the house and into the orchard. He looked up at the darkened sky. They let him go.

    On his knees, he asked God, "Why is life designed to break your heart?"

    He went to his fig tree and hugged its bark, begging it to take away the ache that burned like a fire in his heart. Stefano's weary body was ready to fall into the earth and be swallowed up for all of eternity. The curse of loving Maria had become more than he could bear. He looked up at the moon and she was not glowing on this very night, but hidden behind the dark clouds. He cursed her for hiding her light from him. He fell to the earth and into a deep sleep.

VENTITRE

Days later, under an exacting sun, Stefano labored in Giuliano's rose garden, each petal of each bush seeming to wither in his hands, a stabbing in his heart like a thousand thorns. Suddenly, a shadow loomed over him, blocking the light. Looking up, he thought perhaps his eyes were playing tricks on him. A nun in full habit appeared to be standing above him.
"Sister Camilla?" he gasped.
"Stefano, it's been so long." She held out her arms.
"I can't believe you're here." He rose from the soil and, wiping his brow, embraced her tenderly. "I thought you were an angel. I was afraid I was seeing things."
"Well, I hope you'll think I'm an angel after I tell you why I'm here." She laughed. Age had not changed her features, but laugh lines had etched themselves deeply in the corners of her bright eyes.
As they walked under the pergola to find some shade, Sister Camilla thanked Stefano for all of his letters and kind donations to the orphanage. "Mother Giloria and I followed your successes and we always kept you in our prayers and hearts," she said.
"How is Mother Giloria?" Stefano asked, recalling the stern face and loving heart of his other guardian.
Sister Camilla lowered her head and emotion trembled in her voice. "Mother passed away just recently," she said "She went peacefully. And you should know that she was so proud of you, that you have used so well the gift God gave you." Deeply moved, Stefano found his manners and offered Sister Camilla something cool. When she accepted, he went inside and came back out with a *limonata*. Sipping the drink, Sister Camilla told Stefano the reason for her visit.
"I had a letter from Signore Mancinelli," she began

"A letter?" Stefano thought this strange. The Mancinellis had always been regular visitors to the nearby orphanage, dedicated parishioners. Why would they need to write her? "Is he all right?"

"Oh yes. He and his wife have gone to America!" she said.

"America?" Stefano gasped.

"Yes." Camilla went on to tell Stefano that Signore Mancinelli had taken his wife to an estate on the Hudson River in New York. He was pursuing new business opportunities there. But the couple had not been able to find help they could trust. His wife yearned for the gardens in the villa they had left behind. Would Stefano consider returning to work for them? The Mancinellis would pay all his expenses to come to America.

Stefano realized that he had been asking God for a sign. Was this his answer? His mind raced with a million questions. Maybe he should leave this place. Maybe if Maria knew he was leaving she would be forced to finally make a decision, and choose him. He had an opportunity to go to America, an endless pain in his heart, and the woman who had been like a mother to him asking him to go to a family that had already given him so much. Any place would be better than here, he thought. Every corner of every property reminded him of Maria. Each sunset reflected her smile, all the birds sang her name, and every flower held her scent.

"I will think about it, Sister," Stefano said. "Thank you."

* * *

That night, Stefano shared the news of the opportunity with his friends over a simple dinner of *spaghetti aglio olio*. He felt nervous, not wanting in particular to abandon Giuliano. At first, he could see, they were stricken at the thought of him leaving. But the Giulianos felt that this could be a blessing, as did Prima. The three of them knew that staying in Castellina would kill Stefano.

"You'll be missed. But you should do it Stefano," Giuliano urged. "America holds so many new opportunities. Our work together is done. And there's nothing here for you anymore, only ghosts."

"Colombo!" Prima exclaimed, "Go discover America! There you can begin a new life."

* * *

The night Prima told Maria that Stefano would be leaving in two days, the young woman felt the walls of her house pressing in around her. Her heart raced like never before and, holding Donata closely, she ran into her ruined garden, frantic for a sign of what to do. From the hollow of the willow tree, she took the ring he had given her. Reading once again the inscription, she sobbed and threaded it onto a chain she placed around her neck.

She would go with him to America. How could she do otherwise? She had been a fool to try and separate herself from him. They were already one.

She took Donata to Prima's. "We will leave with him," she exclaimed. "Oh, Prima, do you think he will have us?"

Prima, rocking Donata in her arms, looked at Maria curiously. "Of course he will."

Together they planned how Maria could pack up a few things for herself and the baby that night, how she could meet Stefano at Giuliano's and escape. "Martino hardly ever comes home before midnight," Maria told Prima. "That will give me time to see my father one last time. We can pack and go before my husband even suspects I'm gone."

* * *

That night Martino came home earlier than usual. Maria was not there but he found Angelina preparing dinner in the kitchen. Coming up behind the young girl, startling her, he demanded, "Where is my wife?"

"I don't know, sir," she answered meekly. When he grunted in frustration, she felt compelled to add, "She sent word that she didn't need me tonight, but I came anyway."

"Why did you come anyway?" Martino asked her. This was something strange. As far as he knew, Maria always needed the extra help Angelina provided.

"Well, sir," Angelina answered. "Forgive me, but I could not do without the wage. You know, like that time you went to Rome?"

"What about the time I went to Rome?" Martino was breathing quickly now, dread spreading through his chest.

"Why, that time you went away to Rome. She told me not to bother coming to work."

Martino was shocked. His mood turned black.

"So you didn't work while I was away?"

"She said she was sick and that you wanted to save the money."

"Hmm," Martino managed.

"But I thought it was strange."

"What was strange?"

"Why she didn't ask that gardener to stay away as well. After all, I could have helped her in the kitchen. What could he do for her?"

The blood seemed to drain from Martino's face.

"Signore Ricci, are you all right?" Angelina asked, putting out a tentative hand toward his face. "You don't look so…" Abruptly, Martino pushed her hand away and darted to the sitting room. Opening the armoire, sweat pouring from his brow, he tried to control his trembling hands. Mixed with his anger was the wound of betrayal. Obsession had captured his mind and all he could see was his Maria, his wife, sleeping with that fool of a gardener. But who, really, had been the fool?

He opened the drawer and pulled out his pistol. Angelina followed him. "I knew it!"

"But what are you doing, Signore Ricci?" she screamed.

"Get out of here," he shouted. "Now!" Terrified, Angelina ran out the front door. It closed with a slam.

* * *

Martino waited for hours for Maria to return. He knew she would be back. All of her things were untouched, as were

Donata's. When she came through the door, humming, he sat at the kitchen table with an empty bottle of brandy before him. Donata lay asleep in her mother's arms.

"Oh! Martino!" she gasped. "You're home early."

She kissed him on the cheek, but he did not respond. Her heart was sticking in her throat and she felt panic seeping into all her limbs. She began to stroke Donata's hair nervously. "She was such a good girl tonight, but I think she missed her Daddy." She smiled at Martino, but he frowned in return. Not knowing what else to do, hoping he might go out again, she put Donata to bed. When she walked down the staircase, Martino was waiting. He lunged for her, knocking her to the floor, the pistol in his hand. Maria screamed, but he covered her mouth.

"You listen to me. I can kill you right now, but you're the mother of my child, so I will spare you. But what if it's not my child?"

"What's happened? What's come over you?" Maria sobbed, fearing she already knew the answer.

Martino brought his face close to hers and hissed. She felt his saliva on her skin. "If I ever find out that it is true, then I will kill you and your precious gardener."

Maria trembled beneath him. She prayed he wouldn't notice the chain around her neck

"But I promise you this, wife. If I ever hear about you even seeing him again, I will kill him. Do you understand?"

Maria froze and Martino slapped her hard across the face.

"I—I understand."

* * *

The day dawned and Stefano, who had never known of Maria's plan to come to him, felt an overwhelming longing to see her and his daughter. He knew no good could come of it, but he couldn't stop himself. He was leaving his homeland, the land that he had loved and nurtured, the land where he had fallen in love. He had to see Maria and Donata one last time.

He walked up the road and past the Ricci residence, careful to note that Martino had gone, and approached up the cobblestone driveway. Maria saw him coming from her arched window and panicked. God forbid anyone saw him! If Martino got word, he would surely murder Stefano. She grabbed Donata and rushed outside, but Stefano was walking away from the house.

Surveying the ragged edges of the topiary and the absolute lack of flowers in the garden, Stefano's heart sank. He realized that it reflected what remained between him and Maria. Walking over to where the sunflowers used to be, he found nothing but a memory. Then, from behind him, the baby's laugh caught him by surprise. He turned to find Maria standing like a figure in a fresco, Donata wrapped in her arms. Maria smiled, but tears followed quickly.

Stefano found himself paralyzed upon seeing their faces, speechless. Maria handed him their daughter. Gently he drew Donata to his heart, pressing her little chest to his, feeling her tiny heart pulsating. She gurgled and smiled a big, happy smile.

"She knows her papa." Maria covered her mouth and turned away, breaking into tears. Her eyes darted across the way, nervously checking to see if the Finellis or the LaPortas were watching. Mercifully, she saw no one.

Stefano kissed Donata's tiny nose and then her forehead and each cheek. Tears streamed down his face. Donata opened her mouth with excitement, cooing happily.

"You are wrong, Maria," he said. "She does not know who I'm. She never will know me." His heart broken, bitterness came through in his voice.

Maria kept her eyes on Donata and avoided catching Stefano's gaze.

Grabbing her arm, he turned her to face him. "Tell me, Maria," he went on, "please tell me that I was not alone in my feelings." She kept her eyes down. "What about the time that we shared? Was it not wonderful?"

"Yes it was full of wonder," she whispered. "Magical. I felt things I have never felt before…and will never again."

Incanto ~ The Singing Gardener

She held her stomach, pulled her arm from his grip and, gathering Donata from him, tried to walk away.

"So I offer you a love unlike any you have ever known," he pressed, ignoring her distress. "But you reject it! Instead you embrace the indifference, arrogance and lack of respect that your husband offers you?" Stefano raised his voice. If only he could wake her up! "How can you stay here and live with this man and pretend that this is your child together? I don't understand how you can betray yourself. And you betray me Maria, and Donata."

With that, Maria pulled herself upright and gathered Donata more tightly in her arms. The baby began to cry as Maria marched away from him.

"Maria, please don't walk away from me."

But she would not stop.

"I gave you my heart and you took it. Why? Why would you trick me like that if you had no intention of being with me? You can't play with a man's heart, Maria."

At this, she stopped, turned, and cried out, "I didn't play with your heart! I meant everything I said. I felt every thing you felt." She began to run. He chased her. With the baby in her arms, she could not go very far.

"Maria, you know that I'm leaving for America tomorrow."

Maria stopped and turned around. "Yes, I know, Stefano. So why come here now?" she was screaming now, unable to contain herself. "Why don't you just go and leave me forever! That's what you're going to do. You'll never return!"

The commotion had caught the attention of the Finelli's and the LaPorta's, but neither Stefano or Maria seemed to care.

Maria cried, her sobs mingling with Donata's.

"I would not be leaving if you chose me," he shot back. "But I can't stay in this purgatory anymore. My soul wants nothing but you, yet you keep yourself in a prison of your own making. Choose me Maria and I will stay here with you and Donata forever."

Donata's eyes widened and her cries subsided. Stefano stood

before them both, completely surrendered. "Or better yet, you can come with me. We can start a new life in America. Nobody knows us there. Please look at me, Maria. Why won't you look at me?"

"Because, Stefano," she said quietly, keeping her eyes on the ground, "If I look at you I will fall apart for eternity. You must go. Please, Stefano, leave before it is too late."

"Maria, I don't understand. Please, what is it?" Desperately, he tried to reach her. He put his hand on the baby's soft cheek, then on hers. She pushed it away. "Look at me, Maria."

"No." She shook her head back and forth as if hypnotized.

Gently, Stefano took Donata from Maria's arms. He brought the baby to Prima's door and, when his friend opened it, asked her to watch Donata for a moment. Prima obliged.

Angrily, Stefano strode back to find Maria on her knees by the willow tree. "Maria?"

"Please, Stefano don't make this any harder. You'll never understand. It's complicated." She would rather save his life than tell him the truth. She stammered, "This is my home. I can't just leave, and I can't stay in Castellina with you. I would shame my daughter, my husband and myself. No one would ever look at me the same way again. The guilt I feel is already eating me alive. I've sinned. I have committed adultery, and I know God will punish me."

Stefano lifted her up and held her face to his. "Look at me, Maria! Please."

Finally, she looked into his eyes and melted into hazel.

"I can't Stefano," she murmured. "Please. It's out of my control." She closed her eyes, fighting the desire welling up in her like an ocean. "I'm too weak when it comes to you. This was never supposed to happen. We should have never done what we did. No, this should have never happened." She said it over and over, as if trying to convince herself.

"But it did happen, Maria," he countered. "You can't pretend that it didn't. It was our destiny. You have to face that. But what happens now is up to you. We are in love, Maria, are we not?" He put his face close to hers and his sweet breath covered her. "I know I'm in love with you," he whispered.

She grew weaker and weaker, and could no longer fight. She opened her eyes and locked them on his. Her entire body collapsed in agony. She fell down to the soil and Stefano joined her. Together, they wept under the willow tree. She saw in his eyes everything she could ever want and all the feelings she tried to forget stirred up, gripping her like a vice. She began to run her fingers through his wavy hair, to kiss his face everywhere.

"Oh, Stefano, why does it have to be this way? Why?"

Stefano kissed her mouth. Only her lips could quench him. In that kiss, they recognized that all the feelings they had for each other were as alive as ever. Nothing would ever be able to change the fact that their bodies belonged to one another. Maria could fight it and deny it but it made itself known in their kiss. For a moment she forgot about the neighbors. This would be their last kiss. She let herself indulge.

"Please, Maria," he murmured into her hair, "Don't let this die. I have never felt anything like this in my life."

"Nor have I, Stefano." Her body ached for him.

"Then be mine, and let me be yours, now and forever," he whispered.

"How, Stefano? I don't know what to do." She couldn't tell him about Martino threatening to kill him. She knew Stefano would stay and fight. She couldn't risk his death. She was trapped.

He pulled away. "That is all you have to offer me, still? You don't know what to do?"

"Please don't get angry, Stefano," she pleaded.

"Maria, just answer one question for me and this will be the last thing I ever ask of you. Will you leave Martino and be with me?" It took all the courage he had to ask.

Maria's body recoiled as if she were going to be sick. He watched her struggle, and this alone broke his heart. The answer should be so simple. Choosing love seemed like the only way. She looked up at him and held his eyes in hers. Neither of them had ever looked sadder.

"I cannot leave Martino, Stefano."

Disappointment washed over Stefano like a wall of water, drowning him.

"Then I must take my heart back from you now, Maria," he said, his voice cracking. "You've had it for so long, but it is no longer safe in your keeping."

His words pierced her like the thorns of a rose and he hated to hurt her. But maybe saying this aloud would give him the strength to reclaim his heart. "I must go now." He turned from her and walked toward Prima's. She watched his long, lean body drift away from her like a phantom. Sickness spiraled up, and she turned into the willow, sobbing.

He did not turn around. How could he? Stefano walked lifelessly into his Prima's warm kitchen.

"Look, Donata, it's papa," Prima prodded. Stefano's eyes told Prima everything she needed to know. Donata looked at Stefano and released a happy gurgle like a song. Stefano gathered his baby girl in his arms and held her tightly.

"Donata, I must go, my angel." His voice cracked. "But I'll never truly be gone." He felt like a liar. America was a world away. He pulled the baby in to his chest one last time and whispered into her ear. "I don't want to leave you, Donata."

He could not bear another moment. He kissed Donata over and over and then handed her back to Prima. Then he kissed Prima on both cheeks. "Forgive me, dear friend. I can't make sense of anything right now."

Donata grabbed at his wavy hair. Stefano buried his head into Prima's shoulder for a moment and then, uncurling the baby's little fists, ran from the house. He ran down the road that he had traveled every day, his legs moving faster than they ever had.

The LaPortas watched him running and, turning to each other under, they cried for the pain they witnessed in the garden. Signore Finelli watched the gardener fly by and waved to get his attention,

but Stefano did not stop running.
He ran as if to extinguish himself.

* * *

That moonless night, feeling his way in the dark, Stefano walked back to the garden he knew so well. Like a ghost, he approached the willow tree and, resting his hand on its mighty trunk for strength, set something inside it and turned away. Maria, Donata beside her, stirred in her sleep but did not wake.

Trish Doolan

VENTIQUATTRO

In New York, despite a short growing season and stubborn soil, the Mancinelli estate was quickly becoming famous for its beautiful gardens. Inside the estate the rooms were filled with Italian hand carved furniture, sculptures and artwork that made Stefano feel somewhat at home. Dark hardwood floors extended throughout the estate, with imported silk area rugs to accentuate the shade of each room. Signora Mancinelli insisted on having each room painted a different shade and picked colors as rich and bright as Portofino. She had imported as much of Italy into New York as she could. Several maids and a butler tended to the home regularly. It had been many years since Stefano had last seen Signore and Signora Mancinelli. They had grown even more alike and finished each others sentences as if it were once voice speaking. Now, both grey and more wrinkled, they moved a little slower, but still had that familiar sparkle that Stefano had grown to love, shining through their eyes. What he admired most was their great love and appreciation for each other. They had brought their chef from Italy with them and everyday made sure that the help was fed properly and happy so that they may do a better job because of their good treatment. The chef was always creating masterpieces, as classical music from the great masters streamed through the radio. The kitchen was constantly flowing with food and an intoxicating aroma that brought Stefano an inexplicable comfort.

 Signor Mancinelli and his wife had welcomed Stefano with open arms, and, sensing his broken heart, urged their favorite young gardener to make a new life in America. "There are many beautiful women here, Stefano!" Signore Mancinelli told him one day as they walked the grounds of the large estate, the river shining like a satin ribbon at the property's edge. Stefano nodded into the kind, round face of his *padrone*, but his heart never wavered from

Incanto ~ The Singing Gardener

Maria.

He could not seem to shake the grip that she had upon his soul. She haunted him in his sleep and drifted through his spirit when he was awake. Each night, lying in the single bed in his quarters in the carriage house, he prayed before resting his head on the pillow. He prayed for God to help him move on from her and take away all of his memories. But love was not kind. Love was a slow and arduous death that suffocates the heart, beat by beat. It had fed him with a delusion, he saw now. He had been satisfied for a brief moment in time, but that moment cost him the rest of his life.

Signora Mancinelli loved to entertain and people of all backgrounds came to visit the Mancinelli estate. Plenty of women expressed their interest in Stefano. But Stefano would not let himself fall in love again.

The butler for the estate, an enthusiastic young Frenchman the Mancinellis had hired on a whim, took a liking to Stefano. He had been in America for only a few years more than the gardener, but took it upon himself to act as Stefano's guide. "There are places in the city a man in need can go," he told the heartbroken Italian. When Stefano shook his head, the man insisted. "*Mon ami*, we are only human."

So from time to time, Stefano began taking the train to the city, his hollow face reflecting in fast-moving windows. He wandered streets in Hell's Kitchen looking for tenderness. Little gratification and a thin sense of comfort could be found in the company of the women paid to take away men's loneliness. His eyes searched theirs to find Maria's green gaze. He sniffed their skin and turned cold with disappointment. His fingers traveled along their bodies, searching for Maria but never finding her. None could compare to her, and he always left lonelier for trying.

Only one woman captivated him body and soul. In the end, he found it more satisfying to touch himself and imagine Maria. His days were full of work. He wanted to make sure that Signora Mancinelli was happy and felt at home when she looked at her garden. So he found every flower and plant that reminded her of Italy and made it a point to create a masterpiece garden. She was delighted with his presence on her estate and he was grateful for the task. Unfortunately his nights seemed to go on for eternity and each night felt like a year. The only time Stefano could visit Maria was in his dreams. When he woke to reach for her the only thing he could collect, in his outstretched hands, was the air.

* * *

Though he did not know it, Maria shared each and every feeling Stefano had. Despite the thousands of miles that separated them, they remained connected, their souls intertwined. Stefano could not share his torment, and vowed to never speak Maria's name aloud again. Just hearing her name caused pain. Stefano cursed the day that he laid eyes on her, and then felt thankful he'd been allowed to love so deeply. He surrendered to the fact that love like theirs came around once in a lifetime. His time had come and gone and that window was now closed. To live without Maria meant to live without love, and to live without love was meaningless.

He longed to return to Italy, but could not be there if he could not be with her. Summer loomed and Maria's birthday was coming. He wanted to surprise her, to touch her somehow over all these miles and passing time.

* * *

On June twelfth, nine months after Stefano had left for America, Martino left the house without a word to his wife. These days, he could hardly be bothered to smile at Donata. Maria took Donata to Prima's to drown herself in one of her sinful *torta's*, hoping to push the pain down a little with something sweet.

"Prima, I am such a fool. How can I have let him go? Shoveling *torta* into her mouth. "I am dead and nothing else matters. I should have let him kill us both with his pistol. It would have been easier than this hell we are in."

"Maria, you did the right thing." She covered her hand

delicately, but her eyes were betraying her words.

"Have I Prima? If you were me would you have let him go? Would you have let Paola walk away if the rest of the world told you that you should?" There was no answer from Prima. "I am wracked every day with regret. Each day I feel a little piece of me dying, a sickness eating at me like vultures." Maria grabbed her stomach. "It is my birthday and all I can do is curse the day I was born." With that Donata let out a healthy cry.

"You have much to live for my friend and much to look forward to. There are surprises waiting for you if you just let them happen." Prima smiled.

When a large truck pulled into Prima's driveway, her neighbor rushed to Maria's front door. She knew from Giuliano who had ordered this delivery. Stefano had written to his old friend for help in fulfilling a promise.

Maria came out with Donata in her arms, and Prima smiled and welcomed the movers. They ripped off the canvas cloth in the back of the truck, revealing a shiny black grand piano decorated with a huge red bow. Seeing it, Maria felt a thrill up her spine. But she quickly dismissed the feeling. Did Prima have a secret admirer?

Handing Prima an envelope, the men unloaded the instrument. "Where shall we put this?"

Prima led them into her dining room where the other, upright piano had stood for many years. "Can you move this one next door and put the new one in its place?"

The deliverymen looked at each other. Moving an old piano was more than they had bargained for. But when Prima indicated a fresh cherry *torta* on the counter, they agreed. When the moving was complete, they left with the pastry in hand.

"Who has sent you such a beautiful piano?" Maria asked her friend, handing the baby to Prima and running her fingers along the smooth black wood.

"Silly woman, don't you know?" Prima pressed. "This is from Stefano. And it's not for me it's for you! *Buon Compleanno*,"

Maria sunk to the piano bench and rested her cheek on the keys. Her heart swelled. Prima led her to the table and fed her a second cherry *torta* and espresso. Then she opened the envelope and read Stefano's letter aloud.

"Prima,
I trust that you are well and know that you are always in my heart, as I feel I'm in yours. Life is unpredictable! Who ever thought I would be in America? I miss your kind face. I long to sit in your kitchen again, to relive the comfort your home always brought me. I've enclosed a letter for Maria and Donata. Please give it to them. Also, you will find some money. Make sure Maria buys a present for the baby."

Prima finished and then turned to the next page. "This one is for you." She handed it to her friend.

Maria trembled. "Please, Prima, read it to me. I can't." Prima nodded and began,

"For Maria,
Burn this if you must, but before you do please burn the memory of these words into your heart. There is so much I long to say, but shall not say it all, for I do not know which way your heart turns at this time. I have words buried deep inside of me, words you will never have to hear unless you ask me to share them with you. I do not want to cause you harm or confusion. But after seeing you in the garden, the last time we met, I realized that you were torn. I believe that no matter how much damage your husband has caused you, there must be a part of you that loves him or you would have been able to choose me. It's been hard for me to accept your choice because the answer seemed so clear to me. But I am learning not to believe everything I see, not to trust everything I feel. Life is not what it seems and life is not the same without you.

I have a comfortable existence here, but the truth is it is killing me not to be with you. It kills me not to see Donata's smile and watch her grow. America is a place where everything is new and the people are as innocent as children. Yet nothing here moves me since I cannot share it with you. Nothing is real to me, sweet

Incanto ~ The Singing Gardener

Maria, but you. I reflect on the days we shared together and your beautiful fingers dancing along Prima's piano keys."
 Donata had fallen asleep. Maria rocked her and wept as Prima continued.
 "For your birthday I wanted you to have your very own piano and make love to it the way you made love to me. Whenever you play these keys know that I'm singing a song to match your music, and together our hearts will be dancing across the garden. Come to me, as you always do in my dreams. I will always be happy for the love we shared and I will never be happy for the love that we've lost. Play, Maria, with all of your heart and teach Donata the meaning of music.
 Oh, my love! I know I shouldn't ask again, but I must. Please come to me, find me. We will forgive all of the past."
 Forever yours,
 Your Gardener"
 Maria placed Donata on the little bed Prima kept for her and walked over to her new piano. She wiped the tears from her eyes and, ripping the big red bow off with a mighty pull, sat down at the black and white keys and began to play. She touched the keys with confidence and created a song that grew from her love for Stefano. Prima swayed to the heavenly music while Maria played, stirring up all the passion she had been suppressing. She surrendered to the keys and let herself make love to him in that moment, on her birthday, through the music.

* * *

 Maria did not burn the letter. She sat in the arched window for hours, reading it over and over again. She went up to her bedroom to hide it. Looking around her room, she searched for a safe place. She settled on her lingerie drawer and shoved the envelope far into the back. There it would remain.

Trish Doolan

VENTICINQUE

Maria found solace in the piano and it lifted her heavy sorrow. After Stefano left, she had not touched piano keys. Now Donata looked forward to her time at the piano with her mother, and had even begun to play on her own. Now there were two pianos for Maria and Donata to practice on. The two spent more time at Prima's than in their own home.

One day, Giuliano went to Prima's and was happy to find that Maria and Donata were enjoying the piano. He pulled Maria aside. "Here is the address you asked for," he told her. With gratitude, she smiled into his eyes. Late that night, when Martino lay snoring in the guest bedroom and Donata slept peacefully, Maria penned her reply.

"*Dearest,*

I cannot thank you enough for my beautiful birthday piano. I have been playing every day and hope that you are singing lyrics to accompany me. Donata has been learning to play, too. She's a natural. You would be so proud of her. I don't know how much I can say in this letter or if I should even be writing at all. I can offer you nothing right now but my thanks. But please know that I'm dancing on the magical keys that you gave me. And write me again if you can bear to.

All of my love,
Maria"

Receiving the letter weeks later, Stefano sequestered himself in his room in the dark carriage house and opened the envelope carefully. Though she had not said much, he felt a surge of hope. She could offer him nothing right now, she said. But maybe later, in just a little bit of time, that could change! He wrote back immediately to tell her that he was waiting for her, that there was still no one else in his heart but her and Donata. He wished she had

Incanto ~ The Singing Gardener

said something about seeing him again, or being together. He sent his next letter through Prima, telling Maria it was safe to say whatever she wished. With baited breath, he awaited her next letter.

The day his letter came to Prima's, Donata had just taken her first steps, walking from the piano bench to her mother's arms. Maria and Prima were clapping for her, spinning the baby girl around the room, when the post came through the door. When Prima put the letter from America in Maria's hand, she trembled. As she read, her mind had begun to churn with possibilities. A window had opened in her heart, and she felt she might breathe sweet air again. It was a new day, full of hope. Like a child excited to give her first Christmas gifts, she wanted to send him special treats. She bundled Donata up and went with Prima into town. They wandered from shop to shop, giddy, buying chocolates, books and small records. Maria hoped he had a phonograph to play the romantic songs Maria picked especially for him.

The next day after Martino left for work, Maria and Donata walked through the gate to Prima's. There, in the warm kitchen of her best friend, after sipping espresso and nibbling her breakfast, Maria said a silent prayer. Prima took Donata into the sitting room to play piano. As her daughter tinkered with the keys in the next room, Maria blessed herself and, a great heaviness leaving her body, began drafting the perfect love letter. Losing herself and all sense of time, Maria wrote and wrote.

It took weeks for her to formulate her words of love. But she didn't care. She felt as if she were building a work of art. She added poetry, pressed dried flowers into the growing pages, and set down lyrics to songs she had written hoping someday he would sing them to her. Finally, she was ready to send the package. She asked Prima to bring it to the post office, to be safe. God forbid one of the postal workers told Martino that his wife was mailing a package to America. He might kill her after all. Prima added a letter of her own and handed the package to the postal worker in

Castellina to be shipped to the Mancinelli estate in New York.

* * *

The package never reached him.

* * *

Stefano was trimming the rose bushes in the east garden one day when he saw the round figure of Signora Mancinelli bending to smell the full, colorful blooms. "*Buongiorno*, Signora," he greeted her.

"*Buongiorno*, Stefano," she replied wistfully.

He could hear the sadness in her voice and could not help but ask her if everything was all right.

"Oh, Stefano, it's my mother," she said. "I heard from home today that she is crossing over soon. How I long to return to our home there—you remember it well, don't you? I can close my eyes and still hear the sound of the surf and smell the air so fresh! "She took a deep breath in. "I need to be with her. America is nice, but there's no place like the place you were born, *vero*?"

Stefano knew just what she meant. When the next day Signore Mancinelli sat him on the leather couch in the study, shared a cigar, and told him that they would be selling the estate here and returning home for who knew how long, the gardener was not surprised. For the Mancinellis, family had always come before business.

"Please, come back with us," Signore Mancinelli implored. "You know our gardens at home better than anyone, and my dear wife will need the solace of their beauty at this time."

He paused. Might Maria be ready to receive him? Her letter, though sweet, had given no indication of this. And no reply had come to his latest letter months ago. His heart had formed its own scars now. Though dearly tempted, Stefano knew he couldn't risk being any closer to Maria when she might still not want him.

"I'm sorry, Signore," he told the kind old man, "Maybe some day. But for now my fate is here."

* * *

Incanto ~ The Singing Gardener

Within a month, the estate was sold and, since no reply had come from Maria, Stefano convinced himself that her last note had been only a cordial thank you for the piano. He, in his yearning, must have read too much into it. She was indecisive as always. He took her silence as a message for him to carry on and forget.

Months passed and Stefano had found work with a new family. When their garden flourished, he moved on to another job, and then another. In this way, from year to year he buried himself in other people's gardens. His name became synonymous with beauty, but he refused positions that might lead to public recognition. Moving often, he never let himself become attached to any one place or person. Only the flowers knew him well.

In Castellina in Chianti, Maria awaited a reply to her heartfelt package and her letter, which unbeknownst to either of the lovers, had languished first in the sluggish hands of the Castellina postman, then in the cargo hold of a slow ship, for months. When she did not hear from Stefano, she assumed the worst. He must have found another love. She had come around to him too late. Well, she thought, sobs racking her body, didn't she deserve what she got?

* * *

Stefano decided he would never return to the soil that he loved the most. He did not try to contact anyone in Castellina in Chianti again. It would simply be too painful. He wanted to erase his life in Italy. In America, tending to other people's gardens and never his own, he lived like a monk, as his hair began to weave in threads of grey. His hazel eyes that once shone with hope now were outlined by crow's feet leaving their imprint and framing his sadness.

* * *

As Donata grew older, Maria tried her best to go on and be the best mother she could be. Always making sure Donata had all the things in life that she herself missed out on. She watched her garden die a little more each day, the death of her own soul swooping toward her like a predator.

Martino had given up on the idea of a son, and even told Mama Ricci to stop pressing for one. Maria's body began to wither, and she too began to turn grey. He had become a politician in Siena, well known for false promises and expensive campaigns. This also meant that he left the house earlier than ever, and returned even later. Martino, less discrete than ever about his drinking and cheating, hardly saw Donata. The little girl never felt his affection. How could she? He was incapable of expressing himself. Martino wanted to be able to love Maria and Donata, but he did not know how. The fig does not fall far from the tree, and all Martino's life, his mother had done nothing but dictate what he should do. She'd never given him tenderness of any kind. He never mentioned his suspicions about Maria and the gardener. His ego would not allow him to. And when he was home, he barreled around screaming and banging into things, without ever really knowing why. Donata tried to pretend that she didn't care.

The girl found comfort at Prima's, becoming an accomplished pianist. One day, she opened her mouth to sing, a simple song of love, and Prima clapped, her eyes lighting up. Donata had inherited her father's gift, a voice of pure gold.

Donata tried to bring happiness to her melancholy mother and was sometimes able to bring a sparkle to Maria's eyes. When Donata sang, Maria forgot that the love of her life had left her, or did she abandon him? The truth was it didn't matter whose fault it was anymore. The end result was that the two people who belonged together more than anyone in the world were apart and that is all! Wise beyond her years, Donata knew her Mother suffered from silent demons. Try as she might, she could not penetrate the thick walls that kept her mother secret. Thanks to Prima, though, Donata never sank into melancholy herself. "Your mother loves you dearly," Prima told her. "It's just that her anguish is stronger than her joy."

Every night, Donata knew, her mother would walk in the garden and cry. The soil, as dry as dust, grew nothing but weeds.

Incanto ~ The Singing Gardener

Martino did not care anymore. He knew that the garden would never be the glorious haven it once had been. "Why should we bother spending money on a ruin?" he said. It didn't matter to him that the garden brought Maria happiness. In fact, this also served as her punishment for his suspicion that she had been with Stefano.

Over the years, Donata watched her mother wandering the barren garden and felt helpless. There is nothing worse than living with regret and Maria was filled with the constant reminder of her fear to choose love. The only plant that remained strong? The willow tree.

* * *

One wet November evening, Martino had just left one of his women. Drunk as always, he climbed behind the wheel of his new coupe and began to drive, struggling to keep his eyes open. The sleepier he got, the more heavily his foot pressed the gas pedal. He raced through slippery streets. Suddenly, oncoming headlights were beaming brightly into his face. His eyes widened in horror, as, slamming on the brakes he careened into a divider, spun out, and crashed into the oncoming car. His face hit the steering wheel as blood gushed from his nose.

The other car smashed in on itself like an accordion. Shattered glass and specks of blood littered the street.

Martino stumbled out of his car and approached the car he'd hit. Inside, he saw a family of three. A father, a mother, and their young son, who had been asleep in the back seat. Martino passed out on the road.

When the two cars collided, the noise had alarmed everyone in the area and other cars stopped on the slick road to help. Giuliano happened to be driving home when he heard the terrible crash. Pulling up to the scene, he stopped and ran to help, and was stopped in his tracks by what he saw. The father, covered in blood, turned to see if his son was all right, but the boy's head was crushed, and the impact had killed him. His eyes turned upward in his head, his small mouth gushing with blood. The boy's father moaned in agony, and then turned to his wife, who remained unconscious, but alive. The father cried, reaching out to touch his son's body.

Giuliano approached him, "Don't move! I'll get help. Don't move!" He ran to find a telephone. When he looked over and saw Martino's car on the other side of the road, Giuliano's heart sank.

* * *

Maria and Donata had gathered at Prima's to play the piano and finish off one of Prima's *tortas*, pecan with chocolate sauce. Donata had just turned seventeen that August and was growing into a beautiful young woman. She had begun to talk of studying music in Rome, and she dreamed of a career in the opera, though she had told no one of her idea. Maria was repeating for her an intricate phrase on the piano when suddenly a loud, rapid knock came at the door. Prima answered it only to find Giuliano standing on her threshold, a worried look on his face.

"Is Maria here?"

"Yes, she's inside with Donata." She invited him in. When Maria saw her old friend, she stopped playing. Donata's pure voice carried the last line of the song without accompaniment, and she stopped, confused. Following her mother's gaze, she took in the figure of Signore Giuliano in the doorway. He looked as if he'd seen a ghost.

"I was just in town and there's been...an accident," Giuliano stammered. The women waited for him to finish. "Your husband was driving drunk, and he crashed his automobile."

Maria did not feel surprised. Indeed, she noticed that she felt relief. Donata watched her mother carefully.

"Is he dead?" Maria asked, her tone matter-of-fact.

"No," Giuliano replied. "He's in critical condition in the hospital. But there's more."

Donata was confused. She didn't feel much of anything and realized Martino, her father, was a stranger to her. She thought of Mama Ricci and imagined how upset her grandmother would be if

he died. But this was as close to worry as Donata could come.
Giuliano continued. "Martino killed a little boy."
"Oh my God!" Maria cried out. "So he is a murderer after all!"
Prima quickly blessed herself and, at this, Donata began to cry. What did her mother mean, 'after all'? And why did Martino have to be her father? She felt shame just knowing that she shared his blood, then a pang of guilt for having such thoughts.
"*Bastardo*! He should die!" Maria looked at everyone and, realizing what she had said, covered her mouth and blessed herself. Nobody said a word.
"The boy was twelve," Giuliano went on. "The press is all over the story. They say that if he lives, Martino will surely be removed from office." Giuliano got up and took Maria's hands in his.

* * *

Martino remained in a coma for several weeks, but the doctors gave no hope of recovery. When he died, Maria felt nothing. She tried to muster some tears when she saw Mama Ricci at the funeral, but the truth was, she felt tired. She had spent her whole life pretending and did not want to pretend anymore. Mama, distraught, blamed Maria for Martino's drinking and cheating. "You could not satisfy him!" she kept crying. "If only you had been able to keep him happy at home." Finally, Maria could hold back no longer.
"Your son finally got what he deserved," she yelled, stopping the funeral procession, not caring what anyone thought. "But not before he robbed an innocent boy of his life and ruined their family forever. And not before he robbed me and my daughter of our lives." She spit on the ground.
Maria's behavior shocked some, but anyone who knew the truth was glad to hear her finally speak it. Mama Ricci shook her head and raised her hands to her ears. She took Donata aside.
"Donata, your father was a good man. He loved you very much." She held her face with her hands, as she wept.
"Really? I never felt it." She stared coldly into Mama Ricci's

eyes. "I hardly every saw him, but when I did he was always threatening my mother."

"That was because your mother deserved it my dear." She assured.

"No she didn't. No one deserves to be treated the way he treated her. And honestly Nonna I cannot remember even having one conversation with my father and that's the saddest part about this day." She removed Mama Ricci's hands from her face and walked away.

They gathered at the gravesite. But when her mother nodded that it was time for Donata to sing the song she had practiced for the funeral, she found she could not sing. She had been singing joyfully the night she learned her father was on the edge of death and had felt nothing. Guilt and confusion churned inside of her, strangling her voice. Mama Ricci shot her a look of pain, as if Donata had set out to do her harm.

Silence hung heavy in the air. Prima patted Donata on the shoulder and whispered, "It doesn't matter."

As Maria threw the dirt onto the coffin, she realized she had been praying for this day to come for years. Finally, she was free from her prison, but so much damage had been done. Damage that had been building and growing inside of her like a twisted vine since that day so many years earlier when she'd said goodbye to Stefano.

VENTISEI

In spring, Maria had become very thin and Prima and Donata, home for Easter from her studies at the opera in Rome, grew quite concerned. Maria had lost her color, and felt exhausted every day without any cause. Prima and Giuliano arranged for their friend to be seen by a specialist in Siena. "Me, see a doctor?" Maria protested. "Why? I didn't even see a doctor when I gave birth to Donata!" She thought they were all overreacting. It was not until she saw the silent plea on her daughter's face that she agreed.

The hospital ran a serious of blood tests and x-rays and asked Maria to return in a week for the results. Maria, Donata, Prima, and Giuliano all went together like a family to the large, modern building. Maria joked and made Prima promise that they would all go back to her place after to celebrate her clean bill of health with some wine when this was done. "Donata will play the piano and sing for us. After all, she'll be going back to Rome soon. We must have her perform before she's too famous to indulge us!"

Donata blushed. Her mother knew that, ever since Martino's death, despite her dedication to music, she suffered bouts of nerves that stopped her from singing and kept her in supporting roles, though her voice was better than so many of the leads. Still, Maria never stopped having faith that Donata was a born star.

"Of course we would love to hear Donata sing," Prima said, glancing at Giuliano, who shook his head. "But do you think you'll be up to a celebration after the long drive home?"

Maria smiled and answered lightly, "Of course!" Nervously, they all agreed it would be a wonderful idea.

The Doctor sat down with them all in a small white room. He laid the X-rays on the lit screens. "Are you her family?" Giuliano and Prima nodded. "Well," he said. "Well." Maria's father had died years ago and her sisters were never heard from after they left

Castellina.

"Well, out with it, doctor. I'm an old woman and shouldn't wait too long for anything," Prima pushed.

"Maria," the doctor said, looking only at the X-rays, "You have cancer."

Donata gasped. "Where is it?" she managed. Prima and Giuliano put their hands on her shoulders.

"It's everywhere. She's probably had it for quite some time." He took a stick and pointed to several tumors that had built up over time, originating from no one knew where. "Slowly, they are eating away the healthy cells."

Prima was on the verge of tears and Giuliano could hardly contain his shock. Donata had gone pale as a sheet. Only Maria seemed to have surrendered. She almost smiled when she heard the word, *cancer*, as if she already knew. Donata collapsed into her mother's chest and cried. The doctor spoke about treatments and remedies, but also explained that she probably didn't have much time.

Maria thanked the doctor and, smiling, addressed her loved ones cheerfully. "Well, we made a deal. Let's go back to Prima's and celebrate."

The doctor, pulling down the X-Rays, was writing prescriptions on a notepad. Prima, Giuliano and Donata could only stare at Maria, speechless.

"Don't look so surprised. I don't have much time to waste. Please, take me home."

They returned to Prima's, met by Filomena, who kissed Maria on both cheeks. They were all despondent except for Maria. As they entered the house, Maria sat at the grand piano and attacked the keys with vigor.

"Come, Donata, sit by me. Let's play." She smiled into Donata's big, sad eyes. "Prima, open one of your famous bottles of wine. I'll drink anything tonight. Surprise me!"

Prima went to the basement and, staring at her wine collection, began to cry in earnest. She could not imagine life without her best friend. She never dreamed she would outlive Maria and had never wanted to. Scanning the scalloped wooden shelves that lined the walls for a miracle elixir, she despaired. Nothing here could heal Maria. "God takes souls to His breast when he chooses." She whispered to the wine bottles as her voice cracked with despair.

Then a bottle with a bright label called to her and she pulled it from its place with a cry of satisfaction. Yes. This was the one. It would not cure her friend, but it might help Maria just a little to live the remainder of her life happy and with no more regrets. Prima wished that Maria might escape the pain and suffering that goes along with illness. She wished for her to feel only love and for her to let Stefano back into her heart, to celebrate the love they shared together.

Prima held the bottle, crying and laughing. Giuliano came down to check on her.

"Are you all right, Prima?" he asked. When she nodded, he looked at the bottle she was holding and then questioningly, back at her. "Are you sure that's the one you want?"

"Oh, yes."

He nodded, then rested his head on the cellar wall and began to cry himself. "She's so young."

Prima held him and tried to be strong. "I know, but I guess she's ready or else she wouldn't be leaving us."

Giuliano looked at her curiously. "Do you really believe that?"

She smiled softly. "Yes, I do. I hate it, but I have to accept it. But I'm worried about Donata."

"Thank God she has you, Prima."

Prima grabbed his hand. "Now. Let's stop this gloomy talk and celebrate."

Prima and Giuliano joined Maria and Donata by the piano. Mother and daughter sat playing a lighthearted duet. Prima uncorked the bottle and poured four glasses of red wine.

Maria stopped and smiled. "Ah, did you choose something special for us tonight?"

Prima smiled. "Yes, you could say that."

Maria looked at her friend with curiosity. She knew Prima well enough to know that something hid behind her words. Raising her glass, Maria's eye caught the label on the bottle. Painted yellow and black, it was covered in hand-drawn sunflowers. A chill went up her spine. She looked more closely at the label. Reading it, she exclaimed, "I didn't know you made your own wine, Giuliano!"

"Oh, Filomena and I, we experimented a little for a time. Some bottles came out all right." Giuliano laughed and studied the label carefully as if remembering a precious day. Maria, too, ran her hands wistfully over the sunflowers.

Maria raised her glass to toast. "Here's to life! It's not always what you thought it was going to be, but it's full of surprises." Recovering herself a bit, she said, her voice full and rich with love, "I feel lucky to be sitting here with four of my favorite people in the world." She touched Donata's cheek gently, as tears ran down to meet Maria's fingers. "I have the most beautiful, talented daughter anyone could have ever dreamed of." She turned to Prima. "To the best friend and neighbor in the world, to her magical wines…"

"You never know what you'll get when you swallow!" Giuliano laughed. They all joined him.

Maria smiled and addressed the Giulianos. "And to the sweetest couple in Tuscany, who have always shown me kindness I will never forget."

She held up her glass, as did they all. Fighting tears, they tried to let Maria be in the happy place she wished to be in. "Because of all of you I have had a blessed life and I shall have a blessed death." She moved her glass into the center and they all joined her, touching the glasses together to seal the toast. Maria took a sip of the wine.

She closed her eyes and let the rich, fresh taste swirl in her mouth. Her eyebrows rose in surprise. How could a wine taste of sunflowers, tulips, lilies and roses? How could it taste of him? She could not help but let out a groan of pleasure as she swallowed and

Incanto ~ The Singing Gardener

the beautiful memories permeated her body.

"*Delicioso*," Giuliano admitted. "Thanks to our gardener." Filomena nodded. She remembered the grapes they had harvested from the field that had once been filled, so long ago, with Casablancas. Stefano had already gone to America as they harvested, but his power had still surged through the earth he'd once touched.

Maria sat back down at the piano and played. A wave of sadness welled up in her, but Donata thought she should wait until she was alone to have her feelings. She hated pretending, but wasn't it more important for her mother to have fun than for her to fall apart and spoil the moment?

As the night progressed, Maria became more and more affected by the wine. She turned to Donata, watching her daughter and listening intently as she sang a soft, low aria. Donata noticed how intensely Maria stared, almost as if she were looking through her. Prima and the Giulianos sat listening to the song. Maria stopped playing and sat in silence as Donata finished a cappella. Donata smiled, and Maria saw Stefano smiling back at her. He was standing in front of her in the form of their beloved daughter.

"You look exactly like him." Prima and Filomena looked at each other. Giuliano cleared his throat nervously. Maria went on. "You have his eyes, his smile and his voice. My God, his voice!" Maria began to weep, but still she felt happy.

Confused, her daughter responded, "Mama what are you talking about? I never looked like papa, and he didn't sing."

Maria starting laughing, and Donata gave her a puzzled look. Prima and the Giulianos stood up to go into the other room.

"No, please I want you all to stay," Maria asked them. "You're family and I need you to help me." They all sat, as Maria began to tell her daughter the story of her and Stefano. Prima poured the last of the wine for everyone and went into the basement to crack open a different vintage, this time one for stamina. They had a long night in store.

Drawing herself up straighter in her seat, Maria told Donata the story of how she was conceived, and how in love she and Stefano had been. "You were created out of pure love and that is why you are so special."

Donata did not know what to say. She had not felt special. She looked around her at Prima and the Giulianos. "And all of you knew?"

They nodded.

"Martino and I were never meant to be," Maria tried to explain how she'd felt she had no choice and settled. "Don't ever do such a thing, Donata. You will know your true love when you see him. Don't let him go. And never deny love in any form, even in your work." Now she became emotional. "Never choose money over love. I believed because Martino was wealthy he would provide a better life for you. How wrong I was. I blame myself, not him. It wasn't his fault, but his mother, *Dio Mio*!" She laughed through her tears and they all joined in.

Maria told Donata about the garden and how Stefano had come to her, both of them knowing they were meant to be together. She told the young woman, too, of the many obstacles that had been in their way. "It was I," Maria said sadly, "Who was the biggest obstacle."

With so much to tell Donata, it could not be done in one evening. Maria had opened the door so Donata could get to know her real father through stories before she passed on. Maria wanted to be honest about everything, even if it hurt Donata, because she felt that she deserved to know the truth. She wanted her to know her father, and that he was still alive somewhere, and had always loved her very much.

Donata rested her hands on the piano for balance. At first she didn't know how to feel. Her mother had betrayed the man she was married to, and betrayed her by keeping the truth hidden all these years. That was hard to swallow. But as the night went on and Prima and the Giulianos added their own stories of Stefano and all of his powers in the garden, Donata began to realize why Maria

Incanto ~ The Singing Gardener

could not have told her any sooner. All things in their season. She realized that she felt relief. Martino and Mama Ricci were not her flesh and blood. A tension in her throat began to ease. Perhaps it was time to find her true voice?

* * *

In the weeks that followed Maria spent most of her time with Donata. She shared all of her stories about Stefano, lingering especially on the details of his love for their daughter, the pink sweet peas, the rain after the drought, and the way he had held her heart to his the last day he saw her. "He is your flesh and blood no matter what," Maria said.

Everything had become a little more difficult for Maria, who was growing weaker each day. Her body failing, her spirit nonetheless soared. Talking about Stefano brought her so much joy. Reliving the memories with Donata was the best medicine she could have.

One night, Maria asked Donata to sleep in her bed with her. She went to her dresser drawer and reached deep into the back, pulling out the hidden letter.

"Read this, darling," she said, and Donata fell upon each word. After she had folded the letter and put it back in its place, Donata longed more than ever to meet her father. She was falling in love with him a little more each day, with each story. With her mother, too.

"I don't want you to leave, Mama," she cried. "We're just getting to know each other." She buried her head in Maria's thin chest.

"I know *figlia mia*, I'm sorry that I have to go, and I'm so sorry we didn't share like this before. But let's squeeze it all in as quickly as we can so that we don't miss out on one single moment together." Maria laughed and tickled Donata. They hugged and cried all through the night and Maria held her as if she were a young girl again, in a delicate embrace. "Oh my beautiful Donata. Your father named you the moment he saw your face." Donata smiled as she drifted to sleep dreaming about meeting the man that created her.

When the morning sunlight hit Maria's eyes, she was surprised to find that Donata had gotten up already. She made her way downstairs to the kitchen. A pot of strong espresso and an apple *torta* sat on the table, evidence that Prima had already come. But no one could be found in the house. Where were they? Maria looked out her arched window, and could not believe her eyes. Her lifeless garden was filled with workers. Amidst the men, Giuliano stood with Filomena, Prima, Donata, the Finelli's and the LaPorta's.

Maria didn't know whether to laugh or cry. Pulling her robe tightly around her, she went outside to greet them. Carlo ran up to her with a loaf of bread. "Please, try, you will be happy I promise." Maria broke off a small piece and sampled it. "Carlo, it's delicious. I mean it! At least you got it right before I died." No one knew whether to laugh, but Maria broke out so they all felt comfortable to chime in.

Guiliano grabbed her hand. "Now listen, it will never be the way Stefano had it, but let's get it into shape for you." He kissed her on both cheeks. "What are your favorites? I'll have them plant anything you want."

Maria began to cry. Donata held her. Maria walked through the garden, picturing in her mind's eye the way it used to be. She walked over to the spot where the tall sunflowers had protected them as they made love. "Sunflowers right here, lots of them," she said, smiling a private smile. She turned to Donata and whispered, "This is where you were conceived. Right in this spot." She hugged her daughter tightly.

Giuliano ordered the workers to come over to where Maria stood.

"I want sunflowers here! As many as you can fit. I don't care if you have to go rob them from somebody. I want them here by tomorrow morning."

Maria laughed with delight as she held Donata's hand. She

stopped in another familiar spot.

"Tulips here, all different kinds. My God there were so many, all different colors!" she said. Turning to Donata, she added, "I had no idea there were so many different kinds of tulips until he showed me." Giuliano marked the spot. "And the corn field he made so high to protect us."

"Ah ha, there was a cornfield." Turning to Elena, Finelli gloated. "You see, I knew all along."

"I'll find tulips for you." Giuliano promised. They walked around the property all morning, as Maria tried to recreate the garden that she once had and loved. She remembered how much joy just the mere sight of it used to bring her each morning. It would be nice to feel a little of that again.

Maria grew tired. She and Donata went inside to lie down.

"Where is he, Mama?" Donata blurted.

"In America."

"Why don't you contact him?"

Maria sighed. "I tried, believe me. After the letter you read, I sent him a thank-you. He sent another letter back and I, I replied. But..."

"But what?"

"He never answered." Maria began to cry. Donata held her.

"When was that, Mama?"

"Years ago. You were just a little girl. I can't blame him."

* * *

Maria found that it was getting more and more difficult to get out of bed. The cancer was growing, eating away at her time. One morning, she made her way down to her arched window. Prima and Donata waited for her with a morning pastry and espresso.

Maria looked out and saw the garden. It had been dead for so long, but now Giuliano had pulled off the impossible. All of Maria's favorite flowers had been replanted. The dark faces of the sunflowers seemed to smile as they wished Maria a good morning. The array of tulips swayed gently in the light breeze, and multi-colored roses were lined up in attention. Daffodils, tuberose, birds of paradise, hydrangeas, stargazers, orchids, peonies and gerber daisies. Oh, and the Casablancas! Giuliano assured her more would come. Grateful, Maria suddenly felt very much alive again. She called Prima and Donata to her.

"I do have one request, but I don't know if it is possible." She grabbed Donata's hand.

"Tell me, Mama, what is it?"

"I would love for you find your father and bring him to me before I die. I want to see his beautiful face again. I want to hear him sing once more. I want him to sing to me." Tears welled in her green eyes.

Donata jumped up. "I'm going to find him, Mama. I know I can."

Prima chimed in. "Maria, how will she do that? The address Giuliano gave you is nearly twenty years old. He's no doubt moved on from there.

"Go to San Salvatore, first," she told Donata. "Look for a nun, Sister Camilla, she'll know how to reach him."

"Then it's settled. I will go. I'm going to find him Mama and I'm going to bring him back to you, and to me." Donata determined to do it, but she cried through her conviction. "I won't be long. I promise. I'll call you every day."

"I have plenty of money I've been saving for I don't know what," Prima broke in. "But you take it, Donata. Find your father and hurry back." There wasn't much time.

* * *

Preparing to leave, Donata felt torn. She didn't want to miss any days with her mother, but wanted to grant her last wish. The Giulianos, seeing her off, had given her money to travel. Donata could not believe everyone's generosity, but they assured her it was nothing in comparison to the gifts that her father had given them and everyone else in Castellina.

"I will bring him home to you." Donata smiled at her mother

and then at the rest of them.

San Salvatore still functioned as an orphanage, and young boys were playing soccer on the grounds, young girls squealing at jump rope, when Donata arrived. The buildings, though covered with crumbling plaster, had a pleasant air about them. She entered a side garden and prepared to meet Sister Camilla, who, she learned from the housekeeper who received her, had become the Mother Superior.

Donata sat on a stone bench and tried to imagine her father as a boy, tending the beds of irises, winding the grape leaves through the pergola. A cardinal flashed red as it darted from a rose bush to a tree branch, and Donata looked up to see an old nun in full habit approaching her. She rose. The woman came to her immediately, her skirts brushing the stone walkway. As Donata started to introduce herself, Sister Camilla greeted her with a calm, knowing smile, extending her two hands and taking Donata's hands in hers.

"*Cara mia*, I know who you are just by looking in your eyes. You are Stefano Portigiani's daughter." Sister Camilla beamed as Donata admitted it was true. The nun did not seem to care about the circumstances of Donata's birth. She took the young woman to the same dormitory where Stefano used to sleep, then to the study where she conducted the business of the orphanage. Sister Camilla told Donata stories about Stefano, how he had a gift in the garden apparent from a young age, how he had been the kindest boy she'd ever known. These stories made Donata proud to be his daughter, and hungrier than ever to meet the man responsible for her existence.

Donata told Sister Camilla what brought her to the convent and how she must find her father in America.

Nodding somberly, the nun went to a cabinet in the corner and pulled the letters he had sent over the years. "Your father always donated a part of his salary to the church, so that it would continue to thrive. He never forgot how we saved him through the kindness of the parishioners offerings." Donata poured over every word, noting the familiar curve of his handwriting—so like her own. But the letters were brief, filled only with cordial greetings and general descriptions of his life in America. What was worse, they had no return addresses. The last letter Sister Camilla had from him was over a year old. Donata tucked the envelope into her pocket hoping it could somehow help her find him. Then the nun showed Donata the newspaper clippings of the drought, with pictures of Stefano healing the land. Dizzy with information, Donata needed to take a breath. Sister Camilla sat in the garden with her. "And the people he first worked for in America?" Donata asked her. "Are they still in the same house?"

Regret filled Sister Camilla's brown eyes. She explained that the Mancinellis had returned to Italy, and that both of them had passed away in the same year. "But go to America," the nun told Donata. "Your faith will help you find him."

As she drove the winding road from San Salvatore to Castellina in Chianti, Donata reflected on the twisting paths that had kept her from knowing her father. She thought of all the wasted years her mother had lived and fear gripped her heart. Was she in the same danger? Her life in Rome was a safe one. She dated now and then but seldom saw the same young man more than twice. The truth was, she hesitated to share her thoughts and dreams with any one person, and pretended to be content when her date told her of himself, his life, his dreams. The same was true in her work. Hiding in the wings, lost behind the costumes and swelling music of the opera, she did not risk expressing herself fully.

Yes, she decided, she would go to America and look for the man who had once made her mother so happy.

VENTISETTE

Donata bought her ticket for New York, agreeing to return in one week with or without Stefano. In the meanwhile, Giuliano nurtured Maria's garden more each day, while Prima, Filomena, and Maria sat watching from the arched window.

Arriving at the airport in the city, she hailed a cab and, not knowing where else to start, had the driver taken her on the hour-long journey north to the Hudson valley address of the former Mancinelli estate.

Arriving in a light rain, she saw that, as expected, the sprawling property was under new ownership. A placard with the name of an American family had been erected at the open gate. Donata drove in and parked in front of a carriage house. She asked the yellow cab to wait. Walking to the front door, she knocked on the solid mahogany and looked around her at the grounds. She tried to imagine her father tending the plants and flowers in this enormous place. When an older man in formal butler's dress opened the door, she informed him that she was looking for the Mancinelli's former gardener, Stefano Portigiani. "I have come from Italy," she told him.

The man paused and then nodded, but she could not tell if he recognized the name or was merely being polite.

"I was hoping that someone here could help me find him," she went on. Having been ushered out of the rain into the black and white tiled foyer, she saw that she was dripping rainwater onto the floor. "I—I am his daughter." The butler looked at her closely and pursed his lips. Then he bowed and asked her to wait.

"I'm sorry," he said, coming back to her in the front foyer carrying something under his arm. He spoke in a thick French accent. "He left no forwarding address, and it has been so very long."

Donata glanced around at the pristine surroundings. Everything looked new and clean. From the large paned windows, she saw that the gardens were straight and sharp. No signs of Italy here. No signs of her father. Her heart sank, but she thanked the man and turned to leave.

"Mademoiselle?" the butler stopped her.

"Yes?"

"Can you wait a moment? I may have something to help you." The butler indicated to Donata the package he was holding. It was wrapped in paper that had yellowed with age. Reading the label on the box, he asked her, "Do you know a…Prima D'Amato?"

"Of course," Donata answered, surprised, "She is like a second mother to me. Why?"

"Well, I have worked at this estate for twenty years, under the employ of different owners, including the Mancinellis. This package came from her for your father, many years ago. I put it in our storage room. I hoped he would visit again." Donata searched his face and found a wistful look there. "But he did not return. The package never reached him, but maybe it will help you."

"Thank you." She smiled at the butler, took the parcel and left. In the car, she was tempted to open it, but stopped herself. Instead, she vowed to find the man it was meant for and give it to him.

* * *

The cab took her into the nearby town, which had little to recommend it but its perch above the river. The sky loomed gray and dark and she checked into a bed and breakfast, where she was shown to her room by an older woman bright blue eyes who identified herself as the owner. "And where are you from?" The woman asked politely. Donata told her she was from Italy, and the woman opened the door to the room with a nod. Sitting on the single bed, Donata racked her brain. She tried the phone book, but no Portigianis were listed. Where could she find him?

After a fitful sleep, she woke to another gray day and came down to breakfast. The small, papered dining room smelled of

Incanto ~ The Singing Gardener

lilies, and Donata noticed a splash of color in each of the vases on the tables, beautiful bouquets of fresh flowers in an array of whites, violets, yellows and reds. Inexplicably, she was cheered.

"What beautiful flowers," she remarked to the owner, who was laying a plate of eggs, fruit, and homemade bread before her.

"Oh you Italians certainly know your flowers!" the woman laughed.

"I thought we were supposed to know food," Donata answered, smiling.

"Maybe so, but the man who brings me these, he's Italian, too," the woman went on. "And I don't mind telling you, I have a little crush on him. He delivers once a week and at the end of the week the flowers are as fresh as they were the first day. Since he's been bringing me flowers, my guests have never once complained about a thing. I think he's put a spell on them!"

A chill ran up Donata's spine.

"This man," she said, her voice full of air. "Can you tell me…who he is?"

"Well, his name is Stefano Portigiani," she said. "I believe he told me he's from Tuscany."

"Can you please…" Donata felt she might faint. "Can you please tell me how to find him?"

"And why would you want to know that?" the woman asked, suddenly suspicious.

Tears welled in Donata's eyes. "I'm his daughter." A pause lingered in the air. "Do you have a number for him? An address?"

By some miracle, the woman didn't fight her. She didn't object that this information was private. "He doesn't have a phone," she said. She studied Donata's face, went to another room, and came back with an address written on a small piece of paper.

"Thank you," Donata breathed. "You're an angel."

"No," the woman said. "It's your father who's the angel."

* * *

Donata drove up one crooked street and down another, arriving at a modest Victorian with geraniums of every color wilting in every window box. When she knocked on the door, she was greeted by a sour-faced landlady. "He's not here," the woman told her. "Our flowers haven't been the same since he left."

Donata felt she would crumble. "Do you know where he's gone to?" she asked.

"He has a plot of land somewhere where he grows his flowers. He's always disappearing there from time to time. I don't know where it is. No one does. And there's no telling how long he'll stay away."

Donata felt she would collapse on the threshold. The landlady put a thin hand on her shoulder. "Don't look so sad, dear," she said. "He always comes back."

This, at least, was something.

* * *

Donata called Maria and told her the news, explaining that she had not gotten in touch with Stefano yet. Maria tried to stay hopeful and hang on, but Donata could hear in her voice that she was wavering.

"Mama, please wait. I promise to return him to you."

"All right, Donata, I will wait. I love you with all of my heart."

"Me too, Mama." Donata hung up the phone and knew she didn't have much time. She went back to his building in the morning, but the landlady just shook her head. The following day was the same. And as much as Donata wanted to find her father, she did not want her mother to die without seeing her once more.

On the day before she had promised them all she would come back to Italy, Donata wrote a letter to Stefano explaining everything. Her only hope was that he would return to his building soon, find the letter, and fly to Italy. She gave the letter to the landlady, who promised she would give it to Stefano the moment she saw him. The package Donata kept. She felt it was too valuable to leave behind.

Donata called home and Prima picked up the phone.

"*Buongiorno.*"
"*Buongiorno*, Prima."
"You must come home at once." Prima wasted no words. "She isn't doing well."
"Can I speak to her?" Donata pleaded.
Prima held the phone to Maria's ear. Very sick, she could hardly speak. "Donata," she managed.
"Mama, please wait for me."
"And Stefano?" Maria used all her strength to say his name.
"I tried, Mama. Maybe he'll come. I left a letter for him." Her voice sank. "The landlady promised to give it to him. Mama, I love you."
"I love you, too, my angel." Too weak to speak anymore, Maria gave the phone to Prima.
"I will try to keep her until you return," Prima said.
Donata went directly to the airport and begged to be put on the next flight home.

* * *

Arriving at his address the next day, Stefano listened as the landlady told him about Donata. She handed him the letter the young woman had left for him. His hands trembling, he opened the envelope. The geraniums came to life in their boxes as he read and, when he was done, Stefano ran up the street like a boy on Christmas morning. The landlady called after him. "I have the rest of your mail!" But he never looked back.

* * *

When Donata got home, Maria was lying in her bed, but it had been moved downstairs in front of her arched window. "We wanted the garden to be the last thing she saw before…before crossing over," Giuliano explained. Donata rushed to Maria's side, grabbed her hand and kissed her.
"Mama, I'm home." She assured her that he would come once he received the letter. Maria smiled, but Donata could see that she

was weary.
"I'm here with you, Mama."
Maria smiled and gently touched her daughter's face.
"I remember the first time I ever touched this face," Maria whispered. "Donata?"
"Yes, mama."
"I need you to go out to the garden to the Weeping Willow. Ask Guilano for a ladder. There are two things in the hollow of the tree. Please go find them and bring them to me." Maria quickly fell asleep with the effort of speaking.

Donata remembered the package and, unpacking it from her bag, handed it to Prima. As soon as Prima laid eyes on it, her eyes widened and filled with tears.

"Prima?"

"I'll explain everything later," she told Donata. "Now go."

* * *

Taking a stepladder from the shed, Donata went to and climbed into the ancient tree, its tendrils swirling around her in the breeze. She rested inside the crook of its trunk and, looking out at the valley of lush fields and winding roads lined with tall cypress, stillness filled her. She ran her fingers through the leafy hair of the tree until she came upon the hollow. Reaching around, she took hold of the ring. And there was something else. A small wooden box? She took hold of that as well, and saw it had a flower carved into the top. Climbing down, she ran to her mother's bedside.

* * *

Meanwhile, Prima sat in a chair at Maria's side, as though on guard duty. After all these years, Prima could hardly wait to share Donata's news of the undelivered package with her friend. Finally, Maria opened her eyes and saw Prima beaming above her. Prima could not waste another moment. Without explanation, she placed the worn package Donata had given her on Maria's stomach. When Maria saw it, confusion filled her mind at first. Then, when she noticed that the package had not been opened, understanding flooded her heart. Stefano had never received her package! Never read her heartfelt letter! Electricity ran through Maria's worn body. Maria held the package in her arms as if it were Stefano himself. She whispered to Prima.

"Prima, please make sure he sees this."

"Of course I will." Prima's eyes filled with tears.

At that moment, Donata ran in. "Mama, I think I found what you wanted."

Maria motioned for Donata to come beside her. She took the ring from her daughter and pulled it onto her own ring finger, which had shrunk in size. Then she motioned to the box and told Donata to open it.

Donata pulled the tightly sealed lid off the top of the box. Inside was folded a letter, the paper yellowing.

"Read it to me," Maria said weakly.

Donata began.

My Sweet Angel,

How can I say goodbye to you when we barely said hello? My heart breaks as I leave you, and yet I have no choice. You are truly the most beautiful wonder I have ever laid eyes on. Please know that if it were in my power I would have been here with you each and every day. Like the Weeping Willow I always wanted to protect you and shelter you from all storms, but life is not always the way you wish for it to be. Sometimes it rips us away from the ones we love the most. I'm so sorry for the way things turned out, but nothing can ever change my love for you. You are the one thing that breathed life into me once again. You stirred my soul, gave me purpose and a will to carry on. I'll cherish you and hold you in my heart all the days of my life. I know that you were the reason God chose for me to exist. You may think that I left you, but that is not possible, for I'm always with you and you, with me."

Donata finished the letter and began to cry.

"Mama, what a beautiful letter. I only hope someday I can be so lucky to receive such a letter."

"You just did." Maria smiled up at her. Donata looked back, confused.

"What do you mean?"

"He left that for you." She looked to Prima, who sat quietly on the other side of the bed, nodding. Maria showed her daughter the inscription of the words *per Donata* on the inside lid of the box. "The night he left," Maria told Donata, "Stefano must have came back to the garden. I—I thought I sensed him that night and when I went out to the willow, I found this in the morning. He must have hoped that someday you would get it, but not before you were ready."

Donata scanned the words on the page again and tucked the letter back in its box.

"I want you to keep this ring, too, *cara mia*." Maria slipped the gold band off her finger. "It is my true wedding ring."

Donata cried even harder as she read the engraving, "From this day on we are forever." This was her parents' wedding vow. And now, with Maria dying, they would not have another chance.

"No, Donata, don't cry," Maria said, resting her hand in her daughter's. "I'm always going to be with you, always. You can find me in every flower and every garden. Just call to me and I will come."

Prima took her other hand. "She's right, Donata, we never really leave each other. My Paolo still comes to me whenever I call to him." Prima smiled into Maria's beautiful green eyes. Maria's smile said the words she did not have the strength left to say, but Prima knew them all already.

"Prima, you've been my angel." Prima tried to be strong, but soon became teary-eyed. Maria let out a weak laugh. "Not you, too." Prima wiped her eyes quickly. Giuliano and Filomena emerged from the kitchen, where they had been preparing food for Donata. They said their goodbyes to Maria, who thanked them for all the love that they had given so freely to her and to Donata over the years. She asked them to take care of her daughter. "We'll look out for her as if she were our own, Maria," they assured her. Maria knew that between them and Prima, Donata would be fine. Her daughter was much stronger than she had ever been. Maria prayed she would fight for the things she wanted in life.

The time had come. Maria felt ready to let go. She called for Donata, who sat down and took her hand.

"If he comes, darling, tell him I was wrong for ever letting him go and ask him...ask him to please forgive me."

Donata tried to stop her. "Mama, please..."

Maria gathered her strength. "Please, let me finish." Donata nodded, listening closely. "Tell him we will meet again...in the garden."

Then she indicated that she wanted Donata to play for her. Donata wiped her tears and kissed her Mother for the last time. "I love you, Mama." Maria smiled.

Donata walked over to Maria's piano, which had been moved to the house after Martino's death. She began to play a song on the black and white keys, and Maria's face glowed with serenity. She drifted into endless sleep with a smile on her face. A breeze blew in the window and through the garden, and, as her soul crossed over, all the flowers bowed their heads.

EPILOGUE

Standing by my mother's casket, the stranger wept as he sang and I wept with him. The others, too, could not help but cry. By my side, Prima whispered to me through her tears, "That, my dear, is Stefano Portigiani." My heart rose to my throat. Another cardinal flew past, a flash of red in the corner of my eye.

I liked to think I knew something about music. I had studied at my mother's piano all my life, and though I suffered terrible stage fright, I had been singing in the opera in Rome. But I had never heard a voice like this. Bitter with grief, so sweet it collected the sadness with a smile, his tenor permeated the garden. It lifted my heart then pulled me under, swallowing me whole with a melody that haunted my soul so that I, too, felt I would be buried. The rich voice seemed accompanied by an orchestra, yet the man stood alone singing my mother's name over and over. "Maria," he sang, along with the word "farewell."

Rain fell onto the grass, weighing on the leaves of the willow, the petals of flowers, and my skin. He opened his arms, singing and smiling as if he were being baptized. His song drenched us all. The priest gave the signal and, with Stefano's accompaniment, my mother's body was returned to the wet, dark earth.

Stefano finished and raised his eyes from the ground where her casket had been lowered. He bent to the earth and gathering the soil in his hand, sprinkled it lovingly into her final resting place. The mourners filed away and Prima, Giuliano, and Filomena all moved to greet him.

I walked over, awkwardly at first. But he held his arms out to me, smiling through his tears.

"Donata, my angel. I've missed you all of these years." He hugged me and I collapsed into his embrace.

"I have missed you too, Papa." He held my face in his hands, looking into my eyes.

"You're so beautiful, just like your mother."

I laughed through my tears. "She said I looked just like you."

We all went back to Prima's after the ceremony. The Finellis and the LaPortas joined us, as did the man I'd seen writing in the notebook. My father greeted Dante Deloria warmly. "How are you, my old friend?" Stefano said, clapping the man on the back. "Have you finally become a poet?"

"How did you know?" Deloria asked him, smiling, and an expression of surprise on his thin face.

"How did you not know?" My father laughed.

After all the years, there seemed no need to hide the fact that he had loved Maria, and she him. In fact, our closest neighbors were not surprised that he would come all the way from America for her funeral. All of us shared stories about Mama, drinking glass after glass of Prima's wine. Everyone was happy to see my father, and he them. Still, I caught his eye more than once and saw in his face the devastation he felt. When our friends had gone, and Prima was upstairs in bed, we sat next to each other on the old piano bench.

"I'm proud you're my daughter," he said. "Your mother did a good job raising you." He held me close, and I felt the power that lived inside of him, that everyone had spoken of. Although his embrace was full of strength, it was also the most gentle I had ever felt.

"I have something to give you," I told him, "Something Mama sent you years ago. It never reached you." I pulled the package from a shelf in Prima's kitchen. He looked at the package, and the date, stunned. Opening it, his hands were trembling. To my surprise, when he unfolded her letter to him, he read it aloud, but nearly whispering.

"For the Gardener of my Heart, Stefano,

It has been far too long, my love, and, torn from yours, my soul is not satisfied. Please forgive me. I made a grave mistake. My heart has been paying the price. I was afraid, Stefano, and this is my biggest regret. Fear and indecision have led to a living death. I have not really lived since you left. I have been frozen just waiting for your touch to bring on the thaw. Oh, Stefano, please let me come to you. I will be yours, no matter what anyone thinks."

The letter went on to describe the reason Maria had not left with him for America, the threat of murder Martino had made, her fear for Stefano's life. He read on.

"But I see that none of that matters now. I can't live in fear. I have been living a lie for so long that I did not know how to live in truth. You are my truth, Stefano, you and Donata are all that I care about and I will do anything you ask. I will leave Italy. I will follow you anywhere.

Donata and I shall wait for your reply.
Per sempre il tuo amore,
Maria"

He looked at me, his hazel eyes brimming. In his gaze, I saw wounds healing over.

"I have to walk now," he said. "I have to walk in her garden alone."

"It's there she told me she would see you again," I remembered.

He nodded. "I'll be back."

I watched him as he walked out Prima's door and climbed over the low wall to our property. Under a forgiving moon, he approached the willow tree where she was buried, singing up to the stars. In his voice, I heard my own. As he sang the last words of his tribute, the willow branches held him. The tulips swayed, the sunflowers turned to listen, and the roses opened their hearts to the night.

* * *

Since my father came back, I have come to understand that life is a garden, and each of us has our very own. We can choose to nourish and care for it so it grows to its full potential, or we can choose to deny and destroy its beauty. I do not hide my voice anymore, and the world has begun to know my true name. I know now that I was created out of pure love in the garden on fertile soil, under the sunflowers by my mother and my father, the Singing Gardener.

I know this now. We all have our song to sing.

FINÉ

Trish Doolan

Sample from Trish Doolan's Upcoming Novel
Me and Five Guys
ME AND JFK

It was November 22, 1963, and all the good democratic Americans of Dallas gathered on the streets to see John F. Kennedy and his elegant wife, Jackie. They rode in their motorcade smiling and waving to throngs of loyal fans. JFK was the inspiration for America, the man who saved everyone from the Cuban Missile Crisis and invoked citizens to take pride in themselves and our nation. He represented hope for our country. Everyone was in awe of the President who would change the future for their families and put men on the moon. He was my father's hero, especially because he was Irish.

Me, I was in Queens, New York, pushing my way through a very small passageway called the birth canal. The pressure was great and my mother was howling in pain. All of a sudden a special bulletin came over every television and radio station. JFK was shot.

The world stopped. My mother's labor stopped. Nurses and doctors were hysterical, crying and running around the hospital aimlessly. My mother was screaming bloody murder; everyone had jumped ship. The televisions were on everywhere catching the scoop, even in Astoria General Hospital where I was trying to be born.

My father, Ryan Finnegan, was at his home away from home, McTierney's Ale House. His eyes were glued to the news broadcast and his hand was glued to a glass of whiskey. My oldest brother Ryan, named after Dad, went to tell him Mom was in labor, but he didn't care. JFK was much more important to him. He needed to know if his hero was going to pull through.

The whole world awaited the unfortunate conclusion to this day. It was confirmed, JFK was pronounced dead at 1:30 pm, New York time, and Mom had a baby girl at 1:34 pm. Born into a world of uncertainty was how I entered into the world. I was told the only one happy to see me was Mom. And no one was happy to witness Lyndon B. Johnson sworn in to fill JFK's shoes; an impossible feat and everyone feared the worst.

For the rest of my life, my birthday was a day of mourning. In my father's heart, his daughter was not another year older, but Kennedy had been dead another year.

My mother was my hero. Isabella Finnegan was, of course, her married name. Five foot five, green eyes and red hair, which she styled exactly like Sophia Loren and had the figure to match. She was off the boat from Italy where she was known as Isabella Juliano. I was the only child my father allowed her to name. Mainly because I was a girl and he had already named the four sons they had before me. She told me she longed to have a baby girl and that my birth was the happiest day of her life, despite the horrific day that God sent me down. The name came easily to her. Francesca. She pronounced it so beautifully in her Italian accent. It was like music when my mother called me. There is nothing I wouldn't do for her because I felt her love so strongly. When Mom told Dad my name, he said, "Alright, I guess that will do. Frankie." To him I was just another one of the guys.

From a very young age, my mother taught me Italian, but it wasn't proper Italian, it was Neapolitan dialect, which is kind of like slang. Neapolitan dialect was frowned upon by true Italians, but in Naples it was the language of the street peasants. Mom could pretty much understand most Italians and converse, but when her and Nanny Juliano went at it (fast and with the hands and all) no one could understand them. It was fantastic, their very own secret code, and I wanted in. It was really fun in the food department. For example, MOZZERELLA would be pronounced MUTZ-A-DELL and RICOTTA was pronounced RA-GUT, SOPRESATTA SALAMI, was SOUP-A-SAD. For whatever the reason, things were added and changed in dialect. I didn't know why and I didn't care. It was the way Mom talked and I loved it. None of my brothers wanted to learn. My father told them that it was for sissies. "These stupid Guineas come to our country and expect us to speak their language. You want to be in the U.S. of A. then learn our language and don't be pushing that crap on my sons."

My mother would shake her head and tell me in Italian, "Your father is a very ignorant man and tonight I'm gonna pee in his soup and he won't even notice!" We'd laugh.

"Hey, what the hell did you say to her?" Dad would get all defensive.

Mom would just smile. "You don't want to know my stupid language, remember? So don't ask me what I said."

He wanted to make sure she wasn't talking about him and she always was. It was the only way she could release her frustration about Dad; out loud, in Italian, passionately and angrily without him understanding a single word. We were comrades, Mom and I, girls against the boys. We were constantly fighting for our rights. Bathroom privacy was an impossibility. You could be in the middle of important business on the bowl and they would think nothing of coming in, brushing their teeth, having a conversation, and even jumping in the shower. When dinner hit the table, the cannibals were attacking anything with a smell. I was so little I couldn't seem to get a forkful. My mother started to put a plate aside for me before she put out the guys' food. No one spoke at the table. They just swallowed, drooled and smiled.

The food was always amazing. Mom cooked Italian food like nobody's business and let me tell you, there were no complaints about my Mom being a guinea when it came to her cooking.

Even though we lived in Queens, under the El, Mom managed to have the most beautiful garden in the backyard. There was basil

Incanto ~ The Singing Gardener

so green it was Irish; rosemary, oregano, sage, red and yellow peppers that glowed like a sunset. Her tomatoes were so red and juicy you could squeeze them over spaghetti. There was zucchini, portabella mushrooms, parsley, garlic, eggplant and spinach. The woman brought Italy to Queens.

Breakfast was like a small wedding. Salami and provolone omelets with fresh garden herbs, hand shaved Parmesan cheese, and sausage she made herself at home and french toast made with homemade Italian semolina bread that she baked every night. The neighbors would always ring our bell and make believe they just wanted to say 'hello,' but really they were hoping Mom would give them a loaf. She did when Dad wasn't home. He would always yell that he wasn't made of money and let them go somewhere else for a handout. What he didn't understand is that this was Mom's pride and joy.

We all asked her why she didn't open a place of her own. She said it would drain the love out of her, especially if she had to do it for money. See, Mom believed her cooking was a gift. Something she could give people. Pouring a piece of herself into every meal, mom was a true artist in the kitchen. The kitchen was always my favorite room in the house, because that's where I saw Mom thrive.

The black and white Zenith TV, framed in light brown wood with rabbit ears adorned the living room, but was off limits to Mom and me during peak hours. The boob tube was monopolized by the guys so they could watch sports, sports and more sports. If it wasn't a game of some kind, it was a show talking about a game that would be coming on soon. Dad's mood would change dramatically depending on which team won and so would his alcohol consumption. Mom said it was because he made bets with some bookies and it would determine what would be on the menu for the upcoming weeks. If he won we could eat Steak, maybe veal, but if he lost we were looking at hot dogs, or peppers, eggs & onions, a popular dish in our house. I didn't care because Mom could make Spam taste like prime rib. Sundays were the worst for TV domination, especially during football season. Mom and I couldn't wait until all the games ended so we could snuggle up, finally, and watch our favorite show together; Ed Sullivan, 8 o'clock on CBS, every Sunday night, it was our religion. Thank God there were no sports on early in the morning because that was our time to spend with Jack La Lane and his fancy one-piece spandex jumpsuit. I figured I needed to buff up so I could become big and strong like the guys. It was no fun being the runt of the litter.

    I learned at a very young age if I wanted to fit in with my brothers, I'd better learn to play sports. I wanted desperately to be part of them. I even let them rough me up to prove I could take it. One time they played hot potato and I was elected the potato. It was initiation time. I was five, Patrick was eight, Seamus was ten, Ian was twelve, and Ryan, thirteen. Ryan and Ian were Irish twins, eleven months apart. Ryan picked me up like I was a potato. He was so strong. Dad said he took after my Uncle Jim, his brother, who fought six men at once and sipped on whiskey in between. We weren't allowed to see Uncle Jim or talk to him if we accidentally bumped into him, and we weren't allowed to ask why. All we knew was he was built like an Irish plow, demolished anything in his path, and had a terrible drinking habit. It seemed to run in the family, like diabetes.

    There I was in Ryan's hand, he tosses me to Ian who tosses me to Seamus and then to Patrick who wasn't as big and strong as the others. He dropped me flat on my face. Out popped my two front teeth and blood was everywhere. As I lay on the concrete, I felt the pressure of my gums sticking to my lip. The taste was comforting for some reason. It hurt like hell, but all of a sudden I felt tough, special. Secretly, I had wanted to get hurt. I was just afraid of how it would happen. All my brothers had stitches, scars, bruises and war wounds to show off.

    Not a sound was made. I couldn't speak. I think I was in shock. I could hear my brothers arguing. Ryan thought maybe

Incanto ~ The Singing Gardener

they killed me because I wasn't moving. Ian said, "Dad is gonna kill us all and Patrick shouldn't have been playing 'cause he's too weak." Patrick got defensive and said that he was just as strong, but his eyes were closed. Seamus didn't say a word. He knelt down beside me, felt my pulse. "She's alive!" All my brothers cheered, "Thank God, whoa, that was close." Seamus placed his hand on the back of my neck. The touch of Seamus' hands on me was so comforting.

My brothers were all concerned about me. For the first time in my life I knew they loved me. I didn't feel like their stupid kid sister.

Seamus asked Ian to help him turn me around. They moved me ever so gently, like I was a wounded baby bird. As my eyes hit the light I squinted.

Seamus was relieved. "She's conscious. How you doin' kiddo?"

Ian said he couldn't believe I wasn't crying and that if that was Patrick he would've been. Ryan told Ian to shut his trap or he'd shut it for him. Ryan was very protective about Patrick, who was so little.

Seamus softly said, "Can you hear me Frankie?" I smiled as big as day. I was so proud to be wounded. Seamus saw the gap in my mouth as his eyes widened.

Ian screamed, "She has no teeth!" then turned to Patrick; "You knocked her fucking teeth out."

Ryan smacked Ian in the head, "I'm gonna knock your fucking teeth out if you say another word." Ian zipped up quickly. When it came to fighting, no one would cross Ryan.

Patrick stood crying, "I'm sorry Frankie. I didn't mean it." I was so touched by his little face.

"Don't worry, Patrick. I'm okay."

"Let's get her to the hospital, her lip is split and stitches are definitely necessary." Seamus insisted. I was queasy and wanted to cry, but no way in the world would I shed a single tear.

When we got to the hospital the lady at the desk immediately called for a doctor then took our information from Ryan explaining that she had to call our parents. The doctor took one look at me and cleared a room.

"I'm Doctor Silver." His name sounded shiny and pretty so I trusted him. He asked that the boys wait outside, but Seamus said, "I have to stay and make sure you do it right. I'm gonna be a doctor someday."

Then Ryan said, "That's my baby sister and I ain't leaving."

Ian said, "I have to stay because wherever they go, I go."

Patrick pouted. "I'm the one who did this to her so I have to be here." The doctor smiled at all the love they showed and told Patrick he must have some right hook. Ryan laughed and tousled Patrick's hair. Patrick didn't get it, but since Ryan laughed, he knew it was okay to laugh. We were all together, a family, and I was one of them, even if I was a girl.

Twelve stitches later, I was ready to go home. Mom and Dad ran in and saw my lip. Mom started swearing in Italian. Dad wanted to know how it happened. I couldn't speak too well because my lip was swelled up like a golf ball. Ian started to tell the story as Patrick hung his head low.

Ryan jumped in, "I had her on my shoulders, Dad, and she fell."

We all looked at him in amazement, knowing Dad was gonna give him a beating. Dad told Ryan he was a careless ape, just like his brother, and shouldn't go near me because he didn't know how to be gentle with anything. Dad called Ryan a 'bull in a china shop.'

That night we all waited atop the stairs as Ryan took his beating with Dad's infamous belt, thick, dark brown leather; the third notch wider than the rest. You could smell the musty hide of the animal as it whipped around your skin like a leech. That old belt seemed to get a lot more use on us than it did on Dad's pants. This time Ryan was the victim. He never even said ouch, but he walked upstairs slower than usual. Patrick asked him why he lied to Dad.

He answered, "He can't hurt me, but he can kill you."

Incanto ~ The Singing Gardener

Dad was like two people. When he was drinking he didn't even know what he was saying or doing. He could give Mom a beating so bad and the next day ask her where she got the black eye. He'd even go as far as to tell her that she looked like shit. He had no recollection of any of it.

When he wasn't drinking he was kind, funny, a philosopher. You just never knew which one he would be. It was like Russian roulette. Mom used to tell me that someday he was going to kill her. I believed her.

I always seemed to be at the wrong place at the wrong time. Particularly when it came to Mom and Dad. All the boys were in school, but I hadn't started yet. I didn't want to 'cause I knew it was going to take away my special time with Mom, so I wanted to enjoy every minute of it while I could. More often than not Dad came home drunk and I would be dancing with Mom. She loved her victrola and her dancing. She had boxes full of 45's and bags full of the yellow plastic disc that went in the hole in the middle so they could spin round and round on the turntable. I loved popping those little yellow suckers in and getting the next record ready for me and Mom to dance to. I was her DJ of choice and knew all of her favorite songs. There we were dancing and singing to "What A Difference A Day Makes" by the great Dinah Washington. It was such a hopeful song about how twenty-four little hours could change anything. I wanted to believe that, but then Dad came in sloshed, saw us dancing, as he did so many times before, and ripped the needle across the record scratching the vinyl. He wanted to make sure Mom wouldn't play that one again, and then he threatened to break the goddamn victrola. I never understood why my happiness with Mom made him so furious. He told her that she turned me away from him and that she loved me more than him. "You're being ridiculous Ryan." That was all he needed.

"Ridiculous, I'll show you ridiculous." He'd smack her in the face; she would hit him back and start swearing in Italian. Then it became punches, "You guinea bitch. You ever raise your hand to me again and I'll break it."

She was down, I would jump on him, but he would fling me off like an insect. The rest of the night would be silent. No singing, no dancing, no music. Just the sounds of forks hitting the plates as me and five guys sat around the kitchen table eating my mother's Italian food while she wept upstairs, longing for a better life.

Connect with Trish Doolan Online

The Singing Gardener

http://thesingininggardenerbook.com

Facebook:

http://www.facebook.com/trish.doolan.77?ref=tn_tnmn

Twitter:

https://twitter.com/curlyred817

My LinkedIn:

http://www.linkedin.com/profile/view?id=124537822&trk=hb_tab_pro_top

Made in the USA
Las Vegas, NV
15 February 2025